Free the Puddles
by Pierre O'Rourke

To Cheryl —

That's a wrap!

Hugs —

Pierre O'Rourke

12-22-19

ELM Tree

ELM Tree Books

Published in association with TechPress Publishing

6611 N. 64 Place, Paradise Valley, Arizona 85253

www.TechPressPublishing.com

ISBN 978-0-9996243-0-2 (Paperback Edition)

Free the Puddles / Pierre O'Rourke

Editing by Sherry Hays, Judy Worman

Front cover design by Edward Ellsworth

Front cover photograph by Pierre O'Rourke

Cover model, Noah Kraus

Author photograph by Ashleigh Samira Hays

Book design by Edward Ellsworth

Printed in the United States of America

First Printing May 2018

DEDICATED TO

my 3-M Angels

Esther Smith O'Rourke, my mother,
for teaching me the value of respect and
unguarded love…

Og Mandino,
for teaching me the power of a parable
and for respect of words…

Michael Landon,
for teaching me of the value of a good
story and the limits of time.

MUSINGS ABOUT PIERRE O'ROURKE

Meeting someone special in life is a rare and wonderful gift. And you never know how those meetings will happen. With Pierre, it was rather normal: he picked me up in an airport.

Well, our encounter wasn't exactly as I've made it sound. He did pick me up in an airport, but my then husband's publisher had hired him in his role as a Host to Authors to do so and to escort us around the Greater Phoenix area.

While my Ex did his author thing, Pierre and I bonded over shared silliness, butter cookies and a love of dogs.

As of today we've known each other a very long time—I refuse to count the years. And our friendship has grown with time.

And now, Pierre and I do our own "author things." It's been really great to watch him grow and evolve as a writer. To each story, each project, Pierre brings the things that are the glue to our friendship: his big heart, his wonderful take on life and people, his love of animals, and his incredible compassion for everyone.

Pierre is impossible to pigeonhole in terms of genre or style, but I know that each time I pick up a work of his, I know the characters will be rich, the voice real, and the heart very evident.

Please give him a read. I know his work will touch your soul.

Deborah Coonts

Author of Lucky O'Toole Adventure Series

www.deborahcoonts.com

"In a world of cynicism and anti-love, it is so wonderful to read your words filled with such unguarded caring. You have a gift, you have an obligation. Write."

Michael Landon - Actor / Producer - "Little House on the Prairie" and "Highway to Heaven"

"Free the Puddles made me think and laugh. I held it together until I reached the part where his phrase "pissful angel" jumped out at me. After that I couldn't stop laughing."

Rita Mae Brown - *Me & Rubyfruit Jungle, Southern Discomfort,* and *Whisker of Evil*

"This author is one of the most intriguing people to bless my 30 year media career. His writings always manage to stir me deep within, and I have been one of many waiting for him to jump to novels. To answer the age old question, Who would you choose for company while driving across the country? My answer would be Pierre O' Rourke."

Dave Pratt - Talk-Show Host and author of *Behind the Mic*

"Pierre is a consummate story teller, verbally and with a pen. I have been a fan of his columns with their hidden insights and am so glad he has finally turned to novels. In the vein of legendary Og Mandino, he entertains while drawing the reader in – whether a comedy or mystery, allowing them to enhance their essence by the time they reach The End."

Rita Davenport - Former President of Arbonne International and author of *Making Time, Making Money*

"Pierre O'Rourke writes like Og Mandino's kid brother. His heartwarming Free the Puddles takes us on a classic Odyssey, when two travelling strangers enter the world of a young family, leaving their world changed for the better. Laced with metaphysical wisdom, a little bit of magic, and endearing characters. Enjoy the journey."

Susan Alcott Jardine - Artist of Green Door Editions and author of *The Channel: Stories From L.A.*

"Thoughtful, humorous, engaging, observant, sensitive, and well spoken, Pierre is an excellent storyteller and writer!"

Gary Puckett - Formerly of The Union Gap with "Young Girl" and "Lady Will Power"

"I really enjoy Pierre's pieces. I love that in each one he has something to say - simple but working on many levels - profound and poignant, moving and muscular."

Mrs. Robert (Joan) Parker - 'Spenser for Hire' novels & TV series and 'Jesse Stone' novels & TV Movies

"Pierre's style is magical, pure and fresh, biting in the way of true spirit, uplifting in the style of real soul."

Ken Bruen - *Tower, The Guards,* and *Headstone*

"Pierre is a gifted writer with a flair for insight and humor."

Randy Wayne White - *Sanibel Flats, Everglades,* and *Night Vision*

CHAPTER ONE

HE SAID, SHE SAID

JUST LIKE COITUS INTERRUPTUS when a child walks into the bedroom before a couple reaches climax, counseling sessions can end before a happy ending.

Brian picked at the faded label on the magazine cover, black ink turned gray. *Dr. Elwood Richard Feldman, Ph.D., LPC.* Allison nervously straightened the worn dog-eared magazines.

"That's about it. That's our time for today," said the counselor as he glanced at his gold wristwatch. "You two did a lot of good work. You both opened a lot of territory. Don't be afraid to go out on a limb. That's where the fruit is," offered his hollow quotes

As the couple rose to leave, Dr. Feldman placed his hands upon their shoulders to guide them. "Why don't you go out this way? It's a private room with a separate exit."

"The magazines any newer than in your waiting room?" cracked Brian.

The therapist focused on Allison. "Sometimes after a session, couples still have some talking to do and this area is more private."

Brian held the door open for his ex-wife-to-be.

Dr. Feldman's false laugh was as fake as the plastic plants amid the landscaped wallpaper in the windowless room. "Take your time; don't rush."

"Can we send out for meals?" continued Brian in a fruitless effort to ease the tension, avoiding contact with Allison's reddened eyes.

The counselor forced another laugh. "Same time, next week. Remember, it's like floating in water. You have to relax." He hugged Allison.

Brian sat quickly before an embrace was offered to him.

As the door closed, she was seated and he was standing again. "Relax to stay afloat. Struggle and you'll sink. It's easy for him to say with his $150-per-hour hugs and Dr. Phil one-liners." He shoved his hands into his rear pockets.

Glaring at the ornate mirror on the wall, he was suspicious of all. "Struggle or relax. Hell, we're going down either way! Folks on the *Titanic* had better chances with half of their lifeboats missing."

Allison took a tissue from the end table, dabbing at her eyes as she tried to smile.

He saw her reflection in the mirror and his heart went out to her. He tried once again to lighten things but his grin was as false as the counselor's. "Your mother was right. You don't have the greatest taste in men."

"She never said that. She just wonders why you don't act like a normal husband."

"Again with the *normal?*"

She had hit a raw spot most certainly. "You know she loves you."

"Yeah, read her book, *Men Are from Mars, Their Heads up Uranus.*"

He had the knack for making folks laugh in the darkest scenarios, a defensive skill developed as a child trying to cheer up his mother. Her chuckle calmed him enough to sit down. "You know it doesn't help matters when you side with that Dr. Phil-wannabe, anymore than when you and your mother preach to me about what's *normal.* I never claimed to be normal; never looked for it."

"We just meant...what's working for everyone else," she offered timidly.

He leaned forward, elbows on his knees, voice low, continuing before she could speak a word, another habit of defense. "So who're all these normal people you all keep talking about? Your family?"

His satire loomed. "Your folks don't even touch anymore, let alone share a bed. Lillian always citing the way they faked it through hard times." He looked at the fluorescent lighting. "And why? Just so we can end up like them, as just... friends?"

Silence prevailed, so he plowed on, bitter satire rolling off his tongue. "Or, how about your sister? She's one of the most loving folks around. Your brother-in-law is, too. Yet she's wound up tighter than a clock, and he can't let go of his grudge for that company that screwed him. They know they'll never get the money. They should cut their losses and move on." He leaned back as if deflated by the energy.

"At least they still make love." Her lip trembled.

"When their schedules permit. They're so worried about making plans for next month that they're missing all the moments of today."

"Maybe," she reached for the knee of his faded blue jeans, "maybe if you just back off on your workload. Turn some over to Jason or skip a few bids."

He placed his hand on top of her fingers, looking her straight on. "When was the last time your dad came over for a full evening without arriving late, in a separate car, and not wearing that blamed phone plus a paging gizmo?"

"Brian," she claimed almost in a plea, "I don't need all that to be happy."

"Sure you don't." His mind nursed a wound he kept fresh. "I suppose you're ready to dump your new Pathfinder, garage-sale all your antiques, and find a nice little three-bedroom apartment. It would be like the dam that broke before we were married when I refused to go on your family's yearly vacation due to my work."

He felt guilty for spewing his thoughts. She never really demanded much in material things. Never asked directly anyhow.

He couldn't get her to understand when she told him what others were doing, it left him feeling as if he weren't providing enough. Comparing him to others felt like she was throwing it in his face. The same tactic Lillian used.

Allison felt her own guilt. She was often accused of demanding that things go her way with having tunnel vision, but she worked hard not to believe it. When her material desires were ones Brian fulfilled, her joyous display of thanks was one of her most powerful tools to get more of what she wanted. She'd show happiness in hopes of being treated that way again. A habit she developed, rather than learning to ask for what she wanted directly.

While her tactics often proved successful, it actually took a great deal more energy, more energy to get the other person to figure out her desires. And even more energy to hide her disappointment when it didn't work. Her disappointment often broke out in the guise of moods she didn't understand. Biting winds of disappointment exposing hurts and feelings she had buried. Her mother shamed her for airing dirty laundry with a stranger such as a counselor.

Brian softly resumed. "I'm not saying that you and Lillian don't deserve all you want. I know what she went through to support Hughie in their early years while he busted his butt. But face it Allison, you've always had them as backup, that safety net. You deserve having what you want, and what's more, you're used to getting it."

Inside she agreed but felt shameful when she heard the words out loud.

"No offense, but if it all collapsed, I don't see you staying with me. You're hanging in right now 'cause of the way you think it should be."

He seemed so blind to her. Her reply was framed in a glare. "I love you."

His head hung down. "That oughta be good for a few house payments."

The solution seemed so obvious to her. Maybe if she said it

enough times, repeated it enough, loud enough, he'd get it. "You're *not* committed to this marriage!"

"So why am I here?" He turned in a small circle facing the mirror. "Committed. Like in jails and nut houses. Maybe that's it. I should be committed for not knowing what committed is."

"Committed," she repeated helplessly.

He threw his arms to his side, turning to her. "You don't get it. You, your mother, your sister, all say I'm not. You tell me what everyone thinks but give me no direction."

"It's making it work," she interrupted.

"But how?" He dropped to one knee, almost in a whisper. "I don't see the action, don't see the colors; I don't get the picture. Maybe I don't know what commitment is supposed to look like. I can't imitate something if I don't know what it is."

Her anger was on the rise. "I think you're stuck hiding behind being confused."

Delicately pronounced words oozed through his clenched teeth. "I am confused, I admit it, and stuck on the fact that I don't understand."

"The counselor says you hide behind being stuck and being confused. That you get stuck on needing to know the reason why and needing proof."

The vein protruded in the left of his neck the moment her words left her lips, and he glared as he straightened up.

"Sorry, I did it again," she said.

"You just don't get it. I feel like I'm failing on all fronts. Skip fatherhood and husband. Just being a good provider for the three of us." He toed at the nap in the carpet. "Then making sure there's enough work to keep the crews going. Each of 'em represents a family I'm responsible for."

"I care for them, too."

"But I have to do more than care. I'm responsible for finding the work and if the payroll's tight, then I'm the first to go without. Just try going without. I did. I grew up that way. In good times, there was enough, just barely enough. Bad times were devastating. So I've been there. I wouldn't notice tough times like you would."

His thoughts came quickly. In the mirror he paced like the animals behind the thick glass at the Brookfield Zoo. Walls too close, pacing the cage. "You've no idea what it feels like to be worried of putting someone else at risk, making someone go without." His jaw went slack.

She began to stand to soothe him. "Brian, we'll always have enough."

He countered her abruptly. "I don't want to be teaching our son that there's *only enough*, just barely enough to get by."

Allison saw his dilemma, for once seeing the weight on him. But instead of just showing she understood, she felt stumped and remained silent.

"Worse still, I'm scared Benny's gonna see me become like my dad, so buried in his work to be The Great Provider."

She snapped, "Or like Benjamin. He quit and ran away. That was a fine example."

CHAPTER TWO

FLYIN' DOWN THE HIGHWAY

HINDSIGHT CAN BE A BITCH. Seldom is she a friendly reminder. We're always moving from the known into the unknown, each moment defining a future moment down our highway. I wish I could've remembered that bit of wisdom on this trip. That might have made it easier, but I reckon every path has a few puddles in it.

Sometimes I suffer brain farts where everything goes into slow motion, as with me studying the texture of the porous yellow peel before biting it, the stinging acid biting back, making my nostrils flare. See how I digress? I blame the dyslexia.

"Hey, Daro, knock off with the facial," George squinted from the misty spray.

"Sorry," I chuckled.

He looked at me in silence, scrunching his face slightly at my habit of eating lemon wedges peel and all. Only Bette has come to accept it but heck, you get all the vitamins that way.

I braced my drink and reopened my journal, hoping for ideas to use in *Arizona Highways* or *True West*. Ironic, looking back now, what I wrote as I rode from the known into the unknown. *Hindsight. What a bitch.* I began to scrawl with my pen.

I wonder if I'll suspect or sense the day I'm going to die?

Do we receive a clue, knowledge prior to beginning that last day?

Do we hear a slight alarm before we turn that street corner and have a fatal accident?

7

When the universe wants to get my attention, I seem to get my messages in groups of three, like the way I met George and us hanging out together.

George Valmore Mazen was older than me but in darn good shape. We met on a forest fire in New Mexico where he'd been a smoke jumper and I was working helitack. A few years later, I saw him at the Barrett-Jackson Car Auction in Scottsdale. Between Clive Cussler and Craig Jackson, I get all-access passes. George was eyeing a late model 1965 Mustang and gave me the rundown as I tried not to drool on it. Cars like women, I can appreciate, enjoy their beauty... even though I don't understand either.

Dynasty Green with a 289-V8. Back then, Ford had also offered other greens, such as Ivy. George was animated pointing out changes Ford had made in late 1965, such as the way the generator was replaced by an alternator, which was like telling me the difference between Iran and Iraq. The horns and the oil filter were relocated, and the chrome gas cap was placed on the tail panel, center above the bumper. A wire ring was added so it was harder to swipe or lose.

Other changes in 1965 included the AM radio, interior completely carpeted up the rocker panels, full headliner, and floor-mounted shifter which were considered *features*. Front seats were buckets and the rear a bench. Rather than metal like most cars of the era, the dash was vinyl-covered. And this baby was pristine.

Clive, quite the car connoisseur, explained this later model had the décor group called the Pony Interior, exemplified by the running horses embossed across the back of the seat covers. This also included a wood-grain steering wheel commanding a five-gauge instrument panel with wood-grain trim. Door panels were special, too. Arm rests and door handles with pistol grips.

James Bond drove an Aston Martin chasing Tilly Masterson's white convertible Mustang in *Goldfiner*. It was the first magor motion picture to show a Mustang and Ford needed three plants to keep up with the demand. And while Sean Connery will always be the only Bond to me, 1965 will be the only Mustang even after Steve McQueen's '68 in *Bullitt*.

Third time the tapestry of life brought George into my life was the summer after the car auction when I received an email from him regarding one of my newspaper columns entitled "Who Holds the Key?"

A teacher shared a parable creating both conflict and awareness for me. A wise man and student were walking. They saw a man in the water. "Master, that man is drowning. Aren't we going to help?" The master softly replied, "He has not asked for our help."

I have trouble asking for help, and a tendency to help before invited. I admit, too, my nose has been bent and broken. I have difficulty correlating 'Destiny' and our 'Freedom of Choice' – like this incident at the McDonald's near the Sedona turn-off.

Three young guys and two gals had a mini-tailgate party going in the rear parking lot. A macho white Jeep towed a majestic jet boat; invasive speakers blared out music. Among Big Mac cartons were alcohol bottles, obvious that the three gents had consumed far more than burgers. I verbalized my hope one was the designated driver, subtle as painting a target on my nose. After less than complimentary remarks about my age and drinking abilities, I went inside — where I noticed one of the young ladies. At my smile, she nervously approached.

"They've been drinking the whole way. I can't get them to quit."

"Take the keys. Friends don't let friends drive drunk." It sounded good on commercials.

"Right! I don't even have a license — I just turned sixteen."

I looked at her short blond hair with spikes, blue eyes about level with my chin. "Sixteen," I repeated, "awfully young to die."

"Maybe you can talk to them. Even my girlfriend won't and she's sober. Can't you help?"

"Find a phone, don't get in, stand up for your rights." All my suggestions sounded even colder as I left. Then I realized how she reminded me of another sixteen-year-old I knew.

Headed back to my car, I rounded their group and commented on the boat. "Mind if I sneak a peek?"

"Just stay out of our ice chest," laughed the barrel-chested kid, bigger than in my school days.

Stepping up on the trailer, I leaned over the right side. The key with a red float was inserted below the curved mirror on the dash. I saw the young girl in the reflection — before I palmed the key.

On the other side, I pulled the float loose and dropped it in the boat, figuring it might keep them off the lake. While pondering what to do with the key, one guy stepped over the trailer tongue. His faded purple tank top hung loose, revealing big arms that flexed with the mere gesture to his comrade. "Hey, help me toss these empties. Don't want to make it too easy for the cops!"

He threw a wad of keys upon the open driver's seat and began scooping up bottles from the floorboard, which took a few minutes. Looking past the roll bar to the guys at the trash bin, I stared only a moment at the unattended keys.

We can have 2,000 thoughts for every 2 seconds of time. Mine included wondering if the expensive Jeep was Daddy's, if the ladies told their folks they were going, if any of the five were legal age, and how the heck to get the little knob off the end of the key ring.

I pulled what resembled car keys, three in all. On the visor was a clear plastic holder with registration and business cards, typical realtor cards, not the kid's face. I shoved it all in with my new key collection. Then I tossed the remaining keys back upon the blue bucket seat watching them bounce once before I slipped into my car.

The next day I used an envelope to copy the name and Scottsdale address, taped the keys on the realtor's business card, folded it in the registration, and placed all in the mailbox with the little red flag up.

A red flag, I questioned if I intruded on 'Destiny' or her 'Freedom of Choice.' I knew folks on the roads and lake. I wouldn't want someone letting me drive in that condition. Maybe I should have just hoped the kid got pulled over. And then...I remembered the young lady.

I wondered how the disappearance of the keys and registration would be explained. I've had strange things happen with no explanation. I decided if I were the father or employer, I'd want to know how my keys magically came back to me. And I wanted that young lady to know that *sometimes you only get help by asking for it.*

But most of all — I wanted you to know that someone was listening to your plea — so I wrote this column to let you know that I hope your life is a spectacular one.

So anyhow, after George's email, we met for lunch at Pischke's Paradise on First Street. Over a crunchy Drinkwater Burger and Green Chile Pork Stew while sitting beneath *Lakota*, a serigraph of seven warriors by Rob Stern that my buddy Lloyd threatened to swipe, George was about to make an offer I couldn't refuse. He'd closed a deal with Craig Jackson on the Mustang, and had just picked it up.

We'd entered summer in the Valley of the Sun. It may be a *dry heat* but the hinges of hell still get hot, so I took him up on the chance to cruise from Scottsdale to a cooler climate. I knew my assistant, Emily, could handle it if any publishers called with an author on a book tour. And as aunty to Nubble, she'd spoil him with dog treats.

George had to deliver the Mustang to Illinois and wanted me to be his co-pilot over the 1,750 miles. Said if I were game, he'd cover food and lodging, and then fly me back. My dyslexia was not a big asset in reading maps but we were enjoying a good time and I'd gained some material for a few columns.

After the dry heat of Arizona, I appreciated the cool breezes of Flagstaff and Winslow, passing truck stops in Albuquerque and Gallup, through Oklahoma City, and across to St. Louis, as we headed east across the central flatlands of America in that sweet Dynasty Green 1965 Mustang hardtop.

Gravel thrown by a truck's knobby tires had sounded a distinct snap in the windshield, at eye level, of course. Figured we'd fix it once delivered. The rest of the trip, we peered around the blasted crescent chip in pursuit of the shields tipped in red denoting *INTERSTATE 55*.

I really dug George. His ice-blue eyes were unmistakably his most notable feature. I can say that as a guy with no homophobic fears. Eyes accented with ample crows' feet, half equated to laugh lines while the others were earned from years of squinting through clouds of smoke. His pepper-colored hair with a mind of its own fanned out as he drove.

My arm hung out the window, occasionally grasping at the gentle raindrops, wetness exploding in my hand, accenting the grain of my fingerprints. I pulled down the sun visor, enjoying our ride into the unknown. Of course, if I'd had a clue, guess it wouldn't be the unknown. I journaled when I wasn't serving as his hapless navigator.

The cross-country road trip was a great place to let my thoughts take an unbridled journey. With a trusted buddy at the wheel, no kids aboard, and abiding an occasional pothole, it provided a favorable atmosphere to record my thoughts. Plus, the silence of writing creates a safe arena for me to be verbose. It also helped me practice *reticence* which George had explained as selective speaking, having no need just to be heard. Not one of my strong points.

We rode on in stillness. I was staring in my notebook at the blank sheet staring back.

Pesky page. Teasing tablet. Journaling and keeping quiet aren't characteristics that come easy for me. Luckily, George broke the silence when he noticed I was fidgeting.

"Thinking is the hardest work there is. Henry Ford said that's the probable reason so few engaged in it. Did you ever think of all the thoughts in you just waiting to be thought?" He paused to let it sink in, something he did a lot.

The wind tickled the pages of my journal as if seeking attention, waiting for my pen to answer the call, teasing me until I began to set my thoughts down in ink.

I used to wonder if God was a guy or a gal.

Wondered what I'd do if I came face-to-face with God. I wondered if I'd even recognize Him or Her.

I paused and reread my scribbles, tapping my pen between my teeth. I shifted in my seat, toying with the chrome latch on the wing vent until the glass wedge forced the air into my face to clear my thoughts. I released a sigh.

Then George asked, "Have you ever thought of how much

you actually know? Maybe attempt to inventory what you really *know* versus what you *think* you know?"

The pen made a hollow sound bouncing off my cheek while he continued casting. "I find it interesting, all that exists which can't be touched physically, such as feelings, beliefs, and emotions, like love," he suggested.

I swiped at the air as if to catch the elusive idea. "You can't touch a thought, can't put a feeling in a briefcase." Felt as if I were onto something. "We can stick a brain in a jar, but we can't do that with a mind."

"What's in our minds is untouchable. *Mind* is an activity. *Brain* is a thing."

I turned toward him having already learned a great deal from this sage. "Is that due to that right-brain, left-brain stuff? Such as, where it loses something in the translation to take it from right-brain to left-brain? The right side is the place where music comes from, right?"

"The right side is our creative side. It's also the place where some say God speaks to us. That's the reason some folks see God as *separate* from us, rather than *in* us. We create in our right-brain, the home of our being, our essence."

My guesstimate was on track, so I resumed. "And our left-brain deals with memorization and ciphering, important but boring stuff."

"*Stuff*, as you so eloquently put it, like our five senses plus memory, habit, and reflexes. Pretty important stuff I'd say, but from the left-brain. The right-brain side creates our pictures, imagination, songs, inventions, and also true prayer as opposed to memorized jargon. And you're correct. It's difficult for the images born in our right-brain to make it successfully to the left-brain and vice versa."

"Is that the reason a dream that lasted a few minutes takes me forever to explain?"

"That, and the fact you like to talk," he grinned. "We can have 2,000 thoughts and images for every two seconds of what we call time."

That made sense because I knew that Handel had said he'd come up with all the music for *The Messiah* in moments, but it had taken him almost a year to have it transcribed into a musical score and such. I chewed at my cheek. "So, what am I using when I journal?"

"I'd say your writing is left-brain when you rehash ideas, but right-brain when you actually have a thought as opposed to just repeating or thinking about something you already learned. Knowing how to write, to spell, that's memorization, that's left-brain. And there's no limit to which a person will go to avoid the labor of thinking. Thinking is left brain, having an actual thought is right brain."

"Thinking versus thought. Is that what you meant about a memorized prayer rather than a genuine prayer from the heart?"

"What's *your* thought on that question?" He grinned before nodding. "Wonder how we'd prove feelings actually exist to someone from another planet?"

CHAPTER THREE

DIVORCE AMERICAN STYLE

BRIAN'S REACTION TO HER COMMENT about his brother was slow. His shoulders rotated first, head following in a deliberate turn. His stare was frozen on her. Right arm stiffened, raised gradually first in a point, then his finger curling to join as a fist until his knuckles went milky white. And just as slowly his hand returned to his side as he turned away.

"I'm sorry, Brian, I didn't mean that," Allison said.

"Sorry." It was his turn to interrupt. "Sorry." His face looked pitiful as he paced in circles, knowing the floor was his. Emotion and temperament can blindside the best of folks, releasing uncontrolled words like an angry lynch mob. His tone rose, breathing fire into his words.

"Want to talk of brothers? How about your oldest one? He's making more money than all of us put together. He stays in touch with your family just to put them down. He leaves you and Lillian in tears every time he calls."

"I appreciate your going with me to the counselor," she offered as she gestured for him to sit on the couch. "Dr. Feldman says he credits you for being a strong man." She completed on the tail of a smile, "But you're stubborn."

Brian grinned. "Some call it tenacity." Stubbornness was a trait he incorrectly associated with strength.

"Whatever."

"I take it you've a point to make?"

15

"Well, the counselor says you're too stubborn and too proud to seek advice or help." Quoting the opinions of others, she believed would strengthen the reason he should agree with her.

"I ask for their input but their words don't make any sense," Brian said. "I ask for directions in a strange land and they tell me about landmarks I've never seen. I ask for verbs, and they give me nouns."

"He says you ask because you have to know all the answers. Not knowing allows you to remain stuck, to make you look like you're trying."

"Sure, I admit I need the reason *why* when someone gives me an answer they expect me to accept blindly. Folks telling me to trust, yet their own lives are in chaos. You, and I quote the counselor, *are afraid of the unknown.* That's the destination we're heading into, a big unknown. Fear of the unknown kept my mom with my dad." He dropped his forehead into his open hand. "The unknown had to be better."

"We're not like your folks."

"We're headed there. We've begun to argue, not just discuss. We bicker and we fight. At least we all seem to agree that we don't communicate."

Allison inhaled deeply as she sat up straight, not liking to look inside herself. "Fine, you've walked into the darkness more than I have. And I don't see a future with us apart. I admit it's easier for me to move on when I see something in progress and know the direction I'm going in." She gazed at her own reflection, wishing it were Queen Grimhilde's magic mirror in *Snow White.*

Admitting faults didn't come easy for Allison, admitting her own faults anyway. She struggled, "I handled relationships that way, making sure I had a backup. I only fought with my sister when I had someone else to play with." She looked to her feet. "I overlapped boyfriends when I knew one was going sour. I just couldn't be alone. Even when we started dating, I didn't get clear of my last boyfriend until I knew I had a chance with you. Todd and I were on the way out but you didn't know a thing about it."

He chewed on this factor before tossing, "So, go date."

She swiveled as if he'd slapped her. Early in their relationship, his never acting jealous hurt her ego. He encouraged her to remain friends with her old boyfriends, which her mother said wasn't normal. And to be comfortable with his lady friends was considered foolish by her sister and mother. Now once again, Allison began to replay the old tapes, the tape of her believing that he really didn't care.

"I couldn't date. I won't," she said defiantly. "And I won't give up. This marriage is going to work. And I'm committed to you even if you aren't committed to me, even if you want to date around." The jab was unnecessary.

"Allison, I don't want anyone else. Right now, I don't even want me. I'm afraid, afraid I'll taint anyone I'm around. Afraid I'll hurt them."

"Like this doesn't hurt?" She prepared to lay a guilt trip on him. "I'd think you'd at least want to stay together for Benny."

"Benny? Stay together for Benny? Like my mom did for me, right?" His laugh was vindictive. "Look how well it helped me! See how well adjusted I am?" He waved his arms. "Hell, Allison, Benny's only four years old and he knows what's going on."

"How could he?"

"Just as I did. I remember the vibes, the energy, the anger between my folks. Their silence was as loud as their yelling. Same with my father and brother even if I couldn't put it into words back then. Once Benjamin was gone, I knew something was wrong with my folks being together even if I didn't know the words for *affair* or *separation* or *divorce*. By six, I definitely knew I wanted something different, something to make my mom happy even though I didn't know what the hell was going on."

This was the reason Brian communicated so well with little children. He remembered what he felt and how he saw things at their age. So what if they were just kids? They were still people, little people with emotions, feelings, and brains.

"But if Benny sees us together, how could you..."

"Why lie to him? Why try to make Benny think all is well with me lying in a bed, *lying* in more ways than one because we're not really together in there."

"But I want to be together, to make love."

"But I don't. I mean, it's not you." He knew she had trouble believing this fact but he was getting to the point where he was tired of her lack of self-worth, especially as his was eroding. "It's not you. I just don't feel attractive. I can't even get myself to do something about the fact that I'm starting to disgust myself." He poked at his belt line.

"I think you're being too harsh on yourself. Besides, I love you!"

His face came within inches of hers. "And I love you, but it isn't enough."

She longed for his touch. "If you'd just…"

He straightened up. Being needy repulsed him. Whether true or false, it was his belief and his truth. "Just try making love and it'll all be okay? That's what an animal does. It might be okay for you but too hypocritical for me."

"But…"

"But right now, I just don't feel sexy, so making love or screwing or even making out isn't even on my mind. I don't like being with me, so I figure no one else would want to either. And when you say you do, it makes me wonder what's wrong with you."

He stretched his arms, knowing they'd had this conversation before. "Darlin', what little I am and the little I've done are due to my faking it. From the time I was picked on by the big kids until I got a lucky punch on Ray Wazzack." He had a tendency to fall into telling stories and caught himself. "It's just that I learned to fake being tough and faked being tough ever since, until I believed it."

"So fake it now," she pushed.

"It's gotten to the point…to a point that I can't tell when I'm faking it anymore. I'm so tired of it all. Lately I'm wondering if that's all I've been doing my entire life, faking it. I don't really trust myself anymore, can't hear my intuition, don't trust my behavior or my instincts. Some days, I just feel plain dumb."

"I know the feeling," she offered, wanting to understand. "When we bought the new computer, I couldn't even fake it. I felt so stupid, slow, retarded."

"You're not stupid."

Her eyes glistened. "My dad used to call me stupid and my brother still does."

His voice was soft to hide the anger he felt for any parent who would act so foolishly. "Your dad didn't mean it."

"Then he shouldn't have said it," as she wiped at fresh tears.

"I know. To do that was stupid of *him*. As for your brother, he's an insecure asshole." He rolled his tongue against his lower lip before he spoke. "Folks show love in weird ways, like me cutting you free. It's just because I love you, you and Benny."

She didn't see it that way.

He tried to console her. "I don't want to take you down. I think I'll make it, but I don't know. And it's not fair to ask you to wait, especially when there's a damn good chance I'll fail. I don't want that for you, or Benny."

"What about me? I shouldn't even be a parent."

He felt their son so blessed to have her as his mother. He cherished watching them together, feeling it so unfair that she and his mom had never met. His reply was brief. "Why?"

"I'm afraid to have another child," she looked away.

Having another child was the furthest thing from his mind. "But, you love kids. Love those cards by Anne Geddes. You love babies."

"I love chocolate and Kit-Kats, too, but they're no good for me." Her face wrinkled as she forced a smile.

"Couldn't tell it by me," he eyed her in a flirtatious manner.

"I'm serious." She stomped her foot, an action to drive points home that only resulted in his chuckles. "Benny listens to you more than me even though I'm around him the most. You know how to play with him, and I only imitate you." She felt fear in her throat. "I'm afraid he'll turn out like me."

"I pray he does."

The words shattered her. "Then why don't you want me?"

A long pause ensued as he looked at the tall plaster lamp with the vine pattern, cheap attempts to make a sterile room feel homey. *They should've hired Allison to decorate*, he thought. He broke the silence in his guise of humor. "It's not a case of not wanting you. I just feel like your checkbook, over-extended."

He sighed as he sat on the edge of the table. "It's me and my environment. I mean I didn't need some Dr. Phil or some bald bouncer cop-turned-counselor telling me that I'm not responsible for Benjamin leaving or Mom dying." He tossed his head back. "The first blunder goes to my dad and the second one to that stupid surgeon. God, I wish she'd gotten a second opinion."

She patted his hand.

"I just don't know how to be a parent or a husband and barely know the way to be a businessman." His eyebrows darted as if telling a secret. "I was lucky in the people I hired. Lucky with you and then we had Mary Jean to figure out the books."

Her tears preceded his words.

"I really want to know the right way." He sucked on his lip. "I pray for miracles, just a small tip-off or partial realization. Even to find out I'm wrong would be a relief. Maybe then I'd know the opposite thing to do."

"You're such a good man with such a loving heart. I see that. Everyone does." She grinned mischievously. "Even my mother."

He blinked back the moisture welling in his own eyes. "I know I'm a good guy." He took his hand back. "I'm a good guy who doesn't know the answers."

She gingerly reached for his hand again. "Are you worried what you'll look like?"

"Yeah some, I used to deny it, but Mister Counselor won that round. He helped me see that aspect." Brian tilted his head in a futile effort to release the tightness in his neck. "I'm afraid I'll look weak, unskilled, or dumb. Then folks would find out I've been faking it even more than I was aware of. Then, they'll lose trust in me."

"So," she prodded, "why leave me and Benny?"

"Because I know what it feels like to be left and alone. And if I can't prevent it, I don't want to prolong that pain for both of you. It's the difference between using a butter knife or a scalpel to remove a poisoned limb. Waiting makes it worse. I could even keep faking it, until you woke up one day and found me out."

"I'd never leave."

"No, because of Benny and you've been taught what's normal. What a wife's supposed to do and your dogged determination to get what you want at all costs."

"But…"

"You and Benny would find it even harder down the road to leave. You'd think like my mom and so many other mothers." He raised a defiant fist. "Gotta stay together for the kid. Gotta stay together because of all the time invested." She saw she was losing the battle.

"Time is all we have, Allison. And your time would be wasted when you awoke one day to find out I wasn't giving you all you wanted, all you deserved. You'd see all the opportunities you'd missed. Some pain now would be far worse later." He fiddled with his wedding ring.

"I look into the future, and I can't see being without you," she said. "I'm looking and all I see is the reason it isn't working."

Anger altered her approach. "So, you just want to give up? What about Benny? Is that what you want to teach *your* son?"

Brian's eyes popped. "Good. That's very good. *My* son. Like garage sales and vacation bargains, you know how to get the most even in the guilt trips you lay!" He stepped away to shift to gentler gears.

He began. "I want to teach Benny when to quit and try another path rather than uselessly banging his little head against the wall. Teach him if he plants corn, not to expect alfalfa."

"Please. Haven't you learned anything in counseling?" she baited.

His hands went to his head, dragging through his hair. He forced his clenched jaw wide as his palms pulled the skin taut across his temples. "I know my limits. I never did before."

"So teach him to be a quitter," she said through her tears.

Brian spun around as if someone was holding his child hostage. "Quit laying it on Benny! What do you really want, Allison? Do you want to be a smart quitter or a dumb loser? I want to teach him not to remain stuck. You'd have us all stand on the shifting deck of the *Titanic* in a sing-along so we could sink as a family rather than leaving me and climbing into the damn lifeboat with Benny to save you both."

She sought to calm the torrid sea. "Want to get some coffee and talk?"

"I've had enough, of both. Besides, I have to check on the jobs." He shook his head, revealing the truth. "I just need to be alone for a while, to chill." He read her mind. "Not to get away from you, just to be alone. Don't take it so personally for once. I'll see you later at the house. Enough struggle."

The air-release mechanism on the door sighed. "Clever," mouthed Brian. "Can't slam the door." It didn't matter in this instance. Anger had drained away his energy. To slam anything else would be too much of an effort.

Allison sought clarity about the difference between his wanting time alone versus his not wanting her around. She sank back into the couch, her long blonde hair engulfing the pillow as she crushed it to her chest, doubling over and crying. It took no effort.

CHAPTER FOUR

HERE'S YOUR SIGN

I SUCKED AT MY CHEEK as I looked back to the blank page taunting me, that stupid page. I put pen to paper.

It seems that so many of the things we take and accept as TRUTH or FACTS are merely BELIEFS. While many of them can be proven as facts, most are really just beliefs, stuff we consciously or unconsciously accept as facts. So, since we all have different beliefs, do we all have different truths?

I barely lifted the pen as George surprised me. "What about miracles? Are there really any?"

"Guess it depends a lot on where someone is in his beliefs, regarding his view of what a miracle is."

He glanced toward my notebook and challenged me. "Good point. Now have a thought... don't think."

I returned to the pad on my lap.

Miracles are rare. Then of course so is gold. In some places water is a rarity. Both gold and water are considered commodities, and companies exist to market both. The greater the abundance, the less things are recognized for their value. Could miracles be rated the same way? Maybe we don't notice them as much like back when the Bible was written because we take them for granted. Miracles happen all around us — a child's birth, blooming flowers, chirping birds, even the simple act of me breathing but I have to remind myself to think of them as miracles to notice them anymore.

I served my conclusion with pride. "A miracle is an uncommon occurrence that defies facts and natural laws."

My guru driver digested this without the slightest facial expression. "Roger Bannister ran The Miracle Mile breaking the four-minute barrier in 1954. Within ten years, 336 more runners had broken the four-minute mile. Now more than 1,000 have performed that feat. In fact, Jim Ryun was the first high-school student and Eamonn Coghlan, the first man over forty. Bannister proved the experts wrong and hundreds ran free.

"The world is round and we can sail around it, now. But folks once knew that circling the globe was impossible because they'd fall off the earth…until a breath after the beginning of the sixteenth century. Some people believed that for humans to fly would take magic…until a shade after the beginning of the twentieth century. Humans knew it would take a miracle for a man to walk on the moon, until 1969, just four years after this Mustang was manufactured.

He continued. "Now, what do we have? Ocean cruises around the world are advertised on an apparatus called a television. We defy gravity and fly so much, we collide in the clouds. And we've lost count of how many have walked on the moon. The news media skips gracing such space-age magic and miracles on the front page unless someone is killed." He paused to give his own silent respect to those galactic pioneers. "And now the moon has been cast aside to train our telescopes on Mars and we've renounced poor Pluto as a planet."

"You mentioned magic *and* miracles. What about magic?"

"Well, the word comes from *Magi*, which relates to God."

"Hmmm." That sound always sounded smarter when I made it. "Strange the way that inventions like flight and electricity were often linked to magic and miracles."

Without returning my look, he asked, "What is really invented? Inventors enlist the basics, the facts, and natural laws that were always here. Things like birds and lightning and gravity have been around since before we had calendars. It took humans time to learn the basic laws of nature, and then find a way to harness them into controlled electricity as well as manual flight. Nobody *invented* electricity or flight."

I offered another long, "Hmmm," as his comment crawled through my hearing and teeter-tottered between my left and right brain. To listen is to know for a moment; to hear is to know forever.

George resumed. "God speaks in many ways. We hear of angels, now a trendy topic. The word *Angel* comes from the Greek culture, a derivative of the word *Angelos.*"

"What's it mean?"

"Means *messenger of love, servant of God.* If God were to walk up and introduce himself, many would not believe it. Some might virtually turn to dust out of their self-imposed personal shame or fear."

That remark shook me as I glanced back at the words I'd just written. *What would I do if I came face-to-face with God?*

"Remember being a youngster and hearing in Sunday School about the Trinity?" I nodded.

"We hear of the Father, the Son, and the Holy Ghost. Most agree or recognize, no matter their faith or religion, that the Father is the Supreme Being. I see it as The Father, The Mother, The Creator of all, *The* All. I simply believe that some part of the human self or soul is not subject to the laws of space and time."

Passing a road marker, he turned back to me. "To me, the Son or rather the Son and Daughter, means mortal man, mortal woman, all children. Jesus said He was no more and no less than mortal man, just another child of God although He may have had His act together better than you and me."

We both chuckled.

"I figure the Holy Ghost or Holy Spirit functions as a conduit or translator between God and mere mortals. A kind of messenger helping us to hear the news we might miss."

I thought of some of the people I'd been blessed to befriend. "Like when they come in the guise of a coincidence. Og Mandino paraphrased *coincidence as those things upon which God does not choose to sign openly.*"

"There was also a book by SQuire Rushnell entitled *When*

God Winks. Richard Bach with *Illusions* and Albert Clayton Gaulden detailed such things in *Signs and Wonders.*"

I interlocked my thumbs with my palms open, mimicking wings in flight. "Birds are one of those wonders. They've always fascinated me. If everyone we meet is indeed a mirror of ourselves, it makes sense that this'd also hold true for animals, for birds. Birds and angels are similar in the way they operate, besides both having wings. I can see birds being messengers of God, each species with its own personal method for relaying the messages."

The jarring of a pothole knocked the metal ashtray free. Picking up the spillage of coins, I saw the image of an eagle. "It's scary that our nation's symbol has been placed on the endangered species list, in jeopardy of not surviving far into this new millennium."

"Maybe eagles have the duty of reminding us to become more conscious and aware of the things we have. The Native Americans taught that eagle medicine was the power of the Great Spirit connected to the divine. The ability to live in the realm of spirit and yet remain connected in balance within the realm of earth."

"That reminds me of the left-brain, right-brain connection. Yin-yang stuff. So whatcha think about crows?" I asked.

"The Indians told a story that Crow was fascinated with her own shadow and ignored all around her. She kept looking at it, pecking at it, until her shadow woke up and came alive."

"And?"

"It ate her. They say Crow became dead Crow."

"So, what did the Indians make of that?"

"Looking deep into the eye of the crow, some say they found the gateway to the supernatural. Crow knows the unknowable mysteries of creation, keepers of the sacred law. They can bend the facts and natural laws of the universe. Sometimes leading lost souls or sometimes being an omen of change. The cult movie covered some of that."

My eyes grew large as I stared at him.

He turned to me, released the wheel and threw his arms up. "Crows are able to shape-shift, too." Then he grabbed the wheel.

"Man, sometimes you creep me out."

"Ah come on, I was answering your question from the wisdom of the Native American Indian."

"You'd enjoy my buddy Lloyd. His grandma is a Lakota medicine woman. So what about a smaller bird? What about sparrows?"

"Oh, I'd say sparrows serve as one of the most heavily relied-upon messengers. Their job is to point the way to enjoy the moment. It's probably from those little balls of energy that the phrase, *a little bird told me so*, was derived. The first bird of the day and last to speak at night is generally the sparrow. They're entertaining, too."

"Remember at that outdoor café when we watched them beg for treats?" I tossed my shoulders to and fro. "They bounced tirelessly all animated with their little tan bellies. Their back and wings with a rust brown cloak."

We drove for a piece. As usual, I spoke first. My mind was still on the possibility of birds working for God. "It seems that pigeons catch a lotta heat."

"For some reason, pigeons have been saddled with the reputation of being dirty and unsanitary."

"I've heard them called rats with wings."

"That probably has something to do with city folk. Maybe because of the calling cards pigeons leave on edges of rooftops, windshields, white-draped statues, and unsuspecting people. Proof cities need more trees and parks. Maybe pigeons are teaching that we all have to work together. By the way, God made rats, too."

"What about flamingos?"

"Pink flamingos are meant for decorating lawns. Enough said."

I chuckled as I watched the wind toss the raindrops and

massage the tree branches along the highway. It made me think of the Indians who lived here long ago when Mustangs weren't metallic but four-legged creatures that came from God and not Henry Ford. I wondered how many lives went on before me so I could be on this road at this moment. Maybe an article for *True West*.

Unknown to me at the time, the same breath that tossed our hair and fluttered the pages of my journal in the back seat, now carried three crows to deliver their message. Their wings in sync with the fluttering pages, three feathered messengers were bearing down toward a mid-eastern highway for a juncture in time.

The light summer shower continued, not quite enough to wash the vintage car but enough to smear the chipped windshield with wet dust. The map rustled annoyingly from beneath my notebook as I reached to pull it free.

Tied to the rhythmic *flap-flap* of the windshield wipers was the low rumble of a traffic helicopter. As its rotor beat the air into submission, the sound piqued George's attention, his eyes more on the helicopter than the highway.

Three sounds, rhythms all the same, but each evoking different emotions. Swishing wipers, relaxed. Fluttering pages, annoyed. Whooshing helicopter blades, tension. All sounds coincided with the unseen but steady flapping of the black-feathered messengers.

My face was buried in the map as I muttered instructions. I scanned it in a helter-skelter fashion to disguise my futile dyslexic attempt to figure out the direction in which we were headed. The roads looked like bloodshot eyes. Frustrated by my inability to navigate, I barked, "I don't see why we need this map."

"We need it to find our next job. Just find Hinsdale. That's all you have to do. It's outside Chicago. I know we're near."

George, still wary of the helicopter, examined the skies as if in search of a sign. I felt his amusement when he looked at me, his bewildered co-pilot, clenching the edge of the worn, frayed map.

Suddenly, a virtual black cloud entered my peripheral view. "WATCH OUT!"

Our car veered to the left as the birds altered their flight path in an impressive aerial climb. The tires of the Mustang bit the disapproving gravel before releasing the car back to the shoulder of asphalt with a rough jerk and finally onto the highway again.

He appeared unruffled by the incident as if he had been in another world. But the stunt scared the crap out of me.

"Don't you have any better directions?" I peered over the top to watch the highway and the road map at the same time.

"I knew where Illinoise was."

"Ill–in–oy. Ill–N–noy," I said slowly. "It's not Illinoise. Why can't people get that right?"

"Ill–in–NOY."

"So how come you don't know where the blamed town is located?"

"Hey, do I look like Charles Kuralt? Besides, you'd take it for granted if everything came easy."

I'd lost count of the number of times I'd heard that one.

A flash of light followed closely by a clap of thunder and increase in rain pellets gained my attention. I raised my eyebrows looking out the windshield, then to the rear, finally coming to rest my cheek on the window. "Aw, and this rain, I can't see anything."

"Come on, Daro. What's the matter? A wise man taught me that the sun warms our bones and the rain cleanses our spirit."

I tried to ignore the Zennish smarty-pants, but he continued.

"And it helps the flowers grow. It fills the streams, rivers, and lakes. Each and every solitary drop uplifts the entire ocean. Rain is the giver of life."

My voice softened slightly. "Thank you, Mr. Wizard."

His temperament oozed patience as his face gave way to a slight grin. "It gives kids mud puddles." A rare moment of silence occurred before he continued in a slightly distant voice. "I don't know.

I really enjoy the rain." His hand windsurfed out the window as his fingers toyed with the wet downfall. His voice became softer still. "I feel relaxed. Warm, almost…loved."

I think the last statement brought a puzzling sensation even to him. Possibly intoxicating and keeping him from noticing the highway's pavement give way again to the asphalt, the gravel shoulder, and then the grass.

"GEORGE VALMORE!"

He calmly regained control as he surveyed, via the mirror, the tracks the tires had made in the grass. He offered a humble, "Sorry 'bout that."

"You tryin' to get us killed?" I know my face turned an embarrassed red as we both looked at each other. The leather squeaked as I sank lower into the bucket seat, wishing I could retract my statement. My voice trailed off, my face reburied in the map.

As we looked upward, we spied several sparrows seeking shelter on a large overhead sign of green and white. *HINSDALE 63 MILES.*

He mildly eased, "No one gets out of here alive."

"WHAT?" The map ripped as my face burst through it.

There was a chuckle followed by a smirk upon Mr. Cool's face. Both halves of the torn map crunched loudly as I wadded them up and began to unconsciously roll my window down. Feeling his watchful eyes, I flung the balled-up map pieces onto the back seat, as if that were my plan all along. I doubt he was fooled.

CHAPTER FIVE

NAME THAT TUNE

I ADMIT THAT I'M UNCOMFORTABLE with silence. That's one reason why meditation, prayer, and woo-woo stuff is sometimes difficult for me. As George drove, I fiddle-farted with the silver knobs on the radio but all we got was static. Having only an AM radio cut down the choices. Be okay if Pat McMahon broadcast this far. Or hearing Dave Pratt or Beth 'n' Bill. I really missed hearing my buddy Trent on his morning show. Hey, we were in the Heartland. I figured we could hear some good old country music or just anything in which I could at least understand the words, so I kept spinning the dial.

I tuned in John Denver's recognizable voice singing, "What One Man Can Do." Normally not a song getting radio play time. I'd met John on one of the fund-raising events I'd produced. I remember he'd said he wrote the song as a tribute to his friend, Buckminster Fuller, a man who truly walked the talk of change and peace for the planet.

I agreed with the Buckminster's comment. *I am convinced that all of humanity is born with more gifts than we know. Most were born geniuses and just got de-genius-ed rapidly.*

George's steel blue eyes followed a plane as he spoke ever so softly. "I suppose Bucky was there waiting to greet John."

More static popped until I finally struck country pay dirt. George Strait's deep voice on "Heartline," galloped into "The Road You Leave Behind" by David Lee Murphy. R.J. Vandergriff swore "This Cowboy Ain't Dead Yet." And Brad Paisley's "Mud on the Tires" had me grinning. We hummed along, recalling the lug nuts

31

from strangers' cars we'd wrenched along the way, radiators we'd cooled with our water, and the crayon drawing a freckled-faced kid had given us as a thank-you after we repaired a blown hose on the family automobile. Then at the last note of the song, static cut the broadcast short.

I automatically punched one of the hard black plastic buttons, figuring the diesel truck roaring past had cut the reception. The blond cowboy at the wheel reminded me of the likable down-home sidekick in the Burt Reynolds' movie, *Smokey and the Bandit.* Maybe it was just a coincidence to hear Jerry Reed's southern voice and straight guitar licks mount the airways with "What Comes Around." *Maybe, just maybe.*

The next clear station I found offered a complete opposite on the spectrum of singers as the high intensity of Dishwalla pleaded, *"Tell me all your thoughts on God, cuz I'd really like to meet Her."* So went much of our drive: music, static, tune in another broadcast…music, static, turn the dial, and seek again.

A hard-banging piano backed Rod Stewart's strained voice. I'm not a big fan of the rocker, but I like anyone who preaches to "Hold onto Your Dream," no matter how raspy the voice. The song meshed into static at the end. And I searched, once again until joining to sing a vow to *"sail my vessel, till the river runs dry."*

"Who sings that?" "Garth Brooks."

"Let's keep it that way," he chuckled.

George says I have a knack for singing in the key of R-flat. Funny guy. Then he dumped some more of those facts he has overstocked in his head.

"I think 'The Dance' is my favorite. Garth once shared a story about a lady who stopped him outside the gates of his home in Oklahoma. Always in service to his fans, Garth exited his vehicle and went to greet her. She used her open hand to push him back against the truck."

"What happened?"

"It kinda shook Garth up. Then she told of a point in her life when she'd given up, like so many do. Her husband had been gone for several days and she'd placed their three-month-old baby boy in his crib. Went and pulled a pistol from their nightstand, returned to the kitchen and sat on the linoleum floor."

He faltered as he looked through the window. "Strange the way the mind works. She felt this would be the easiest place for folks to clean up the mess."

My eyes widened. He was good at story-telling.

"Sat on the cold floor and placed the gun in her mouth. Told Garth that a gun barrel tastes just the way it smells. As she cocked it, "The Dance" came on the kitchen radio. She sat there like that, gun barrel in her mouth with a lead bullet waiting to have its destination determined. Sat for three solid minutes like that."

It seemed like an eternity as I awaited his finish.

"At the end of the song, she removed the barrel from her mouth, gently un-cocked the pistol, stood up, put the gun away, and retrieved their little baby from his bed. Turned out that the older of the two kids in their truck was once that little baby, and the man was her husband."

I sighed deeply. "The ripples we cause and yet may never know of the good we've done." It took a second for the static at the end to grind into the depth of my thoughts.

I turned the dial as I thought of the relatively short time that I had actually known George, those three circumstances that had brought us together. I thought of my columns and the uncertainty of time. I agreed with the next lyrics.

"Because we're ONLY here for a little while."

I had fallen into an automatic routine of station surfing when static followed each song.

A deep bass electric guitar vibrated the dashboard.

"When I die, and they lay me to rest; gonna go to the place that's the best."

George sang with me. *"When they lay me down to die; going up to the Spirit in the sky."*

"Quick! For the washer and dryer, name that tune," I prompted.

"That would be 'Spirit in the Sky'." Norman Greenbaum. Number one hit in 1969."

I wondered why I ever tried to stump him.

"He lives in Northern California. That landmark song has been good to him with the added royalties from movies using the tune in their soundtracks."

"Such as?"

"Such as *Apollo 13, Wayne's World II, Maid to Order, The War*, and *Michael.*" As usual, I wasn't disappointed by the onslaught of info, but he didn't stop there.

"Greenbaum has some trouble getting around nowadays, having broken both his legs twice. He says he has so much metal in his legs that he can pick up reruns of Wolfman Jack broadcasts from Texas."

The push of the next button had Elton with "The Circle of Life." The lyrics conjured up an image of a circle of friends, arm-in-arm back in Phoenix gathered in a former printing company warehouse converted into a virtual university of spiritual wisdom. Not religious but extremely spiritual, and home to another special *George*.

Following this myriad of talents and diversity of styles, it seemed fitting to hear, "We Are the World." I did my best rendition of a rock star, a type of Bruce Springsteen melded with Mister Rogers and Joe Cocker. Not a pretty sight I was told.

Static interceded at the end as I adjusted the old chrome dial. I still hadn't caught on. Next voice was a bit nasal, a bit scratchy, and I cranked up the volume as I cheered, "My man Willie! Hey, you don't hear this one often."

"Nice version. 'Somewhere over the Rainbow' is one of the

most popular tunes that folks like to re-record."

"Maybe Willie should have re-made a version of 'The Taxman' by The Beatles." I hoped to skirt another outpouring of trivia, but I was too late.

"Judy Garland recorded several renditions of 'Somewhere over the Rainbow' on her own. Then there are versions by Tony Bennett, Glenn Miller, Frank Sinatra, Patti LaBelle, soul-man Sam Jones, Liberace, Wendy Webb, Barbara Streisand, Brad Paisley, Kathi Kamen-Goldmark, Taylor Dayne, Arte Shaw, and even Jerry Lee Lewis. Over 283 versions have been recorded."

At moments like that, I just stared at him blankly. The next station, graced by Peter Cetera's voice, was giving directions to listen for "One Clear Voice."

"Appropriate," said George, "the place we're heading and the song's message."

At the end, no static or music filled the car. No matter, I was deep in thought scrutinizing my words before shifting my tongue into gear. Seeking to master consciousness of my thoughts would make me master of my words. I had a long, long way to go. Reticence, don't leave home without it.

"Strange the way an action in a scant moment defines time, defines the future." I began to forge the way for my true question, looking to his understanding eyes. "I find it so damn impressive at the way you just accept folks, and the way people open up for you. Hell, I thought I was good with folks, but I really didn't know the way to talk or listen to others. Not like you anyhow. Around you, I've learned to be open when I talk." A span of silence prevailed. "I used to be such a manipulative S.O.B."

George merely chuckled.

I ran my hand through my hair. "So how come it isn't any easier? Besides those pearls of wisdom you drop, I don't see the advantages I'd expect hanging with you."

His reply came without missing a beat. "How many times

have you had to fill up the tank since we left Arizona?"

My eyes flashed to the white needle on the gauge, pegged steadily on *Full*.

"What about all those times you said we wouldn't find a motel vacancy, and we did?"

I felt my eyebrows rise, temporarily satisfied, mumbling, "Probably explains the reason we never have any dead bugs to clean off the windshield either."

The rain finally subsided as the sun peeked around the clouds. I began to fidget. "Pull into the next gas station. Please."

"Why?" he asked glancing at the fuel gauge. "My kidneys are full too."

"You mean food time," he laughed.

"C'mon, I need nourishment. I care about keeping my strength up and taking care of my body." I reached for the paper sculpture that was once a road Atlas. "Besides, we need a new road map. I kinda killed this one."

George pulled off the highway into a truck stop and right into an open slot near the storefront. Seemed we never had any trouble finding a parking spot either when he was at the wheel. He shut off the engine and hopped out, making friends immediately, as usual. Folks never appeared hesitant or concerned about his approach. They were almost attracted to him, such as the husband and wife traveling with three kids.

I watched him for a moment before un-crumbling the map, which I found to be in one piece. The markings, erratic red lines, light pinks, blues, and yellows joined perfectly. The orange hi-liter marked our way. My eyes ping-ponged from George to the map.

I stretched it out holding it upward, studying it against the sun as I walked slowly toward the restroom until I blindly bumped into a gas-station attendant. The kid sported a moustache of not much more than peach fuzz.

"Pardon me," he offered.

"I'm sorry, Bubba. Hey, would you mind scoping out our radio?" I pointed over my shoulder. "The fuses or something must be blown. We're getting a ton of static." Remembering that George had been driving, I added, "Keys are in it."

Then I continued searching the map while wandering across the parking lot.

CHAPTER SIX

U.S. MALE

ASPHALT BLACKENED DARK by the rains, the heat traveled up through the soles of my tennis shoes as I returned from the restroom. I took the seat behind the wheel. The tan leather squeaked as I tossed an opened bag of junk food on the dash, and then moved it to the seats. A safety measure drummed into my head by Michael McGarrity when I drove him on his book tour. The simulated odor of cheddar cheese filled the car as I paused, wondering. *So is the cheese fake or the smell?*

I had to pull twice on the door to close it securely. 'Course George never seemed to have any problem with it. Reaching for the window crank, I grasped only air. More things needing to be addressed before delivering the car.

Butting my shoulder into the door, I leaned out and picked up the chrome window crank, slammed the door for a third time, and put the crank back on the gear spindle. The fleshy side of my hand stung from the smack I gave it.

I saw the attendant step off the curb toward me. George met the young man halfway to the car. I watched as the worker wiped his blackened hands on his orange shop-worn towel. They were out of earshot as I crunched on some snacks but I knew George was making a friend.

"SORRY, SIR," the attendant said to George. "Your buddy had me check the radio. Said it was getting a buncha static. Wanted me to see if I could fix it."

George stood in silence, awaiting the rest.

The confused attendant continued. "He must've heard something else, maybe just the engine rattling. See, the radio isn't even hooked up to the antenna. And even if it was, the speakers aren't hooked up. I mean, there ain't no speakers, just holes behind the covers. Right now you couldn't even get static." He shrugged. "Want me to check the engine?"

George eyed the stitched name and smiled. "Nah, that's okay, Ricky." He offered the young man a few bucks but the attendant would only accept a smile.

Ricky turned away and had taken a few steps when his silver tire gauge bounced off the pavement. He bent over and spotted the crisp, lonely, brand-new, twenty-dollar bill waiting beneath his oil-covered work boot.

I WAS STILL SHAKING MY HEAD, as I rolled down my window with a jerky motion. When George climbed in, I handed him the old map, neatly folded. He didn't bother to open it and merely motioned onward. Placing the map between the seats, he gestured to my snacks. "So, I suppose you figure Cheese Puffs are considered a dairy product and a part of a balanced diet."

I reached for my seatbelt and ignored the health jab, turning the key as the Mustang sprang to life. I accelerated up the on-ramp. As we sped down the highway, the clouds disappeared, revealing an assortment of puddles.

I guess I proceeded more carefully with my mouth than the gas pedal but I was in a good mood and I loved razzing him with his middle name. "Looks like it's clearing up, George Valmore."

He grinned. "So, you glad you came along?"

"I am. I waffled on deciding. How do you make those decisions…when you just don't know?"

"You figure smarts comes with age? I can only speak for me. It's a feeling, a belief. A sort of inner knowing." He paused to see if the explanation was sinking in as he added, "It's being tuned into my intuition."

"Like instinct?"

"Nope. Intuition. Instinct is learned; intuition is inbred, a true knowing. Kind of like hints from my inner-self, that little voice folks refer to. God Whispers some say. Others say the instinct and subconscious are located in the left-brain, and the intuition and super-conscious in the right." He probably sensed the wheels turning in my head. "Didn't you use that as a fireman or now when you write articles and news stories?"

"Uh-huh, yeah, yeah. Used that in a crisis a lot. Sometimes it felt like a warning even when doing a column. And, I eventually learned if I didn't listen, it could be a disaster."

"Crisis can be good because it gives you the chance to take a risk. Can be viewed as an alert to danger or an opportunity to change. The Chinese symbol for risk contains the marks for *danger* and *opportunity*."

George was careful to walk the line between informing and lecturing. "Maybe intuition or coincidence is one of the ways the Creator or the Holy Spirit or the All speaks to us. You know, how we run across things. Maybe a book is used to send a message. Maybe we stumble across a specific magazine or bump into a stranger who seems to shed light on a situation."

"Sure, like my buddy Lloyd and his grandma. They're Indians, or Native Americans to be politically correct," I grinned. "So for them there may be an owl on a moonlit night. To a Baptist it may be Billy Graham at a revival meeting. Or it might be someone flipping the TV to Joel Osteen at three in the morning. To a Buddhist it may be a pattern in the sand. All are messages. I figure awareness can come through a rainbow, an animal, a magazine, movies, and certainly through music.

"I don't guess only one way exists to get a message from God any more than there being only one way to pray to God. My mom opens the Bible when she has a problem and seems to turn right to the passage she needs. Some call that coincidence."

"Sir Winston Churchill often turned to the Bible for divine confirmation in overwhelming times. A prime example, he was about to lead the entire British Navy into a world war." George quoted from his expansive memory.

Hear, O Israel: Thou art to pass over Jordan this day, to go in to possess nations greater and mightier than thyself . . . Understand therefore this day, that the Lord thy God is he which goeth over before thee, as a consuming fire he shall destroy them, and he shall bring them down before thy face, so shall thou drive them out, and destroy them quickly, as the Lord hath said unto thee.

"The Bible along with many others are instruments with which He sends His message. Ways He, or She, finds to enter our right brain in order to communicate without getting right in a person's face. I think the help is always there like a radio transmission. What matters is, if we're tuned into it or not."

George thought for a moment then admitted, "You know what? I'm really not quite sure, and even if I was, I'm not sure I could explain it in a way that it'd make any sense. I'm not even sure where you get the idea I should have all the answers."

"Maybe it's your knowing things such as how many versions of 'Somewhere over the Rainbow' are currently on the market."

He humbly accepted being the butt of the joke. "All I can say is that my not answering is simply because it's all I know at this point. However, I do know, now, before delivering this Mustang in Chicago, that we're looking for a young man named Brian Poppy. He lives in Hinsdale, Ill-in-NOY. And his family is having a crisis, headed for disaster."

"Having a crisis?"

"It starts with a divorce."

I cringed at the mere mention of the word. I cast a side-glance, waiting for the rest of the story.

"Period. That's all I know."

"All right," I shrugged.

He began again somewhat gingerly. "I get frustrated too, just living my life relying on faith. Not knowing if I'm hearing my intuition. Sometimes I receive static, like on the radio. I don't understand anyone's problems any more than I know the solutions. It could be someone is attempting to succeed at something and do great things."

"You mean they have potential to succeed?"

"*Potential* is an overused word. It's an escape word. Potential is like a peach pit sitting in the refrigerator. It's not yet a tree producing bushels of peaches and can't be eaten. But," he raised his finger, "it has potential. "Maybe someone's about to give up, can't handle all the pressure. Least that person *thinks* he can't, so he can't. He loses his faith, loses belief in himself and just needs someone to lift his spirits."

"Sounds kinda like the way Og was a Rag Picker." I pushed the chrome turn lever on the column down and a small wedge flashed green as I switched lanes.

"Imagine a person and his goal. That's a beginning and an end. It's very linear with a first and second force at work. I see it as being energy."

"You mean as in the natural laws of the universe in which everything has to have an opposite force?"

"Right, and with the application of a third force, creating a triangle, miracles are sometimes born. That third point makes us capable of being non-linear. That third force can make or break things. Andrew Carnegie was once questioned about the worth of labor, capital, and brains. His answer was a question: *Which is the most important leg of a three-legged stool?* Remember that the Father, Son, Holy Ghost form a triangle."

"You think it really matters what we think, or do you figure it all just kind of works out…for the highest good?"

"Turn signal's still on," he nodded as he collected his thoughts. "I don't buy the popular belief of man being tied to predestination. I don't think this whole thing down here is like some scripted and choreographed movie. Destiny isn't a matter of chance or pre-planning. It's a matter of choice. God gave a great gift, the freedom of choice, the power to choose.

"We have the power to say yes or no, to take action, the greatest freedom in the world. Man and woman have the power to dream and the power to make their own choices. To make their own decisions, to make their own dreams come true." He was emphatic with his belief. "Man can control his attitude, and that can be the energy of the third force. Man has attitude to use as his own force."

"What about positive thinking?"

"Positive thinking works if linked directly to action. It doesn't work when we use it just to avoid negative thinking. When we use affirmations to try to magically overpower, cover up, or change a situation we don't like with no action, we're just giving more power to the negative by denying and suppressing it. Have to walk the talk."

"So you figure natural laws prevail even for miracles?"

A somewhat relieved sigh escaped his throat. "That's right, I suppose. And it's the same thing right now with us heading blindly towards this Brian guy because I received a rather aloof message that we might be helpful. Sometimes you just have to believe. That's all you have left. Different stages and levels exist, higher levels to everything. Belief, trust, dreams, action, friendship, even love.

He paused. "And sometimes as we're growing and learning, all we can do is believe. Have faith. Keep the faith. Handle the attitude with attitude adjustments."

The vibrant roar of the approaching diesel truck interrupted us. I hoisted my left arm out and made a gesture as if pulling on the cord of an air horn. The driver, a willowy red-headed lady, gave two short blasts with her horn and one long grin. I may be growing older but I'm in no rush to grow up.

HINSDALE NEXT EXIT.

"There's our turn."

I tapped the turn signal as I eased the steering wheel to the right, and then pulled the silver knob to turn the wipers back on. I launched my next question, an old one for me. "So where do you figure all the problems come from?"

"Well, because it can't come easy. Not because it's supposed to be difficult, but I mean there's that second force. Not a bad force, just one opposite of the first."

"Like competition?"

He avoided a linear discussion of good and evil. "Well, no. It's as I said, it's not a bad force. Just the opposite of the first one opposing it. Not the reverse, but the opposite."

I thought about the time I drove Rich Eisen, the host on the NFL network. "Like football? Though God doesn't control everything, He can see it all from up there in His regal box seat. He can see all the players and all the forces at work."

"Go on."

"And like any manager or coach, He may be able to see the action and even call the shots. But it's up to the player to listen to Him and to make the right choice in order for it all to happen. Maybe there're even some cheerleaders to help keep their attitude up."

"Cheerleaders?"

"Animals. Pets. Friends. Counselors. Rag Pickers."

Somewhat amused by my sports-take on life, he opted for an apprehensive "Okay," gesturing to make a left turn at the base of the off-ramp.

My speed slowed only slightly as my speech gained momentum. "And He can see this guy has been getting tackled, that things aren't working. Second force is gunning for the dude, so He sends in someone to run interference."

"Interference?" His head spun toward me. "Turn again, the next street, a right."

"Yeah, interference. Maybe the Holy Spirit passes off a signal or two through intuition to the Higher Self, to the super-consciousness for the third force. Runs blocks for the dude. So that's how they got the name." I exclaimed as I bounced my hand off the top of the steering wheel.

"Name?" he asked, wondering where he had lost control of the lesson as I whipped down one of the side roads.

"Guardian Angels. Guards running blocks to help people. Just like in football and hockey." My voice hit a crescendo with, "Guardian Angels. MAY THE FORCE BE WITH YOU!"

I remember being quite satisfied with myself as I turned to face George but he never had a chance to respond. A loud thud interrupted my jovial musings when our car abruptly thundered over a mailbox.

And as abruptly as we stopped, the rain lifted to reveal a startled lady standing with a child in her arms on the front porch. Both of them were staring inquisitively at us, unamused.

CHAPTER SEVEN

MIRACLE ON THIRD OR FOURTH STREET

SHE APPREHENSIVELY stepped forward, a white apron over her floral dress. Her auburn- tinted hair was pulled up, crisp with hair spray. The elderly woman slowly descended from the porch. The rain soaked wooden stairs had a soft hollow resonance beneath her. At the bottom, she gently lowered the small child. They moved along the walk, approaching our car parked atop the spot where their mailbox had stood.

Embarrassed, I shut off the engine. The vibrations stopped as I moved reluctantly, butting my shoulder against the driver's door, feeling a tingle race down my arm. George was already out with his right hand extended and making his way toward the lady and child. Her lilac perfume filled the air, stronger than the fragrant roses lining the walkway.

"George, George Valmore Mazen," he offered.

Her face softened as he removed his cap in a gentlemanly fashion, his blue eyes looking purposefully into her eyes of green. Doing his magic.

"Hello," she began with caution. "I'm Mrs. Eades. And this young man," placing her hand atop his head, "is Benny, short for Benjamin. My grandson."

The boy, clad in cuffed blue jeans with a red and white striped tee shirt, wrinkled a freckled nose as he squirmed out from underneath her protective hand.

George looked down, appearing even larger in his bulky, drab flak jacket. He brushed his hair back and smiled. "And how old are you, Benny?"

Benny answered by proudly holding up four fingers with one hand while the other pushed his own curly hair from his eyes.

My buddy squatted down, one arm hanging loosely over his knee as he held out his hand again. "Benny. I have always liked that name."

The child beamed and immediately stepped forth. He politely extended his little arm to shake hands, pleasantly surprising us and temporarily setting me at ease.

George looked over his shoulder to me. "This here's my friend, Daro. Daro Brónach. He went to the Helen Keller School of Driving."

The lady laughed but Benny remained standoffish, suspiciously eyeing his grandmother's mailbox and me. Normally I do better with youngsters. The boy dug the toe of his red and white sneaker into the mud as he studied me, as I in turn was studying the damage.

I walked around the car twice, running my hand over the fenders, gulping air as I saw the way that the car was precariously perched on their mailbox. When I peered under the back of the car, I saw Benny on his knees mimicking me, wide-eyed and peering back. The gravel crunched as he shifted for a better look.

Lillian and George were obviously amused at the show. The rattling of a three-wheel mail cart shattered our concentration as it pulled up. "Where's your mailbox, Lillian?" asked the government worker clad in blue.

"He kilt it!" Benny brazenly pointed toward me bent over the car bumper.

The mailman stepped out as he grinned at the pointing child, and then winked to Lillian and George. He shuffled the mail together in his right hand, lifted the Mustang's windshield wiper, and tucked the bundle under it. He nodded to us onlookers, three of whom chuckled before he rumbled off in his noisy cart.

I resumed my silent survey of the predicament as I dug in the tight pocket of my jeans for the keys.

"Where you boys from?" asked the lady as she stepped to avoid the puddles for a subtle examination of our license plate from Arizona.

Appreciating her concern for safety, George pretended not to notice her deliberate walk to the rear of our car. "Of late the western part of this nation, Arizona and California, to be more exact."

"Aren't you boys a little old to be gallivanting around the country on some kind of road trip, all foot loose and fancy free? No jobs?" she prodded.

I wondered where she'd culled such an opinion of us as vagabonds. Deciding I'd rather be doing what I was doing than fielding this lady's interrogation, I popped open the trunk, moved the toolbox, then threw a faded canvas tarp down on the moist ground.

Few things ruffled my traveling companion. "Quite a bite you placed on us there. We're not quite hobos, though it might be fun," he added with a grin. "Daro there is a columnist, and I was asked to deliver this car to someone in Illinois. I do contract work for an entrepreneur. Anyhow, too many things are disappearing from life. Since Daro writes and hasn't seen old Route 66, we're checking it out on the way to our next job."

The mention of the historic highway caused her face to light up. "We traveled that road in its heyday, my husband Hughie and I." She sighed deeply as images flooded her mind. "That highway has lots of memories for people all over the country. Shame they just let it go to waste."

George then addressed her other comment. He wasn't irritated, just aware not to leave new accounts pending. "As to our gallivanting around at our age, age is just attitude and some pages off the calendar."

Lillian wasn't sure how to take his comments. The man had a silver tongue all right, but something about the very essence of George Valmore Mazen set her at ease in spite of his outlook on life. He often did that.

It seemed a safe place for me to enter. "Sooooo," I began as I mopped my face and stroked my chin. "I've determined the damage… is…fairly minimal, both to the vehicle and mailbox." I kinda expected to have my hand swatted. "The post is clearly pulled out of the ground, but it ain't busted.

"And we, I mean, me…well the aluminum box was knocked cleanly from the top of the post." The box lay with its red flag as if sending an S.O.S. "I can fix that." Then I pulled the keys from the trunk and climbed back into the car to pull it forward.

"Seatbelt," Benny reminded me with a boisterous yell.

Cute kid, I thought.

As he followed me back over to the defenseless mailbox and pole, I picked up the post. "We've some tools in the trunk. Would you have some white paint so I could touch this up right, Mrs. Eades?"

My genuine concern transformed Mrs. Eades into Lillian as she directed Benny to take me to the garage where I found paint cans stored on a metal shelf. Rather than a two-man project, it quickly became a one-man-and-a-child endeavor as George continued his conversation with Lillian. I figured I had the easier end of the deal.

"Do you boys have family to visit out here?" she resumed.

George handled her effectively. "No Ma'am. As I mentioned, we have a delivery job, near here." To avoid complicating matters with too much information, he added, "We don't have to report for a couple weeks."

Benny guided me through several bent nails and a slammed thumb before we finally applied a fresh coat of paint. It took longer than necessary due to fresh lemonade, perfectionism, and constant questioning. The boy had inherited his grandmother's gift of gab and her fine art of directing. 'Course, some would call this *bossing*.

"That's quite a lad there," George observed as the active child kept a taut rein on me. He knew his compliment would be fuel for any proud grandmother. We soon learned considerable details about all those related to the owners of the refurbished mailbox.

"I watch Benny three times a week as my husband travels," the barriers of defensiveness falling away as the woman began to divulge such information to strangers. "Benny's mother, my Allison, married her high school beau seven years ago." Her deep sigh clearly signaled something did not meet with her approval.

"Allison and her husband have a successful construction company which specializes in restoring older houses."

"Sounds nice," led George. "You must be very proud." When she remained silent, he added, "Has Benny any brothers or sisters?"

A shift occurred in her look.

"No, Benny is their only child. And sadly, he's probably their last." She concluded with dramatic emphasis. "Their marriage is doomed."

Folks poured out their hearts to George with the slightest nudge. I wasn't certain I would want folks to be that open with me. However, I admired, even envied the trust he could instill in people.

As I secured the post back in the ground using the shovel handle to pack the dirt, Benny coaxed his grandmother into telling us about his dog, his cat, and his tree fort as she nodded along.

"They're good with children, with Benny. They know the importance of a child helping in order to feel important. Sometimes his daddy takes him out to the job sites."

"I bang nails," bragged Benny.

"Always plenty of nails to make sure are pounded in all the way." She smiled broadly. "His grandfather and I gave him his own little set of tools. Even made him a tool belt like his daddy's."

While in constant conversation, Lillian remained observant as I worked with her grandson. She was impressed with my repairing it better than its original condition, coupled with my earnest temperament with Benny. And few people, especially women, found George difficult to like. He wasn't flirtatious but maintained an air of being safe. He held an inner confidence in himself, most unpretentious yet gracious to all. Even to animals and plants for that matter. And I swear they noticed too.

Soon the silver mailbox stood proudly erect atop the brightly painted post, again awaiting deliveries for *Hughie and Lillian Eades*.

"Finished M'am-maw," shouted Benny as he pointed at the upright mailbox and patted the post. "Now, les eat. C'mon, c'mon," he tugged at my finger.

Lillian looked sheepish, natural to feel awkward in such a situation. Then her smile connected with George. Based on the actions of her grandson, she countered, "Well, I do prepare the Wednesday night supper. And I always make way too much."

"I wouldn't think there would be that much for two ladies and a little boy."

"Wednesdays the whole table is full with room for more. My husband Hughie will be joining us, and Benny's father still eats there regularly." She added in a low voice, "Mainly to help with the changes and adjustments for Benny." Then she smiled with pride, "especially when I'm cooking."

"S'mtimes Justin eats too," squealed Benny.

"His little neighbor friend," she clarified.

I was a little hesitant to accept, and cast a look at George. Although always hungry, especially for a home-cooked meal, I was basically winging it. I wing it a lot.

George sought assurance that we would be no trouble when a sparrow perched atop the mailbox and glanced upwards as if checking the weather. George smiled. "Well, Daro, we do need to eat. After all, we're only human."

Lillian rushed backward up the walk. "Of course, just let me call my daughter so we don't catch her off guard and she can have the table ready."

With that, Benny grabbed my hand and dubbed me with a

new moniker. "C'mon Daaaw- oh. You fixed dat most as goodly as my daddy. You come eat."

"Okay, squirt but first let's put the tools and paint stuff away."

"Squeert," howled my tiny assistant.

After we cleaned up our mess, we helped Lillian carry a couple of containers and a pie to our Mustang. Once the trunk was loaded, I held the passenger door open as George tilted the seat forward and rotated his shoulders to climb in. Although the plan was for Lillian taking the passenger seat, Benny and his car seat wound up in it, determined to sit by his new buddy. Me. Good ol' Daaaw-oh.

The skies had cleared to a blue that made me think of a snow crest before the last ski run of the day up in McNary, and then it triggered a brilliant double rainbow. The violet hue of royalty and spirituality clearly held the other colors aloft.

George leaned between the bucket seats, tracing the rainbow with his finger as he spoke softly to the child. "Noah looked out from his ark and saw the rainbow and said it was God's promise to man." Benny appeared to understand while Lillian was reassured at the mention of the Lord's name.

As we drove, the light of the sky began to wane as the conversation alerted us of the situation brewing at Benny's house. Sometimes folks find it easier to talk to strangers and Lillian found an inexplicable confidant in us. Her talking was not as much gossip as a mere release, distraught that the young couple was giving up on their marriage. Although always deep in conversation, she still managed to direct my driving, a mannerism I subtly acknowledged.

"You're pretty good at this mother-in-law business," earned me a curt look from George in the mirror.

Lillian did not catch the jab. "Turn up here. It's the third or fourth street. I always forget which." She laughed, "My forgetter is getting better and better with age."

We smiled sympathetically. Her comments reinforced her

challenges rather than diminishing them.

"Here," she commanded with no warning.

Turning at her verbal signal, the home immediately came into view. The sun setting behind the large house painted a powerful backdrop to accent the teal blue, green, and white two-story home as she continued to talk. "This was one of the houses Benny's parents remodeled. It was a mess."

"Victorian," deduced George, impressing Lillian, but no surprise to me.

As she continued to direct, she told me to park in the front, which prompted a holler from the cautious Benny.

"Daaaw-oh, look out!"

After hitting the brake and lurching forward, I turned to Benny.

"Fer arr mailbox," the child helpfully pointed to it.

My left eye still squints at the memory. I ignored the muffled chuckles from the back seat and then carefully parked next to the mailbox, beside which stood a sheet-metal sign that wobbled in the breeze as it reflected the setting sun.

FOR SALE

LESLIE McDONNELL

Two phone numbers were listed below.

I felt for the key with the round head and opened the car's small trunk, the whiff of the home-cooked food escaping. I bent down to hand the pie to Benny.

"Careful, Benny," Lillian directed as she hovered.

"He can handle it," I winked, bestowing a confidence in the small child as I seized the plastic bag full of incidentals. George grabbed the rectangular glass dish with the meatloaf, and then noticed my look of surprise.

At first he thought it was his not using a potholder with the hot glass dish; then he realized I was staring past him, to the brown bird atop the mailbox. He turned to see Benny standing by the mailbox, pointing.

"Me. Me name too."

We saw Benny's name had been added in a childlike script, below the neatly stenciled names of *Brian and Allison Poppy*.

While I stood in confusion, George merely glanced upward with a slight smirk as the sparrow lifted its wings to fly in a low circle overhead.

CHAPTER EIGHT

GUESS WHO'S COMING TO DINNER?

AT THE SLAMMING of the car door, a white flash curbed the corner of the raised porch. Claws clicking across the wood, a large dog with lush fur bounded forth to greet Benny. The pie bounced in his hands as he ran towards the dog. Although each stair reached his knee level, he managed to scale them without delay.

The first thing I noticed about Brian was that he and his son shared the same electric-blue eyes. A slender man in his early thirties, he also had the same thick dark curls. A smile exploded as he crouched, his arms open, scrambling to use one to stabilize himself and the other to save the pie. "Benny, your mom says we have guests."

"Yeah," the excited reply came while pointing at us. "They mashed M'am-maw's mailbox but I he'ped Daaw-oh fix it."

"Daaw-oh?" came in unison as one of the loveliest ladies I've ever seen joined them. She reached over his shoulder for the pie, as he remained kneeling, his hugging turned to snuggling with his son. It was obvious where the kid got his freckles.

Her blonde hair hung to her waist, thick with as many flecks of color as grains of sand on the beach. Shades of Claudia Lund. Cheerleader. Fantasy. But Hal Mayer beat me to reality. As her hair brushed across them both, I felt a twinge of envy. A couple of twinges. How my mind wanders.

Then the dog focused her attention on us, the two strangers. Although non-menacing in temperament, she effectively blocked the stairs. Attitude is everything.

"Oöso, stay," ordered Brian.

"We come in peace," George laughed, seeing the protective pooch.

She stood erect, tail straight. Her medals included a silver nametag in the shape of a bone that jingled from her hot pink collar as she panted.

Careful not to step in the festive flowerbed, George placed the container he was carrying atop the wide porch rail. Nearing the dog, he cupped his hands and breathed into the cavern formed, offering them palms up. "You're gorgeous." He moved his own nose within inches of the big animal's nose as she sniffed.

"Her's Oöso. Her's a woof," hollered Benny as I immediately slowed my approach along the brick walk even more as I eyeballed the creature.

"Half Samoyed and half Timber Wolf," Brian elaborated as he noticed her acceptance of George, nuzzling nose to nose.

George proceeded to introduce us to the couple, and at the wag of her tail, to Oöso. Then he offered a laughable explanation of my new nickname, thanks to Benny, of *Daaw-oh*. And he became *Jaa-urge-val-more*. Quite a mouthful.

Their house was genuine Victorian, enjoying an exterior scheme of five colors including teal blues, lavenders, and a hint of foam green over a base of white. Applied in tasteful conjunction was maroon gingerbread and lace molding. The large L-shaped porch ran the full length of their home, cornering along the western wall. The plank decking had a slight slope to channel the rainwater away from the home. Matching dormers from the upstairs bedrooms reached out of the roof to the front as well as the rear. Two were added to expand Allison's sewing room and one of the guest bedrooms.

As I looked closer at the ornately carved tops of the railings and pillars, Brian explained they had to sandblast decades of paint coatings just to free the pattern. He pointed out the three supports that had to be custom-made to replace ones which had rotted beyond hope. Perfect matches.

The entrance was a wide Dutch door with an antique ivory doorknob and the old-fashioned keyhole left for effect. Elaborate carvings and the stained-glass window provided a welcoming feel. "This door was Allison's find," began Brian proudly as he reached for the handle. "She found it in an old garage. Folks were using it as a shelf with a sheet of wood over the glass. We only had to replace a couple of pieces."

The glass shards were intact, secured by masterfully placed gray leading. The diamond-shaped clear glass was intermingled with those reminiscent of amethyst. It caught the light and created prism colors on the floor and walls as the door swung open.

Benny rushed past us to help his grandmother in the kitchen. The interior smelled as fresh as the outside with an array of flowers arranged in various vases. An open plan encompassed the living room, family center, dining area, and kitchen. The exposed stairway in the center had a landing situated halfway up or halfway down, as the case may be. Either way, an abrupt awakening for sliding down the wooden banister with two sharp turns. To the left of the front door was a window box adorned with patchwork pillows. Moving past the window, the western wall brandished a large rustic hearth.

"Most of this fireplace was original, just a bit dilapidated," gestured Brian.

"A bit?" laughed Allison.

It was a random collection of river rock and old red brick, excellent for the atmosphere only a fireplace can create. Having built a couple in my time, I especially appreciated the craftsmanship.

She placed her hand on the massive yellowed oaken beam that served as the mantle with several family keepsakes sitting on it. "This was a rafter Brian pulled from above here when we opened up the room and had to shore up the ceiling. Silly me, I'd have thought it was trash and now, well, he amazes me."

Diagonal to the living room off the corner of the stair landing was an over-stuffed couch of deep blue. George looked at the coffee table cleverly converted from the base runners of an antique sleigh. "More of Allison's magic?" he rightfully guessed.

Beyond the fireplace to the left, the living room had been opened to include the dining area where the ceiling dropped just past the first stair landing. Both rooms offered passage into a large country kitchen that rested in the eastern portion of the home. Shelves bordered the upper walls displaying small antiques. The dining area and kitchen shared a view across another porch into a mammoth backyard scalloped with seasonal plantings, ample toys, a huge tree… and a tree fort.

Browsing about the Poppy's home revealed an abundance of things that made me smile. A handsome grandfather clock stood serenely swinging his pendulum with the slow animation of an old man. A bowl of carved fruit came from an outing to an arts and crafts festival, complete with a realistic bite in one apple.

The home contained ample wall space, even with the floor-to-ceiling bookshelves running along the wall between the dining area and the fireplace. I noted typical family photos. Many were of their photogenic four-year-old. Several were of Brian's and Allison's early years together and of Allison's family. Some pictures revealed her youth but none pertaining to Brian's early days.

Then Benny pulled me by my finger, anxiously dragging me past the large refrigerator that had his artwork in ever-updated fashion held in place by magnets gathered from weekend getaways. Past this hung a collection of pictures about three feet above the floor, comprising Benny's gallery, and each picture had a story attached to it. My tiny tour guide led me through the breakfast and kitchen area with George in close pursuit, and Oöso never far from her boy-child.

Warmth of the heart and family abounded. The personal touches let any guest know that caring folks lived in this charming abode, and loving animals as well.

Case in point, the eastern wall of the kitchen leading to the breezeway held a narrow shelf, beneath which sat Oöso's dishes. The water bowl was a treasure Allison discovered at another crafts show. Pale-blue ceramic with an inscription in the bottom reading *Furr Face*. A yellow tennis ball lay by the dog dish, as did an orange one near the fireplace, and lime-green one by the front door. The tail-wagger made sure no one had far to go in order to find something to toss for her.

Scotch-taped to the wall above her dishes and beneath the shelf were news articles about dogs and other animals. One reported a dog giving litter to thirteen puppies. A clipping of a column by Dr. Marty Becker hung next to it. Another one was a picture of a German shepherd that had saved a child from a swimming pool. All of them hung at eye level, a foot above the baseboard, eye level for Oöso, and Polly, her cat.

While Allison explained Oöso's and Polly's changing collection of newspaper articles taped to the wall, I stooped to see as Benny looked intently at a new clipping of two Labradors staring into the camera. He looked up to me after a bit.

"Ya know what, Daaw-oh? Ya jus' can't nebber tell wot a doggie's thinkin' from a pitch-yer." Then he strode off leaving me with my eyebrows high, pondering the little man's observation. Not a child but a little person with thoughts all his own.

As I rose, I looked at the lone shelf just above. At one end was a small dish. At the other, were the distinctive black and yellow covers of *Dogs for Dummies* and the cat version as well. Then books like *Chicken Soup for the Pet Lover's Soul*, *The Healing Power of Pets*, and *The Art of Raising a Puppy*. The deep blue-gray bookends were a Buddha cat and a Buddha dog, appropriate for the animals' library.

The typical Welcome Tour for Company continued with me sighing in relief once we passed the restroom near the family center. Meanwhile, Brian assisted Lillian in preparing the dinner table. A festive arrangement of sunflowers and dry foliage graced the center of the large oaken table that stood upon elegantly carved claw legs. I heard Lillian musically voice, "Dinner," while I was still making a pit stop.

Oöso remained within her self-induced protective zone, somewhat mellowed. Polly, however, attempted to join us. The shorthaired cat had straight eyes and a body of light brown fur, with her tail, ears, and paws as if dipped in dark chocolate.

"She tries this act with company," said Brian. "Come get her, Benny."

Allison walked into the breezeway and placed a treat for both animals in their dishes, Polly's on the narrow shelf with the books. "Her dishes are attached with Velcro. Otherwise," she glanced into the attentive brown eyes below, "she feeds Oöso."

"That's quite a Sia-"

"Shhh," interrupted Brian as he whispered cautiously. "She doesn't know her pedigree," alluding to a Siamese's alleged temperament making us laugh.

Benny set her near her dish and then ran back to George. "Her's Polly and t'inks her's a woof too. WATCH!" he squealed before Lillian could stop him. "Get da kitty."

Ears of both animals peaked as the cat took flight, triggering Oöso to scamper from the breezeway across the kitchen. I barely jumped from their harried path, shocked when the dog's white paws flattened the cat to the ground at the end of the kitchen as both critters slid across the shiny wood floor of the dining area until they hit the carpeted edge of the living room and tumbled into a heap.

The wolf dog with kitty-held-captive, turned back with as near a happy face as an animal could muster. And the sound from Polly wasn't a cry of pain. Oöso's lips were taut above her gums as she began nuzzling the cat with her teeth as a wolf nuzzles her cubs clean. Soon the cat was as wet as Lillian's dishtowel.

"It's okay. It's their game," Allison reassured me as I stared in disbelief.

My tongue slipped but my, "I'll be da…" was cut short by the pivoting head of George, effectively censoring my statement.

Conversation around the dinner table was pleasant, especially for a family that had a pending divorce. And the meal was delicious. The "mashed taters by M'am-maw" were Benny's obvious favorite.

Lillian's husband Hughie arrived late. After closing his cell phone and kissing the foreheads of his daughter and grandson, he pulled his chair back as I was met with another shock. "What happened to our mailbox?" he asked. "The door's on backward."

I swallowed my drink, narrowly escaping an involuntary gush

of water through my nostrils as I saw the mischievous grin on Brian's face.

Chat typical of new acquaintances continued with George explaining our planned delivery of the car and the way we left early to travel and perhaps find an odd job or two on the way. He effectively sidestepped Lillian's commentaries, "Sounds like gypsies" and "Doesn't sound like a responsible way to live."

"Where've you traveled lately?" interrupted Hughie who had wanderlust himself.

"I spent quite a while around Scottsdale and Phoenix. That's where Daro writes for a newspaper and a couple of magazines. I also worked on a couple of projects."

"What type of projects?" Lillian asked.

"I did some construction on a restaurant. Wiley, Ken and Denise worked together before. They decided they were restaurateurs in rehab, so they created Rehab Burger Therapy. Then Harvest for Humanity was another project. Before that, was some work with Dan Harkins who owned a few movie theaters. His daddy, Dwight, would be proud of him today."

"His father's gone, I assume?" Lillian asked, prying without being obvious.

"Been gone since the early '70s but that's a whole other story about the way that we never know where the ripples will end up when we make a splash."

"Tell them about what you did with Dan," I urged.

"Buildings have personalities, and the Cine Capri Theatre was a true lady. Majestic. A thing of grandeur. She'd stood for more than thirty years at the corner of 24th Street and Camelback in Phoenix. Dan's company had assumed the lease, but the property owners decided to tear it down to build another high-rise office complex."

"In the name of progress," I added with disgust.

"It sounds like it was practically a landmark," said Brian.

"It should've been. Trying to make it so was the way I met Dan Harkins and another friend of Daro's named Pat McMahon. The original theatre was a 16,500-square-foot facility with sculpted dual colonnades flanking both sides. These concrete columns weighed more than seven tons each and supported overhangs with copper fasciae cured to achieve an antique green patina. Quite the popular look in the Southwest now. The lower building face was overlaid with imported Italian jade hexagonal tile."

"What about inside?" asked Allison.

"Inside was a spacious two-level lobby with a beautiful stained-glass window. The auditorium was enveloped in 4,000 yards of lustrous gold fabric covering the proscenium and walls from floor to ceiling. The electronically synchronized cascade drape moved on cue at different speeds to reveal the title curtain behind. And that opened horizontally to expose the film on a giant curved screen, curved to the point that it extended out to the fifth row of seats."

"It opened in March of 1966," I added, knowing a fair amount of the Cine Capri's history, especially after being one of the folks who'd supported a grass-roots movement with Pat to save it. "When it opened, it was with all the hoopla of the best Hollywood event. Charlton Heston was starring in The *Agony and the Ecstasy,* the first movie shown in the new theatre. He arrived in an open convertible and officially launched the theatre with a ribbon-cutting ceremony. It remained one of the most popular movie theatres in Phoenix, showing such films as *The Godfather, True Grit*, and most notably, *Star Wars.*"

"How'd you get involved, George?" asked Allison.

"Some would call it silly, but I found I was working with the group going to tear it down, so I quit. Then I ran down Dan Harkins and joined with him and his vice-president, a man named Wayne Kullande, to work with on that grass-roots effort of gathering 250,000 signatures to save the Cine Capri. During it all, Dan and I became friends. It wasn't until a few years later when I got to know Daro that I found out his older brother had been friends with Danny in high school."

"So, you saved it?" asked Hughie.

"Nope." George hung his head. "The wreckers arrived in February and now some complex occupies the space. Hardly something that'll be remembered through the ages or stir the imagination of so many as the Cine Capri had done."

I stepped in again. "A couple of ironies were that the final film showing in '88 was *Titanic*. The last curtain lowering was at 2:12 in the morning, about the same time the real *Titanic* slipped beneath the waves of the Atlantic. A month later, the wreckers arrived, and Cine Capri joined *Titanic* in being a memory."

"So, what all did you do work-wise then with Dan and his theatres?" asked Lillian. "Signature-gathering seems an unlikely job."

He chuckled. "Guess I did wander off the path a bit. I worked with Dan, Wayne, and their team to collect as many bits of memorabilia as we could to be used later in the brand new state-of-the-art theatre he erected in the north end of Scottsdale, proudly bearing the name of Cine Capri again later that same year. Its design included the same famous portico columns, built from the original 1960's blueprints. It includes a museum dedicated to the original Cine Capri. The interior, with its gold curtains, are also duplicates of the original theatre. As I said, Dan's daddy sure would be proud of him."

Brian, trying to move the conversation off fathers and sons, passed a plate of food and asked, "What was that harvest thing you mentioned?"

"Harvest for Humanity was created by a fellow named Homer Piatt," George answered. "I met him at a training seminar."

"Training?" quizzed Lillian.

"Self-awareness stuff," he casually passed.

"This guy Homer was pretty impressive," I joined. "He's this former jet pilot who fought in Viet Nam. Now he fights hunger with an army of volunteers he recruited. He goes around the city, finds unused land, and obtains permission to farm it. They've raised tons of food, all of which is donated to local food banks and shelters for the homeless on the day it's picked."

George shrewdly redirected the conversation into Allison's court. "Your mother, here, has been bragging about your business," he initiated, "sounds very interesting. I've done quite a bit of carpentry work, and Daro there has bent a few nails in his day."

Brian happily detailed the work of their remodeling and restoring Cape, Colonial, Federal, Georgian, and Victorian homes. Allison joined in, elaborating on their increase in business and recent rains compounding a tight calendar. Lillian took the initiative, suggesting they add their two wandering dinner guests to Brian's work crew.

At her suggestion, Allison's head spun from assisting Benny. Her long hair fanned out across her shoulders. "What about it, Boys? As payroll clerk, I can guarantee the wages are fair and as innkeeper, the lodging is clean."

"Plus, the meals are excellent," promised Brian with his raised fork.

"And," Hughie chuckled, "no mailboxes to be installed."

George and Brian reached their long arms across the dinner to shake hands. Even Benny raised his glass to a ceremonial toast as a light evening shower christened our business agreement. It could be argued who welcomed the dessert more, Benny or me. We were quite the dynamic dining duo, the first to dig in and the last to finish.

I ignored Lillian's orders not to help as I carried dishes to the counter and scraped them. I could tell she appreciated the quality of politeness, especially in a man.

Allison was filling the sink as she noticed Brian looking out the large bay window. She'd grown accustomed to watching him when he was unaware. "It doesn't look like the storm will hit tonight," he said.

"Then we should be able to get in a full day's work, Boss," smiled George, sensing the darkness about our new employer.

Brian shrugged his shoulders, his voice like a murmur. "I could use a good rain." He sighed deeply as he returned to the kitchen. "The silver ships of souls."

Allison smiled weakly at his approach. We figured out later it was because they had their own schedule for the next morning. The couple's personal restoration was hinting of collapse and failure.

The laundry room off the breezeway included a large cupboard containing guest linens. I grabbed our canvas bags from the car while George got our jackets as Oöso watched closely.

Allison took the time to deliver a quick loving pat to the pooch, pulling out extra blankets and two large fluffy towels for us. We followed Oöso as she galloped up the stairs to one of the two guest rooms until we heard Polly screech from downstairs.

"Benny. Are you pulling on the kitty's tail?"

"No. Me holdin' it. Her doin' da pullin'."

"Mother!"

"I have it, dear. Show our guests to their rooms."

The room at the rear of the house was quite spacious. They'd expanded it, furnishing it with two queen-sized beds. It was painted in colors of blues, grays, and white. A slanted ceiling dipped opposite the doorway within a few feet of the floor where a large dormer window allowed a person to peer over the backyard.

Allison rushed about, making sure we were comfortable. "The dressers are empty. A few of Benny's winter things are stored in the closet," as she slid them aside.

"That's fine." George moved to the bed by the window and placed his cap atop the wooden bedpost. He tossed a jacket on each bed. "We don't take up much room."

"Anything you might need will either be in the hall closet or guest bath, just outside to the right. Don't be afraid to poke about," as she politely excused herself.

Both of us noticed the way her mood had become subdued with nightfall. She feared and hated being alone.

Brian saw her returning down the stairs as he straightened the throw rug by the kitchen counter. Now their conversation consisted of a more private nature.

"Tomorrow's pretty busy, what with starting the new guys." He paused, "And, then I've got some errands to run, so I won't be able to pick you up."

She already knew he would have errands. Their moods generally weren't too great following their counseling sessions. "That's fine. I told mother I'd be right home since she's watching Benny. Good night."

She leaned to kiss his cheek but he had already turned away and was headed out the door for his apartment.

CHAPTER NINE

THE START OF A PUDDLE

ALLISON HAD A KNACK for raising the spirits of other people, and doing so was a way for her to raise her own, a necessity after another counseling session. Mixing the music of Randy Crawford, Dan Fogelberg, Christian Kane, Wendy Webb, and James Taylor helped her mood with setting the table to follow our first day on the job.

She used a few slender tree branches to form a base of rich green tear-dropped leaves to fill a blue-and-beige vase and then placed several yellow roses surrounded by multi-stemmed buds of purple and pale yellows protruding from the center with daisy types of deep orange.

Next she busied herself with the food preparation. In peeling and dicing the fresh elephant-eared garlic, she popped a crescent-shaped clove into her mouth. The hot flavor burst made her eyes water. She sucked on an ice cube to ease the pungent taste as she held the cobalt-blue goblets up to the light to be sure they were spot-free.

She always enjoyed having her parents join them for a meal, plus efforts to prepare a special meal for guests shifted her thoughts from her confrontation with Brian. As the day wore on, her hopes had returned, clinging to reconciliation.

Dry weather held throughout the day, allowing us a full day's work. For being in what I considered great shape, I was moving slower than normal. Maybe the good showing I made for our first day was a bit too showy. My feet were heavy as I stopped to lean on the stair rails before going up to wash and I felt Benny's eyes on me.

"Wotsa matta, Daaw-oh?" the little squirt asked as I grimaced bending to retrieve Oöso's fuzzy tennis ball.

Following dinner, George helped clear the dishes around Benny and me as we finished our dessert, able to feel the muscle throb when he patted my shoulder. Allison was the first to notice her soon-to-be ex-husband staring absently out the dining room window.

His beloved rain clouds were hovering lower, creating a charred ceiling. Clouds melted in dark shadows of violets to blues with a periodic flash of white lightning followed by thunder. Brian smiled. "When I was Benny's age, I thought that was God turning on the lights in Heaven and his dogs were growling."

As the droplets trickled down the windowpanes, each one became its own prism. Allison interrupted his silence. "Go on," she coaxed. "Mom and I will do the dishes."

He turned with a grin as he looked at us. "This is one of my idiosyncrasies that both ladies have come to accept."

She supported his comment. "Besides, he does the dishes a lot of the time."

Looking content and even younger, he brushed a kiss on her cheek as he placed his dishes on the counter, heading for the breezeway.

"Actually, I used to go too. I couldn't break him of the habit, so I joined him." Her laugh was melodic, "He says he's on a mission from God."

Out of earshot, Brian pulled on his boots as the ladies dealt with the meager leftovers. As usual, Lillian made him a care package. When the screen door gently slapped behind him, Allison pointed past the central stairway to the long rustic mantel. Among the photos, a simple wooden stand held a small yellow rain cap.

"He says he has to free the puddles." She animated her comment in an exaggerated, hollow stomp on the wide tan planks of her dining room floor.

As George moved to the window, the image of his face

reflected in the panes. With rapt attention, he watched Brian turn almost childlike, walking unconcerned, oblivious to all else, wandering in the rain. His hair gleamed, as his curls resisted the moist weight, face raised to the heavens with each drop gently caressing his skin.

Allison saw me cross into the living room, my curiosity focused on the child's rain cap setting to the far left. She answered my unvoiced question in a reverent voice.

"Brian loves the rain. His brother started that ritual. Benjamin, that is, Benny's namesake." She paused to clarify, "Freeing the puddles." She looked at the rain cap. "Always took Brian out to play in the rain and puddles. Guess he was afraid of the rain and Benjamin helped him overcome that fear. It turned out that their mother had done the same with Benjamin when he was little." She smiled, "So years later, Brian inducted Benny into freeing puddles."

Two panes above the windowsill, George's open palm pressed against the glass as if sending energy. Brian's arms were stretched wide, his body turning slow circles, mouth open wide to taste the sweet rain, his eyelashes like grass touched by early morning dew.

Allison peered over her double sink out the window, a soft look appearing on her face. "He still misses him, his big brother Benjamin, and his mother. Both left the earth too early. Sometimes the rain's his only link to them." Her eyes grew misty with the weather as she traced a raindrop. "*Silver ships of souls*, he calls them."

Hughie cautiously approached the breakfast bar. "Excuse me, Hon. It was delicious, but I need to finish some phone calls." This allowed him to avoid the upcoming topic and leave.

Lillian had turned to help Benny with his coloring, joining the conversation in a tone of disappointment and irritation. "Allison met Brian in high school but he never asked her out until college. He was a good boy. Unfocused, but we thought he'd come around." She emphatically leaped ahead. "They should've dated more people."

Allison attempted to soften the atmosphere. "C'mon, Mother. We dated others but we didn't have as much fun with anyone else."

"Some of those other boys had their minds on their careers

and families. More responsible about finances," her mother shrugged.

"Kind of dull, smooching money," I popped, which prompted a glare from Lillian.

Allison finished filling the sink with hot foamy suds, a formality before placing the dishes in the dishwasher when her mother was visiting. She whispered, "Brian was shy. I had to ask him out first. We married a few months after he turned twenty-five, older than when many others are married."

She hung her head as Lillian dramatically dished up a touch of guilt. "They became parents in their third year. Now, just past the seventh year and they're relinquishing their bond for life, and heading for divorce court."

It was an effective guilt trip as Allison picked up the thought. "It was hoped that it would be a friendly divorce." The words caught in her throat. "The most frustrating thing," as she looked at her son, "is the fact that we're very much in love. Brian, we, it's just that we're unable to make it work. I don't know why."

"It's Brian," began Lillian with judgment fueled by disappointment.

"What've you done to make it work?" asked George, returning the focus to her daughter.

"Counseling," she shrugged, "but it seems to be too late." She shook her head and her voice trailed off.

I was surprised to hear my own voice as I looked at Lillian while touching the slick vinyl of the rain hood. "Sometimes, we find it easier to work on improving others instead of working on ourselves." I lifted the small rain cap as if talking to it.

"It's like trying to empower others. We can only empower ourselves. I've met, I mean, we've met people…husbands and wives who pray together, who visualize the kind of life they want together. They've learned to support each other in a healthful way. These couples focus on doing the *Work*, with a capital *W*. They work on sharing, creating, and repeating their goals together. I think it keeps everything, everybody more aware. More conscious, more focused."

George turned to the ladies. "Imagine sharing things with your spouse that you normally only share with your best friend." He let them think. "You know it's possible, spouse and best friend can be one and the same."

Allison hid her emotions well. Both ladies were aware of subjects they'd shared with friends that they'd never shared with their spouses, or even with each other. She leaned on the counter, her arms out straight. "Benny and our business will be our only link. Although he's moved out, he often has dinner with us. We hoped it might bring us closer together." Under the strain, her voice was barely audible. "We're just, just so damned scared."

It was clear that Lillian was uncomfortable with weighty or explorative topics, a trait she'd passed on to her daughter. This lack of discomfort in Brian had attracted Allison yet clashed with Lillian. Although he had trouble voicing his problems, he seldom dodged the issues or hid his opinions, rarely ran from a fight or a confrontation.

While Allison had succeeded in stepping away from a few of the limiting mannerisms she'd inherited, it was obvious that her mother remained a slave to them. Such was illustrated when the grandmother attempted to divert the conversation with her animated suggestion of a blue crayon to the active grandchild.

Benny shoved it away. "Don't want boo sky."

She pushed for control. "Benny, this blue crayon is the correct one for skies. It's the color artists use."

Once again, I spoke without forethought. "Actually, every child's an artist. The problem is remaining an artist as he becomes an adult."

"Says who?" she snapped.

"A dude named Pablo Picasso," I quipped.

Some learn a lesson and just keep coming back for more. Or maybe it's just me but I had to grin as Lillian continued to orchestrate Benny's coloring, an exercise he found out-of-tune.

"Benny, dear, here's a big piece of paper that you began coloring. Do you want to work on it? It looks pretty. What is it?"

"I makin' a pitch-yer of God."

The silence was as deafening as if the archangels were bowling.

Her eyebrows arched as she cleared her throat, almost apologetically. "Benny, dear, no one knows what God looks like."

"I not done. Wait 'til I finishes the pitch-yer."

Two lessons seemed enough for Lillian so the grandmother resumed the previous topic. "Benny was named for Brian's brother. I don't know why because he was never around."

Razor blades flashed in Allison's deep green eyes, her voice loomed in defense. "Benjamin was a wonderful brother. He had to be to have left such an impact on Brian." She turned to us. "He was quite a bit older. Benjamin was named after their father, and it was naturally assumed Benjamin would follow in the family business."

Lillian smugly interjected, "Guess Brian *is* like his brother. He never does anything normal as one would expect someone to do."

Without missing a beat, Allison resumed. "Their father owned a construction company. It began to consume him with a major remodeling job on The Village Market in La Grange. Lots of prestige and recognition came with the job. Meanwhile, Benjamin grew more disenchanted with his father's expectations. The business nevertheless thrived, compelled by their father's vision of success while less time was spent with the family."

"Except one night," chirped Lillian. "Brian's what one might call a surprise."

Allison drew in a deep breath. "Benjamin was already seventeen and graduating from Hinsdale High when Brian was born." Suddenly a flash of lightning followed by a hearty clap of thunder caused Lillian to look out the window. Her daughter reassured her. "He'll be fine."

Lillian shrugged. "Come help me, Benny. We'll load the dishwasher."

"She's worried about Brian," whispered Allison. "She sounds rough on him sometimes. The truth is, and she hates this term, he does *piss her off*." Her freckled nose crinkled as we laughed. "But he only bugs her because of how much she cares for him. Although they've had their share of quarrels, he loves her very much. He adopted her in his heart as his mother, too."

"Quite a tribute," I noted. "I hold a special place for moms."

"One of his saving graces," she smiled. "Another is he always asks my mother to dance when we're out for the evening. And he never gives her a book he hasn't read and inscribes something inside. Big hit with my mother because she reads a great deal."

Lillian pretended to be oblivious to the conversation, concealing her smile.

"Truth is," sighed Allison, "she'll miss him."

The smile faded.

George noted in a low voice, "And she probably feels betrayed. Sees divorce as his failing and disappointing you. Therefore, it allows her to be disappointed too."

This gave Allison an added view of burdens placed upon Brian. Sensing her desire to keep talking, we moved into the living room. As she settled onto the overstuffed chair, we learned how the new baby's arrival had affected Benjamin and the family years ago.

"When their father heard that they'd be having another child, he relentlessly began to strive for greater success. I don't think he ever felt secure in the role of a father, especially after his disagreements with Benjamin."

"What disagreements?" I asked.

"Fights, actually. I imagine their father felt somewhat deserted without any interest from Benjamin to assume the family business."

George said, "When someone disappoints another person, they let down that person's *expectations* by not doing the things they're *expected* to do. Sometimes, the first person becomes defensive to raise his own ego. I imagine seeing less of her husband and getting less of his attention led Brian's mother to become more withdrawn. Probably the only way she could protect herself from the pitfall of loving a husband with no time left for her and their family."

Allison nervously moved on quickly. "Benjamin was really affected by all this upheaval, adding to his already rebellious behavior. Pushed to assume control of his father's business, he became more conscious of his father's actions. By the comments I heard, his father no longer seemed to enjoy his work, but became almost a slave to it."

"So," I summarized, "here's Benjamin, a youngster who wanted to spend time with his dad as father and son, rather than boss and employee or founder and heir. On top of that, he saw his mother being ignored."

She nodded in agreement. "Evidently from what his mother told Brian years later, she discussed her feelings with Benjamin, but never her husband. She also felt guilty that Benjamin rejected scholarships from out-of-state to be near her and little Brian."

"Quite a weight. Friend instead of son, counselor and confidant rather than merely being a child," observed George. "It must've placed quite a burden on him."

"And?" I get impatient easily.

"Years later, their mother regretted not listening to Benjamin's suggestions to leave her husband. By the time Brian was two years old their father was little more than a bread-winner for the family. Benjamin, at nineteen, was filling in the missing gaps. Almost a father to Brian and as you said, a confidant and friend to his mother. He took Brian on errands, wrestled with him, and played with him in the rain. Even after renting his own apartment, a day never passed without Benjamin seeing Brian."

"So what ever happened to Benjamin?"

"As you heard Mother blurt out, having Brian wasn't planned. Benjamin turned twenty-one when Brian was four."

"That's an important developmental time for a youngster,

between four and five, same age as Benny. Learning music, numbers, language, colors. Parents are already thinking of him growing up, attending school. The energy around him is felt, if not spoken." George looked toward the window. "So what happened?"

"Their father was a control freak. He never related to people. Ironic, as people skills are Brian's best trait." Nervously she toyed with a pillow and then her hair. "The pressure on Benjamin to join his father's business became too great a burden. Almost a curse."

All I did was raise my eyebrows to get her to continue.

"Their father would manipulate things to have his own way. Whenever Benjamin came to him for help, the father considered it a favor the son owed him. His father made deals with his son in order to trap him into working for him."

The crack of George's knuckles filled the room.

She clenched the patchwork pillow. "The education Benjamin received and the jobs he worked merely made him realize that his and his father's reasons for making money greatly differed. Yet he was afraid that he'd fall under his father's control. He knew he had to escape his father's shadow and seeing his mother had failed to accomplish that, he decided to escape by physically severing the relationship. And she supported it."

"Sounds like Brian's brother was brave, considering how scared he was of the old man," I noted. "What'd he do?"

"Benjamin knew what his father's reaction would be." Turmoil was evident as she folded the pillow in half. "You have to understand, this was a man more concerned that his son be a quarterback than a scholar, more adamant he take ROTC than English. Benjamin figured he'd continue to hound him, no matter the direction in life he chose."

No one spoke for several moments, and then naturally I broke the silence. "Sad. People seek love and respect, and try to find it by using fear and intimidation. Then they seem so surprised, offended even, when it backfires."

"Backfire it did. After he was forced to take ROTC, he forged his escape plan. His senior year, he secretly passed exams to join the Army Air Force."

"Thumbed his nose at the old man," I chuckled. "So much for the Marines."

Allison nodded. "Benjamin shared his plans with his mother right before the school year ended, so when it concluded, he could discreetly leave for boot camp. He'd lied to his father but wouldn't lie to her. He respected her and she supported his lie. She was even willing to sign permission papers if necessary."

"If nothing else, to avoid another confrontation," I said.

"They concocted a story that Benjamin was taking a road trip with friends before continuing Business College. In truth, he went to boot camp in Valdosta, Georgia."

"That'd be Moody Air Force Base," George announced. "Her support showed some backbone on her part. She had to know the way her husband would react."

"She'd already lost her husband. The marriage was finished, no more than a charade. She feared losing her son, too."

"How'd Benjamin do?" I asked.

Allison's mellow laugh crinkled her freckled nose. "I've heard the story so many times. His mother finally shared it with Brian in his teen years. Benjamin's ROTC grades allowed him to skip Airman Basic Training, entering the service as an Airman Third Class, with one stripe at the head of his class." Her voice held pride.

"Good career base," George nodded.

"I feel at times I knew his brother and mother. I'm sorry that I didn't get to meet them."

My expression admitted I was lost.

"Since Brian and I didn't date until college, I never had the chance to meet Benjamin nor Mrs. Poppy either." She smiled. "I'm ahead of myself." She regained her composure and her place in the story.

"Benjamin knew his mother's will power was weak around his father, and he feared his dad's controlling reach could even extend into the service. Having excelled when he enlisted in boot camp, he had his choice of training and duty. He opted to focus on a stint overseas and became part of an elite team of servicemen."

"Low self-esteem is often a catalyst to take on dangerous roles," said George as he ran a finger down the windowpane. "He hated his father, yet sought his approval. Probably hoped he'd make him proud. When did the old man discover his enlistment?"

"Benjamin returned home from boot camp at his mother's insistence. She hoped that her husband would accept their son and bless his career choice. Evidently Benjamin thought a chance existed because he came home for a week. All decked out in his uniform," she laughed, "with one of those horrid haircuts, having graduated at the top of his class."

We waited.

"Rather than proud, their father felt betrayed. The father went ballistic. He almost became physical with Benjamin but I guess his son had beefed up in boot camp."

"They use a lot of push-ups for discipline," George chuckled.

I winked at him. "He still does 200 push-ups every morning."

"An old habit, but for different reasons now."

She forced a grin. "When their mother took Benjamin to the airport, their father went on a rampage. Destroyed everything associated with his black-sheep son. In his rage, he destroyed direct links to Brian's life, too." She looked at the mantle. "That's why you don't see any pictures."

We finally understood.

"Any mementos, high school awards, photographs, newspaper clippings, even baby books. All gathered in frenzy and trashed. Brian swears he can remember, even though he was only four, coming home and seeing spots on the walls where photos had hung for years.

Everything had been thrown into his father's truck and carted away. He pitched anything and everything that bore any association to Benjamin. It all just, disappeared. Benjamin's twenty-one years and Brian's fewer than five, they just ceased to exist."

"What a jerk." I snapped as I flexed my fingers. "What'd their mom do?"

"The day that this…upheaval greeted her, she built a cocoon around herself. Never forgave her husband and stayed married only because of little Brian. Benjamin, like Brian, was persistent. He made one more attempt to reconcile bad feelings about six months later, before leaving on tour. I think he did it more for Brian's sake."

"And?" asked George.

"Benjamin returned to Hinsdale unannounced. It was Brian's fifth birthday. Training complete, he was about to ship out to some remote place."

"And?" I prompted.

"His father saw him just long enough to disavow him. Benjamin only stayed for the day. Brian says he still remembers it was raining." The anger rose in her voice. "Within his first year of service, their father began to deny he even had another son. Or, when it helped business, he'd say Benjamin had died a hero in some battle." Her voice was deep, breathy. "Such an evil man."

CHAPTER TEN

THE SINS OF THE FATHER

MY HEART WENT OUT to Allison. It took her a few moments to regain her composure. She toyed with the bright yellow rain cap, taking in deep breaths. "Their father diverted all mail to his office. He forbade their mother to mention Benjamin, which she basically obeyed for years."

The comment grossed me out and stirred a rage. "How could she?"

"Fear," hushed George as his fingers drummed the ledge in time with the water dripping off the roof. It was an answer to the question, not an acceptance of the actions.

"Did Brian know then what his father had done? Trashing stuff, obstruction of mail?"

"No. Not then. She wanted to spare him more pain. Not wanting him to hate his father," she bit her lip with enough force that she left a mark, "even if he deserved it!"

"With the stunt the old man pulled, no way could Benjamin know that Brian and his mother weren't receiving his mail. Only that he wasn't hearing back from them."

She sighed deeply as she wandered to the window. "I guess Benjamin grew tired of hitting a brick wall. He finally gave up trying to reach them."

"I don't buy that," said George.

"Maybe he figured it'd make things easier on his mom and Brian if he stopped writing since he knew his father held grudges," I offered.

79

"The fact is…it's all history now." She wrung her hands. "I don't think their mother ever recovered from thinking that Benjamin assumed she'd disowned him too." She stepped away from the window. "Maybe she was too afraid to track him down. Didn't know a way to find him or afraid to make more waves. For years, she never told Brian what their father had done. She never even mentioned Benjamin to Brian until he was a teenager."

"A child feeling guilty could feel deserted," mused George. "Lotta walls could go up."

"You're right. Brian never learned that Benjamin hadn't deserted him until it was too late. Benjamin made the Army Air Force his family and excelled." She nodded toward Brian and Oöso outside in the rain. "His only memories of Benjamin are of him always having time to play with him, and freeing the puddles. Memories he was forced to keep to himself."

"No constructive memories of a father, a poor example of being a husband, few memories of a brother." George frowned visibly.

"How'd he find out what really happened?" I asked.

"More than ten years had passed since his brother's name had ever been mentioned. After Brian and I were dating, he said he sometimes thought he'd imagined he'd ever even had a brother. A whole life lived, not knowing." Abuse came in all disguises.

I felt my temper rise. "Did Brian try to find Benjamin?"

"Not before it was too late." Allison breathed deeply. "One day Brian's mother received her first contact with Benjamin in twelve years. Rather, a reference to him. Prior to Brian's seventeenth Christmas, a telegram arrived from the War Department. It began with the words *We regret to inform you*," her voice broke. "That was it. That's all they received. No remains to bury, not even a body to bid farewell to."

The tears from Lillian's eyes fell silently into the dishwater, unnoticed. She quietly lifted Benny in her arms and solemnly walked towards the stairs.

George spoke. "They say death is final. It's not true to those who remain behind."

"Surprisingly, his father took the news hard. It drove a spike deeper into his heart."

"How was that?"

"No physical body. He'd last seen his son at twenty-two. He couldn't even imagine him in his thirties, let alone dead at thirty-five. In part, he felt responsible for his son's death as if he may have preordained it. And his wife kept silent rather than throwing barbs at him."

She rose to pace near the window. "Their dad then became partners with some big investor. Work became his grave, shallow but packed firmly. Unable to make up for Benjamin, the son he'd loved and lost, and Brian, the son who'd remained but he didn't know, their father focused on his work. It allowed him to escape the condemnation he felt he deserved from his wife. Even if she'd wanted to forgive him, her love was blocked by him moving around too much for their relationship to do anything but stagnate."

Allison looked tired from this chronological journey, one she'd traversed many times. "Brian tried to punish him for the loss of Benjamin by breaking things off with their father."

I walked closer. "How'd he do that?"

"A year after learning of Benjamin's death, Brian left home at eighteen. No one stopped him and no one gave him a reason to stay. His taste of love and the open affection of an older brother had been taken away when he was only four years old."

I used my fingers as I figured. "So he had one good example for less than…one-eighth of his life. One of Brian's greatest challenges is that he never had a decent role model for fathering or for being a husband. He can imagine it, hope for it, but not visualize a healthy one."

She concluded in almost a whisper. "The counselors say since he never really had anyone to talk with, he has trouble talking about his own problems. He listens way better than sharing. His mother was nurturing, but he couldn't talk about Benjamin. Therefore, he keeps to himself at times. He feels as if he has to go it alone."

Lillian crossed back into the room, having put Benny to bed. She interrupted gently. "Allison, dear, make sure you tuck him in."

Upon her return, Hughie entered, hanging up his phone. He kissed his daughter and took his wife's arm. "C'mon, Hon." He led her to the door. "Nice meeting you fellows."

With them gone, talk continued and we learned more about Allison's side of the family. Early home life had been unstable as her parents maintained a pretense of a perfect marriage, the only way they knew to cope. Pretend, fake it. It did little to create a picture of communication skills for Allison and her siblings.

Death and sex were among the topics that remained off-limits. Lillian had only grown close to Allison since Benny's birth, and that relationship had been forged through osmosis with little, real, verbal communication.

Hughie took care of his family financially, and wasn't a talker. He was the provider. Money was seen more regularly than he was, even after he was well established. Actions create pictures, and duplicated, they become habits.

Allison looked out to Brian still playing in the rain. "It's as if he can't let go and be a father and a husband. We're great friends. But my love isn't strong enough by itself," she whispered. "I don't know what to do."

I breathed the answer, surprising George and me. "Belief. Plus faith, in yourself."

"You make it sound easy."

Half satirically I countered, "If it were easy, it wouldn't be worth the effort." Then I nervously raked my fingers through my hair. "Choose one. The fear of failure or the fear of being left without." I shoved another cookie in my mouth.

Moments later, a sopping wet Brian re-entered the house looking at peace from his rainy sojourn. He wiped Oöso before drying his own hair with a dishtowel. Then he ran upstairs to kiss Benny good night and share in a tickle. After a collective, "Night," he headed for his truck.

ONCE WE WERE UPSTAIRS in the guestroom, I reached for my notebook as George stepped to the window. Too tired to write, I tossed it on the dresser and pulled my green sweat pants and a couple items out of my bag. I leaned over checking in the oval dresser mirror for whiskers and then threw a towel over my shoulder. We could hear Allison leaving Benny's room, headed down the wooden stairs.

As I passed George at the window, we shared the view of the backyard. Brian sat beneath the shelter of the tree house, his arms wrapped around his knees, his head down so low that only his shoulders were visible.

I patted George on the shoulder. "Well, Bunkie, looks like your boss and your intuition are correct. I'd say we have our work cut out for us." I headed down the hall.

LATE THAT NIGHT WHILE George and I rested in our bunks, the rain resumed falling on the peaked roof. Well into slumber land, I woke for a second. My quilt was twisted, my foot sticking out as my personal barometer. I looked toward the window but made no sounds.

George appeared restful, lying on his back, completely dressed. His sheets remained un-rumpled and smooth. When the green numerals of the digital clock on the nightstand gleamed *12:06*, his eyes popped open. He glanced at the time and then stared intently at the ceiling.

Unknown to me, the movie screen in our minds played the same scenarios of Brian putting on his boots and Benny playing in a mud puddle. George's eyes darted to the trail of rain on the window and then quickly closed. I stretched, pulled up my blanket, and went back to sleep.

CHAPTER ELEVEN

SOMETIMES WHEN THE TEACHER IS READY, THE STUDENT APPEARS

THE RAIN HAD SLACKENED by dawn. The trees looked crisper and the air smelled pure as the sun made the dark mud bake before drying to a tan and cracking later in the day. On the second floor, new lumber was cool to the touch.

I was assigned to work with Tom, a teenager from New Mexico, who had only been on the crew a couple weeks. Apprentices often try to use the largest hammer, hoping to impress, like the greenhorn gunslingers of the Old West carrying long-barreled pistols. Both generally presented more danger to themselves than others.

Pimpled and insecure, he carried a brand new twenty-eight-ounce East Wing claw hammer that he had to grip halfway up the tan handle. We immediately had a rub. The teenager told dirty jokes, figuring it would gain admiration from the crew. He tried levity whenever he messed up, actually bringing more attention to his shortcomings.

Tom bent another nail, his heavy hammer thudding hollow on the wood as he cursed and resorted to an old carpentry joke. "Hey, Daro, here's my problem." He held up several dark nails. "Half of these have the heads on the wrong end."

"Those are for the other side of the house," I slammed.

The kid was a slow learner and I had a few years on him. He soon found reason to take his humor downstairs. I was relieved as I was having my own problems, building a channel joint to attach a short wall. I rattled the nails in my pouch as I studied the situation.

Brian stopped on his way to the truck. Without a word, he altered the positioning of the 2-by-6-inch lumber and smiled. "There. Now nail it," and he was gone.

I was appreciative but my glance to George showed my embarrassment. "Does being shown the way to do something bother you?" he asked.

"Sometimes it does. Like when I feel I should've known." I paused, mid-swing with my hammer. "Frankly, most of the time I just feel plain dumb, and when someone has to show me something, that feeling gets worse."

"There are always smarter folks. Otherwise, look how dull it would be. You tell me how much you learn from me, but do you realize how much I learn from you?"

I assessed the channel I'd built as I evaluated the conversation. More to stall than anything else.

He looked at me. "To be taught…to be a student, is no lesser place to be. We just tend to notice the point of learning because it's something new. Teaching is often a more natural or automatic action because we already know it. Remember when you repaired Lillian's mailbox? How difficult was that?"

"C'mon."

He leapt ahead. "Sure, it was easy for you. And I could have done the same repair. But what about Benny? What about his helping you?"

"George, be real. The kid's only four."

"Go back, go deep. What was Benny really doing?"

I replied without thinking. "He was watching me. Imitating me. When I walked around, he walked around. When I looked under the car, he looked... Hey." I drove the nail in with one swing. "He was learning. Benny was learning. He couldn't repair a mailbox but he'll remember some of what he saw me do. He was learning."

George holstered his hammer into the ring of his tool belt to applaud my realization. "And you didn't know you were teaching. It was automatic. So, while Benny didn't know the difference between learning and teaching, even his wee mind knew he was doing something new, and it didn't bother him. You helped develop a new picture for him. The role of student and the role of teacher are both honorable, and for it to work, we must have both."

"Is that like the first-force, second-force thing?"

"Yeah, somewhat. There must be moments of exchanging titles, whereby teacher becomes student and student becomes teacher." He grasped a handful of nails from the water-stained cardboard box to refill his leather pouch. "At one time a person's credibility rested upon the endorsement of a teacher or university. This necessity is being lost to ego and vanity as a result of the arrogance of individualism afoot on this land. People have this idea that they have to do it alone or are too good to be taught. Socrates taught Plato, Plato taught Aristotle, and none of them was embarrassed."

"Aristotle?" I repeated. "*For the things we have to learn before we can do them, we learn by doing them.*"

"Very good."

I pursed my lips as I mentally reviewed his example of Benny and me. "So, part of Brian and Allison's problem seems to be that they are both trying to be the teacher."

"We're always students, always learning, and always teachers. However, proper teaching leads to understanding, understanding leads to love, and love leads to service."

"Okay, so Brian had poor teachers and learned the lessons that didn't work."

"Because that's the only picture he'd seen."

"Like when you say, *don't look*, rather than, *look this way*. So, he's trying to teach himself by looking only at the ideas that didn't work and with no guides."

"That's pretty much it," said George.

"Until now?" I squinted.

"Maybe," George grinned.

The only sounds made for some time came from our hammers and saws. He was ripping through a sheet of plywood when I felt a smirk cross my face.

"Hey, George, you just did it to me. I was the student and you the teacher as you explained that whole mess. After learning Benny's position, I saw I was his teacher. Now I see Brian's predicament at this point in his life, by being your student."

He resumed his cut, halfway along the chalk line on the plywood, spewing sawdust. The twinkle in his eyes showed through his goggles as he rewarded me with a wink. I didn't expect to complete the wall and supports until the next day, but I finished the project with finesse, surprising Brian when he returned, which felt really cool.

"Looks good," he reassured me. "Maybe I should put Tom in your hands tomorrow." George laughed as I coiled the orange power cord, trying to focus on dinner rather than the pending dilemma of the next day's work saddled with the new kid.

Brian dropped us at the house and then headed to meet with his neighbor. Walking past the breakfast counter, I noticed the dining room window was a natural frame for a priceless picture. Allison and Lillian shared the moment.

The normally white Oöso wore dark socks, complements of the moist Illinois soil. Benny was soaked past his knees. A dog and his child at play, both with a special mission of freeing the puddles. But Lillian was concerned that Benny might catch a cold.

"Oh, come on, Mother," chided Allison. "We play at Timber Lake so Oöso can swim and Benny's just fine."

"And how 'bout them Indians? Barefoot all year. Hardly wore a stitch," I laughed.

"Just watch those two," marveled George, oblivious to all else.

The Poppy's yard was home to several puddles. Those near the tree house offered the most mud because of the grass worn away. The two had their ritual down pat. Oöso bounded gleefully until she heard Benny's call.

"Oooo-so!"

The dog then scampered over to the child who had staked out the next captive puddle for them to rescue. Benny placed his hand on her back that stood level to his shoulders as the half-wolf anxiously waited for the signal.

"One. Taa-ooo. TWWWEEE," he hollered as they both leapt into the air, landing as far into the center of the puddle as possible.

His laugh was enhanced by her bark while the water settled over their ankles. Then a joyous screech sounded as he insured the puddle's freedom with avid marching steps, forcefully applied in quick succession. Oöso circled about her playmate in bouncing mannerisms. Then they were off to stake out another trapped puddle and set it free.

"Like father, like son," Allison shook her head with a grin. "He used to be so afraid of the rain, but before he could stand, Brian had him outside on his shoulders. As soon as Benny could walk, it was a contest to see who jumped the puddles first." She glanced at her mother, the jab was playful. "And they never caught a cold."

Lillian laughed, hoping to change the subject. "Well, I must admit that dog sure loves that little boy. She's shadowed him since he was born."

Allison added, "Brian refers to Oöso as Benny's white shadow. She was especially protective when he was…"

"Still a squib," concluded Brian as he entered with Jason. Jason Johnson was his crew chief and neighbor, who still blushed at the retelling of the story.

"I was alone watching Benny. He was just a couple months

old in his crib by my desk. Oöso was in an old easy chair when Jason came over to see the baby. We never thought anything about it when I went down the hall."

Jason shrugged. "See, when Brian was single, I used to watch and feed Oöso when he was out of town. I'd play Frisbee with her and Zorro, our black Lab. So Oöso and me, we're supposed to be buds."

Brian resumed the narration about Jason reaching in the crib to touch the baby, which evidently didn't meet with Oöso's approval. Silently and swiftly she was between him and the crib with his forearm clasped in her mouth.

"She wasn't hurting me," Jason recalled. "But when I tried to move, she'd clamp down tighter, and her tail would quit wagging, so I stood there in this bent-over position," he demonstrated, "waiting for Brian to return. Finally, I began to call Brian's name really soft-like, not wanting to upset the dog. Her eyebrows were twitching as if she were thinking, evaluating the whole event. And the entire time she had those big brown eyes focused on me…and those big white teeth on me, too."

It was obvious Brian enjoyed telling this story. "So here I was at the end of the hall and I see Jason," as he imitated the pose. "Bent over at the hips, right arm to the crib out of my view, he was looking down the hall at me, but only with his eyes, not his whole head. I could see all of the white in his eyes."

Our laughter propelled him along.

"Here's Jason. His jaw is clenched with only his lips moving in a high voice. *Brian. Briiiaaan.* So I run back to see what's happening. I said Oöso's name, and over the top of her head I could see her eyebrows twitching." He leaned his head back, imitating the dog with his eyes turned big and wide. "She's trying to look at me without releasing Jason's arm."

Laughter intensified with his gyrations of coaxing Oöso into releasing Jason's arm by petting his hand while reassuring the dog that everything was okay. "As soon as she released it, she shifted directly between him and the baby, staring up at him."

"Attitude," I mumbled.

"It was a whole year before I even held the baby," murmured Jason, absently rubbing his right wrist.

Our chuckles were interrupted by a tiny knock from the backyard at the French doors, followed by Benny's boisterous request for puppy treats. Allison handed him three dog biscuits. "We're going to eat soon. Make him work for them, Honey."

"*Her*," corrected Benny.

"Make *her* work for them," she amended.

Six legs scampered down the porch steps as he called over his shoulder, "Gonna show Madmoe her tricks."

Lillian's head fell back. "Madmoe," she repeated with obvious disgust. Clearly the grandmother disapproved of his fantasy friend.

Allison had prepared a wonderful dinner but Benny played with his mom's mashed potatoes rather than devouring them as he did when they were his grandmother's. All the coaxing was to no avail. It didn't help matters when the boy sneaked a spoonful to the dog, and she refused them. Concerned about Allison's feelings and still a bit of the rescuer, I loaded an extra scoop of potatoes on my plate. They weren't...bad.

Following dinner, Brian carried the last of the plates to the sink, stopping to kiss Benny being taken to bed by his mother, until he squirmed free from her arms.

Somewhere in the genes of a child exists the DNA assemblage to prevent him from going to bed when asked. Benny found the aquariums adequate to stall the inevitable bedtime as he pulled George and me along.

In the living room were two large salt-water fish tanks. One held 75 gallons, sitting on an oak table, and another holding 125 gallons built into the bookshelves. It may sound silly that I think of such fish as being incarcerated against their will in brightly lit synthetic underwater worlds. As Benny pointed to each fish, Brian helped.

The most noticeable finned captives were the lumbering big flat Yellow Tangs. Darting about the corrals of rust red and bright white was a school of blue Damsels, much smaller with luminous blue and dark blue trim. The Flame Angels were named because of their orange with black stripes. The gray-with-blue Humma Hummas were Benny's favorite, simply because of the name. They were hanging close to three ornamental silver dollars whose spirits had left them in California, their shells lying in the gravel. But the young tour guide saved the best for last. His very own fish tank.

Actually, a two-gallon bowl manned with a little helmet-clad diver releasing a regular flow of bubbles for the two inexpensive fish. A gold one with a black companion darted about as the child placed his open palm gently against the bowl. "Penny 'n' Blackie," he proudly introduced.

Allison re-entered, successfully re-scooping Benny up in her arms. Everyone offered their own good night wishes as she held him out to deliver hugs while Brian wrapped the clingy cellophane around an extra slice of Lillian's blueberry pie.

"G'nite Daddy, I luff you," as he snagged another kiss and a tickle. He turned and leaned into me, giggling with, "G'nite Unca Daaw-oh." Then he turned and voiced, "G'nite Unca Jaa- urge-val- more. Luff you."

I noticed that George's reaction was a blend of surprise followed by aloofness.

CHAPTER TWELVE

THE THINGS WE READ AND SEE

UPSTAIRS AFTER TWO REQUESTS for a drink, the first being for "kishin' waa-er" and another for "baffwume waa-er," Benny finally began to settle down.

I was eyeing the plasma TV that sat in the corner between the window box and fireplace. So big it reminded me of back home at the Round-Up Drive-In. The custom book shelves held ample DVDs and I flirted with them and a couple of books as I browsed some of the titles, attempting to ignore my buddy's somber mood.

"Hey, George, did you see this collection?" He barely turned so I continued. "Allison showed me a section of books Brian's been gathering for Benny for when he's old enough. She said they all have notations and inscriptions explaining why he picked them for him."

All were alphabetized with colorful spines. I put a fresh bandaid over my blistered finger, running it across the titles. Beneath the books were more DVDs, also alphabetized. Stored in two rows, classic and current ones. Many contained similar notes from Brian.

"Look at these movies. *The Ghost and Mrs. Muir, Hans Christian Anderson, Harvey, Jack.*" I skipped around. "Good choices. *It's a Wonderful Life.* And here's the 1947 one of *Miracle on 34th Street*, not that terrible remake. And *Mister Roberts.* What a cast. Cagney, Fonda, and Lemmon. They just don't make 'em like that anymore."

George was fiddling with the fire as I turned back to him. "She told me that Brian's plan is to present them to Benny when he turns fourteen. You've said before that we mold ourselves only by the things we read and the people we know."

"Great idea," he mused absently, "but it wasn't my thought, I quoted it." His attention was diverted to the enormous amount of rain being dumped outside.

I glanced heavenward with a satirical comment. "Hope God isn't pulling a déjà vu with forty days of rain."

Silence. Difficult crowd. Now he was mesmerized with the crackling fire.

"Hey, George, you okay?" I prodded gingerly. "You sure got touchy when Benny said good night to us."

Still, no reply was issued.

"So, what's the matter?"

He barely shook his head. "Nothing."

"Didn't you take an oath or something not to be telling fibs?"

A soft chuckle finally escaped him, more of a breathy release. "I have a job to do. We, I mean, I can't become attached."

"Attached? You mean to tell me you didn't feel anything when you were feeding that boy, huh? Besides," I teased, "I thought we were only human. You mean we're not supposed to feel emotions?" I continued to prod. Patience isn't my strong suit.

He looked as if to speak, but no words came out.

I was frustrated although I kept my cool. "I thought I was a tough nut to crack. What kind of family did you come from? Just realized that after all we've talked about, that we never talked about your upbringing."

George almost whispered, "That was a long time ago." Embers flared as he poked at the fire, his voice slightly more audible. "Yeah, okay. I care about them."

I felt terrible for the way I had spoken but he continued.

"I see Brian's pain, his confusion. I see the way his path led to this point in his life and the direction he's headed. I can feel the uncertainties, the fears. I can feel, I can feel," his voice began to trail off. "Already, I feel so close to them. To Benny, to all of them, to Brian."

"You sure got a funny way of showing it. My old man was a tough old bird." I mimicked my dad's gruffness. *"If it ain't bleedin' or bent funny, you cain't cry."*

With his laugh, I felt a bit better, so I asked, "What was your pop like?" Again, he began to speak but only silence came from his mouth. "C'mon, I'm always blabbing. Was your pop a good one or a jerk?"

"I don't, I don't…never mind." He lowered his head.

"Oh sorry, I didn't realize." I stumbled again, thinking he was illegitimate. "I had normal parents…I guess."

"Did you know them? No offense. Don't tell me that you lost your memories. I mean, I did some things I'd like to forget but there's a bunch I want to remember." I paced around the couch. "Is that the meaning when they say, *you can't take it with you?*"

After each outburst, George's face revealed only love and understanding for my concern. Frankly, that look bothered me more. I realized how little I knew about him. Knew he had been an MIA-turned-POW. Later he fought oil rig and then forest fires. But we'd never talked of his growing up or family. Just mine.

"Hey, George, I would think what happened to you when…" I floundered for words. "Well, that it would help you in your job now. I mean I know nobody knows everything but I learned all sorts of things when I was a fireman. Met all kinds of people. That was an education. And this running around with you." I stopped short as if molasses were caught in my breath, speech, and walk. Fear stepped into the conversation. "Hey, now, does this happen when, I mean, you know." My voice squeaked, "Die?"

An incredibly long pause before he calmly replied. "I can't tell you certain things."

"Why? You can't tell me 'cause you won't, or can't tell me 'cause you can't? Is it them rules? At least files were kept on us at the fire station." Frustrated, I headed for the stairs. "Someday I'd like to see the files on you."

George whispered, "You will."

I spun around, then I saw the grin. "You really enjoy that out-of-this-world humor." I turned back at the first landing and smiled. "Well, this mortal is heading to bed. See you in the morning, Kemosabe."

With no response, I slowed my ascent. "See you...in the morning?"

He paused, allowing the anticipation to build and then let fly with a toothy smile beneath his moustache. "Yeah, Daro, see you in the morning."

My sigh was loud as he rose to follow me up the stairs. My footsteps echoed hollow in spite of my efforts to be quiet. He walked on past me to the bathroom.

GEORGE TOOK A REALLY LONG SHOWER, rocking his head beneath the torrent of water as if to wash his thoughts free, pondering his mission. He placed his arms against the tile wall, leaning his head forward to allow the hot water to flow over the rear of his head. It channeled down his neck and strong back. The run-off cascaded down his chest and attempted to flatten the thick crop of hair, funneling down along what a lady once termed his *happy trail*. Facing into the spray, he breathed through his mouth, opening his eyes and allowing the water to distort his vision as if swimming under the ocean's surface. He was glad he no longer needed contacts.

I struggled to stay awake to chat more, but by the time he entered our room, I was close to snoozing. The moon was caught in the branches of the trees, quivering in the wind. Peering through the second-story window as he approached his bed, he mentioned the stars were hiding behind the clouds.

My buddy Lloyd's grandma is a medicine woman. She taught us that the Indians called this a *female rain*. Easy and constant, nourishing as dreams should be. I felt my body drift off into slumber. I used to apologize for snoring. George said it no longer bothered him, that it had become a type of rumbling lullaby. 'Course, he'd been taught to meditate in a soup kitchen.

THE RAIN CONTINUED in gentle massages, the birds beneath the cover of trees with their heads tucked under their wings. The leaves acted as natural gutters making waterfalls. Puddles formed as the illuminated clock beamed *12:06* in the morning.

George's eyes burst open, his body as still as the previous night. He stared at the ceiling as if seeing through it. When he rose to go to the window, not a wrinkle creased his bed. From the French-paned window, he watched the rain, beheld the way it distorted the view.

Focusing through it on the tree house. Under it sat Brian, alone again, in thought and prayer. I missed the view but kinda remember him pulling the blue patchwork comforter up over me before he walked into the hall.

Walking lightly, he peeked in on Benny. Oöso raised her head to check out the intruder. Her paw lay over Polly. Content at George's smile, she nuzzled back into the small of Benny's legs and closed her brown eyes.

Passing the fireplace, only embers and aromas remained. The rear door made no sound. Once on the deck, he looked upward and then ran his hand over the wicker furniture. The woven reeds had absorbed the moist air, making them cool to the touch with the scent of sweet straw. He saw Brian's face down in his hands, the young man totally unaware of his presence on the porch.

Delicately, George continued down the steps. A few paces into the mild rain, he stepped into a mud puddle. Startled, he recoiled. Glancing upward again, he turned and re-entered the house. Crossing past the couch at the base of the stairway, he spied the rain cap on the mantle above the glowing coals. Then he stared at the embers until they were only a memory.

CHAPTER THIRTEEN

WHITE RABBIT

WHEN CHILDREN WERE SENT into the stench of sweatshops rather than his open-air plays, Shakespeare shouted, *"Ignorance is the curse of God: knowledge is the wing where we fly to heaven."* Four-hundred years later and mentioned often in my columns, I think illiteracy remains one of the strongest means of censorship.

I had to credit Benny's family. They strove to avoid such atrocities, an exercise that Lillian enjoyed. Although unable to tell time, Benny knew. One chubby hand held a book and the other still sticky from amber pancake syrup, patted the soft skin of her face with the familiar, "M'am-maw, time to weed."

Settled with his grandmother in their habitual reading spot on the overstuffed sofa, he always sat to her right. That day, Dr. Seuss's classic *The Cat in the Hat* supplied the missing piece of a puzzle regarding Benny's request.

She read aloud as his stubby finger followed.

"The water ran out.

And then I SAW THE RING! A ring in the tub!

And, oh boy! What a thing!"

Benny excitedly patted the picture. "Pipe hat. Madmoes's pipe hat."

The commotion caught my attention as I slurped at a sweet peach slice. I walked from the kitchen licking my fingers and peeked over their shoulders. Benny had wanted a *pipe hat*, a repetitive request that left everyone in the dark, until that moment.

On page 15, standing in the bathtub with the stubborn pink ring, was the famous lanky cat. Water dripping from his trademark red-and-white striped hat. I had to laugh. "That's pretty good. I get it now. A pipe hat. A stovepipe hat. A top hat. You're pretty sharp, kiddo. Pipe hat. You're right."

Benny beamed but I suspect his higher self questioned us adults, slow to figure it out as he repeated, "Madmoe's pipe hat."

"Madmoe," Lillian sighed under her breath. The mere mention of his imaginary friend caused her concern. It didn't help her demeanor that his folks were merely amused.

Two days prior, while rummaging through a carton of clothes for the homeless, Benny had found a loudly colored necktie of his grandpa's. He had wrapped it around his neck, rambling in a musical voice. "Madmoe, Madmoe."

"Probably the divorce," Lillian muttered.

Her worry was beginning to wear on Allison who motioned for Brian to join her in the kitchen. "Do you think we need to worry? Benny acts as if this Madmoe is real. Says he protects him and Oöso, and sleeps in the tree house."

"C'mon, Allison, I had an imaginary friend and I turned out okay," he quipped while making a grotesque face, rolling his eyes with his tongue lolling to the side.

"Benjamin, no doubt," Lillian snapped, insulted that her concerns be taken so lightly.

I noticed the brusque looks both Brian and George returned over their shoulders. Still the rescuer, I offered, "It'll be okay, Lillian. I'll take Benny out to play later and see what's going on. I think it's worthwhile that you're concerned, but I'm sure it's nothing to worry about." My patronizing gesture temporarily pacified the grandmother.

George headed for the fridge, bending to find the coldest water bottle. As the couple talked, he heard her ask Brian how his morning runs were going. It was her method of checking if he was still exercising. *Snooping* is another term.

Brian admitted, "I just have no drive, no push."

She understood all too well, but she remained silent and turned her attention to other matters, mechanical behavior at its foremost.

Rescuing is a habit many folks find difficult to break. George has better self-control than me. While he was tempted to offer to run with him, he had the wisdom not to become a crutch, so he offered another tool. He leafed through the newspaper until he found the section he wanted, rolled it up, and then tapped him on the shoulder with it.

Brian turned to reach for it. "What's this?"

"An obituary. An old friend taught me this. Keep it near your bed. When you find you can't make yourself climb out of bed in the morning, read it. Any one of these folks would gladly trade places with you."

Before the depressed father could comment, a scream ignited a new calamity. He shoved the paper in his rear pocket while bolting for the front door. Benny and Oöso raced from the living room. The dog charged through the screen door to chase Zorro and two other dogs from the porch as we rushed outside and saw Allison's ashen face.

"Oh, no," groaned Brian, seeing the ruffled prone body of a dead rabbit. And not just any rabbit, but the Johnson's pet rabbit.

Benny caught up to his father as the screen door slammed. He stared, not comprehending the doggies' actions that left the rabbit soggy, muddy, and motionless.

Lillian could not bear the thought of explaining the violent death to the neighbors and certainly not to Benny. Allison was faring no better. The grandmother ignored Brian's protest when she knelt and told Benny, "It's all right. The bunny is just sleeping."

George came to Brian's support. "Death is often kept as an unknown. People fear the unknown. Don't do that to Benny. Death is a natural order of events."

"Death is *not* natural," snapped the grandmother.

"You plan on skipping that part of life, Lillian? Life and death form a circle. Without the circle, we have a broken link. Children need to know this in order to be able to handle it when it happens. We never know when they'll be exposed to death."

"He's too young. He's too young, he'll never understand."

George crossed over the rabbit and settled on the rail of the porch, never taking his eyes from the ladies. "Eggbert and Eggbertha were unborn twins who'd spent several months in their mother's womb." He scrunched his body with his arms about himself.

Brian's eyes rose in wonderment as to the direction this tale was headed. "The womb was all Eggbert and Eggbertha knew. It was home, warmth and nourishment. Suddenly, after nine months, came discomfort and change.

"A tiny white light appeared and Eggbert was drawn to a narrow passage into a tiny tunnel, into the most peduncle of all peduncles." He stretched his arms as if crawling. "This was the tiny crossing-over as birth began."

He stood upright. "Outside in the light the doctor announced, *Congratulations! You've given birth to a son.*"

His shoulders slumped. "Inside in the dark womb, *Eggbertha cried, Eggbert is gone. He's dead.*"

Allison and Lillian remained deaf to his parable as a plan began to hatch, as opposed to a hutch. Lillian used a dishtowel to carry the dead rabbit into the kitchen. There she began to fill the sink with warm water as she instructed Allison to get the hair dryer.

Brian took his son out to the truck, concerned about the mother-and-daughter Good Samaritans.

Aware that Jason had just pulled out of his drive and was headed first to pick up Tom gave the ladies ample time before he returned to get George. Bath completed, the two female allies sneaked into the Johnson's backyard with the fluff-dried rabbit wrapped in a clean towel, avoiding the rambunctious Zorro who wanted to play with the dead critter some more.

Allison turned the silver latch on the wire mesh cage, pulling the wooden frame open. Lillian carefully laid the white bunny on its side although the stiffness of death allowed no other position.

"At least he looks peaceful," said Allison as a breeze stirred the animal's soft hair. She looked questioningly as her mother pulled the gray plastic water dish from the cage and rushed over to the garden spigot to refill the bowl.

The reply came before she could ask as she tried to shush the inquisitive black dog away. "So the Johnsons won't think the poor thing died of thirst."

Satisfied with their work, the women closed the cage and quietly returned home.

Brian and I had already left, avoiding a useless clash with Lillian. Jason arrived and Tom climbed from the cab into the truck bed as George approached. They drove Tom to one of the sites and then headed for another project.

George was quieter than usual, feeling like an accomplice to the recent rabbit ruse as they sped down the congested street. Jason was tense, preoccupied with a meeting he and his wife had scheduled with the doctors about their son. Before reaching the busy intersection, the left rear tire blew, causing the small truck to lunge.

Jason swerved into the right lane, the metal rim scraping loudly against the concrete curb. "DAMN!" as he slammed his fist against the steering wheel. A shutter went through the dash. "Now, we'll be late for sure."

The physical act of changing the tire was good therapy for Jason. The hubcap popped off easily as George guarded against the hectic onslaught of rushing commuters. Adjusting the scissors jack, Jason inserted the worn iron bar, standing on it for leverage as he loosened the fourth nut and tossed it in with the others in the overturned hubcap.

George looked at the property behind him. The tall cyclone fence tapered inward, trimmed with barbed wire, leaving an ominous feeling in the pit of his stomach as if recalling a bad dream. He doubted Michael Kelly and Joseph Glidden foresaw such a use for their invention of barbed wire. "What is this place?"

"The nut, I mean, the asylum," corrected Jason, embarrassed. "The state's mental place where they put folks a few bites shy of a can of chew."

George noticed three patients approach, looking more like inmates. He sent silent love as the three leaned into the fence, their fingers clenched through the small diamond shapes created by the interwoven wires.

As the last lug nut was tossed in with the others, a car struck the hubcap with a loud metallic clang, flipping it high above the traffic. The lug nuts careened through the air, shooting haphazardly into the intersection.

Lug nuts bouncing, traffic uncaring, Jason jumped to his feet and began violently slamming the tailgate with the wrench. Amid his cussing and the flagrant rage inflicted upon their vehicle, a non-elegant almost childish voice pierced the commotion.

"Mither. Mither," it chirped impatiently.

"What?" snapped Jason spinning in his insane fury as he stared past George. "What?" he screamed again, short of breath.

"Mither," returned the stuttering voice from beyond the fence. "Why on't you take…take a nut off each of the nother tireth. Then, then…then you can drive to the gath-thation…and you…and you, you can buy more wheel-thingth."

It seemed even the traffic grew silent. George bit his lip as a blank look dawned on his downtrodden acquaintance, lug wrench turned war club held high in the air, his knuckles still white from rage.

Jason looked at the busy traffic and hubcap crushed like tin foil, then the nut-less tire, then the inmates who merely gazed back, then randomly to the traffic to his left, then into nothingness, then to the battered fender, then back to the innocent inmate who cocked his head to the side with compassion. Then he committed his next error. He looked at George, whose shoulders were shaking, trying to contain himself.

Jason slumped over the truck bed and grinned in embarrassment. It was more a statement than a question. "Why am I allowed to run loose, while they're locked up?"

Even the three patients joined in the laughter, and neither of the free men questioned if they knew the joke.

Sweat beaded on Jason's face as he rolled his neck, until it crackled in his ears. He removed a nut from the left wheel as George handed him two lug nuts from the passenger's side, never noticing that he worked with no wrench.

ON THE OTHER SIDE OF TOWN in the Poppy's driveway, Lillian buckled Benny securely into his car seat as Allison opened the door behind the driver's seat for Oöso to hop in. Every other week, the four of them had a standing date at Whispering Pines, a center for the elderly in LaGrange.

Pets & Pals was an innovative program that enabled Benny and Oöso to provide love therapy for so many whose families had forgotten them. Allison initiated the visits to instill love and respect in Benny for his elders. Initially, these trips made Lillian nervous, too close to home with the passage of time perhaps. However, she was relieved to have the bunny rabbit ordeal behind them.

Benny's squeals of joy were a happy echoing medicine throughout the sanitary halls. He brought an onslaught of paintings and drawings from home that he gladly distributed, even to the old folks who remained silent and distant. On a few magic occasions, one of the forgotten would even color with him.

The observant child often noticed when one of the elderly residents was missing. Lillian and Allison still believed in the sanctity of white lies, as with the white bunny. They dismissed such absences with, "They must have gone home."

Oöso's behavior in the nursing home always remained her gentlest. Allison swore the dog was a seventy-pound angel wrapped in fur who understood their mission at the center. The hour of providing unconditional love always passed quickly.

Love task for the day completed, Allison backed from one of the *VISITORS* spots that she found always more vacant than full, an asphalt commentary on the treatment of the elderly. As they entered the street, she spotted the police car accelerating from behind and uttered another phrase her mother detested. "Crap, this really sucks."

"Wot cwap? Wot cwap, Mommy?" spouted Benny.

"Oh, your father's been telling me to replace the tail light and I procrastinated."

"Wot's kass-in-ated?"

"I didn't do it," came her abrupt answer as the telltale flashing lights pulsed with the pierce of the siren. "Now, Mommy will probably get a ticket."

Pulling ever so carefully to the right side of the road, she turned off the engine and avoided her mother's stare. She rolled down the driver's window as the officer removed his mirrored sunglasses, approaching the vehicle.

"Good day, ladies," tipping his broad-brimmed hat, the officer surveyed the interior of the vehicle. Turning to Benny, he smiled, "And how are you today, young man?"

"Cwap. Dis weewy thuckth," parroted Benny.

Lillian playfully slapped her daughter who already had her forehead resting against the steering wheel.

THAT EVENING Benny was the first to run for the door at the sound of the bell. His buddy Justin entered first, followed by his parents. Denise was holding their little baby with a look of guilt on her face.

The Poppys had been adamant, plus Brian pulled rank as Jason's boss, citing the flat-tire incident. They insisted the couple make time for a night away from home, alone. Since Rio's birth, they had become homebodies, focused on fear and his health. Allison had made reservations and arranged an overnight stay in a quaint bed 'n' breakfast they'd later be remodeling. Brian called after her, and prepaid for everything.

Ample neighborhood teens were anxious to earn babysitting money but this called for all night and Denise was over-protective with Rio. Rose, their regular sitter, didn't do over-nights.

Jason and Rio's big brother Pete had an out-of-town ball game and was staying at a friend's house. However, Lillian was willing to babysit, or as Justin preferred to call it, *kid-sitter*. She and his baby brother would share the bedroom downstairs.

Lillian was eager to hold the baby. Once Denise released him, George and I joined in offering the couple several goodbyes in an attempt to start their evening. I think even Justin knew his folks needed time alone.

We were unaware of the details at first. As the parents' footsteps cleared the porch, Lillian began to explain as she cautiously bounced the child in her arms. "Poor child. Three months old and they discovered he has a cancerous tumor behind his left eye."

"Retinal Blastoma," added Brian in a low monotone, with distaste for fanciful medical words.

"Surgery is scheduled in two weeks. Brian insisted they spend one night alone before then." Her son-in-law's concern for others was a trait she supported.

Brian resorted to humor when the situation became heavy. "It was cheaper than having him take it out on the vehicles." His eyes wandered to his bookshelves.

George watched through the window-pane as the solemn couple stood by their car, obviously hesitant to leave. He placed an open palm against the glass. Jason was showing the greater strength out of concern for Denise. Fortunately, once inside their vehicle, they were unable to hear Rio begin to cry from the swelling behind his eye.

As Brian spotted the binding of *When Bad Things Happen to Good People*, he stepped to pull it from the shelf. He'd read the book before his own mother's fateful trip to the doctor. "We are so blessed with Benny." He slipped the book into the baby's bag. His own eyes glistened as both he and Allison touched the kicking feet, toes smaller than the tip of his little finger.

Lillian drew the infant close. Rio grasped Brian's finger as Allison began to stroke the soft minuscule knuckles. I imagine we were all sharing the same thought, afraid to guess whether or not the child would be alive in two weeks, let alone for his first Christmas or birthday.

With the red tail lights out of view, George walked back from the window box toward Lillian who was growing frustrated at her inability to appease the fussing child. As he placed his thumb to the child's forehead above the faint blond eyebrow, the babe instantly quieted. Clearly Rio's right eye functioned as he reached for the mustached face of the stranger. Moving naturally, George opened his own arms.

Although happy to see Rio peaceful, Lillian released him with some reserve. She kept a hand upon the tiny shoulder, maintaining her vigilant watch as he began to bond with the child no longer than his forearm.

Benny wrapped one arm around the waist of his teary-eyed pal Justin and leaned his head against my leg. Slowly his free arm wrapped around my knee. He sighed as I placed an open palm atop his head.

It was only a moment, a Kodak Moment, one might say. But a photo would not have shown our gentle sway or caught the tear that fell from George's eye onto Rio James's tiny forehead.

Allison nervously giggled through her own tears, as a loving mother spared such worries and grief. George asked softly if the parents had requested a second and a third opinion. His question was colored with the touch of a loving command.

CHAPTER FOURTEEN

DARE THE DARK

THE BOYS ARRANGED THE OVERSTUFFED couch cushions into a virtual fortress to await the baby. Soon as Rio was asleep, George gingerly laid him down on the rust-colored cushions. Lillian smiled, seeing the ever-watchful Oöso remain behind as we humans gathered around the table for dinner.

Rio's health occupied a fair share of our dinner conversation. As the grandfather clock chimed seven times, it was evident that Allison was anxious to put her little jabber-box to bed. Benny declared it "not fair" that Justin was allowed to stay up just because he was older. I agreed to go fetch a couple of my tee shirts for both kids as night-shirts. George offered to carry Benny upstairs, promising the tyke that he would clear the closets of monsters.

We'd heard Lillian's beliefs about the causes of Benny's imaginary friend as well as his fear of the dark. She also thought it was poor taste to let them sleep in my *rude* tee shirts.

Finally, the elder lady voiced that there was no sense in George attempting to dispel the little boy's fear of the dark. Certainly she was on a roll.

The close-minded grandmother's eyes widened when George explained he had no plans of dispelling Benny's fears. "Rather than trying to convince him that something he feels is real, is not real, I'm going to accept Benny's fears as real, for him, and give him some tools in which to believe. Strategies he can use against those fears." Before the ladies could comment the big man and the little man headed upstairs.

Benny's bedroom was down the hall from our room. Originally rectangular, it had been modified into an L shape with a bit of an alcove housing shelves and a small desk. The higher shelves displayed his collectibles out of reach of little visitors. He was quite mindful of breakables, respect had been effectively instilled. One shelf held several colorful ceramic clowns belonging to Brian's mom whom Benny had never known. He kept a framed photograph of her at one end. Sometimes the actions of his little man made Brian swear his mother and son had met. Perhaps a dream or in another life.

Above the bed hung a shelf with Allison's collection of children's antique shoes, stylish high-tops in glossy brown and black leather with long laces. It took a few times to explain to Benny that these shoes were not for him to wear.

His bunk was a French sleigh bed of farmhouse cherry, another treasure from a garage sale. She had completely refinished it herself. The finely veneered curved head and foot panels made it the perfect spaceship or racecar for an imaginative little boy, and large enough for two extra youngsters to sleep over. A huge down comforter with fabrics the colors of the rainbow kept him warm. Plus Oöso. Plus Polly.

George sat down on the edge of the bed, tucking the comforter under the little tyke's chin. They played "What color is this?" as George selected red, orange, yellow, green, blue, purple, and violet. Benny named each one correctly, allowing for "geen, boo, buwple" and "eye-o-let." George smiled as he spied Mercer Mayer's *What a Bad Dream* lying on the nightstand atop several children's books.

"You know," he delicately began, "I used to be afraid of the dark."

The little pupils eyed him suspiciously.

He slid Benny farther over to the center of the bed, so he could lean on one elbow and speak at the boy's level right next to him. "Whatcha scared of, little guy?"

"Mon-sers," was the succinct reply.

"Suppose the folks already tried to tell you that they aren't real."

"But dere weeeeel to me," clasping his tiny hands defiantly over his chest.

"What about Oöso? She'll protect you."

"Dewe's ony onea her," came the quick reply.

Thoughts flooded George's mind in moments when he stroked the small forehead as Oöso wandered through the door and leapt up to assume her normal spot on the bed, right corner edge nearest the door.

Mental thoughts can become real in the physical world. Inventions and sicknesses began as thoughts. But, in the world of the abstract, thoughts are already real to each other. To overcome the struggle with fear means one has to *dare the dark*.

Along with many other children, monsters were stored in Benny's belief system. Therefore, since he believed in them, they were real to him. Real in his world of thought. Truth and facts, however, can be overpowered by belief. Monsters of all sorts exist for most people, not just youngsters. That's the reason a placebo can work to heal someone. A sugar pill can cure them because the person believes it can.

Real is real in its own plane. Faith healers illustrate bridges between illusion and reality. But bringing the belief of an illusion into the physical world can be harmful. Voodoo dolls stuck with pins have a much easier chance of inflicting real pain on the person who believes in and fears such magic.

Death and darkness are two places where many children have trouble seeing, from their own fear of things they cannot see. George continued to brush the child's forehead with his finger. "Want to talk about it?"

Benny turned to look directly at the man as he clutched his covers. "Inna dark, me not see how beeeg or how cwooose or how scaawy mon-ser is."

"Would you feel better seeing the size of the monster?"

The question caught the child off-guard. This adult was not attempting to convince him by saying nothing was there that could hurt him. He wasn't saying it was all in his imagination, not telling him monsters weren't real.

"You know the reason I figure monsters only come out in the dark?"

The child was indeed curious.

"I reckon they're afraid of the light. Our light time is their dark time. They can't see us in the light, so their imagination starts going and they get scared. Like a fish feels at home in the water and a bird enjoys the sky."

Benny wasn't letting on if he was buying this, but he liked the sound of it.

Oöso raised her head when George sat up. "Once the monsters know that we know this, they back off." He moved to the closet and placed his hand on the brass door pull. "So where the monsters feel safe and tough in the dark," he flung the door open, "the first flicker of light and they hide. Now they're in their darkness, and they figure we're the scary ones."

Benny sat up and clapped his hands together, then quickly frowned. "M'am-maw sayz me too beeeg for night-light."

"She says that because she knows the secret, so she can look tough." He paused as if he could hear the tiny wheels turning in the child's head. "Besides, why do you think she keeps the light on in the hall after she goes to bed when she *kid-sits* you?"

Benny bit his lip. "Her sayz iz so if some-un needth go bafwoom."

George's smiling reply triggered one on the little boy's face, followed by a giggle.

Pulling one pillow free, George fluffed it. He bent over and flipped on the night-light, leaving a suggestion, actually, a request. "Don't grow too fast little guy. Nighty-night."

Benny rolled over on his side and placed his arm over Oöso, after he blew the man a kiss.

His yawn muffled his, "Ni-nite, Unca Jaa-urge-val-more."

George looked around, then back towards Benny. The words didn't sound so scary this time.

CHAPTER FIFTEEN

FIRST FORCE, SECOND FORCE

FOLLOWING A GREAT night's sleep, the morning began with *Waffles á la Daaw-oh*. Then Allison began to pack the bags of our little overnight guests. 'Course that was after cleaning up the sticky orange juice the chef had spilled on the floor. She insisted the floor needed mopping anyhow, bless her heart.

Brian wanted to see how Jason and Denise's date went, so he stalled by hosing the front porch before work. He leaned over to inhale the sweet fragrance of a pale yellow rose. Flipping open his buck knife, he cut the stem just above a bud. Then he popped off the thorns but not before one pricked him.

Placing the flower on the banister, he uncoiled the light green hose, pulling it up the wide wooden steps. The water ran off in small sheets and waterfalls with a fresh fragrance as it seeped into the black dirt of the flowerbeds as Jason and Denise approached the split-rail fence. Obviously their date had been a success. Jason hollered greetings, thanking Brian for the prepaid surprise. They crossed through the shared gate to collect their sons.

"Congratulations," grinned Brian in a wink, handing her the rose. "The gals said you only checked on Rio twice the entire night."

Her laugh was refreshed. Placing the soft petals against her cheek with morning dew on a leaf, she gave Brian such a hug, his back popped. Their voices brought the ladies outside.

George had skipped breakfast and was lying in the hammock with his eyes closed, checking for light leaks between flipping the pages of a blue pocket book. Intuition is often associated with extrasensory perception. He had opted to be within range while waiting for the proverbial other shoe to drop.

Walking to the stairs, Jason gave a bewildered look to his boss. "Hey, Brian, the weirdest thing happened while we were away."

The female Good Samaritans rushed back inside the house near the window, silent, not a breath between them.

"You know Energizer, our pet rabbit?"

"Sure, sure," stammered Brian, "Energizer," beginning to spray the hose absently.

"Well, we arrived home this morning and Zorro was kind of wound up, so I went into the backyard to throw the ball for him."

"Yeah, Oöso likes that too," drifted Brian.

"Anyhow," Jason continued, "I found Energizer lying on his side in the cage."

"Dead?" I grimaced preparing to console him.

"Yeah. The weird thing is that Pete and I buried him in the yard the day before."

The ungoverned hose soaked me before my startled yell caused Brian to divert the surge of water...through Allison's kitchen window.

"BRIIIAN," followed her scream as a hysterical George was flipped from his hammock to the ground.

After assisting with the second mopping, Jason and Denise returned home with their boys in tow, delighted to see Rio content and playful. Once home, Jason hugged Justin then sent him to brush his teeth. At his truck, Jason halted, spun around, and stared at his home before bounding up the stairs to knock on the door until his wife answered.

"Hey, Lady, I just wanted to thank you for the date with me. I enjoyed myself tremendously. Hope we can do it again soon."

She peeked innocently out the door. "I look forward to it. But we don't have to go out to have a good time," with a slight blush.

He took his wife's hand, caressing her wedding ring between his thumb and forefinger. "I've been keeping to myself a bit, putting in extra hours to take my mind off things. We lost quality time. Something tells me that we need to be together more."

Justin stood silently in the background, a smudge of peppermint toothpaste on his left cheek. He watched his parents embrace until his father spied him and motioned for the youngster to come join them.

BACK AT THE POPPY'S place, I rushed out with our lunches at the sound of George hitting the horn. "I think I settled Lillian a bit, and I asked Benny to draw me a picture of Madmoe. You saw how tense she was earlier."

"And?"

"Aw, the boy jumped at it once he heard it would hang on the fridge. His mom loaded him with crayons before walking him next door to spend the day with Justin."

AFTER WORK we found Lillian fretting. Not really new, but troubling still. Allison stood close to her mother.

"It's a good thing Benny isn't home yet." She was dipping a long yellow spoon in his fish bowl. "I've poked him and everything, but he won't move."

We looked at the small globe housing the boy's pet goldfish.

"That's because he's dead," I blurted out. "Blackie is now sushi."

George popped me, trying to control his own grin.

"Can't you do something, George?" Asking only gained another poke in my ribs. "You're the specialist at rescuing and saving critters," he countered.

Allison took the spoon from her mother and dabbed at the fish lying sideways. Even dead, it eluded capture. Finally, Brian reached his hand in and collected the scaled creature, heading to the bathroom for a burial at sea.

"I know," exclaimed Lillian, running after the fish pallbearer. "Let me look at him. Yes, we can buy another like it before Benny returns. He'll never know."

"Wait a minute, Lil," began Brian. "We've been through this before. Benny needs to learn about death. I'd rather he learn from a pet's death than a parent's."

George reminded her about the last time they tried to pull the wool over somebody's eyes about death, to no avail.

"That time was different, and besides, Benny's only four." When she insisted I accompany her, I turned to George but at his nod, I reluctantly left with her tugging my arm, following the flush of the toilet.

Within the hour, Blackie the Second was swimming with Goldie, minutes before Benny burst upon the scene. While he made the rounds greeting everyone, Allison softly warned the Johnson family of the fish ruse.

Benny hugged Oöso, catching a mouthful of fur in the process. Then running by his fish bowl he halted, staring intently at the glass enclosure.

Oöso stared at the child staring at the tank.

We adults stared as well.

"Hey. You not my Bwackie," shouted the boy suspiciously, pecking his finger on the glass, looking up to his mom and grandmother, expecting answers.

"Think they'll ever learn?" George whispered to Brian.

"I just hope they're not around when I die," replied the smirking father as he headed to join me reviewing some new artwork on the fridge.

The drawing of a man by a child less than a fistful of fingers old is not one in which the police would place much faith in order to identify someone. Benny's colorful rendition was festive to say the least. The hours his artistic parents spent with him were evident.

A mix of magnets held the rendering on the upper left corner. The paper ran vertically with the tall lanky figure hitting the top and bottom edges of the sheet. Little more than a stick figure, it left ample negative space to both sides of the page.

"Skin-neee," Benny described.

The face was a tall oval with an expansive smile formed by a single line. A violet jacket hung almost to the long feet. A narrow neck housed a tie on which Benny had used every color at his disposal. The tie hung as long as the coat. Atop it all, high upon his head, rested the pipe hat.

Brian praised his son on his fine artwork as he warmed us a couple of Gardenburgers, implemented into our new routine of an after-work snack. Plus, it made me think of my buddy Paul Wenner. But I puzzled in silence over the childish rendering as I slowly munched. Then I puzzled with several homemade chocolate chip cookies, unable to escape my déjà vu feeling of the child's drawing.

Happy that we liked his artwork, Benny headed to his fish bowl. Quickly recovered from the loss of Blackie, he was telling the new fish all about his new home.

Allison was working at the dining room table on her latest garage-sale acquisition. Soon after Brian left, Oöso began to nuzzle her arm. She was happily detailing her latest treasure to Lillian and me as she rewired the double student lamp. She was a wonder. I watched her skillfully remove the second of the gold opal cased-glass shades. The hand-rubbed bronze bore nary a scratch.

"It's an authentic Crist-Lundberg," she exclaimed, which I figured must be good.

The first force of Oöso's cold nose and impatience for attention began to wear on the second force of Allison's nerves. "Oöso, go. Play with Benny."

Visions occur differently for each soul. Images are triggered by, and for, a number of reasons. All of us heard the doorbell, yet in

Allison's mind she saw a busy street, a speeding truck, and her son.

"BENNY!" she screamed, jumping up to run to the door, dodging furniture as Lillian caught the rolling opal shade.

The doorbell sounded again as we reached the heavy door that led to the porch and front yard. Allison whipped it open effortlessly as we all crowded to look and were greeted by no one. Then we looked down into the smiling face of Benny as a large cargo truck roared past the driveway raising dust.

The relieved mother hugged her child, wondering amid her kisses how he'd managed to cross into the front yard and ring the doorbell. Oöso, now calm, merely peered outside, front legs on the porch and the screen door resting against her wide frame.

"C'mon, Oöso," I had to repeat the command. "Oöso, come." She looked up at me twice before responding reluctantly.

I thrust out my lower lip as I glanced up and down the front porch. Once, twice, three times and then I followed the dog inside. But, the moment the screen door slammed, I bolted back to the porch. My eyes went to the far end of the long block.

I wondered how I'd missed that silly purple coat that hung well below the lanky person's hips with the split-tail swaying in the opposite direction of the bobbing black top hat. However, the physical image had disappeared by the time it registered in my head. Vanished before I had stuck my noggin back outside. Gone before I could be certain he or it was ever there in the first place.

CHAPTER SIXTEEN

GO FLY A KITE

THE BREEZY ARRIVAL of Saturday marked the end of our first full week as the adopted workers. Leaves rustled and the air blew fresh and clean, accented by the tantalizing aroma of toasted muffins and fresh eggs. Benny was baptizing bits of banana in his pool of cereal and milk. Tiny white droplets were splattered on his orange Tigger placemat. The "Hi-ya' boys" from the tiny boy's mouth brought a howl to us all.

I devoured my plate of *Eggs Benny-dict* and then cleared the table. Hey, I'm a thoughtful houseguest. While I poured a tall glass of water, Allison cheerfully asked one of us to assist her and Benny going to buy picnic food and supplies. "The party's not for a week, but I don't want to be rushed."

"You choose," Brian said as Benny took the cue.

"Daaw-oh," he bellowed, mushy mouth full of banana and hands open wide.

"Settles that matter," grinned Brian. "Good choice. We know Daro likes to eat. You," he pointed to George, "barely eat enough to keep a body alive."

Allison ran to pat my back as I coughed. "Arms up, arms up," repeated Benny.

She took Benny to his room to change into his favorite coveralls while Lillian announced she was doing laundry. Besides gathering Benny's and Allison's clothing, she headed to grab our dirty clothes too. I was glad I had emptied my pockets.

Finding only one denim shirt from the entire week for George, she looked into the hall to make sure no one was near. But she missed me around the corner, peeking in the hall mirror. I watched as she sniffed at his shirt, surprised to find it smelled fresh but gathered it anyway. She used the lack of dirty clothes as just cause to search his zippered canvas bag which irritated me. Unable to open it, she was plagued by frustration that fueled her curiosity. She turned to my dirty wardrobe easily gathered from the closet floor. It was unnecessary to sniff-check. I had to chuckle.

The essence of sweaty labor filled her nostrils. A pair of dusty jeans, several bright boxers, a tangle of gray sweat socks, a heavy work shirt, and my dreaded *rude* tee-shirts collected in Arizona from Pischke's Paradise and Oregano's Pizza Bistro.

One bore a color shot of three scantily-clad female derrieres seated on barstools and the inscription: *We Get a Little Behind at Pischke's*. Ones from Oregano's were inscribed with *Pick Your Seat on Our Patio* and *Menu Can Trust*.

Reaching the bottom of the stairs, Lillian's verbal tee shirt review continued, a joust between the two female generations as she briskly sorted the clothes by color. The volley was interrupted when a tiny white swatch of cloth attached to the underside of George's sole shirt caught her eye.

Her attention was diverted when Allison embarrassingly said, "Really, Mother. Are you washing their clothes or critiquing them?"

George seized the moment to release the small safety pin and palm the half-inch square of cloth as he scooped up one of the baskets.

Inquisitively Lillian turned, "What was that?"

"Oh, just something from the manufacturer, I reckon," as he carried the basket to her car before she could question his lack of dirty clothes.

I immediately followed in silence with the second basket and waited near the garage until Lillian was in her car before returning to the kitchen. Mom might have raised a fool but she didn't raise a darn fool.

The prevailing attitude between the ladies had been obvious. As Lillian drove off, I nudged Allison. "Frost seems a little early this year." I correctly read her notion that she was looking for the opportunity to talk, initiating the conversation with questions about my life. I answered each one with, "And you?"

Allison was one of four children, two older brothers and a younger sister. Both girls were groomed to be ladies, influenced by Lillian. "It's frustrating to realize the beliefs and habits I have are my mother's but are ones that I don't want. Some are convenient but not the way I really believe or want to believe."

"Convenient? Like what?" I baited.

"Like repairs being considered male responsibilities. I don't like doing any of that nonsense but when I actually manage to do it, I get a satisfied feeling. It's sort of a self-reliant feeling. I can remember as little kids, my brothers could help my father work on the car, but if my sister or I asked to help him, *Oooh noooo.*"

"What happened?"

"Mother would proclaim: *That's a man's job*. And if we made it past her objections, our dad blocked us. *Get away, you're a girl,* she cracked disgustingly. "Even as a little girl, I wondered *who made these stupid rules.*"

I understood. "Their type of belief doesn't help a woman later in life."

"No kidding, especially as a single mother. It leaves us easy prey to unethical mechanics and sinister repairmen." After a moment she smiled, "I loved learning to do carpentry and fixing things with Brian. He's a great teacher and fun to work with. And patient, like the time he taught me to snow ski."

Her laughter surfaced. "He liked going to the hardware store and watching me tell the clerks what I wanted, asking by proper names rather than some dumb blond with a peroxide- saturated brain." Imitating a whiny voice, theatrically tossing her hair, *"Can you help meeee, pleeeze? I need a dealie-bob gadget to hook this whatzit together and maybe a thingie to go with it. Some kinda round, you know, thingamajiggie."*

I convulsed in hysterics. Damn, I enjoyed her energy and wit. Plus, she was gorgeous and smart. I figured eligible guys would line up after the divorce, waiting for a chance. "How'd your mother take it, you working in construction?"

She tilted her head. "At first she thought it was *cute*. Then she made it clear it wasn't ladylike, wasn't normal, and it didn't help that Brian was self-employed. To her it meant the work I did wasn't real. Once she saw my tenacity, she couldn't bring herself to tell her friends that her daughter worked in construction." Chortling, she added, "We began to call it the 'C' word."

I used the counter as a seat. "So how'd your folks handle it after they saw you were sticking with it?"

"Daddy was actually proud although sometimes I think he enjoyed chipping at Mother's ego. She would tell folks that her daughter was working in home design, a decorator." She mimicked a haughty tone, raising her nose, "*A procurer of antiques*." Allison then gave a dainty wave with her dishtowel.

"Daddy would burst her bubble at their dinner parties," assuming a deep voice. '*Hell, Lilly, she hits garage sales and buys old things.*' Inside, I knew he was proud."

Feeling a bit guilty and a touch ashamed, she added, "I love her, and I know she means well, but I see her being just like her mother. And I'm sure I could describe my great-grandmother even though I never met her. Like I'm entangled in, in what feels like a chain." Her jaw clenched, "And it's a real bitch to break free."

Silence hung for a moment before I softly underscored her statement, "The chain and the sins of the father are the same thing."

"The chain? Sins?"

Gently I began to share some of the wisdom gleaned from the insightful road trips with George. "The sins of the father and the mother forge a chain. A sin is not so much a sin when it is a one-time mistake or something such as an accident due to ignorance. However, when the sin, the action, becomes a habit, the repetition makes it a sin. That's your chain. The trick is breaking it, and following your spirit. The spirit is the ribbon within the chain, within the self."

She said nothing, concentrating on my words.

I slyly wrapped a dishtowel around my wrists, holding the ends in my fists. "If the habit is an unhealthful one and allowed to continue, it's as if it were a sin. Negative habits, repeated, fall in that category. Children pay for the sins of the father or mother because they are continuing as they have seen. Hence, the actions or the sins continue."

I snapped the towel tight, effectively serving as handcuffs. "And the chain continues unbroken until some noble or determined soul chooses to take action. Otherwise, the children and their children and their children's children continue the repetition, chained to the sins of the father or the sins of the mother."

She pondered a moment before turning away to stare at the massive ash tree. "Dag Hammarskjöld said: *'Raise yourself above the times you were born into'.*"

I was impressed that she knew of this great statesman. "It's like a fine ribbon runs through the links of the chain in each one of us. Difficult to break the chain and save the ribbon." I walked over and placed my hand on her shoulder.

"Lillian's a smart cookie. I know her ways seem strange sometimes. We know the spirit and body are one, yet few manage to live it. Beliefs, truths, facts, are all difficult to align. She behaves the way she's been taught. I bet she sees this pattern and when she was younger may even have felt as you do. Bet she had plans to be the best mother ever, probably frustrated at having failed to break the chain. Now she's been entangled in it so long that she almost doesn't realize it. Although she wants the best for you, all she knows is this one way to behave."

I stretched the towel tightly. "The chain. And when we change our behavior," as I released one end, "folks close to us become nervous. Maybe they fear they'll be left alone or behind, forgotten. Nothing scares someone stuck in a habitual rut as much as seeing someone close to them escaping that rut."

Allison drifted away before her eyes revealed a moist sheen of realization. "And while I'm bogged down in the sins of my mother, Brian's dealing with the sins of his father." She continued, "I wish Brian were here; I don't think I can explain this."

I bit my lip, wishing George were here, too, but I had seen him head for the garage where we had spotted a red kite resting on the rafters above the vehicles.

THE BREEZE CAUGHT QUICKLY and held the rich red diamond in contrast against the bright blue sky. "Ever hear of a place called Acabar?" quizzed George, looking upward.

"Sounds familiar," said Brian, letting out more line. "Africa? Arabia?"

He smiled that familiar smile. "Check in the bookstore sometime. The kites in Acabar soar so high," he focused his handsome eyes beyond the horizon, "they could snag a star." He ignored the side-glance from his boss and redirected the conversation. "So, how'd you do in school? You and Allison earn good grades?"

"I'd say Allison is definitely the brighter one of us. Hope Benny takes after his mother. She used her brains while I passed more on persistence and smiles."

"Like your father?"

"How'd you know?"

"Someone once said: *The acorn never falls far from the tree.*" Seeing his mood dip with the kite's descent, George reached over to assist the maneuver. "That's the reason why partners are so important. That's one of the thoughts in the Bible about God being certain to hear when two or more are gathered in His name."

He watched Brian squint at the kite, knowing it was a gesture behind which to hide, so he continued. "You've never been in military service like me but remember when Daro was telling his fire-fighting stories? What did they share in common?"

Brian took a guess. "Never being alone? Even when working solo, he was part of a team. Others were around and he knew even in the midst of danger if things went sour, another team member would be close behind. He had faith that one of his team would at least attempt to reach him, attempt to save him, as he would them."

"Faith," George repeated, following the string as the crimson kite began to catch more air. "Two islands exist, the Land of Despair and the Land of Peace. Faith becomes the bridge. Our reach exceeds the moment we have in hand. That's the meaning of heaven. For a man with faith, without knowing the way, can overcome and reach any heights. Raise your will to meet virtues and gods rather than changing your values to accommodate your will and strength." The string grew taut, the kite soaring, as if on cue.

Coincidence, thought Brian as he looked at the kite higher than he'd ever seen it ascend in the sky. "I've always been kind of a loner," he mumbled.

George sensed that he was going to have to work more diligently than he had planned. I felt good to later learn he was confident that I was working with Allison.

CHAPTER SEVENTEEN

THE LINE AND THE CIRCLE

I MAY NOT KNOW A LOT but I do understand body language, and Allison's language was loud and clear as she edited her grocery list. It was the mechanical rattling of the chain many experience when they get close to finding the ribbon.

"Okay if I make an observation and ask a question?"

She nodded.

"You seem as if your heart isn't in this, in getting a divorce. Are you certain it's the solution you want? Certain it's the right way to go?"

"I'm certain I'm all out of answers," she snapped as the yellow-lined pages to the legal pad slapped the table. Then came an apologetic look. "I don't see any way I'd call it a happy solution. Divorce feels like an escape, like avoiding the answer. No, it's not the answer I want and it doesn't even feel like the right move, but Brian's forcing the issue."

A heavy sigh escaped my chest. "Brian's like most people in this country. He understands divorce better than marriage, so giving up's easier. He's witnessed marriages dissolve more than seeing them work. You're feeling divorce is not right and that feeling's your intuition. I learned in the fire department, even in my writing, that feelings and intuition are one and the same. Intuition is the feeling you can always trust."

"How do you know when you're hearing it? I hear so many voices. It's like a radio station. How do you know which channel to listen to, which voice to hear?" She glimpsed in the cupboards and scrawled on the shopping list.

I moved gingerly feeling the déjà vu. "You build up trust in your inner voice as you do with a partner. All of these folks you ask for guidance and advice, your mother, your sister, even counselors. Each has a whole flurry of voices of their own, all with their own ideas on whether or not divorce is the answer for you, and Brian, and Benny."

The latter name caused her to recoil.

"Such answers are based on linear thinking, looking merely at two choices, namely, marriage or divorce."

I grabbed two six-packs of bottled water from the breezeway, placing them on the long dining table. I struggled to push a finger through the plastic shrink-wrap to release them. I lined up ten bottles in a straight row, blue labels out, using the length of a yellow pencil to space them evenly. "Back, way back, in olden days, we're talking 2,500 to 3,000 years ago. The dude had a couple of names, but mainly was known as Hermes."

"The messenger of the Greek gods?"

"That's the fella. Also god of shepherds, merchants. Had a major hand in weights and measures. Athletics. Even credited with inventing the flute." I'd begun to wander.

"What about him?" she interrupted.

"This Hermes guy talked about *linear thinking* and introduced *circular thinking*." I opened the cupboard and pulled out a couple of Benny's plastic glasses, placing a red one over the bottle to our far left and a purple one over the one at the far right.

"This is the way I always used to look at things, in a linear fashion. Now, I want you to assign each bottle a number from one through ten. Okay?"

She pointed to the left with the red top and counted out loud, ending with ten on the purple top.

"Okay, then number one with the red cup is the least and this number ten with the purple cup is the most."

"So?"

"Be patient with me. I'm still thinking of a way to explain this. With linear thinking, this red one is the ugliest and this purple one on the right is the prettiest."

"I'm sorry, Daro. How does this lineup of bottles help me?"

"I want you to see this like a thermometer or ruler, a way to measure. The coldest and the hottest. The biggest and smallest, the dumbest and smartest, the poorest and the richest."

She impatiently placed her list on the table.

"Remove the littlest and the biggest ones for me, okay? The one and the ten." She removed the bottles from the far ends. "And?"

"Now which is the littlest and the biggest?"

She sucked at her lip. "Well, the second and ninth ones, I guess except now we have only eight, so the first and eighth."

"True. In linear thinking, we have a ruler and have the littlest and biggest, only the extreme points on the line have been removed."

I reached for the large decorative bowl to use as a guide in forming a circle and replaced the two bottles with cups on them to their original spots.

"Hermes was a god of measures, so he took the stick used as a ruler and converted it to a flexible rope. So imagine that rigid line we had as a ruler becomes flexible. Help me make a circle with all ten of the bottles, keeping them in the same order." I began quickly to rearrange them. Then reached in and lifted the bowl leaving a two-foot-circle of bottles. The bottles with the red cup and the purple cup were now side by side.

She slowly walked part way around the table looking for a clue. "And?"

"Which is the littlest and biggest now, the best and worst?

The ugliest and prettiest?"

She glanced about and then focused on the two colored-cupped bottles. "Aren't they all the same? I mean we still have ten points but they're all the same on the circle."

I placed my hands atop the red and the purple cups. "Circular thinking allows us to see the *similarity* in different points, as opposed to focusing on the extreme *differences*."

"Do we still have extreme differences?"

"Sure," as I reached for the bottle on the circle directly opposite the purple one, "But now we see that all points are attached and all points are valid and equal."

She jumped ahead. "So, if I understand your point, at least ten ways are always available to look at things. At least ten solutions exist for any problem."

"That's good. What else?"

"As you look at something, you're merely seeing things from some different point on this circle. And a circle has a minimum of 360 points," she added quickly.

"You're catching on faster than I did the first time George explained this to me."

Next, I placed a quarter face-up in the center of the circle. "That center is the spot where a true observer is located rather than on the line with the bottles, and a *genuine* observer can see any of these points without judgment or attachment to any of them.

"However, in the increasing speed-frenzied world in which we live, we often seek quick fixes. Black-and-white answers, right-or-wrong answers. Seeing only a couple of options and making a move before observing them all. We move in such a hurry, making so many waves, that we might hear the information everyone else is telling us as static."

"So, you mean this helps us hear ourselves above all of the

noise?"

"Exactly, and it helps us see the good *in* the bad."

"It does?" Allison fidgeted with the shopping list before she decided to dare the dark, or at least brave a shadow. "Can we place Rio here? I mean, what is the good of an innocent baby having cancer?" The words brought tears to her eyes. If she could see the good of a child being ill, she might be able to see the good in their divorce.

"Okay. Here's Rio," I pointed to the silver quarter and faced her across the table. "Can anything good be derived from Rio having cancer?" The words barely left my lips.

"Oh, Daro, how could you? I mean he's hurting. His folks love him. His brother adores him. He never did anything wrong. They don't deserve this tragedy!"

"Whoa there Allison. I wasn't taking a stand, but merely looking for a *yes* or *no* to illustrate the way this idea works."

"Then NO. Nothing good comes from Rio having cancer."

I raised both palms toward her in a calming fashion. "I understand. Now pull that bottle nearest you on the circle, slightly back. Okay?"

Calmed, she complied.

"Okay, that bottle represents your point of view. Therefore, looking around the circle, where is the opposite side or opposite point located?"

"The point where Rio having cancer is good?" her eyes wide with horror.

"Skip the emotion. Where is the *opposite* bottle, *opposite* to your point on the circle?" She counted until she pointed at the one that was five bottles away, nearest me.

I pulled it outward. "Now don't pass judgment here, okay,

Allison? I'm not taking a side. I don't want Rio to be sick either, but stay with me here, okay?"

She nodded twice.

I released the air from my lungs on her second nod. "Frankly, I learned this circular thinking using war and peace, and I kinda wish we were using that here. But let's use cancer and just not be so focused on Rio for a second."

She waited.

"Can you think of anything, anything good that comes from cancer?"

She answered satirically, "It gives doctors jobs."

"Yes, Allison, cancer provides medical employment and jobs to nurses and doctors. And scientists, too, even charities."

She looked at me blankly wondering if I were serious.

"Although I'm not into hospitals and drugs, the fact remains that hospitals and pharmaceuticals dealing with cancer is big business."

She eased a bit. "Well then holistic methods, such as herbs and special diets, can also be counted," pausing as her words echoed in her head, surprised at her realization. "So, the people who deal with cancer from that holistic point on the circle gain purpose and create jobs too." She then nodded slowly. "Okay, continue."

"George and I have met folks with cancer who told us they felt lucky in getting cancer as it made them appreciate their lives. Made them take action, today."

Her face held a grisly look. "Population control."

"A harsh reality, I admit, but true. What if the millions who died from cancer were still here? Pollution, resources. Cancer supports population control."

A single tear fell. "It draws us closer."

"Good girl. Sure does! Look at the added closeness you have

with Justin's family now. Everyone is rooting for Rio."

Allison opened a bottle of water and sipped, regaining her composure. "I'm almost afraid to ask this question."

"Yes?" I winked.

"Besides seeing the good in the bad, how does a soon-to-be divorcee apply this technique before the fact? I mean, in gaining solutions. I admit I'm attached to my place on the circle. I want to save our marriage."

"Okay," I prepared, hoping to ease the tension. "Shoot."

"Skip the 360 solutions. Help me move to the center of the circle and I'll settle for ten of those solutions you mentioned, for Brian and me."

"Same answer. Shoot. That's one."

Lost, she pulled her head back as I threw my answer on the heels of her questioning look.

"Shoot him."

She looked horrified as I calmly continued.

"Shoot him. Then you're a widow. That's one solution." I interrupted her irritation. "Sure, I'm a smartass but look at every solution. Some will be ridiculous but valid points on the circle. Examine them, so you can move onto the others, so you can move forward."

I sat on the table edge in order to relax her more. "Ever wake from a dream or have a thought and you struggle, so you won't forget it? If you jot it down, you can release it. Then your mind's free to continue thinking, to continue searching, to continue dreaming."

"You mean, examining any solution even if it's one we don't like, opens doors to see other solutions?" She cradled her jaw, grasping the concept. "So each point in itself can then become the center to examine, around which multiple ways can be accessed to find the solution."

I was impressed because she took it a step further than I did. Surprised, perhaps embarrassed, but pleased with her astute perception. "Before wedlock and once married you and Brian committed yourselves to working full time on your business." I cracked open a bottle of water. "Were you still looking at whether it would work or not?"

She looked surprised. "No. No, we were always looking at all the ways to make it work. We were committed. We looked at our business, planning it effectively to find solutions. Laying out options. Failing or quitting wasn't an option."

Her face transformed. "So, we could place our marriage in the circle. Then look at all the points to help make it work that we may have overlooked. We've been looking at it in a linear fashion which had only the two points of marriage or divorce." Her eyes widened. "Is it too late?"

I was working hard to help her find the answers to her own questions, a lesson George, like Jesus, offered when He offered the *teach-a-man-to-fish* lesson. I took a big breath. "What kind of advice and chances did your family and friends provide for survival of your business? Did their instincts guide you, or did your own?"

She laughed as she looked about the remarkable house they had restored. Then she thought of their business. A memory came to life. "*The power of a dream is supported by belief.* Those were Brian's words early on."

"You have to believe," I agreed softly. "That includes in yourself and often another."

"But how?"

"Sometimes you just have to *believe*, in someone else. You know the way Brian feels about you and Benny. How do you feel about them? How do you feel about the *way* they feel about you? How do you feel about the way he built the business with you?"

"Why, I...he can do anything. He proved, no we proved, we

proved it." Then she was stalled by her thoughts, racing too quickly in her mind. "I always tell him he can do anything. Whenever a new job comes along, it may scare him like the first fireplace he built. A huge beehive fireplace and I mixed the mortar," she smiled proudly.

Touching her forearm gently, I asked, "What about the marriage?"

Tears of anger accompanied the words, "But I just assumed…"

"Haven't you ever heard the meaning of the word *assume*?"

"You make an *ass* out of *u* and *me*," she giggled, collapsing into my arms, sharing a hug. I hadn't held a lady in a long time. Her silent sobs were mixed with relief as my shoulder absorbed her trembling and my shirt absorbed her tears. "Daro, it feels like I'm at war with others, with myself in making decisions."

"Listen to Hermes then. He said that if we only look at things in a linear fashion, then we are faced with only *rights* and *wrongs*. That's looking at things with the mentality of war."

CHAPTER EIGHTEEN

THIS AIN'T PACE PICANTE SAUCE!

THE KITE SHOOK, waving its tail of plaid rags as it passed through a thermal. "I remember," George began, "owning a shirt and was told by some gals that the green shade complemented my eyes. I virtually wore it to rags." He handed the string over to Brian.

"There're probably a lotta closets like that," he laughed, taking the taut line. "The power of another's opinion. Amazing the weight we place on another's opinion." He pulled in on the string, quite unaware of the snare he'd stepped into.

George stopped momentarily to listen to the chatter of a sparrow before he wandered over to the truck and reached for an open bag on the dash to toss a few stale chips to the happy fellow. The feathered friend danced and then took flight. The man's eyes followed upward as he strolled back toward Brian, stopping abruptly when he stepped in a puddle. He looked upward again, and smiled.

SHE WADDED UP the old shopping list that I grasped as a make-shift basketball. "Dunk shot." It bounced twice off the rim then hit the floor, scooped up by Oöso. Tennis balls and paper wads were fair game for the playful pooch.

After having paid some attention to her eye make-up, Allison returned from the restroom with Benny running alongside. He proudly showed me his coveralls. "Look, Daaw-oh. Baa- woons." He pointed to the colorful pattern on his chest.

Heading to her Pathfinder, I opened her door and then helped Benny into his car seat before I climbed aboard. Slowing in the parking lot, she blushed when I asked if she got her taillight fixed, almost as red as the souped-up Camero that whipped into a slot clearly marked for handicapped people. Man, I immediately saw more red than just the vehicle.

She touched my arm. "Easy there, big fella. He has a handicapped tag."

As the guy bounded from the sports car, it was clear I was not a happy camper. "Handicapped. Not even a limp but that sign makes it okay." As I lifted Benny out of the car, the guy was already at the store's entrance. "You know, Allison, I wouldn't mind it but so many folks consider handicapped stickers as their license for convenience."

She wisely allowed me to vent some steam before we ran into the questionable cripple while shopping.

"It just seems doctors give those to folks who don't really need them." I hoisted Benny into a cart with his scampering legs. "Not many doctors have the..," I rethought my words, "gumption to tell their patients, 'No, you don't need a handicapped plate'."

I struggled to hold Benny's arms around my neck in order to work his playful feet into the leg slots on the cart. As he sat, I turned. "It's not as though I think they have to be sitting in wheelchairs or have to drag themselves across the parking lot. Just be honest and conscious if it's a necessity or a desire."

Then I saw the guy rushing out as I raised my voice. "And if the plate is due to a justifiable spouse or parent or child, they best not use it as their own convenience plate!" I made eye contact with the man who slowed slightly.

The guy's skin tone altered, matching his car's red luster as he broke eye contact with me. Suddenly he stiffened one leg, resulting in a noticeable limp.

"Enough said." My knuckles whitened as I pushed the cart.

"Careful," she grinned impishly. "Don't give Benny whiplash."

I shrugged at my own judgment as we entered the market.

Passing the restroom, Benny blurted, "How da gurls wite they names? Daddy can wite his name inna snow. Dat's why me gwad me a boy. Gurls cain't wite they names inna snow unless they wun weewy fast."

Allison's eyes rolled as he added, "I gotta go baff-woom."

"Okay." I scooped him out of the cart. "Let's go tap a kidney."

ERLE PYLETT STEPPED from behind a tree, re-buckling his jeans before climbing back on his motorcycle. The ignition shook the leaves.

At the fork in the road, the biker stopped and leaned the weight to his left leg, deciding which way to go. His decisions hadn't been the best for some time. Of late he felt like a born loser. The type who'd be near a babe when the wind whipped her skirt in the air, only to have the same gust blow a cinder in his eye.

Overhead a flock of ducks caught his eye as he placed his shades on his forehead. Their wedge formation created a natural directional marker. He pushed his sunglasses back in place and aimed his bike in their direction.

AS I EMERGED FROM the restroom with Benny, Allison saw us just as a tall blond caught my eye and a stout pole caught my shoulder.

"Pretty lady," Allison laughed as I rubbed my arm and lifted Benny. "Boys will be boys," danced off her lips. She fretted about the day they had to explain to Benny where he came from. The dreaded *Sex Talk* was one she hoped Brian would handle.

"The way our bodies get here's a snap. We just don't know the way our spirits joined our bodies or the specific time."

She was never sure what to expect from George and me.

"Bodies have a beginning and an end, but we aren't conscious of the beginning or end of our spirit, the end of ourselves. Once the game's over, the king and pawn go back into the same box."

Another lady walked by us, attentive to those who noticed her. Allison resisted comments until she noticed Benny sniffing at the air.

"Whew. If she stood still, her perfume would puddle."

We each pushed a cart because we needed a lot of supplies for the upcoming picnic. The warehouse-style grocery store was packed. We swapped carriers at one point so she could take Benny into the cereal section while she sent me to purchase hamburger and hot dog buns. "The whole grain stuff, not the white stuff," she reminded me.

"As if the kind of bread matters when you're putting hot dogs in them." I loaded the last of the buns into my cart, making sure no holes were in any of the bags. At the far end of the aisle was a young child in a cart being pushed by a tall, scruffy-looking guy. Then, my peripheral vision caught sight of the familiar denim coveralls with the balloon motif on the front of the child's clothes as the cart disappeared.

I abandoned my cart and yelled for Allison, my volume increasing with the speed of my steps. "Allison. Benny." Breaking into a long forceful stride, I rounded the corner, displacing a lady's cart into a pyramid of pork and bean cans. "ALLISON," I hollered above the clatter as I saw the tall man with the child glance over his shoulder at me and then push the cart a bit faster.

I saw he was near the exit and that he stood at least a head taller than me. Breaking into a full run down the aisle and yards from the stranger, I briefly caught a glimpse of Allison as she passed the far end of the aisle.

"Allison," I yelled, causing her to back-step into the aisle. My mind raced my legs, confident she'd grab Benny if I delayed the kidnapper. My blast of "Benny. Hey, you!" stopped the giant, turning to face me. A dozen feet stood between us. My mind raced faster. *Where to hit? High? Low? High, I'll hold his neck and trip the bastard.*

My feet left the painted concrete floor in flight as my eyes saw all. The crowd parting, the massive brute's eyes widening, the coverall-clad youngster's face distorting, Allison in shock clenching her cart, Benny silent.

Magic Johnson is proof that man can stop in mid-air. My mind's eye instantly replayed the scenes I had just witnessed, as I wished for such an ability, to stop in mid-air. I heard the wind escape the mammoth chest of the unsuspecting father as a slow-motion tumble began, when I viewed the two little boys...dressed alike.

Time returned to normal as the startled father, an unsuspecting grocery clerk, and I, all did a combined cartwheel through a tall display of Goldwater Salsa and Barbecue Sauce.

Allison's gasp was audible above the shattering bottles, an ear-deafening commotion I thought would never end.

First to his feet was the gargantuan stranger. Actually, he was the only one to his feet. Strange thoughts flooded me as I noticed the huge biceps and hairy, beefy forearms. Never saw the punch he had thrown, which left my thick hair matted with red.

Both boys were pointing to each other laughing, oblivious to the life-and-death situation. Their laughter diffused the hulk looming over my body and the waylaid clerk whose white apron bore a red stain. Opportunity for me to knock the legs out from beneath the giant had it not been for the sudden smile. Dimples appeared through scruffy whiskers as he looked to his son and then to Benny, then back and forth again.

Two kids dressed alike. Shared by a confused mother, a laughing father, and me.

Kneeling down, Allison extended her hand to my aching head, fearing the worse with the matter seeping from my hair. Delicately she touched my forehead and then my scalp as she searched for my injury.

I glanced down, my Oregano's shirt quickly turning red, so dark the block letters could not be read. Worried, but I figured my wound was deserved.

Twice more she touched my head, combing her fingers through my hair as I moaned theatrically to diffuse the embarrassment. Then she did something gross. She brought her red drenched fingers to her lips and extended one finger to her tongue.

"This ain't Pace Picante Sauce," she said in a twang reminiscent of the TV commercial.

As a monstrous but understanding father extended his mammoth hand down to me, the translation of the comical event skipped through the crowd as quickly as the Goldwater Salsa was staining the clothes of one hero and one hapless clerk.

Everyone in the store was amused, with the possible exception of the felled clerk.

CHAPTER NINETEEN

CENTER STAGE

"IT WOULD SEEM YOU WANT to save the marriage since you're both here, unless you just like wasting everyone's time. You can either take action or hope for a miracle. Miracles are great but they're damn unpredictable." The gold watch reflected as his light blue cuff pulled up.

Brian, sitting erect, his interlaced fingers his fortitude, glared at the counselor.

"I mean, if you're so determined to get a divorce, you'd be sitting with a lawyer."

"You guys charge about the same," Brian mumbled.

"And we both have the same amount of education," a slight edge to Dr. Feldman's voice. "So go invest in him."

Psychologists have testosterone, too.

Allison's eyes began to ping-pong as she thought, *This is going well.*

"Frankly, I'm tired of your insinuations concerning my abilities and fees. And tired of seeing you waste an obviously intelligent mind on only seeking the reasons why things won't work. You've already decided divorce is the solution, so any constructive suggestions on my part are negated outright before they even get past your ears."

"Get past my ears?" Brian smirked.

"Get past your ears, en route to your brain. You listen but don't hear. Hence, you tend to block it before it can enter your mind. Like all the books you're reading. You're not letting the words pass through your eyes into your mind. Instead of running around putting out fires, you want time to design a new fire truck."

"So, you're saying I don't wanna learn?"

"He's saying you're closed-minded," Allison interjected.

Brian's head jolted to face her but the doctor intervened. "I didn't say that, Allison. Please don't talk for me or attempt to manipulate my words for your cause." Husband and wife stilled momentarily with their mouths opened.

"Brian, you've developed a keen ability to think quickly on your feet. You built a successful company. And you did it having had no teachers or associates in business. You had to develop the ability to make observations, decisions, and take action on your own. Right or wrong, you receive primary credit for your company."

"And your point?"

"In an ideal world you'd have proper teachers, peers, and experts. Partners to discuss matters with instead of only your feelings and instincts. You'd have examples."

Allison sat up. "I'm his partner, in business and marriage." Her eyebrows rose. "So, I'm no good for him?"

Before Brian could defend her, the doctor cut her self-worth issue short. "You're his partner *now*. You weren't there, however, when he was building a foundation for his life or initially his business."

Allison saw Brian fidget with his wedding band. *A circle.* Her mind's eye saw herself in the center of a circle, then removed herself and placed Brian there. And in a flood of awareness she realized all of the counseling and observations were focused upon her being in the circle, as though everything centered on her. So, all of the problems had to be about her. How could she have understood the place where he was coming from when her focus was Brian looking at her?

Suddenly in her mind, she saw the center of the circle and even the room appeared brighter.

A *Hug Mug* sat on Dr. Feldman's desk with a shiny helium balloon bobbing just below the ceiling tiles. Brian first saw it as some touchy-feely object, but now it made him think of the kite, both looking down on him.

When observations were offered, he took them as judgments. He couldn't separate the two. They couldn't penetrate his thinking because he was too busy listening defensively to the messenger. What would a kite or balloon see of him? He took their outside view and could see himself as they saw him. Call it imagination or call it an out-of-body experience. He called it clarity and Dr. Feldman sensed the breakthrough in his thinking.

"Thought leads to action. Action is movement. Actions repeated enough times become habits. Some habits can become mechanical and therefore dangerous. Brian, you found an action that served you well early on, a protective action, since you were alone. The personality you've developed and your abilities allow you to begin. You've begun to follow your thoughts with words and turn them into action."

Brian sensed answers near. Could he hold on? Could he keep his mind open?

"But, and remember the word *but* negates the action that follows. *But* you've developed an unconscious automatic action of responding alone and quickly. Therefore, it's only natural for you not to seek observations when you take them as judgments and thus, destructive. So you're unable to digest observations and suggestions. You're *not* stuck. You just aren't used to them being there, and you simply can't translate them, when listening in defense. You've never received proper support or guidance, so you don't recognize help when it finally appears."

Brian registered a slight smile. *Not stuck?* He heard those two little words.

"It'd be as if you were ringmaster when the Barnum and Bailey Circus came to town, and Benjamin was sitting in the crowd watching rather than interacting with you."

Brian stopped breathing.

"You wouldn't expect to see Benjamin there, even if he saw you, because he hasn't been there. He hasn't existed for you in twenty-five years, not since you were Benny's age, a small boy. You wouldn't ignore him. There'd simply be no recognition. You wouldn't expect him. Mainly, though, you wouldn't see him because you'd never know he was there."

CHAPTER TWENTY

PERSISTENCE PAYS

GOD DID WELL WHEN HE created daybreak. I often wonder why I sleep through so many of them. A fiery red sunburst rose that Monday morning and Benny was well into a newly opened box of cereal.

"Mornin' Unca Daaw-oh. Mornin' Unca Jaa-urge-val-more." The smell of fresh toast and his cheerful greeting was dulled by the look on Allison's face. Her eyes were red and swollen, her happy façade revealing cracks. Hope and faith could only go so far.

Lillian dropped off sack lunches. Allison added a note from Brian explaining he'd join us later. *Enjoy the sun while it lasts.* She set the truck keys by the pad and excused herself, taking Benny to his room. We munched the remains of the toast.

"George?" I began crunching. "Maybe your friend guessed wrong about us being able to help. Is it just me or do you feel like we're failing?" My tongue ran across the rough texture, waiting for his reply.

Troubled, his right thumb was drumming a repetitive hollow thump before he spoke. The thought of the young couple calling it quits left him somber. "Yeah," as he drummed some more. "Yes, Daro, I do."

I tried to improve the mood. "That Lillian's a gem. Despite her mother-in-law stuff, I think they'd have broken up sooner if not for her. And Benny's a firecracker."

The radiant thought of Benny triggered a fleeting smile. "Yeah, so what chance do we have? We're not even family." He paused. "It's been almost two weeks. Maybe it was ridiculous to think we'd be helpful."

My feelings ran the gamut of concern, sadness, and anger when I sensed a possibility he was about to give up. "What do you mean? They want to be together. They just can't work out all the wrinkles."

Now he tried to cover with satire. "What're we supposed to do? Buy an iron?"

"No, but you have something else."

"What?" He looked up, anticipating a satirical heavenly retort.

"Me," I said without missing a beat.

He leaned across the table and squeezed my forearm before reaching for the keys and forced a smile as we rose to leave for the day's labor.

THE SCREAM OF A CHILD can pierce the noise of a construction site. Fortunately, it was one of delight as Benny arrived with his mother and grandmother, dropping off the lunches we'd forgotten in our morning funk. In addition, Lillian had news to share.

It took no coaxing for her to explain that Denise had called and Rio's surgery was postponed in order to obtain a second opinion, set for the upcoming week. The insurance company was still stalling but something in the air was giving them a sense of hope.

While on the site, the ladies took some measurements as Benny ran to his dad, wanting to help build something. He kept the boy's little hammer and work belt in his truck. Soon the child was mimicking his father who stood proudly over him.

I basked in my thoughts of being a teacher and mentor for Benny. "That's quite a smart buck you have there. He learns quickly."

"I learned at his expense, how early in life a child *can* learn." The resulting saga was one told often, one of Benny's favorites now that he'd mastered his toiletry skills.

Early on, he happily cared for his son when schedules permitted. His only concern for the baby was the dreaded diaper change, entailing the deadly *number two*.

Although Brian was able to handle the most violent movie, the raunchiest joke, and the most heinous carpentry accident, changing the diapers of his beloved baby was a major challenge. When bowels moved, he quaked. Something about the smell, the texture, caused juices to race from his belly up his throat and forced his tongue to gag involuntarily as his throat teased with actual retching.

Initially, Allison and Lillian weren't very sympathetic, figuring his behavior was a *guy thing*. Only because of his love for Benny, his persistence, and a touch of ego, did he devise a secret safety plan for this aspect of child rearing.

If no one else were around to bail him out when the proverbial diaper change signaled the *big B*, he'd fill his lungs and swiftly carry Benny to the bathroom that had the shower stall next to the toilet. The primary objective was the stall serving as a safe backup holding tank for Benny in case the all too familiar urge to barf forced Brian to the porcelain receptacle. For a father strong of heart but weak of stomach, it allowed him the means of placing the babe with no fear of him falling while Dad was otherwise indisposed. Fortunately, only close calls presented themselves for the most part.

The gals were less than understanding when they learned of his unorthodox method for the responsibility of messy diapers. Therefore, one fine day, ego overran his instinct to continue with the method that had worked so well for several weeks.

The pungent lesson arrived with Benny lying in the stall upon a pasty browned diaper, in motion as most babes are during changing. Brian bit his lip and pushed himself past the point of his pulsating palate, which began to fill his mouth with the telltale acidic juices that often preceded and announced one about to lose his cookies.

Heart, soul, and stomach told him to escape the security of the stall if only to catch his breath. Ego, logic, and brain said to do so was foolish, wimpy, and unmanly. Those and a slew of other discouraging, guilt-laced opinions began to surface. Speaking of surfacing, his stomach won as the flailing beautiful babe was contentedly examining the texture of his own cast-off creation.

Puke, upchuck, gut the gullet, pump the pipes, barf, toss a cookie, spew the stew, heave, throw up, blow chunks. The unsuspecting child knew none of these terms, but it was the action that immediately trained him to lie still when Daddy changed a poopy diaper. And, the shower came in handy for cleaning the puke and poop off baby Benny.

Such mishaps never occurred again as the ladies decided Brian had enough attributes than to condemn him for a weak stomach. He was credited for his efforts and persistence.

Brian chuckled. "So from nine weeks old, if I was changing him, he'd lie still but if he heard the ladies, he'd return to his original flailing, poop-flinging machine." The father concluded, "Imagine what else they're learning when we aren't even aware of it."

BRIAN RETURNED TO THE JOB SITE later in the day with Jason and additional construction supplies. He tossed a cold soda to each of us guys as he checked on the various assignments throughout the crew. He called for George to help unload his truck, having Jason join me. I was wearing a bandana, dark from sweat, kind of disgusted as George walked past. Wiping my brow, I muttered that he could at least sweat a little.

Once on the other side of the building, Brian had George brace the long planks to combat the warp-causing moisture. Normally he was the type to keep his personal thoughts to himself, particularly around his employees. But with George, an essence resonated that penetrated barriers. Their talk quickly evolved to the upcoming divorce.

George avoided offering suggestions and opinions if unsolicited, a trait that most people like me have trouble mastering. He felt that imposing such when not asked was a form of violence. So he voiced this concern that he did not want to be intrusive.

Brian assured him that he not only felt all right in discussing his problems with him but also welcomed the opportunity for any fresh insight. He was conceding any hope of reconciliation with Allison, his fear evident as he talked about memories of growing up among friends who had divided families.

"Everyone else had stepfathers, stepmothers, stepbrothers, and sisters. Kids envied me being with my original folks, having a full brother even though he was gone. So ironic. If those kids had only known that I wanted my folks to divorce so that something would change. For something different. I never knew what I wanted to be when I grew up. I only wanted to grow up, so I could get away from home." His shoulders slumped.

The first years after high school, people were surprised that Brian succeeded in managing his little company with no support from his family, especially as he was considered merely a handyman. The fact was, with his mother's death he had no family. As Allison and he dated, they found a common love of vintage homes and antiques. They shared a respect and reverence, actually an honor, of things that preceded them. His quality work led him to do small, partial restorations on some turn-of-the-century homes.

He fought an uphill battle, however, with her family who hoped he'd find a *real* job. This sentiment increased once engaged and then married. It continued even after it became obvious that their business was destined not only to survive but thrive.

One unforgettable day he persisted in trying to land a bigger fish. Fueled by an ambitious heart versus a logical brain. He bid and bit off more than he could chew, winning the complete restoration of a local Victorian mansion purchased by a man from New Mexico. Brian hired Allison to scour the area for items from antique doorknobs to vintage light fixtures. He also hired three assistants to work with him on the place for a year with her directing the lion share of the decorating and color schemes. On completion, he traveled to Albuquerque on a shoestring budget to meet with Mr. Rod Duke.

"Actually it was more like a sandal-strap budget. We couldn't afford a shoestring."

Mr. Duke was impressed with the work and Brian's integrity not to gouge him or inflate prices. Here was an honest contractor who refused to have his customer cover the worker's mistakes, a person who lived the sacred meaning of *service*. The investor had purchased several older houses around Chicago. Some were earmarked for offices, others for homes. He offered an ongoing contract to begin restoration on twelve early-era houses. Because of the contract size, much more antique hunting was necessary, to the joy of Allison. They assembled a small, full-time restoration crew and that's when Jason became his crew chief.

However, Mr. Duke appeared to have integrity, too. He'd risen through the ranks with his scruples intact and insisted on two caveats. First, expense bids were to be estimates left open to ensure no shortages for Brian. Second, all holidays and most weekends were declared off-limits to work in order for Brian and his crew to enjoy quality family time. Working late was to be avoided in order to allow evenings with loved ones. He strove to impart this on a young man beginning a family.

In their early days, Brian worked out of his truck and their small apartment. Upon securing the Duke account, they were able to purchase one of the initial twelve homes before remodeling it. They maintained an office studio there, working on their home in off-hours while enjoying creative quality time. Soon, with multiple work sites, it was necessary and feasible to lease an office with storage yard and warehouse.

George absorbed it all as Brian reflected. "In high school I was voted *The Most Persistent*, but I've never understood why folks treat the self-employed as unemployed.

"When I first began working for myself, my mom used to call me, asking me to run an errand for her and then seemed offended if I said I was working. After she died and I met Allison, it was the same with her. She admitted it felt to her as if I were only doing odd jobs until she became a partner in the business. Once she was working with me, her perception changed. Then, we both began to experience it with *her* family."

George nodded. "People who've never been self-employed have little to compare such a lifestyle to. Can't grasp the way someone can be working and love their job. They don't understand passion for work creates the energy to work longer hours."

"And," interjected Brian, "they question why continue if it's not bucks up." He shrugged, "Money doesn't make me happy unless the work does."

"It's a difficult role. Sometimes folks are not supportive during the building, not knowing that being successful doesn't happen overnight. They seldom recognize the discipline it requires."

He welcomed the empathy, the fact that someone understood.

"Brian," George spoke briskly, laying a plank down loudly. "Never let anyone rob you of your right to be complete. Only you know what's best for you. This road trip from Arizona often brought us into contact with folks like you and Allison, those seeking fulfillment, wanting to evolve to a higher level. Sometimes it pertained to career paths and other times to personal and spiritual growth."

"I almost feel clearer in dealing with my spiritual path," remarked Brian.

George stared down a long plank. "My opinion in both cases is the same. Spirit isn't to be reserved for Sundays or kept separate from work. At this point in the life of the world with the Internet and all, information is more readily available than ever before and so are people's opinions. I look for a common thread of personal belief in religious, philosophical, and career teachings. Then I focus on those essentials."

"Did you say essentials?" Brian paused with a plank in hand.

"If you opt for personal advice or instruction, always choose someone who's a healthful-minded example of the path you're seeking. Be aware of the goals they teach, preach, or reach. Don't ask advice of friends who are novices in such endeavors. For example, in

Daro's writing he says he's talked with folks like Dave Barry, Stephen Cannell, Og Mandino, Barbara Taylor Bradford, Robert Parker, and David Morrell. Quite a spread. These people are successful in writing *and* having families."

Brian's chuckle began slow and deep as he thought of folks who'd promised but never delivered. "I always had trouble with the get-rich-quick, multi-level programs led by the man with all the answers for the future, and no cash for the present."

"Non-enlightened people can't assist others to become enlightened. They think they can direct someone when they've never accomplished it themselves, just as some folks find it easier to fix others than to focus on themselves. Even valid information is no more valuable than opinion until proven, until applied and verified, until a man makes a belief his truth."

Brian raced through a few more planks.

"It requires honest self-analysis and disciplined practice," George added.

His boss studied aloud for a minute. "It seems so often, what I'm seeking is attracted to me, attracts my attention. So, I try to remain alert for any sign. It seems to have worked in so many other areas. Work, solutions to construction, finding proper suppliers and antiques." He paused. "Worked in everything but my marriage."

George looked into the young man's eyes and paraphrased. "What's important to you will attract your attention. Signs. Synergy. Be prepared for signs of information and realizations. Be prepared and alert." He was cautious about how much information to share.

They continued in silence through a few more planks.

CHAPTER TWENTY-ONE

HERE'S TO THE DREAMERS

"DID YOU EVER HEAR of a magazine called *Success: Unlimited?*" George asked. "W. Clement Stone founded the publication. They later had an editor who took the periodical to greatness. He had a unique, circular manner in researching success stories. He was writing on Hank Aaron who was close to breaking Babe Ruth's homerun record with the Yankees.

"This editor, a fellow named Mandino, called the offices of the Atlanta Braves. They readily knew Aaron had hit 710 homers and needed five more to beat The Babe. He asked the publicity department how many strike-outs Aaron had made, but they had no clue. It took a while for someone to call him back. They found that Hank Aaron had 1,260 strike-outs.

"Mandino figured out Aaron had to step to the plate and strike out almost three times as many pitches for each homer in order to break The Babe's record."

Brian nodded, showing no relief, leaving George feeling as if he'd struck out.

"Ever felt you're not enough? I mean, as if you're good enough, but not quite enough?" The inquisitive, gentle smile prompted him to continue. "I've no family to offer Allison."

"What do you mean?"

"I'm an only child, virtually an orphan. My folks were well into their forties when I came along. Benjamin was already a teenager. I was a cross between an accident and a last-ditch effort. Then Benjamin bit it in 1988."

Obviously he had chewed on this a lot although seldom shared. "My dad was the youngest and his siblings are dead. Same with Mom's. And she died before Allison and I ever dated. 'Course my father was dead by that time too. I brought nothing to the table."

George paused unloading the lumber.

"Allison's folks may not always agree, but they're good people. Through her, Benny gained two grandparents and I gained a father- and mother-in-law. Benny has an aunt, two uncles, plus two more aunts and an uncle as a result of their marriages, and seven cousins from those unions, with more on the way.

"Although he won't remember, his great-grandmother once held him. From Allison, Benny has all these relatives. With me, they only received yours truly." He wasn't looking for sympathy but genuinely felt they'd been short-changed.

"So your sum total and worth, that is, personal value consists of only the relatives one brings to a marriage. So you offer nothing?"

Brian's satire began. "I had a dog, two beat-up trucks, and an armload of dreams."

George countered, "And many dreams materialized with Allison and Benny. I've heard Lillian and Hughie brag about the things you've shared with them, too."

"Things, being the key word," he retaliated as he tried to force some lumber through a tight space. "I bring no flesh and blood, no lives, no family, no bloodline continuation. No bodies to add to family gatherings. All the leaves on my family tree have fallen to the ground."

"Wait a minute, pal," George reached over shoving the stubborn lumber into place. He came to a complete standstill as he defiantly stared deep into Brian's eyes. "I hear you say, you ARE good enough, just NOT ENOUGH. That thinking is baloney, a phony manipulation of your words to sound different but it still translates to saying, You, Brian Poppy, aren't good enough."

The young man tried to defend himself, realizing he'd stand a better chance stopping a run-away locomotive.

"Brian," he soothed, "God loves each of us as if each is the only one. The Creator accepts us all as equals. The problem is that we don't use that same scale. That's where disharmony originates. That's the place where you currently reside."

"C'mon, George, I thought even you knew the importance of family." The comment hung heavily in the air.

"We're all created equals, on the inside. The individual is responsible for making himself successful," he quietly replied.

"All right, I'll give you that round, but I think you'll agree it's pretty obvious I'm blowing it as a husband and father. Just look at this mess."

"That's your problem. You're stymied about looking at things, the way you fault Lillian for doing. You want to change the outside picture, so you're trying to change your behavior. Change your thoughts, your inner thinking, not your behavior. Behavior will follow."

"I figured if my behavior changed…"

"Focusing on your behavior is like memorizing lines for a movie." George leaned against the truck. "Your behavior outside is a barometer of your thoughts inside. You can only fake the outside. But you can't fake the inside, can't fool your way to heaven."

A frustrated release of air came from Brian's chest. "Man! I'm listening to the counselor, listening to tapes, reading books, and thought I had opened my mind. What's the deal?"

George saw the defensive walls crumbling. "The behavior, the listening, the reading…all of that information deals with the outside. Outside is where all the doing occurs. Not the being. We do ninety-five percent of the things we see, imitating what we see around us. We only do five percent of the things we hear, like lectures or reading. See the hollowness of the concept: Do as I say, not as I do?"

Brian's mind tracked his thoughts in silence.

"From what I've heard, you haven't been given the best examples of a father or a husband. But everyone tells you the way they're supposed to be."

"So," winced Brian, "I understand only five percent of it, right?"

"I'd rate you higher than that but I think you could raise your percentage by changing your approach."

"By doing what?"

"Apply it to yourself, to the inner self in you, rather than the physical. Quit beating yourself up for wrongs you've done and re-direct your energy to the way to do things correctly."

"How?" he quickly voiced.

"Remember to remember. Work with Allison to apply that knowledge with Benny, knowledge in action, so you don't have to fix it or so he won't have to later in life as you're doing now. Help Benny develop his thinking and thoughts, and worry less about his behavior."

It was difficult to tell if the spark in Brian's eye was the beginning or end of a fire, or merely a tear.

George diffused the tension. "In San Francisco, I met a couple, a wonderful couple. The funny thing was that when they met, neither knew the other was adopted and neither had ever met their birth parents. Another secret commodity was a fear of marriage because both secretly felt they didn't have enough to offer, no bona fide blood lines, no history, and no heritage."

"I don't see the humor." Brian was annoyed.

"When she told him, he thought her concern was silly. He only saw all the good she had to offer. Nevertheless, he still felt he wasn't enough."

A quizzical look covered Brian's face but he wisely kept his mouth shut.

Lovingly satirical, George mocked, "I'm good enough. I'm just not enough." He resumed. "Pardon me but a Sheriff Leavitt in Texas once told me: 'Nothing's worse than a bullshitter who believes his own bull shit'."

Feeling misunderstood and hurt, Brian countered immediately. "I'm talkin' about reality, even if it's stuff on the outside. I bring no family."

"You make reality. What's the difference between this truck," he slapped the tailgate, "and an imaginary truck in your head? Both vehicles exist. One is on the physical plane, the other in the ethers of your mind. Can this truck smash into another truck and do damage? You betcha. Now can this truck smash into an imaginary one?"

All was silent until Brian's eyes darted away.

"Brian, you, of all people, should see you're focused on the imaginary just like Benny's monsters waiting in the dark. Mixing the real with the unreal, reality, and shadow world, the doing and the being. Like Benny, making your monsters real.

"You can continue to support that belief, telling yourself that crap about being good enough but not enough. Or" as George placed one end of a 2-by-4 scrap on the tailgate and ran his fist through it without even altering his speech, "You can smash through the belief by recognizing that reality comes from your heart. Choose to be bound by the chain, or by the ribbon."

He handed one of the pieces of pine to Brian as he continued softly. "Would Allison be enough if she were an orphan?" He handed over the second piece. "What about Benny? He surely didn't bring much to the table."

Brian stood dumbfounded. The realization couldn't have been more direct if the lumber had been broken over his skull. His jaw dropped.

George grasped the outer edges of four sheets of half-inch plywood and easily hoisted them overhead, effortlessly transporting them through the main entrance.

When he returned, Brian was attempting to rejoin the

shattered lumber, his jaw quivering as he spoke. "Allison and Benny are more than enough. Sometimes my brain works overtime."

George slipped his left arm over his shoulder. "Brian, look at that huge puddle in the hole where the guys began excavating. What do you see?"

"Water. It's full of rain water."

They walked closer. "Now what do you see?"

"Mud," was his simplistic reply. "And patterns in the mud plus a soda can and two coins. No, they're slugs from an electrical box."

Sounding like Master Po from the old television series Kung Fu, he made a wide arch. "Look closer, from all points on the circle around the puddle."

Brian stared a minute, feeling annoyed.

"Relax," he offered.

Becoming conscious of the reflection, Brian answered. "I see the phone lines above…with three crows sitting on them."

George gently squeezed his shoulder before removing his arm. "Very good, grasshopper." The reflection was suddenly broken by the splash of a rock hitting the glassy surface of the water, distorting the images.

Without looking at Brian, George sensed his surprise. His own intense stare at the water caused Brian's focus to return to the ripples. Slowly, the distortion diffused into an image similar to those of a carnival funhouse mirror and then eventually returned to the crystal clear water with images reflected from above.

"When we allow the waters to still themselves, we can see not only the inside but also the reflection of the heavens above."

They watched the birds take flight as if on cue.

ABOUT THAT TIME, I came walking over, having finished my project. He told me to fetch Jason and head to the warehouse to load some lighting fixtures. They'd join us after running an errand in Brian's truck. I knew he wanted to continue talking with George.

Behind the wheel of the truck, George probed Brian's mind with questions about the way he was able to do construction and bidding, and the way Allison had mastered the antiquing, operating the computer system, and the bookkeeping. All of his answers illustrated the reason his high school cronies pegged him as persistent.

Listening for a while, he began to chide him, alluding to his success being all just good luck. This bait didn't anger or hurt Brian who replied, "Man makes his own luck. Folks that are failures brand the man who pursues his dream, sees the opportunity and runs with it as lucky."

George said nothing, hiding his smile.

"You have to take risks. The greatest hazard in life is risking nothing. A person risking nothing, does nothing, has nothing, and in the end, is nothing."

"So why do you think people fail?" tested George.

Brian chewed the question. "Failure's not really an action. People don't fail; they quit too soon. As if they're satisfied with trying. Trying is like an excuse for failing with honor."

So went the talk as the Chevy's tires freed puddles, more than necessary with George driving. They laughed until he asked how this couple had found so many gullible people to believe in their skills. The comment bared a nerve and the reply was curt.

"You know, George, it really didn't matter who believed in me since I believed in myself and the quality of my workmanship."

Only God heard the whirl of the fish line as the mortal bit and swiftly swam with the bait. "Others could sense my faith, my confidence, and I controlled my emotions and my attitude," expanded the human fish with the splash of his fins resounding.

Pretending not to understand, George pushed. "How was that possible? I mean, the construction, the repairs, especially the designs. All were unlike anything you'd ever done. It's not like running track, painting homecoming windows, or being school president. Certainly, a far cry from a handyman repairing a sink or building shelves."

Until that moment, Brian had considered George rather astute. The surprise of his employee's ignorance was apparent. "Maybe some of my learning came from formal schooling, with most from the school of hard knocks. But I learned that I could have anything I dreamed of, anything, if I put my mind to it."

"Dreams?" asked George in mock innocence.

"Dreams," a slightly calmer Brian returned. "Once a person's mind is stretched to hold a dream, it can never return to its original shape. 'Course he has to move past emotion into action to realize it. But the emotion can be used as fuel. Most folks never run far enough on their first wind to find out they have a second one. Give your dreams all you've got and you'll be amazed at the energy that comes out of you."

"What about predestination? Is man predestined for success or failure?"

"God doesn't make failures, humans do. In their minds, they choose to fail."

George successfully masked the pleasure he was enjoying as they drove into the construction yard. He mocked some belief but continued the act as if he were unclear about the reason a person would try something he'd never done before.

Brian felt irritated, "Well, if they don't go for it, it's the same as failing. A salesman too afraid to make the call receives the same end result as receiving a rejection, if he doesn't ask. That fear is worse than failing. No chance is available for success then. At least, asking increases the odds greatly."

He reached a crescendo as they pulled into the job site and alongside me so that I heard him. "You must have faith. I don't care about the place where you find it. You must develop that faith, a belief. And act on it. You have to believe in yourself and sometimes in other people, like the time Allison and I began this business."

He continued, stepping from the truck, engulfed in his own words as the scenario unfolded.

"We didn't listen to others, only ourselves. We supported each other by listening to ourselves." He looked, mid-sentence, into the side mirror, first spying the lunch wagon and then his own face as his words echoed in his own ears. His voice trailed off. "We proved…" and was cut short by the two short blasts of the lunch wagon whistle.

George stepped around the front of the truck. "There's a title for those who tell us something won't work or all of the reasons you can't accomplish a goal."

Brian's eyebrows arched in anticipation.

"Dream busters," concluded George.

The horn sounded again. He squeezed Brian's shoulder. "It's lunchtime, boss."

We walked off, leaving Brian alone. Focused on himself and the echo in his ears, he was barely breathing.

At the lunch wagon, George handed me a cold soda, offering a toast. "Here's to the dreamers."

CHAPTER TWENTY-TWO

MENU CAN TRUST

TO FREE HIS IMAGE from the mirror and to clear his mind, Brian shook his head. Taking a deep breath, the air was a blend of fast food, fresh sawdust, and funky generator fumes. Not bad, but not something Glade would be packaging soon. At the slamming of the metal panels on the roach-coach, he ambled to the spot where we were sitting with the crew for our lunch break.

Tom walked past my back, staring for a moment at the black blocky slogan on my tee shirt. "*Menu Can Trust.* What's that all about?"

"A tribute to ripples and persistence," chimed my buddy, piquing our new boss's attention in anticipation of a luncheon lesson served á la George. Subconsciously, Jason began rhythmically to tap his feet with the pulse of the generator in the background, which seemed to become louder as if on cue. *As if.*

"Our world's full of rhythm," George began, matching the beat with his fingers. "When you throw a rock in the water, it makes ripples. Those ripples have a pattern, a rhythm. One of the tricks of persistence is spotting the rhythms."

The young kid stared more blankly than the rest of the crew. "I don't get it."

"I'll try again," smiled George. "Things happen from *first force* and *second force*. A saw blade turning is the first force in cutting wood. The board resisting becomes the second force."

"Meaning?"

"If you can understand first force and second force, then you can move from having things happen by coincidence, to having synchronicity."

Tom looked even more confused, so I returned to my roast beef sandwich while George switched tactics, mentioning some of the shirts they'd seen us wear.

"Menu Can Trust. Pick Your Seat on Our Patio. Our Meatballs Your Mouth. Our Cooks Are Goosed. Be a Pie-Diver."

The men began to crack up.

"And those are the slogans they didn't censor," I laughed.

"What're they from?" asked Chad.

"A pretty clever restaurant back in Scottsdale. We got to know the guy who started it. But *how* Oregano's Pizza Bistro came into being with the rhythm, the first and second forces and then the third, makes for some pretty interesting ripples."

Bingo. I thought as I watched Tom's curious eyes. *He's got 'em.*

"We just never know when our paths will cross with another's or how the ripples that we cause may wash upon someone's shore. America West Airlines was still around and a young fella named Mark was based out of Sky Harbor Airport in Phoenix. Basically he was a trouble-shooter, dealing directly with the public."

"Great training for the next stage of his life," I added. "Owner/Operator of a restaurant is taking a voluntary bite of a career in trouble-shooting. 'Course old Mark didn't know that."

Jimmy picked at a nut from his PayDay candy bar. "Didn't know what?"

"That the challenge of a restaurant or even having one was in his future."

"So, how'd he end up with one?" asked Tom as he peeled a banana.

"Mark's grandpappy was a gentleman named Lawrence

Gibbillini. When Mark was Benny's age, both father and grandfather were bricklayers back in Chicago. But on the weekends, little Mark could remember the men borrowing tables and tablecloths to take over the kitchen from the women and make some really wacky pizzas."

"So he opened a pizzeria?" asked Tom with mashed banana in his mouth.

"Too easy," I laughed. "Continue, George."

"First force is when something happens that we perceive as *good* or *bad*. Every first force has an opposite and equally strong second force, often labeled as good or bad. *How* we react or not is known as the *third force* that determines the outcome. And each one is a ripple."

"Where's this going?" asked the youngest crew member.

"Good question, Tom. Life moved on until Grandpa Lawrence was gone. Mark then lost his dad, and like a lotta grown-up kids, he had some unresolved issues."

Unresolved issues. Brian chewed at his lip.

Not keeping my mouth shut, I said, "He went for counseling. Can't always go it alone." Brian's eyes showed that the words struck another chord.

"First force, dad dies; second force, unresolved issues; third force, counseling, each one rippling off the other."

"Where's the restaurant come in?" Tom asked bluntly. Youth is often impatient.

"Counselor gave Mark an assignment. Homework. He had him go through his grandpappy's garage where Mark's dad also had things stored."

All waited until George grinned.

"Found it was packed with mismatched plates and silverware, used pots and pans, and the Gibbillini recipes. Mark stumbled upon their dream. To open a pizza place, specializing in the original family recipes."

"So," drawled Tom, "third force of going through their storage became first force? And finding the restaurant stuff and their dream became the second force?"

"Darn good observation, Tom. So what'd be the third force?"

"Opening the restaurant?"

"Actually, the third force is the decision, the reaction or handling of the first and second force. Mark had freedom of choice. Third force is not linear. Not a right or a wrong. Not a do it or don't do it. Want to field this one, Daro?"

"Well, third force isn't linear with two choices; it's circular, meaning many options."

"Like?" asked Brian.

"Like," I began, "Mark could have put everything back in storage, hauled it to Goodwill, sold the stuff and divvied with his siblings, but he chose to breathe life into his dad and granddad's dreams…as Oregano's in Old Town Scottsdale."

Jimmy began to count on his calloused fingers. "Let's see. His grandfather and father make pizzas on weekends, which Mark remembers. His dad dies, kid has a grudge, he gets counseling, is told to clean out his dad's storage, stumbles on his father and grandfather's dream, decides to make their dream real, and adopts it as his dream. So, like ten ripples. And that first, second, and third force stuff is all over the place."

Brian placed his hand on the worker's sweaty shoulders. "Smart guys I have here. More than just nail-slammers," he smiled. "So what's that Oregano's place like?"

"Mark had respect for things that went ahead of him. Plus, he was underfunded. He got a workable lease for this tiny, narrow strip of land that looked out on the main drag, Scottsdale Road. He refused to tear down the little burnt-out building. I helped work on it," said George.

I then rejoined. "Mark has an eye for design. Opened up the ceiling past the rafters to the roof. Used a variation of the Italian colors with a scheme of sandy beige, fire-engine red, and forest green.

Green shelves border the ceiling with antiques, like in Allison's kitchen. Used rippled sheet metal done in red for the counter fronts.

"Sounds trick," said Clay.

"The real trick was to make it chic to sit around the parking lot in the heart of Scottsdale for a couple of hours to wait for a table, and manage to have customers enjoy the wait."

My mouth began to water. "Boom Dip. Fiery wings. Them two-limit Bellinis. Joe Borik painted all three walls bordering the parking lot with murals of the Chicago shoreline. Add a narrow outside bar and a long row of chairs and everyone's happy."

"All that 'cause he stumbled on his dad's and grandpa's dream?" countered Tom. "That ripple thing's kinda cool."

I had to adjust my judgment. I saw a different facet of the young man. "The ripples continue."

"How's that?"

"Ripples going in all directions. The jobs and careers Mark launched. Suppliers he works with. He opened another Oregano's in Tempe and one in Flagstaff. Next is Tucson, which will give him pizza bistros in Arizona's three college towns. All using dilapidated buildings, Mark and Team Oregano put the love back into them. And that love comes through in the food." I licked my lips.

"So, all of this ripple stuff. It means connections like steps?" Tom was actually trying.

I smiled. "Ripples. We often don't know the people our actions will touch or the way it'll affect others or how they'll react. But in all cases, they reach someone. And in *every* case, we have freedom of choice. What we do, matters."

"Third force," echoed Jason. "We may never know the direction of our ripples."

Brian stood to signal time to resume work as if to let the thoughts settle. "So having freedom, we also have the freedom to choose the ripples we make," he mused.

If I could read minds, I'd have guessed Brian was thinking of the former choices made by his father and Benjamin, and the ones he personally still had time to make.

CHAPTER TWENTY-THREE

GONE FISHING

THE CREEKS ALONG WHERE Brian usually ran were seasonally drained to remove trash and make repairs. A strong fishy smell prevailed when the waterways were this low. Hundreds-upon-hundreds of fish perished, trout and carp trapped in small vanishing pools. Painful deaths. Suffocation as the crowded shallow puddles were drained of oxygen or the fish baked in the heat of the sun.

Benny's red wagon sat on the bank holding the large yellow barrel George had brought.

Justin and Benny were in the ditch, trapping the fish with buckets. Then Justin carried the bucket to George who carried it up, emptied it into the big barrel, and tossed the bucket back down. The water in the big can splashed and churned with activity.

"Hey, George?" yelled Justin, catching his breath.

"Hey, what?" came the reply.

"Know the reason why Noah didn't fish?"

"Why's that?"

"He only had two worms." Sometimes Justin was his own best audience.

"Hey, Justin," George yelled back.

"Hey, what?" both boys squealed.

"You're good in Sunday School. Where do they find Holy Water?"

167

"Dunno," laughed Justin. "Where do they find Holy Water?"

"In the pool where the holy mackerel live." George returned with satisfaction. Justin leaned the shovel over his little shoulder.

"Hey, George."

"Yes, Justin?"

"In Sunday school, the teacher told us a lesson where all these people prayed for rain and faithfully waited. If'n they had all this faith, why didn't they expect the rain and dig a ditch to catch the water while waiting?"

Oöso's barking saved George as Brian lumbered by in a half-hearted attempt to run. He watched the proceedings and spotted the active water with dozens of fish that the yellow barrel already held.

"Whatcha doing, son?" he hollered down.

The little fisher of men raised an eyebrow to the father he generally found wise. "Ketchin' fishies," was the obvious reply.

Brian eyed the three fishermen as he gazed into the swirling water and grimaced. "Hey, fellas," he stammered. "We can't eat all of these."

The child's overturned bucket fell with a mighty splash causing ripples as he captured another orange carp. Leaning his short body upon the bucket, he gasped at his father. "Not eatin' 'em. Fweein' 'em. Us guys takin' the fishies to phwim in Tim-er Lake." Satisfied, the child motioned to Justin who slipped the square-tipped shovel under the trapped fish. Together they flipped the bucket over, slapping each other's hand in a high five.

Already Brian knew he'd probably regret asking. "Why?"

Justin shot back the reply. "So's they don't die. So's they'll have a chance to live." He signaled Benny to bring the next empty bucket.

With a bit of exasperation, Brian remarked, "What difference does it make? You can't save 'em all." He shrugged as he swung out his arms. "What does it matter?"

The reply was quick. "It matters to *this* one," as the lad

motioned to George to hoist up the bucket with the latest fish destined to live in Timber Lake.

Upon eye contact with George, Brian grasped the empty bucket and began his descent into the muddy channel to fish with the boys.

WHILE GEORGE HAD BEEN catchin' fishies with the boys, I'd been peeling potatoes. My chore completed and the fishermen home, I agreed to help Benny build a sandcastle to keep him from being underfoot in the kitchen before the Johnsons arrived for dinner.

Lillian was deep in thought as she prepared a mammoth mound of mashed potatoes from my expertly peeled spuds. Fresh crème, a pinch of sea salt, several mashed cloves of garlic, oodles of fresh butter, some parsley for color, and a great deal of elbow grease transformed the dark earthen creatures into fluffy, white mounds.

Outside, major sand construction took shape as the ladies peered out the window. "Lookit wot me 'n' Daaw-oh did," squealed Benny from his sandbox, until the two ladies came outside to look. Allison giggled at me with sand up to my elbows.

"Senior Engineer," I boasted. "Told Benny I'd help but he had to wet the sand."

Both ladies cringed and then their discreet titters rolled into giggles, a couple of chuckles, and finally into outright laughter, leaving them barely able to speak.

At first, I smiled innocently until growing weary of not understanding the joke. George approached as he heard the ladies' laughter and asked me about the commotion.

"I dunno, and frankly I'm starting to get pissed." Rather than my unfavorable comment raising the grandmother's anger, it raised the volume of their hysterics until a contagious chortle began in George's throat. He shrugged his shoulders as I scratched my head with my sand-covered hand, and then I sniffed suspiciously.

"Oh, Daro, you're right," cried the grandmother almost

doubled over in laughter. "We've been having trouble getting Benny to use water from the hose for his sandbox." George collapsed to his knees as I smelled my hands once more before leaping up and running for the garden hose with my fingers outstretched.

FOLLOWING DINNER, I helped clear the table with Justin and Benny, although I was still double-checking my hands for odd smells.

"Kin me put in da bubboos, Unca Daaw-oh?" Benny smiled.

I nodded as Justin placed the stopper in the sink and reached for the liquid soap while Benny dragged his stepstool to the sink.

"Hey, Daro," began Justin, looking at the label. "How come lemon juice has artificial ingredients, and dishwashing soap uses real lemons?"

"I don't know," I painfully admitted, "But you stay away from my iced tea."

Back at the table, the conversation had shifted to a discussion of Rio's birth. Lillian quietly excused herself to check on the youngsters washing the dishes, so she could be more a bug on the wall than a person directly in the scenario.

"When I was pregnant, we were really selective about the music we played," said Denise. "We felt the baby could hear it already."

"They say that plants like to hear music, so it makes sense babies would."

The small voice of Justin was heard from around the corner. "So, instead of talking nice to plants, if ya yell at 'em will they grow up and be all troubled and insecure?"

"That little guy, man, he's a hoot," I smiled as he ducked back.

"Yeah," Jason softly uttered. He was looking at his folded hands while his mind traveled back and his face began to beam as he shared information.

"When Denise was pregnant with Rio, Justin insisted that when we read to him, we read to the unborn baby too. Their big brother was too into girls and sports although he thought it was cool. When Rio was born six weeks early and kept in the hospital, Justin got upset because the staff wouldn't let him into the Intensive Care Unit. After Denise came home one night still without his new brother, his tantrums began."

"Why can't I see him? He's my brother! I'm not sick! You guys can see him. Dad chews tobacco and gets to see him! And I bet those old doctors smoke!"

"So, on Rio's ninth day in his incubated world, I pressured the hospital on behalf of my son, and my own sanity, which was jeopardized by suddenly giving up Skoal."

"Thank goodness," sighed Denise with her nose wrinkled.

"Anyhow, while the doctors said it would be safe to bring Justin in, they hid behind the hospital rules and regulations that stated he was too young."

"So Jason created a disguise."

"He did what?" George asked.

"Although the weather didn't demand a trench coat, few paid attention to my wardrobe as we entered the hospital. But the two small feet stumbling beneath my bulging overcoat snared a few double takes."

"Blue-green industrial carpet flanked the walls painted with cartoons in the hall of the Children's Unit," said Denise. "No matter, this place was still a hospital. Justin stealthily emerged from beneath Jason's long coat and stood in silence, his face and palms pressed against the thick isolation glass. As we pointed out his new brother, his worried voice cracked. *'He's tinier than I was'*. That comment kept us wondering for a full five minutes, the time allotted for the child's visit. And then we noticed his tears trickling down the glass."

"Justin blinked as he saw the minute-hand on the huge black-

and-white clock, knowing his visit had ended. Unaware that the charade was no longer necessary, he resolutely climbed back inside my trench coat, looking up before pulling it closed. Solemnly he instructed us, *'Tell Rio I love him'.*"

"That five-minute visit pacified Justin for another two weeks at which time, Rio was released from the hospital, and tobacco had become Jason's former habit." She patted her husband's hand as we learned more endearing things about the little trio.

Justin and Benny regularly talked with the baby, now three months old. They told him things they'd do together when he was older, as if they were giving him a reason to live. They critiqued the outfits the grandparents gave him. They brought him leaves from the tree house. In addition, they told him to dream happy thoughts, so he would get all better. The baby often cooed as if to acknowledge their words. *As if.*

CHAPTER TWENTY-FOUR

POPCORN PRAYERS

THAT EVENING AFTER everyone had gone to bed and the clocks were ticking in single digits, a solitary crow peered in from the windowsill. Perhaps he was part night owl.

George's eyes popped open. No threat or fear in the air, just an image of Allison. The thoughts being stirred within mother and daughter would cause her to be sensitive to change. The rattling in the chain as tension was placed upon the ribbon could be quite loud and unnerving.

He swung his legs over the edge of his bed. Sitting up, he saw the glimmer of light that eased down the hall. The popping of sap blended with the aroma of burning logs. Remaining close to the wall as he moved, he looked down the stairway. Allison was awake, unable to sleep.

A friend would be nice right about now. Then he grinned impishly.

Returning to their room, he adjusted the door to remain in the shadows. He picked up one of his combat boots and extended it knee high before he let it drop to the floor to stir his sleeping buddy, but it didn't even alter his breathing. Nor did a drop from shoulder height awaken the sleeping man.

His next move focused on bumping the bed and then leaping catlike to his own bunk. Two, three more failed attempts of jarring and thumping it. In fact, lifting the end of the bed and giving it a hearty shaking didn't stir the sleeping beast, but it sure amused Mr. Crow.

Time to use another tactic. Maybe a flash of light. Nope. Multiple bursts from the overhead light or even the bedside lamp held directly over his face achieved nothing, except to make Mr. Crow tilt his head. At this point, George was no longer concerned about being caught by Daro because nothing seemed to interrupt the volcanic rumblings of the human snoring machine.

A blanket pulled down to create a chill, a comforter added to raise the temperature. Nothing. Pulling the blanket over his face only resulted in concern that his pal would prematurely float on a heavenly cloud from suffocation. No discomfort or noise seemed capable of disturbing his slumber.

Whereas George could hear the distant popping of Allison's popcorn, Daro remained unconscious even being popped in the head. Then George grinned.

He quickly pulled the door open, unconcerned about the light swallowing the shadows where his buddy lay unconscious. In reconnaissance fashion, he crept to the stair rail, peering between the hand-turned maple posts. He watched her pace the floor in a well-worn robe. The left cuff of the green housecoat bore loose threads from a night when Oöso wasn't content to be left home alone.

As she stoked the logs, he knew it was time to make his move. Any delay on his part could foil his plan. Another truism of life. Plus, there was the added factor of her being much more cognizant than Daro at this point.

The bare stairs led down, dividing the dining area and kitchen. Old, wooden plank stairs. Glue, screws, and nails had been used a plenty but a minimum of one creak every five steps was a certainty, and twenty-one stairs led to the first landing, followed by nine to bring him to the living room. Then the challenge of his return coupled with the time required. It was most fortunate George was so light on his feet.

Mission completed, he re-entered the bedroom with a handful of fluffy captives, several warm, popped kernels. Burglars could've stolen Daro's bed with him in it and nary a snore would be lost. George gazed down and made one and then two passes with his handful of fresh popcorn over his pal's face.

Within inches of the majestic nose, nostrils flared as the aroma of hot buttered popcorn permeated his olfactory nerves. And before the sense of smell teamed with his auditory sense, the popcorn-napper had leaped back to his bed. To Daro's suddenly alert senses, George appeared sound asleep.

SUPPORTED BY MY ELBOWS, I sat up and spied my green sweatpants and a tee shirt. I dressed quickly, taking care not to disturb George as I followed my nose.

The flames beckoned from the fireplace as I padded down the stairs in my stocking feet. I beat the creak average, making a wooden stair groan every second step. Allison turned in my direction.

Without a word, I walked to the fire, grabbed a log, and pulled the antique mesh open "Will tend fire for food."

She laughed through her mouthful of popcorn and patted the overstuffed cushion. I loved the way her freckles ran across her nose. When she laughed, it was freckle-football scrimmage. The fire grew, mirrored off the fine dried oak frame, the brass studs on the arms of the nineteenth-century English sofa shining like tiny reflectors.

I sat down. "What's happenin'?"

"I have problems and can't sleep. What's your excuse?" she smirked.

"I'm here to solve your problems," was my quick comeback as I reached into the bowl. "Besides, you've made way too much popcorn and we can't let it go to waste." I bluntly quizzed her. "You 'n' Brian had a fight?"

She sighed deeply. "We really don't fight, much. I have to admit, he's taught me how to disagree without fighting." Tears surfaced. "A friendly divorce."

I remained quiet, attempting to understand her remark.

She grinned through her tears. "One of our first fights, actually just a major disagreement, involved Oöso.

"You fought over the dog?"

"No, we'd been searching for a hard-to-find product line and I'd arranged for a sales call from a potential supplier. The lady sales rep left our office and Oöso spotted her from Brian's truck. Her furry ears popped up like radar and then lay close to her skull as her tail went stiff, so Brian stood close as I escorted the lady back to her utility van. As we passed, Oöso began a slow, deep growl, barely audible. By the time we reached the van, her lips had curled into a noticeable, fang-revealing snarl.

"I was embarrassed and apologized to the nervous sales lady. Brian just remained silent with a casual grip on Oöso's collar, who, I must admit, was looking more like a vicious wolf than cuddly Samoyed."

I remembered the way the dog behaved when we met versus the way she greeted me now. When the truck was parked, the dog stood guard effectively, warning strangers away from absconding with any tools. Plus, Oöso didn't show much love for Tom, either.

"When the sales lady drove off, I asked Brian about the dog's behavior. He asked me who she was, so I told him, and I expected him to be excited to hear I had secured a source for the parts we wanted."

"And?"

"He bluntly instructed me not to do any business with her since Oöso didn't like her. He said that the proper supplier would eventually appear. It struck me as strange to hear this rule." In retrospect, she was now able to join in the laughter.

"Rule?" I puzzled.

"Yes. He told me he had a rule never to do business with anyone his dog didn't like. Later after Benny was born, the same rule applied to our son's judgment."

"Guess he overlooked it, hiring Tom anyway."

Allison slapped my leg.

"So what happened with the lady?"

"I worked with her without telling him, and she didn't stand behind her products. As a result, it cost us more than $1,000."

"How'd Brian handle it?"

"I think he expected it, expected me to ignore him, that is. Said he hoped I'd learned my lesson sooner than he had." Then her face became stoic. "If only someone had the answers now." When she nudged my shoulder, her blonde hair brushed my hand.

It had been a long time since I sat alone with a lovely and intelligent lady. Shoot, long time since I was alone with any chick. The fire reflected as crescent moons in those green eyes, and I'm a sucker for green eyes. And her hair. Lordy, I wanted to run barefoot through it. Here could be a most romantic setting. Yet, I'll toot my own horn, being proof there are still men of ethics, a respect not willing to be compromised by taking advantage of a person in pain, of a married woman. Toot my own horn, indeed.

Someone looking through the window might see this scene as suspiciously as a mother later hearing of the situation, but I never thought to make such an advance. Well, barely, anyhow. Green eyes, freckles, and blonde hair, you know.

Those green eyes were drawing me in, so I tried to adopt a big brother role. I sat up taller, stretched out my legs, and flexed my toes in an attempt to return to the moment. "Answers? You already have them, lil' sister. Just listen. Listen only to you."

Her face seemed tiny in a frail, searching state. She was trying to communicate without speaking, questioning without asking, about how to listen effectively to herself.

"Learning to listen to ourselves is great practice for listening to others. I'm still kind of naturally gabby, you might have noticed," I admitted sheepishly.

"I like the things you share, but I've noticed you take quiet times. George does too. Are you praying?"

"Prayer, meditation. I dunno. I see them as at least being

connected. Prayer is talking to God or my Higher Self. Meditation is the act of listening for the answer.

"At one time, I focused on the first with my talking and asking, and then would be too busy to listen to the answer. I couldn't have heard God if He were talking to me or heard any angels even. I couldn't hear someone when I was too busy talking."

"So you learned to listen?"

"Well, let's say, I'm improving. I've adopted some steps to help me listen better which I can share if you're interested...in listening," I chided.

"Okay," she smiled. "I've got the popcorn, if you've got the time. Lead the way."

"The truth of it is quite simple with only three steps: quieting the mind, paying attention, and giving thanks daily."

She stared at me blankly.

"Understand, this method is merely the way it works for me. The first problem I encounter is focus, creating the space to quiet my physical mind."

"You oughta try it with a four-year-old underfoot."

"Let's take it one step at a time."

Her look told me she was apprehensive.

"One reason for developing a process to quiet your mind is to allow you to use it at any time and in any place. The truth is, we need to hear our intuition most when we're locked in a crisis or in the everyday flurry of life." I reached for popcorn, using the momentary silence to evaluate her willingness to understand the topic.

"George had a teacher who placed him in a soup kitchen to teach him the way to focus his prayers and meditations. It's up to you if you want to make it tougher or just want to practice around Benny," I laughed.

"Okay, attitude adjustment here," as she hoisted her cup.

"How do I learn to quiet my mind?"

On the mantle rested a tall clock. The pewter green pine case was hand rubbed and distressed. Classic Arabic numerals were on the face of the shaker-style timepiece. I used the brass pendulum to illustrate my point as she followed my finger.

"I picture that pendulum in my head." My eyes and head rocked slowly to and fro. "An endless myriad of mind chatter precedes absolute silence. Mind chatter…silence…chatter…silence. At some point in between, just as points on that clock last only a millisecond, that sound becomes *The Voice*, one still voice. It seems confusing but if I remain motionless, the pendulum in my head coincides with the one in my heart. Bingo. One voice and my doubt about *who* disappears."

"But slowing that pendulum," she fussed.

"Being alone with the flickering of a fire is a wonderful place of solitude. That's the kinda space you want for the first step of listening to yourself, that is, finding a place to be calm, calming your consciousness in order to quiet your mind." I watched her breathing slow as the defensiveness in her shoulders relaxed.

"Alone, late at night, too late for the telephone, no music playing, Oöso and Benny sound asleep. Let the pool become calm and allow the reflection to reveal the moon and heavens above."

"Not just relaxing?"

"Nope, sleeping isn't being still nor is chilling to music. Nor is praying, especially when you're asking for guidance. Understand the concept? Still is being completely motionless. George has a number of exercises about focus. Concentrate on things such as a candle flame. Or a windshield wiper when you're not driving, of course. A bird chirping, or even chewing a raisin for fifteen minutes without swallowing it. If you can learn to remain focused on one thing. It's just one step away from nothingness."

"Does it require a long time? I mean, to see any results? How long have you been meditating?"

"Whoa, give it a serious effort and see where it leads you.

Try it for ten minutes a day for one week." I munched, "Let's see here." I counted on my fingers. "So, by spending less than one, one-hundredth of a percent of your waking day investing in yourself… more quickly than you might think, you'll be in direct contact with your intuition. Remember that intuition resides in you. It's already a part of your being. Don't make it more difficult by thinking of it as being separate, and out there."

"I still think it may be easier when you're not raising a family."

I was used to the many excuses for not having time, so I jumped ahead with a capper. "How often do you skip taking a shower? Why do you take a shower anyhow?"

The question surprised her. "Well, daily, at least. To remove the dirt and grime from the day's activities."

"Anything else?"

She looked timid as if I might judge her answer. "To relax. Frankly, to remove the negative energy from all the people I deal with each day."

"So you don't skip many showers. Now can you see meditation as that important too? That's why my intention centers on meditating and praying at least twice a day. And like my shower, without a crowd or interruptions," I grinned before continuing.

"I challenge anyone. The president, a rock star, a corporate head, a TV celebrity, a popular teen, some idiot on a reality show, or the mother of quadruplets, not to find ten minutes uninterrupted. Just give it a try." I narrowed an eye at her, playfully raising my finger. "Not allowed to tell me the reason you can't, until you give it an honest shot."

We shared popcorn for a few minutes. Her hand bumped mine when reaching and I felt my heart flutter. Her left eyebrow rose. "You've used terms, such as God and Higher Self, Inner Self, even angels. Are they interchangeable?"

"In my opinion, they are one and the same, connected,

anyhow. Like we all share DNA. You can't divide a sunbeam from the sun nor make God and man separate. But remember, these are merely my opinions, my beliefs, m' lady."

As I walked toward the kitchen, the sway of the pendulum caught my eye. It was almost three in the morning.

CHAPTER TWENTY-FIVE

TOUCHED BY AN ANGEL-INSOMNIAC

THE AROMA OF THE FRESH BUTTERED POPCORN filled the room as I returned. It was obvious she was waiting for me to proceed as I settled back into the warm spot I'd created on the overstuffed couch. I placed the ceramic bowl as a marker between us.

"Let's make a couple of determinations. The five senses: taste, hearing, sight, touch, smell, those fellows. Are they a part of you or separate? Are they inside or outside you?"

"Well," she began with hesitation.

"It's not a test, merely your opinion, no right or wrong answer."

"Well, then I'd say a part of me. Inside me but they extend to the outside."

I liked the essence of this young woman. Nice mix of spirit and beauty. I savored the hot chocolate and popcorn, enabling me moments to reflect. Her insight of our five senses extending beyond the inside to the outside prompted an image in my head.

"So would you say our senses traverse a type of bridge?" I extended a finger to the back of her hand. "That my sense of touch begins inside me and allows me to enjoy the touch of a soft hand outside me?"

At her slight blush, I brought my hand back and drummed my fingers together. "What happens when people lose one of their senses?"

She shrugged. "Like sight? The other senses become better that is, the hearing becomes more sensitive and more sharply attuned."

"Better?" I baited.

"Sharper. The blind person relies on her hearing more, so she allows it to serve her more meaningfully, more effectively."

"Serve her better. Good logic." I realized I was learning too. "And can you see the way a person learning a foreign language improves more as she uses it?"

"Sure," she smiled sheepishly, attempting to gauge the path ahead.

I fidgeted as I continued with my trail blazing. "It's my belief that our connection with God, our Higher Self, is present and as real as those senses we recognize. A sixth sense as well. The Hawaiian Islands appear separate from the United States, but they are nevertheless a part of the earth. The stars appear separate…"

"But, they're all part of the universe. The earth is merely one of the stars."

"Bingo. And this belief is the premise that leads into the second step of listening to ourselves better."

"So, you're recognizing our spirit self as the sixth sense. Saying it's as much a part of us as our five physical senses, and as much a part of us as our minds."

She looked at the fire. "And we're just as much a part of God, as those islands are a part of the earth, and the earth a part of the heavens."

I stared at the burning logs. "We learned in school that the human brain is actually three brains, but they didn't touch on the way it affects our spiritual evolvement."

She giggled as she thrust her arm upward like a schoolgirl. "The three brains: the lower is reptilian. Then comes our left and right parts that we mainly use."

"Good, you receive an A," I laughed. "Our left brain handles our talking, the mechanical stuff, and memorization. However, we have all of our creative ideas in the right brain: music, poetry, and inventions. That's the area in which we take the facts we've learned in the left and find new applications and inventions using our right."

"And the right is home to our intuition?" she guessed.

"Yep. 'Course, the left-brain and right-brain portions are really one brain. Listening works the same if you see God as part of your own self talking. For example, I enter my meditation and prayers with the intent of developing a more effective relationship with my ongoing eternal spirit-self, with God."

I repositioned myself slightly and turned my head to face her. "The One means that God and I are the same, you and God are one, so you and God and I are all one, a part of one, not a separate entity." I stressed, "The Great One. But, sometimes we talk and act as though we're separate creatures from God."

"It makes sense. *Developing a more effective relationship with my ongoing eternal spirit-self.* I like that phrase."

As I grabbed more popcorn, I motioned towards the glow. "Listening to yourself means allowing yourself to hear your own intuition. Some would call it our link with God. A special lady once told me that it was the ability to listen to our own thoughts above the noise of the world."

Swallowing her popcorn, Allison shared that her times of knowingness were ones that she generally stumbled upon rather than deliberately planned, as in much of her life. "So what happens once a person is able to be still and finally knows she is one?"

I tossed my head back as I flipped a kernel, ignoring the fact that it sailed completely over my head. "That's really the whole arrangement, no magic formula."

She dug for a couple of blackened kernels, crunching them loudly. "Is this idea similar to being in the center of the circle like

George taught you?"

"I suppose it is. Frankly, sometimes I just *pretend* not to be attached. Not being the most advanced being, I have to fool myself. I pretend not to care about the way it ultimately turns out. Then I can get unbiased answers from myself. I find solutions, sometimes harebrained ones, but answers I might never have considered."

"Such as shooting the hubby," she recalled with a grin. "So, no investment or agenda in the answer permits other unexpected and possible answers to come to mind." She popped a kernel in her mouth as a reward.

I sailed another kernel over my head, stretching my neck over the curved back of the sofa. "His voice…Her voice…Your voice. Let's just say that God's voice is heard in everything: people, animals, trees, and rocks. This voice is all there is, encouraging us to be one. God's voice appears in multiple forms, messages delivered in every way. Some call it the Holy Ghost or the Holy Spirit communicating."

She mentioned how her mind was drifting to the terms from Sunday School of the Father, the Son, and the Holy Ghost. My next comment brought her back to the conversation.

"When I succeed with my meditations and prayers daily, I receive the answers, the truth, which may come at any time and in any place, provided I pay attention."

"Okay, I have one for you. How do you define the *truth*?" she asked.

I felt I was on shaky ground, wishing George were nearby to field this one, so I opted to rely on him in the best way I could, by quoting him. "George once told me that if the prayer is true, offered in unconditional love, it is answered. But God is not attached to our ego, or the prayers of our ego, or the fiction and drama we use in order to solve the problems we've created, so the answers may not be ones we want to hear."

"The *fiction* we've created?"

I remembered how strange this conversation sounded when

I first heard it. I was thankful Allison was more open-minded than I'd been. "Although not separate, we sometimes treat it all as if we're separate. The body…the mind…and the spirit. The first is what we focus on the most. The latter two are the ones we deal with the least. We become focused on the body." I paused before answering, "Herein is the truth."

She leaned forward.

I smiled to ease the intensity. "It's not as deep as we make it. Operating from our minds focuses on fear and launches us into survival mode. Operating from spirit, however, is a place of enrichment, love, and victory."

Her eyebrows twitched, and I leaned forward.

"Whatever the subject you're dealing with, ask yourself, see if you're in mind or spirit, head or heart. Simply ask each time, what's my motive?"

"And then?"

"You have to act *when* and *if* you're at peace. Knowing your motive can give you that serenity. If you can be at peace based on peace, that's fine, but don't try to force your faith, don't pretend or force peace.

"This concept is so important, especially in our frenzied world. If the peace in your heart isn't there, return to the first two steps of stilling your mind with the intent of being one with God. Miracles aren't complicated. They happen in simple, practical ways. And don't expect God or our true being to answer a prayer that would further separate us from His love, or from Him, or from ourselves."

Our eyes merged with the fire as we stared into it. "What do you make of coincidences?" I asked.

Coincidence was a buzzword with her and she jumped ahead. "Frankly, I don't believe in them. I think that's God working, God's signposts."

I paused to hear myself to be certain I wasn't being ego-driven. "Maybe God used the Holy Spirit to wake me. Maybe I happened to have a couple of the answers you were looking for. Maybe that's the coincidence of why," as I glanced at the clock, "I awoke a couple hours ago with an overwhelming urge for popcorn at a quarter past midnight."

We both munched for a while. Neither of us had the slightest inkling that George was smiling in unison with us.

"So, do you think coincidence happened here tonight?" she asked.

"That's part of my drift. Ever be thinking about someone and that person calls you on the phone? Want information on a subject and you see a magazine with an article about it? Have a problem and open your Bible directly to the perfect verse?"

She nodded throughout my questions as she clicked her fingernail against her lower teeth. "Actually, I've had that happen a lot, especially on my antiquing junkets." She shook her head discouragingly. "Wish I could do that always. Find the right answers as easily as I do with the antiques."

"You can. You've just learned a way to strengthen that ability."

"So I need to be still in order to hear, and that's the place where it begins?"

I clicked our empty mugs together acknowledging her unfolding awareness and then I got up to refill our cups. I plunked several tiny marshmallows into the swirling hot chocolate and sneaked a couple more into my mouth.

She shifted her voice as I returned. "So what's next, Coach?"

I smiled, warmed by the good that God was allowing me to do. No, it was more than allowing me. I realized He was enabling me, empowering more than allowing. I carefully placed the mugs on the coasters.

"The last part, I figure is mere politeness. That is to say, thanks. Thanks for the answer or the coincidence and be patient. It's important that we say thank you. It allows our selves or angels or God to know we heard and that we appreciate their help. It also begins to expedite the proof of the answer that'll bring us peace."

"Meaning, us knowing God wouldn't give us an answer that would separate us further?"

"Bingo. Just allow it to be an answer. Refrain from judgment. I'm finally at the point whereby I know I'll receive proof either way. Expecting it to be one way or the other can force investment into the answer and cloud the message."

Allison snickered, "I'm good at being patient if it doesn't take too long."

"Saying thanks has become a habit in which I catch myself actually grinning and saying thanks out loud. I figure God and self are one, one voice, only one voice. Beginning to listen for that one voice will help filter out all of the mind chatter and help us to accept the answer and practice patience."

Leaning into the sofa arm, she drew her legs beneath her, carefully draping her robe around them. "This really makes sense. What else is needed?"

"Here's the place where many toes are broken," as I gestured with the cup toward her. "It's a classic case of going ninety percent of the way rather than one hundred. Not quite fixed, not quite clean. The trick is remembering daily devotions or meditations in order to hear. Of course, the more you pray, the better it works, but this idea wraps the whole package neatly.

"I still have trouble doing the stuff daily. Imagine learning French but not practicing it, and then traveling to that country and using it. The more you practice even scant moments of stillness daily, the better the habit of listening becomes."

"Consciousness into unconsciousness." She was chewing more on her thoughts as she asked about old habits and ways to deal with them.

"George has told me time and again that the only way to

eliminate a bad habit is by replacing it with another habit, and it'd better not be a half-hearted attempt. It requires conscious thought to stop a habit and replace it with a new one. The odd thing is that habits are unconscious acts. Everyone today is striving to be conscious, yet in some ways our goal focuses on learning to be unconsciously conscious or automatically conscious."

"Unconsciously being conscious," she mused.

I nodded at her. "That's the time when your devotion of ten minutes a day becomes reality." I let fly a few kernels of popcorn until the fifth attempt finally found its way into my gaping mouth, and half-way down my throat.

Regaining my composure, I resumed. "Things as a habit and things as unconscious acts make me think of the little boy angel who came down to visit his earthbound buddies. One of them said, *'Tommy, those are cool wings you have there, but they're huge. How do you get your shirt over them?'*"

"The angelic lad glanced about a few times at his wings, to his shirt, and back to the boys. Finally, under his breath came his discouraged answer. *'I don't know, but I'll be damned if I'll ever be able to do it again'.*"

She threw a kernel at me that I caught to the amazement of us both. "So what do you know about angels?" she asked.

It made me do a double take and fumble. "Oh, angels are kind of a hobby of mine." Nervous to move on, I plucked at another subject. "Hey, speaking of habits. What do you call a nun who sleepwalks?"

She glanced up with a hollow look. "A roamin' Catholic."

A handful of popcorn sailed at me as I leaned back laughing.

After a pause, she asked in a monotone. "Daro, do you think angels really exist?"

GEORGE HAD DISCOVERED a way to slip past the two in their fireside discussion soon after Daro's nose harnessed him into this popcorn-fueled class of teach and learn. As parents might watch their children in school, so George sat outside the open window near the sink.

Daro wandered into the kitchen, rinsed the popcorn bowl with hot water, welcoming the stubborn butter residue to buy him some time. He regretted his wisecrack of angels being his hobby. As a breeze blew across his face, his skin prickled and he relaxed a bit.

She had followed him slowly into the kitchen. As he spoke over his shoulder, he became aware of her presence. "I believe something happens after dying other than darkness and becoming worm food. I remember the time I was helping a friend sort through his dad's belongings. We ran across an old suitcase. I remember looking at it and found myself refusing to believe that old suitcase would have a longer shelf life than my friend's dad."

Daro turned from the sink leaning against the counter. "Whether someone is living here on this physical plane with a physical body," as he tapped the floor, "or living in heaven with a spiritual soul," as he gazed up to the vaulted ceiling, "they're still part of the same universe. But then, what do I know about angels? I've never actually seen a penguin face-to-face and yet I believe in them too."

Sitting cross-legged beneath the window outside, George placed his forehead in his hands, his shoulders quaking in an attempt not to laugh.

Allison stepped closer. "Think angels look like us, that is, if they want to?"

"I'm sure they do. It'd probably be easier to accept an angel in human form than in spirit form like a ghost. Not everyone could handle ghosts as well as Allison DuBois or Jennifer Love Hewitt. Or maybe they're subtle, appearing to us not visibly but as thoughts mixed with our own intuition and our gut instincts. And they don't sleep much."

"What?"

"I mean, I bet their time is different from the time we know."

"So, do you see them punching some sort of a holy time clock?" She laughed.

"No," he chuckled. "I think an angel remains around as long as it remains an integral part of someone's spiritual development." He was eager to end the topic.

"What's it like being an angel?" she mused. "I bet it's a lot of work when you think about it."

"It takes balls," he added, her laugh making him conscious of the words. "What I mean is," he stuttered, "they're dealing with free will, human will, and their own will."

"Their will?" she asked.

"Sure. I figure they could stay up in fluffy cloudland with streets all paved in gold or return to earth and teach that humans and God are one. Help us find our way back to the heart in order to remember to remember. They can take a break now and then or continue to work, but it's their choice. It's not like they'll be missed up there."

"You mean because of their form of time?"

"Sure. The way I figure it," as he moved toward the clock and thumped it, "five years, fifty years, one hundred years could be an instant for them, similar to the number of thoughts and images we can have in a second. They could become angels, return to earth to handle business, and then return to heaven before they're even missed, before the first bed check. Fifty years to us on the earth plane may be moments for them in heaven."

She agreed to his logic but her grin caused Daro to redden as he heard her giggle and say, "Angels with balls."

OUTSIDE OF THE PORCH SILL crouched beneath the window, George nodded in silent agreement as he whispered. "Brass ones, Daro, big brass ones."

CHAPTER TWENTY-SIX

ANTIQUE LOVE AND AGELESS WISDOM

IT WAS GARAGE SALES or craft shows almost every weekend back when Brian and Allison began to date. Later on, the growth of their business enabled them to refine those playful excursions into prosperous antiquing treks. She honed her attentive eye into a trained sonar system for spotting treasures. It originated with knickknacks like tiny bottles and vintage tin cans.

Brian built her a long shelf in the kitchen just below the ceiling on which she stenciled a vine pattern. Setting on the left was a large box of Kellogg's Toasted Corn Flakes, a commemorative of the original 1906 with a young woman holding an armful of long corn stalks. A thick, glass milk bottle with cardboard stopper stood next to the breakfast carton.

Several metal tins of various sizes and colors also graced the shelf. The Raleigh's Cream of Tartar was some three inches tall, a blue canister with black lettering. Adjacent to it were an orange can of curry powder and a red can with white lettering denoting baking powder. Lipton's Tea rested next to Parker's Healing Tar Soap. A large rectangular yellow tin once held the ever- popular Toll House Chocolate Chip Cookies. And because they were both lovers of s'mores, it was appropriate to see a white coffee-can-style container for Campfire Marshmallows.

Aged to a darker brown was her box of Comet, a rectangular container rather than today's cylindrical design. The Gold Dust Washing Powder stood bright orange with two Negro babies peering from the cardboard, politically incorrect in today's marketing.

The dark wooden base of the old coffee grinder had a pullout drawer, iron bowl, and crank. Two black cast iron baking trays were displayed, one with twelve holes for biscuits while the other had six corncob imprints for corn bread.

Nowadays Allison's junkets often required a trailer to haul her treasures back to storage. Chandeliers, sculpted shelves, iron ovens, ornate windows, carved doors. All repaired and then installed in the homes the couple restored.

Today her mission was geared to unearthing kitchen props, such as stoves, balances, bread-boxes, scales, and glassware. As she backed her Pathfinder out of the driveway, a large *whump* on the left fender caused an abrupt stop. As soon as Brian smacked the panel with his hand, he regretted it. His ex-to-be hated that practical joke.

Ignoring it, she leaned out greeting him, "Hey, Bum."

"Hey, Bumette," he returned. Then all was silent.

She drew in a breath. "Care to go exploring for treasures with me?"

"Short on cash?"

She pulled a light green spiral folder off the side seat and fanned the pages. "Don't need any. I have the checks. I'll even treat for lunch."

"How can I lose?"

"It's *your* checkbook," she quipped. "C'mon. It's been a while. It'll be fun."

He headed around to the passenger side. "Tally Ho," he motioned, mimicking a child's voice. "We're goin' on a 'venture."

Once on the road, she reviewed her list. Her personal weaknesses included children's shoes, old leather satchels, and the elusive perfect rocking chair. So far, eight varied rockers managed to pass through their home before landing elsewhere.

Approaching a yard sale, she slowed her vehicle and cast her definitive eyes across the potential booty. "Nope." She accelerated and drove on.

After the third no-stop while the homeowners watched them drive by, he launched into one of his routines from their early days together. "Yep," he began. "Shatter their lives. Slow down and tease them into thinking you're going to stop at their yard sale. Mock and fondle the most precious memories of their lives with your glance."

He built the emphasis. "Discount the memories attached to their simple belongings, let them know with just your glance in mere seconds, casting your judgment. Relay that silent message," he turned up the theatrics, "that their lives are not even worth your time to stop, that their pitiful belongings are worthless to you. Their lives, their petty belongings, mean nothing. Just spit in their humble memory-filled faces."

"Staaawp it," she playfully whined. However, at times if he really milked it, she would actually stop. He snickered quietly as she pulled up to the next sale without as much as an investigative glance. Climbing out and exchanging casual greetings with the owners, he saw her treasure-hunting sonar rise.

Upon an old picnic table sat some hardware. She held up two metal T-hooks and smiled. "Have any more of these?"

The elderly man went to a some red coffee cans, fishing out fourteen as she playfully flirted with him. The hooks were marked fifty cents each. She walked off with all fourteen for five dollars.

As the wife placed them in a small bag, Allison gestured to a mounted poster of an old four-funnel ocean liner. On top in bold letters was *Odin Rosenvinge.*

"Twenty dollars," offered the old gal.

Allison paid with no negotiations. Rare. Brian learned to wait until back in their vehicle before asking. He was humming the tune to the "The Gambler" as he snapped his seat belt. "Fill me in."

"The house we have to do for Jim Stradling's family has that huge study and they like to travel. The Odin was the last of the four-funnel liners." She pointed to the bottom of the ship. "1910 to 1920, surviving the entire war. I think it'll grant them luck, safety on their trips.

Brought us some luck too. That poster was kept out of the sunlight. Reds and yellows are the first to go. No fading." She pulled out and drove on.

He turned and commented on the rich ink colors of mustard and rust orange, set off by the white and black solid tones.

"Once pressed and professionally matted, it'll be worth about $1,200. I'll have to check my books." She added as she pulled to the side of the road about a mile away.

She was into her other find before he could speak, and reached for a small tube of toothpaste from the glove box smearing a dab on one of the hooks where the ends turned up into a delicate bob. The pearly white porcelain contained no cracks or mars. She took a swig from her water bottle, turned out the door, and then spat upon the pasty bracket. "See," she laughed rubbing the dripping piece, exposing the brilliant sheen and smooth finish. "Solid brass, French, approximate vintage 1920 also."

"What value?"

"Figuring low, twenty bucks each, or as high as forty dollars each for this number of them in other parts of the country. Usually you find small, odd amounts. Seldom with the porcelain." *No need to worry about her survival after the divorce* he thought half jokingly, half admiringly. She stopped at a fork in the road and made a gentle fist. "Even or odd?"

"You're pretty odd. Pretty *and* odd. I'll be even." He shook his fist in sync three times up and down. He fashioned a one and she made a four.

"Five. Odd, I win. Driver's side," she bragged, wheeling off to the left.

He mimicked with his hands. "Hey! You're supposed to do a one or a two. Not a three or a four or a five," he muttered. She knew the way to push his buttons too, but at least it was done in fun. He already missed it.

He absently drank in the beautiful foliage of spring. How often he'd pulled off the road to gather and bring her long-stemmed wild flowers, leaves, even unusual weeds, ever amazed by the remarkable centerpieces she created.

"Strange," as she slowed and looked at the dense forest, obscuring a turn. "I've never seen this road, have you?" Before he could answer, they headed down it. Huge trees hung over the country road, shaking their woody hands above the top of the vehicle.

"I can feel it." They pulled up in front of a stylish clapboard farmhouse with an Estate Sale sign displayed out front next to a bright yellow mailbox. It read *343 Sunrise Avenue*.

Apparently, they were disembarking too slowly to satisfy the elderly man.

"Welcome. Everything goes," he cheered as he waved. "C'mon. Don't let the sign fool you. My old gal and I just want to travel. Nobody died."

They joined in laughter as Lonn Smith herded them between the parked cars of bargain hunters, across a skillfully constructed walk of used bricks. Brian surmised they were new when originally laid to the earth.

Some of the larger items had *SOLD* on them, causing Allison to sprint ahead. He spotted two metal milk cans next to a wooden butter churn. Already the ensemble carried her business cards signifying they were now *SOLD*.

He enjoyed watching her in action but in this potpourri of collectibles, he knew all would go best if he headed in one direction and she in another. He'd slow her down. Plus, he'd developed a pretty good eye on his own.

Near the kitchen entrance he spied an old white wood-burning stove and oven that stood on tall metal legs. The porcelain controls and oven pull were all intact. *Wincroth* was printed in blue script with a small silhouette of a bird below. The tall warming back already bore *SOLD*, but it wasn't Allison's. "Ouch," he mouthed. Old stoves were another of her favorites. It was the right time for him to head elsewhere.

Lonn was wearing a broad smile as if he culled enjoyment in folks rummaging through the belongings of their lives. Brian explained he was mainly looking as he gestured to Allison. As he ran his hand along the fine wall paneling, the elder spoke.

"That oak paneling is part of the original structure. The dining room walls were plaster and lathe. Some sentimental carpenter had pressed coins into the wet plaster. This living room and the homestead were built in 1870, five years after the Civil War and two years after Abe Lincoln was assassinated. Andrew Jackson had been impeached. Ulysses S. Grant was at the reins." The man spoke as if it were just yesterday's news. "Course, we weren't here then."

His wife could be seen through the spacious doorway. "She's still a beauty," Lonn said with obvious pride, "although her looks can hide that blend of sugar and vinegar swirling inside her." She stood shorter with luxurious salt and pepper hair. Her age was as misleading as her husband's. Brian marveled at the vibrant smiles this couple exchanged across the expanse. "Love slows the aging process," was Lonn's answer to the nonverbal question.

Brian smiled automatically. "How long have you lived here?"

"A sea captain named Goodlander lived here before us. He was the fourth owner but missed the ocean. We purchased it twenty-one years ago, quite by accident."

"Actually, it found us," his wife chimed in.

Lonn turned to her to share formal introductions. "This youngster is Brian Poppy and his lovely wife Allison," he pointed as the young couple exchanged strained looks across the room. "And this is my gal, Bessie, the love of my life."

"And thorn in his side," Bessie cackled.

"Yep, been that way since 1936. I was a young know-it-all buck in the Army Air Corp. The Air Force hadn't been established yet. President Franklin Delano Roosevelt was seated in the Oval Office. Hitler was preaching gun control. Jesse Owens nailed the Olympics in Berlin. And God blessed a union no man could put asunder." He winked at his wife, "Not that we didn't put 'er to the test a few times."

Allison looked blankly at Brian, then stepped back into the kitchen, resuming her search. He thought of their dirty laundry, how remaining quiet supported a ruse of being happily married. Then it smacked him right in the solar plexus. Maybe it was the timing, the memories of shopping with her. Finding two folks still so much in love was more than he could fathom. Together, more than two of his lifetimes. The Smiths had been married sixty-six years versus the Poppy's seven. He was dumbfounded.

Lonn stepped farther into the dining room out of the main traffic as if listening to the whir of Brian's mind. The gesture caused the young man to follow, absently looking around as the old man looked directly into his eyes, almost into his soul.

Brian blinked. "How'd you do it?" he asked timidly.

"Son" began the man, "eight decades can teach a great deal even to the dumbest mutt or most stubborn jackass. Lived through five wars. Fought in a few, too. World War II, the war to end all wars. Hah! Then the Philippine and Korean wars. Don't let folks fool you. Conflicts, police actions, military suppression, they were all wars. You know the lesson I learned?"

Brian waited.

"I learned that fighting doesn't result in peace. Silence maybe, but not peace. Those government dogs really want submission when they wag their tails, preaching peace while shoving others ahead to catch their bullets. They want submission and control, not peace." He shook his head solemnly. "I'm not saying I'm ashamed of my actions or that there's not a time to fight, but fighting doesn't bring peace. Don't matter the name you call 'em. When you total 'em up, we've had more wars than we kin count. They don't work. We must all learn to live together as a unit, as family, or die as fools."

He kicked at the floor. "If we're to survive, we must develop a new way of thinking. The test of a wise mind is accepting new ideas. If humans were concerned first with what they leave behind, there'd be no wars, no unrest, no pollution, no revolution, no hatred. Nor fear of war because we'd have no war. Wouldn't invest in 'em. They should capture the two warring heads of nations and force 'em to live together."

Brian sensed the old man's concern that he mightn't be around to witness such a change, and lacking such a reform might prohibit survival in the years ahead. Survival meant Brian's and most certainly Benny's. His look was appropriately distant.

Lonn continued. "To change an outcome, we must change our actions. War works the same as two people having trouble. If they don't change the way they're acting that is, change their behavior, they shouldn't expect a different outcome."

Brian wondered if the seasoned gent knew how close to his and Allison's personal family environment he was hitting.

"Me and Bess made many changes. Still do." The man had made good use of his time on earth. He spoke a powerful truth as he pulled down on the edge of his hand-knit patchwork sweater, as if he lived close to the great-unseen powers of the universe.

"We, as a world, must change our actions." He turned to attend to a couple looking at the sixteenth-century bookstand that rose from a tabletop with turned legs and stretchers inclined. He returned to the conversation still on course. "It doesn't take new facts. It's knowledge we already have. The secret to life depends on leaving the woodpile higher than you found it. It's as ancient as the truth in the Ageless Wisdom."

That halted Brian abruptly. It was recently that he'd heard that term, *Ageless Teachings*.

With his hands upon his hips, he locked his eyes on the elderly gentleman, faltering with his words. "A friend was talking to me about natural laws and such. What is that Ageless Wisdom, the Ageless Teachings?"

Lonn welcomed the question. "Natural laws dictate you may command nature only to the extent that you're willing to obey her. As to Ageless Wisdom, it's exactly that. Ageless Wisdom. Wisdom, that's *true* wisdom, doesn't age. Truths change, wisdom never does. It never changes or loses its value. It's priceless in that regard."

Brian hesitated. "Is it Bible-based?"

"No. If anything, the Bible is based on the Ageless Wisdom. The Bible's only 3,500 years old. It wasn't that long ago that He directed the writing of that wisdom in parables. As teachings go, the Bible's a mere pup in this kennel we call the universe. Ageless Wisdom existed long before the Bible and no doubt infused things like Biblical teachings."

Brian was juggling the information in his head as the old fellow continued.

"So effective, so powerful. *True* wisdom never changes, becomes false, nor gets disproved. It never ages. God existed before the Bible. Common sense to me, if people had to be on this earth to write the Bible, didn't God have to be here already?"

He welcomed the insight that seemed to roll so naturally from Lonn's lips. "And God had smart folks here then, too, like Trismegistus."

"Who?" Brian asked.

"Trismegistus." He repeated it phonetically. "Triz–ma–giz–tis. Hermes Mercurius Trismegistus of Egypt."

"Do you mean Hermes, the mythical character?"

"As in mythical meaning pretend?" He laughed. "Trismegistus was the founder of alchemy, astrology, and mystic psychology. Thousands of years ago, in the way we now mark years, before the Bible. Later came modern astronomy, only 2,500 to 3,000 years ago and with it modern chemistry and medicine and psychology. All of the ancient teachings were transcendental knowledge, that is, the inner knowing as opposed to the outer knowing."

"As opposed to simply memorizing facts?" Lonn smiled.

Contemplating that simple point, Brian ran his hand over a rich burgundy winged-back chair admiring the hand carved beech wood, bearing exquisite details etched into the walnut arms and legs. The thick soft leather was held secure by brass tacks. He did better with physical things.

ALLISON HAD NOT YET EXITED the spacious country kitchen. She tagged the large gray ice tongs that had been converted into a paper-towel holder. Her eyes scanned the exposed massive oak-beam rafters. Turning to her left, she was curious about the smile on Bessie's face, standing next to a Victorian spring balance hanging as if bait for the young blond.

"Oh my," Allison touched the brass front. The graduated scales were still clearly marked in half-pound increments for merchants to weigh their tobacco and cotton. Complete, right down to the iron hook and rings. Now she'd truly found a treasure. It was obvious they'd be tagging enough items for a combined tally once finished. As she placed a business card on the balance, the kindly lady commented in a matter-of-fact tone.

"Balance is so important in one's life, as in a marriage. The fun and tedium must coincide. Work and play. Good and bad. First force and second. Prayer and meditation are the great balancers in the circle called life."

Allison backed up without making a reply and turned to look at the huge quilt on the wall as if to divert the conversation.

"One of my hobbies," Bess proudly pointed out. "I find sewing patch-works relaxing. They're like our lives, bringing much together to form something beautiful. Having fun like you two are, building a home, building a business, raising children. Once we start weaving, God and His angels will furnish the skein. Such is the yarn from which memories are woven."

Allison was cautious about not encouraging her, but the follow-up was softly delivered nonetheless.

"Life's just a tapestry of threads and pieces of different materials all woven together like the rag pickers of the Depression. The trick relies on not breaking any of the threads, to blend all together into a common item, like a good marriage."

Clearly Allison was getting more than antiques, but she wasn't certain if her heart and mind could handle these verbal treasures.

CHAPTER TWENTY-SEVEN

SURPRISES

BRIAN FELT AS IF he were monopolizing the old man's time. He was drawn to him like a magnet, and Lonn seemed quite content as he led him into the study and library. Kneeling to check the broad floor planks almost six inches wide and held securely in place with wooden peg nails, one edge of each board was notched and the other side was beveled so they interlocked. Genuine craftsmanship. As he rose to his feet, he saw framed cross-stitch embroidery.

God Grant Me Patience and Grant It Now. He burst out laughing.

"The little miss made me that one while our third baby was baking in the oven." He pursed his lips, emitting a tiny squeak. "I wasn't doing too well as a father. Felt lost in the military, began commanding my children. That needlework's been one of her reminders to me through eight offspring and the death of one, a long tour of duty, living in six states and several posts, two major businesses, and a slew of other things."

"Like one marriage?" Brian quipped.

"Oh, yeah," returned the gruff voice. "Course I found times to share that saying with her too." He winked, "What's good for the goose is good for the gander. Love is like a horse with a broken leg. You can shoot the horse but that won't fix the leg."

Brian saw the colorful linen was hung within view of two relaxing rockers.

Lonn tapped one into motion. "Patience. Seems it's being lost with more people."

"You should know with eight kids."

"That just comes with good judgment. Good judgment comes from experience. Experience, well, that comes from poor judgment."

Brian began to browse the books on the long wooden shelves. One of his favorite pastimes was flirting with a book. He would have been shocked to learn that many in Lonn's library were first editions, signed and inscribed ones no less.

"Everything nowadays is disposable. Everything moves faster. It's rubbed off on our virtues and is eating away at our patience. Too much is focused on this dad-blamed so-called *artificial intelligence* and nothing to nurture *real intelligence*."

Brian smiled. "Will Rogers wrote that *Common sense is not an issue in politics, it's an affliction.* I'm not too sure much has changed."

As Lonn chuckled, Brian finally stepped to one of the fine rockers. The wooden backs were a reddish hue with elaborate carvings. At the nod of approval to his silent request to try one, he nodded back an invitation for the wise man to continue speaking.

"When there were fewer folks and greater distances between 'em, we valued lives more. Folks respected one another. It was more important to make the marriage last for spiritual and practical reasons. Even friends were closer. We helped birth each other's babies. People just did more for each other without being asked."

Brian stopped mid-rock. "I really never looked at it that way. What else do you see?"

Lonn leaned against the bookshelves' wooden ladder. "It's becoming a disposable world. Disposable marriages equate to more divorce. Disposable lives equal more war, gang wars, and world wars. Less respect even for one's own life. You name it. Young people are even disposing of their parents." He shook his head. "Divorcing their parents, even killing them."

Dispose and waste. Actually, this thought wasn't new to Brian. He long felt he was part of the problem and had taken some steps to correct it, but not nearly enough. To deny a hand in raping the rain forests to raise cattle for American hamburgers would be as ludicrous as thinking his lawn mower didn't pollute the entire world.

"More folks and faster times mean fewer occasions to gather together. Decisions are made quicker, looking at only a couple of solutions instead of all points on the circle. Divorce is one of those popular choices where folks don't examine all the alternatives. Many folks figure if this mate doesn't work, more are available. So they eliminate 'em. Dispose of 'em. Discard 'em." Lonn was gravely sincere.

Brian stood up to look across the room. "There're more than two answers to any problem. I'm beginning to understand that aspect lately."

There was no bitterness or disgust but a touch of sadness apparent in the thoughts of the elder. "Folks are forgetting the way to make decisions. Not knee-jerk reactions, but honest-to-goodness decisions. Folks have stopped teaching their offspring the way to make decisions. Therefore, they learn to fear making a solid decision and that fear breeds an avoidance of commitments. Look at the increase in pre-nuptial agreements." Encouragement peaked in his seasoned voice. "But I think you two have a chance."

Brian's expression concealed his thoughts. If he'd looked into the wrinkled face, he'd have known very little escaped Lonn as they stepped out onto the rear decking.

"Look," gasped Brian, managing a loud whisper.

An eagle perched atop a stump at the pond's edge as if to greet them. The property was much larger than he'd imagined, groomed yet natural, as it led to the forest.

Lonn smiled as though the bird were a close friend. "I remember living in California. They cleared out an area, cut down all these huge eucalyptus and olive trees with trunks bigger than I could put my arms around," as he mimicked a barrel, "only to put in a park and replant these little trees. Like gutting the White House and redecorating with knickknacks from Wal-Mart."

ALLISON STOPPED ABRUPTLY as she spied the wall clock hanging by the Dutch door. "Are you both from Pennsylvania?"

Bess beamed. "You have a good eye, girl. My kin hailed from that region but Lonnie's family came from Minnesota." She seemed to travel back in time, looking at the fine timepiece. "That was one of our wedding gifts."

"And you're selling it? What about your children?" She touched the distressed cabinet, the roughness adding to its appeal. Thin metal hands pointed to the bold black Roman numerals against a pearl white face.

"It's a timepiece, and it's time to move on. The real value in life is the way you spend time with those you love, not the lifeless objects you collect. It's the feelings you convey rather than the desires you have. As for our children, trust me, they collected their fair share." She reached for the brass pull to remove a set of color-coded keys of red and gold, slipping them in her pocket, as the clock gained one of Allison's cards.

"Come, child. You'll enjoy these." Bessie stepped toward a large wooden shelf. While the teal blue shelf itself would be a stunning addition to any entry, it was the decorative items atop that she correctly understood would tickle the young gal's fancy.

Allison was ever respectful of other people's property even when offered for sale. "Oooh may I?" At the twinkle in Bess's eyes, she ran a loving finger across the toe of a tiny child's boot, the sole only three inches long. Gently she slipped a thumb in one boot and two fingers in the other feeling the smooth leather interior.

Raising them slowly, she tilted them to inspect. Soft, glossy Italian leather, paddock- style boots with minuscule brass eyelets and speed hooks at the top. The leather tabs for pulling them on were too small even for her smallest finger. She imagined their history, perhaps belonging to the offspring of an early business tycoon.

Next to them was a French coat bag of center-cut cowhide.

The oil tanning had turned it a luminous brown and two of the three small buckling inner straps were intact. The tiny shoes caused her to think of family, of Benny, then Brian and their marriage.

Unsolicited, Bessie offered, "Your heart knows the path to the dream in your mind. Trust your heart, child, trust your intuition. You're never a fool as long as you follow your heart, and to accomplish that feat you must be quiet and listen."

Allison tried to pay more attention to the items than the words echoing inside her. The heavy leather handle and shoulder strap were attached to brass rings that shined vividly. She pulled a card, opened the bag, and placed the tiny boots inside, as Bessie's comments tugged at her soul.

THE MEN RETURNED FROM THE DECKING and back into the library. Brian spotted his first treasure, coincidentally, sitting tall with a slight lace trim. He grinned as he handed Lonn the children's vintage boots used as bookends. Although unaware that the style was called Mayfair, he knew the chocolate leather wing tips would bring a welcome smile to Allison's face. "Do you have a closet that Allison might bypass when browsing?" he asked as he pulled a business card from his wallet.

Lonn placed them in the large side drawer of his desk marked *Not for Sale*.

"SHUCKS," ALLISON STOMPED her sandal-clad foot as she saw two ladies carrying a wooden and brass coat rack. "Those, too?" she asked as one of the women nodded, stacking the collectible ladies' hats. Beaten to the punch, again. The three glamorous toppers would be a welcome accent to any decor.

One lady held a J. P. Hatbox. It contained a St. Petersburg quilted brim of black velvet with a faux mink trim. Next was a Czechoslovakian velour hat as black as the entire ensemble with mesh suspending snowflake-sized black dots of chenille. Most glamorous was a velvet hat with a crushable crown of black watermark taffeta and a shiny black grosgrain band. It bore an iridescent navy sash cover with a seductive slouching bow at the front, matching the frown created by Allison's eyebrows.

BRIAN AND LONN WALKED DOWN the hallway while the younger looked along the wide, spacious corridor and studied the indented shadow boxes.

"I added those," Lonn boasted, knowing of the young man's skills.

He examined the display. An Erigo brass helmet had been modified to serve as a ship's compass. It had a domed brass binnacle a half-foot tall with a small compass that pivoted inside. Distinct black degrees were marked on the white face. A box at the side held a slide-out lantern with a prism to amplify the lamplight.

"One of the things Captain Matthew Goodlander left behind," noted Lonn.

Brian stopped suddenly. He was trying to wean himself from buying stuff for Allison, but he loved surprising her and she marveled at his knowledge of her tastes. No other boyfriend had ever given her presents and surprises that pleased her so much. He knew it was necessary to cut strings and get rid of habits, but it was easier for him to stop accepting gifts from her than to stop giving them to her.

"Empty your lungs," ordered Lonn.

He complied without thought, beginning to feel limp until the old fella spoke. "That's the way it feels to give, but not receive."

He was aware Allison had been looking for some decorative toiletry items to add to the guest bathroom. He'd designed two decorative shelves cut into the wall that she'd wallpapered with batting and upholstery material. As he gasped for breath, he knew the items that'd soon grace those shelves.

A heavy beige ceramic mug with a pale-blue ring held an inverted teak-handled shaving brush. Alongside it sat a decanter of Dominica Bay Rum, bottled by A.C. Shillingford.

Although manufactured almost a hundred years ago, he could still detect the quiet combined scent of distilled alcohol with bay leaves. He knew the container would bring a squeal of delight to the master-treasure huntress. Laura Croft had nothing on Allison.

The third item, he explained to Lonn, would go with her growing satchel collection. The heirloom Gladstone was constructed of full-grain cowhide. The mellow old leather case was almost two feet long.

"We won't hide this one. If I don't return with something, she'll be suspicious."

"Besides, you want to make sure you give her a surprise today. It'll help you keep the other ones a secret," surmised Lonn.

Was Brian so easy to read or was it just Lonn's years of experience in forging a successful marriage?

"Most of this stuff weren't antiques when we got 'em, just old." There was no denying how clear his antique eyes could see either.

Brian patted his latest find with a grin and glanced over his shoulder to the wooden rockers as if to say goodbye. Then he fell in step with Lonn who motioned for him to follow up the stairs.

Once gone, a tangerine-colored book suddenly fell flat with a muffled *thud*.

CHAPTER TWENTY-EIGHT

TREASURES OF THE HEART

THE SCENT OF OLD BOOKS greeted Allison as she was drawn to the regal rocking chairs in the library. The natural sheen upon the wide armrests was a result of six decades of use. She thought about the lives these two chairs had touched as her hand traced the rose-petal pattern carved into the headrests. Wood had carefully been selected so on both, a dark natural knot created the center of a flower. A vine pattern ran across the back, the aged wood darkened in the etchings. She knew the prices were fair but more than she could justify, especially if one rocker sat motionless.

As if the mother of eight, grandmother of twenty-one, and great-grandmother of nine could read the young gal's mind, she spoke. "Our children are receiving plenty. They've been through the house and already carted off a bunch of mementos. We did pretty well with our youngsters. Not overly materialistic, yet each one is successful. They know the value lies in the memories their hearts hold dear, not the material goods they hold in their hands."

Allison attempted to imagine Benny, when she was Bessie's age. She wondered about the way he'd feel if she were to sell such family mementos. She winced at the price of $1,200 each.

"The kids decided on the price. Since no one could decide who deserved these two keepsakes, Lonn intervened. Surmised they could decide the price and if they sold, well then, the good Lord had intended them for someone special. If they didn't sell, then our children could have a drawing for them."

"What do you want to see happen?" asked Allison.

"Those rockers served us well and I trust they'll serve another couple for a good many more years, whether from our blood or a couple connected to us in blood of the spirit. However, we won't separate them. They need a good home. Together."

Allison nodded and turned from the rockers, seeing *Will Rogers: His Story as Told by His Wife* running horizontally on an orange-colored leather binding. She handled it with care, running the book beneath her nose, the aroma of musty pages sweet. Slightly browned at the edges but in excellent shape. A first edition dated 1941 with original price marked $1.49. Her voice waxed sentimental as she opened the cover. "Oh-my-gosh! It's autographed to Lonn from Betty Rogers. Brian would freak."

"My honey and I have lived a life that some might equate to two or three good lifetimes. We've had happiness and heartbreaks. Therefore, in this next phase of our lives, we're cleaning the slate completely. A new adventure awaits us."

Allison stood silent, reverence coupled with astonishment. She couldn't move past her own crisis to picture the next week of her own life. Yet this lady, a multiple of her own age, sounded as if she might outlive Allison.

"When things are seen as unlimited, we take them for granted. My Lonn has collected more than 12,000 books in here. He's given away many times more in support of others over the years." She was quite proud of her mate. "He walled himself in here for a long night and pulled ten to keep for himself. I sneaked an additional three," she giggled like a child. "Later, he selected one for each of the grandkids and great grandkids. Just walked right up to the shelves, knew which ones by intuition."

That word popped up again. *Intuition.*

"Then the children were allowed to claim as many as they wanted." Allison began to notice some of the vacant spots.

"Child, that still left a few thousand books easily." She waved her arm. "Lonn doesn't salt away these books for monetary worth, but their energy value. Energy of the folks who claimed their spiritual greatness, leaving their personal marks on the world with these simple books, leaving marks on others even after they were gone. Motivators are a dime a dozen, but teachers make the real difference."

Dark colors, many with gold trim, lined the shelves. Volumes of books, some horizontal, a few stacked, others on a diagonal tilt, looked like works of art. Each one was a member of an eclectic collection. *The Fun of It* was written by Amelia Earhart. Others by Jimmy Stewart, Robert Fulghum, Jimmy Buffett, Richard Bach, Buddy Ebsen, Dag Hammerskjöld, Jimmy Carter, Wayne Dyer, Gerry Spence, Louise Hay, Florence Scovel Shinn, Stephen King, Johnny Cash, George Burns, Charles Lindbergh, and John Denver. She'd have been even more shocked to know that each had been personalized by the authors.

Bess reached for the Will Rogers book. "There's a difference between fame and greatness. Our children know the difference too." She laughed, "Trust me. I saw the books they chose. Ample spiritual and financial energy are gracing their shelves now."

Allison inhaled the aged aroma. "Yet, of the ones remaining..."

"If Lonn and I weren't having fun seeing who these books go to, we wouldn't be having this sale and handling the operation ourselves. No life form ends until all it has touched has ended."

She looked out the bay window to the trees at the clearing's edge. "Trees are spawned of the earth and supported by the natural laws, just as we are. People produce the written word and these humans and books are as much a miracle as a tree. In this library, the grace of a tree interlocks with the vision of the human mind. A certain book in the hands of the proper person may give birth to a new miracle."

The book was tugging at Allison's heartstrings. She looked up from under her eyebrows and peered in a silent question. She took a deeper breath.

Bess smiled at the young lady's bewilderment. "The books aren't marked with prices. If someone asks, we decide then *if* they're for sale *and* the price." She paused as she studied the young woman's eyes as Allison eased the book back into its spot.

Bess walked between her and the shelves. "Inhale and hold it until I say exhale."

The young woman did so, thinking it had to do with the sweet, musty smell. Her eyes widened when the elderly lady said nothing and grasped the book. "That's the feeling when we receive, but refuse to give, out of fear. To love for the sake of being loved is human but to love for the sake of loving is angelic."

Suddenly the air rushed from her lungs and she looked back at the book.

"I think my hubby will trust my insight on this one." She slipped the book into the drawer of the desk marked *Not for Sale*, smiling as she saw the items it already hid. "This way, my dear, I can fetch it for you before you leave, and you can surprise your man later. To think too much about giving, means trading." Bess was crafty.

BRIAN SPLIT TO THE RIGHT at the top of the stairs. At the far end stood the master bedroom, light and airy, windows on two sides with large skylights above. The homeowner walked past the spacious plantation bed, beaming the grin of a high school student. Brian eyed the bed, both for its beauty and the simple realization that the elder couple still slept together. The old grin let him know their sixty-some-year romance was alive and well.

Opposite the four-poster bed stood a raised fireplace. Lonn pointed to the hearth. "I raised that puppy a couple feet several years ago. Took a bit of doing but we couldn't see it from the bed. A good bed's important. The couple sleeps together, side-by-side. One side is protected by the other in order to hold or be held." He winked. "And never let the marriage kill the romance."

Yep, romance still alive. Brian ran one hand up the eight-foot post of solid mahogany, the gauze canopy seductively draped above the tops, headboard with hand-carved acanthus leaves, Gothic arches, inlaid squares, and a pineapple pattern.

Lonn dropped an aside. "The bed isn't sold yet."

The old man had no idea of the way the comment bit into Brian's heart. Built to last, mortised and tenoned with solid brass fittings rather than nails, obviously more reliable than the union he and Allison had forged. He left a silent blessing with the bed, praying that it find a couple with as much love as its present occupants.

They returned to the exposed bridge-style hallway that led to four more rooms. With his hand caressing the smooth yellow grain of the banister, Brian peered into the family room below. Bess seemed to shadow Allison.

THE BAR WAS DECORATED TO INTOXICATE with spirits from the heart rather than spirits from alcohol. A western touch to the family room with a smattering of unlabeled deep blue and amber bottles, collected from the days of Prohibition. Several held small clusters of dried flowers, such as baby's breath, jonquils, and daffodils with coral, orange, yellow, white, and lilac accents.

The shelf snared Allison because it held several malt glasses of a slight greenish hue. Sizes varied from eight-to-twelve inches. In the center of the grouping stood a silver cylinder, open on one side to allow red and white paper straws to be removed. Holding one glass up to the light, Bessie's sweet voice could be heard. "Imagine the love these glasses have seen, child, all the sodas shared."

The image formed in Allison's mind of a Rockwell print. Two teenagers, eyes locked above the frothy foam, hands gently touching each other, fumbling with the straws and their thoughts.

"Memories can be the glue to carry us when faith grows thin," observed the old voice as another business card landed by the display.

Bessie was draped in love, peacefulness, joyous contentment, and excitement for the future. That attitude fed Allison's curiosity of a marriage lasting more than half a century and finally forced her question. "How?"

The elderly woman appeared to anticipate it. "The scale is

tipped by the weight of what they serve. Prayerful meditation and service. Love or fear, look diligently at that which you serve. Love or fear and then break down each one for *clarity*."

"This may sound funny but could you clear up clarity?"

The slow smile was like the dawning sun peeking over a hill. "Scarcity begets scarcity. People need to spend money for there to be money. Sometimes, we believe in abstinence, saving, or hoarding for solving the problem of scarcity. A child socializes with gangs and becomes a gang member. It takes a strong will to rise above the times into which a person is born."

The last comment Allison recognized.

"Each one contains a value. If we serve fear, we succumb to using fear to scare it away. Fear does not complement spiritual evolvement. It complements things like scarcity, abstinence, and war. Love, true love of the highest essence, holds the power to complement and heal any ailment. The factor that determines such is the amount of resistance we retain. We must dissolve the resistance; we must let it flow through us."

The young woman absorbed the words with a pondering look.

"Think of it as a faucet. You've a mix of hot and cold or good and bad. Turning it off eliminates all. So," eased the elderly lady, "the question to ask becomes simple."

Allison looked up, relieved.

"According to the problem you're dealing with now, do you serve love or fear?" Then she turned away.

The homework was Allison's responsibility.

OPPOSITE THE UPSTAIRS RAILING hung a collection of photos and matted prints. The first was a black-and-white headshot of a dapper star. He blinked a few times, then read the written inscription: *"To my Commander and Friend, Lonn Smith, an honor to serve under you. My thanks and esteem to you always. Colonel James Stewart."*

"You were in the service with Jimmy Stewart?"

It was obvious Lonn didn't like dwelling on war or heroics. Tapping the glamour shot of the handsome leading man. "That picture was taken back in 1946 after Jimmy did *It's a Wonderful Life!* He shot it immediately after the war. Still think it's his best."

Brian's silence beckoned more of the story.

"Jimmy was a good boy, a bit gawky with a nasal voice. One of the young recruits under my command, training as a bomber pilot in WWII. He was always doing magic tricks to calm the other soldiers. Ended his active tour of duty as the highest ranking of the Hollywood bunch. Full Colonel. He faithfully remained in the Air Force Reserve until 1968, finally earning the rank of Brigadier General. And, he remained faithfully in love with his wife from 1941 onward. We were so sorry when Gloria died. Jimmy was merely biding his time 'til he could join her." His eyes glistened.

Above the photos was a shadow box containing colorful ribbons and gold medals. Brian recognized the two purple hearts, each with clusters, not honors easily earned. The others looked impressive but were a mystery to him, in particular the finely etched one on a broad blue ribbon. Before he could ask, Lonn pointed to a gray and tan photo of a lanky pilot holding a leather flying cap at his side.

"His folks' farm was near ours in Minnesota. He was about ten years older than me," the elder man grinned, revealing a piece of history with each moment. Studs showed clearly in the metal sheeting of the biplane bearing the inscription *N-X-ZII* on the tail.

Brian squinted and read the script on the plane. *"Spirit of...*no way." Lonn countered, "A hero and a gentleman."

"The *Spirit of St. Louis.* Charles Lindbergh," blurted Brian.

"Wow, Lindy. Lucky Lindy. The Lone Eagle and it's signed by him to you."

"Those nicknames, Lucky and Lone, reached out to haunt him. Charlie was only twenty- five when he flew alone to fame with that single-engine monoplane. That solo flight turned him into the most famous man in the world, *the* most famous person of that era. He flew to serve humanity, but the flight forced him to serve the fame."

Brian registered confusion.

"Imagine much of the planet thinking you're nuts to follow your dream. Only twenty- five years of age, you take off from Long Island to land your plane in Le Bourget Field in Paris, and more than 100,000 cheering people emerge to welcome you." His eyes turned sad. "That fame cost him his baby boy about five years later."

"That flight, more than seventy years ago," Brian marveled, as he looked closer. The wheels looked as though they were removed from a child's wagon. He stood in silence before he continued along the wall. He stopped at a black-and-white shot of two vintage biplanes. Two men stood against a field of amber wheat. A snapshot of a lady was tucked in the corner. He leaned forward and pointed with his finger to one of the men. "That's you." He pointed to the small photo. "She looks familiar. Is that Bessie?"

"No," laughed Lonn. "That's Leslie Parrish-Bach. She was in the old TV series, 'Star Trek.' That yellow, winged plane with the red body in the foreground is his. The Stearman belonged to me, from our barnstorming days. You might know her husband Dick, better known as Richard Bach."

Brian certainly did know the man, having read all of his books, not just those since

Jonathan Livingston Seagull and *Illusions*.

"And this one?" The name Buffett caught my eye.

A large toothy grin leapt from Lonn's mouth. "That was

J.D., quite a prankster, not to mention a master of mechanics and barbecuing."

"And the story?" Brian prodded.

"Knew him from the Army Air Corps. I'm amazed that we were never put in the brig for some of our shenanigans. Good thing we weren't based together very long. With my connections, we always had the best ale and meat to barbecue. J.D. had a mighty serious side too. Another man of *the right stuff*. Anyway, this picture was taken when he was based in India. That old C47 was almost his last flight."

"In the war?"

"Nah, just some self-centered officers that should never have been at the stick." He saw the young man's blank look. "The controls, an old term."

After staring at the picture for a few seconds, he continued with the story. "He was sent on a test flight in that thing when a fire ignited below, and it weren't no barbecue. He went to tend to it and returned to find the pilot and co-pilot about to bail without telling him. I remained on the base, waiting with a barrel full of lobsters. Master Sergeant was waiting there too in order to praise my buddy and ground the other two dorks." He laughed, "J.D. outclassed himself on the barbecue that night."

Brian sensed Lonn still felt the hangover. He was hesitant to ask the inevitable. "Did he survive the war?"

"Oh Lord, yes. His boy became quite the pilot too. Rare for his career." "What do you mean?"

"As a rock star. I mean the young man is a real pilot and an accomplished sailor too.

J.D. sent me albums and then cassettes of his recordings. New-fangled CDs now." He pointed to the shelf. Music Brian played often although his weren't autographed.

"And his boy is pretty good. As a matter of fact, damn good.

218

Spiritual without being in your face. Even wrote one song about Lindy." He pointed to another picture. "There they both are, quite a few years later when his boy bought a Grumman Widgeon in Michigan. We caught his show too. Old J.D. is mighty proud of Jimmy. My kids and grandkids like his music. They call themselves Bird-heads."

"Parrot-heads," Brian softly corrected as he shook his head in wonder.

CHAPTER TWENTY-NINE

UPON MY SHOULDER

FARTHER DOWN THE HALL hung some frames, double-matted, emphasizing the rectangular sheets of gray, green, and beige sepia tones. They were checks, each handwritten, most of them for amounts less than two-hundred dollars, but much more valuable now.

"*Dry Cleaning: J.F. Kennedy*," read Brian. "President Kennedy? Hey? This one's written to you!"

"Don't know the reason I never cashed that one. Probably closed the account by now," he smirked. "Only it wasn't written for cleaning. Or, maybe it was. Written for the amount he'd lost in a card game," laughed the old gambler. "He was recovering from his famous boat outing in 1943, toward the end of World War II. Later on, he finished his physical recovery in Arizona. Maybe I figured even then that the check would eventually be worth more if kept than cashed."

"Did he like to gamble?" asked Brian.

"Let's say he kept a good poker face. He proved that with the Cubans and his personal activities. I didn't cotton to the last part but I strive to tend to my own business.

They moved down the hall.

"Found this at an auction." He read aloud, "*Building Supplies: J. Carter.* That was soon after Jimmy Carter began Habitat for Humanity. He's an ex-President still serving his country rather than having his title serve him. Will Rogers said that once a man holds public office, he's no good for honest work. Carter is one of the exceptions."

219

"*MGM?* This one looks like a studio paycheck," Brian puzzled. "*Buddy Ebsen?*" "I found that one at an auction too and bid on it because I knew him and gave it to Buddy. He and Dorothy returned it to my collection. I met him in the service when they had us both dealing with Hollywood on some training films."

"Any idea what the check was written for?"

Lonn pointed to the corporate inscription of *MGM Studios.* "Ever hear the story of the way Buddy became the Tin Man in The *Wizard of Oz?* It's the reason his autobiography is entitled *The Other Side of Oz.*"

"Something about the silver make-up made him sick."

"Sick? Damn near killed Buddy, almost smothered him. Poisoned his skin so bad that even once they found a safer method, he was too ill to resume work. I grabbed this one because I knew it was the only check he earned for being the Tin Man. Had he been able to act the part, I bet he'd have nailed the Academy Award for Best Supporting Actor. However, Buddy didn't believe in bad breaks. He said a fork in the road was not the end of the adventure."

"Wow, *T. A. Edison,*" read Brian as he noticed the imprinted address was in Menlo Park, New Jersey. "*April 15, 1883.* The reference simply says *supplies.* Wonder what those supplies were?"

"Maybe toilet paper," cracked the elderly collector. "Edison was no different from you or me. He was merely human, an impassioned human, at that."

"Too cool," breathed Brian, spotting another check. Being quite the fan of Will Rogers, he was aware that the American humorist promoted polo to worldwide recognition. *Polo Feed: W. Rogers.* "His column was read by millions, the voice of the common man. He died way too early. Wonder what kind of an angel he'd be?"

Lonn pointed to a photo of a well-suited man wearing wire-rimmed glasses, caught speaking in animated gestures from a podium. "There's another young fellow who served under me with Jimmy Stewart. He did okay for himself, for a rag picker."

"Rag Picker?" repeated Brian. "*Og*? That's a funny name." Then he noticed the next in the collection, a black-and-white Lockheed Vega. One man was stocky with dark slicked hair, dimpled, and a head shorter than the young man by his side. "That's you," he deduced, then cocked his head. "Who's the older guy with the white eye patch?"

"Wiley Post. And that's the *Winnie Mae.* Taken about a year before his unprecedented solo flight around the world."

The wheels turned in Brian's mind, associating this man with the fateful flight of Will Rogers. Before he could speak, Lonn intervened.

"Sad that last flight with Will Rogers is the way so many folks remember Wiley. He was so much more than a pilot. He broke the around-the-world record twice, once flying alone.

Pioneered flying the jet streams." A slight tear revealed the two men had been close. "I flew with Charlie and the group that retrieved the bodies."

Brian was doing the math as his fingers wiggled with the count. Lonn married at twenty- one, sixty-some years ago. As a fan of Will's, he knew he'd died in 1935.

Knowing he was trying to compute ages against Lonn's good health, he winked. "The answer is *love*. My Bessie and our kids and their kids keep me young. Love and you shall be loved. It's as mathematical as two sides of an algebraic equation." A sly smile surfaced on the old face, still a splendor with his original teeth.

"Wiley had taken me under his wing, so to speak. I soloed before I married Bessie. Flying was more difficult then but regulations were easier. Part of the reason I rose so quickly in the service. Air Force was new. I could feel Wiley for some time after his death. I think pilots become the best angels because they're used to flying."

Brian marveled. "You were right in the main thrust of the aviation age. I'm surprised you don't have a picture with Howard Hughes and the *Spruce Goose*."

"Proof that a genius can be a fool. He was too involved in bigger-is-better. Didn't even leave a proper will." A couple approached them from the bedroom with a question. Before going to assist them, he looked over his shoulder. "What you serve can make or break you."

Brian watched the two ladies visiting down below, generations apart.

Lonn turned back and then looked below too. "Men often gain the glory when they often have women beside them who deserve just as much credit. Will Rogers and Wiley Post used to credit their lady folks. Bette kept Og from an over-inflated ego. Leslie pulled Dick's ass outta the fire and he admits it. Now them are the real heroes."

"Or she-roes," Brian laughed to himself.

The next photo was of another Lockheed. "Speaking of she-roes," as Lonn continued with his narrative. "Amelia had just flown the Atlantic, landing in London, first woman to accomplish that feat. She soloed at twenty and then set, broke, and reset speed and altitude records, 14,000 feet at one point," he noted with pride.

Brian knew little of this heroine, only her mysterious fateful plunge into the South Pacific. Her death, like Wiley Post's demise, overshadowed her accomplishments.

"Amelia co-founded the airline which became TWA. She was quite a fashion designer too. The first lady to earn the Distinguished Flying Cross. Poor GP. George Putnam, her husband. Book publisher and extraordinary publicist. He spared no expense in searching for her. It's hard to say goodbye when nobody can be buried to give closure."

Brian knew this feeling all too well. "Is it bad when a memory still hurts? Does it mean that we haven't forgiven or gotten over the loss?"

Lonn sighed deeply. "A person can overcome an incident, even forgive. But can travel back in time via what is supposed to set mankind apart from the other animals. Selective memory. Our ability to see from another point on the circle or another way in which to handle an incident will not free us from the memory attached to the history.

"To look from present to past and see our feelings won't erase the emotions we felt then, whether fear, hatred, joy, jealousy, love, or pain. Once a mind is stretched, it's impossible to return it to its original shape. Once a feeling is experienced, in some form, it always exists. Our present view enables us to see differently, react differently, in the future. But the feeling exists, past and present." He possessed the wisdom of a sage.

At thirty-one, Brian had enough regrets and events he'd change to last a lifetime.

Certainly at eighty-years-plus, Lonn would have a few. Aviation was an obvious passion, and his related skills and associations with the military had enabled him many opportunities and memories.

Often we can see ourselves in others. Comparatively, Lonn realized that his early days were akin to Brian's present days. Days when his foundation was built in an unconscious nature. He was aware he could not change his past youth. Yet he knew that he could still learn from it and possibly others could too. Teach...rather than motivate.

The next photo was of two men on a pier, armed for some serious fishing. A pontoon plane sat behind them. Brian guessed it was an Alaskan setting. The old man's reply revealed much of history and regrets.

"That's Sinker." He saw Brian's confused look. "Gus. Was Gus. Captain Virgil I. Grissom to be exact, but folks soon learned to call him Gus. You talk of having *the right stuff*. Gus certainly had it, in spades."

"You talking the astronaut?"

"One and the same." He glanced around for a new spot on which to lean, wondering about the best way to explain one story he seldom shared.

Lonn sucked in on his cheek, emitting a slight squeak. "I joined the service, the Army Air Corps, before WWII. Regulations were less restrictive and to be honest, I flew by the seat of my pants. True even when I became a pilot joining the service." He scowled, "True even getting married. It wasn't until quite a while after I'd entered those three lifestyles that I became conscious."

A linear time line began to formulate in Brian's mind. He knew that WW II had run about six years, from 1939 to 1945.

"By the time WW II ended, I'd had ten years of service and a few lucky missions, thanks to a couple of tricky air maneuvers that Wiley had taught me. Like I said, pilots make the best angels." He paused before resuming. "Soon I was pulling a hefty paycheck and enjoying liberal assignments."

"Enabled you to make the barbecue parties?" teased Brian.

A warm smile spread across his face as the living historian continued. "I actually held off on a couple of promotions, so I could remain on active duty flying. I don't desk well where my only stick is a pencil. It allowed me to have my assignments with time I didn't have to account for. Go for the glitz, glamour, and gusto, like I did with the medals and commendations back then."

Brian instinctively turned back to the shadow-box display on the wall. He didn't want to pry, yet he was danged curious and almost felt the elder needed to talk. "Did you do something…you're ashamed of?"

Lonn looked at the medals. "Bessie and the children gifted me with that display when I retired. I'd just been promoted from Lieutenant Colonel to Colonel. At one time, those pieces of cloth and metal meant more to me." He searched for words to wipe the question from Brian's face. "At the end of my tenure, I stored 'em in boxes. I display them now because of the family's gift rather than why they were awarded to me."

"Mind telling me the way you earned them?" Brian hesitantly asked.

"I'm not ashamed of them, but they just don't serve me now. Love of family and life does. I look at things differently today. Did you know that in the days before they had all the ways of dodging the service, colorblind folks were placed as spotters?"

"Because they could see through the camouflage?"

"More directly, because they saw things differently," he said with a nod as he stepped forward to detail the contents of the shadow box.

Scattered about were various rifle badges and combat ribbons. The European campaign of World War II, the Korean Conflict, and Vietnam War were represented. Various embroidered badges designated *AIRBORNE*. One was a dark-blue rectangle with white wings, lettering, and stitching. Another was a shield with the noble profile of an eagle's head and gold letters. He recognized the big silver cross with flared ends as the Navy Cross. And then, looking much like an Iron Cross was the Silver Star. He knew their stature but learned the smaller stars on the neck ribbon denoted additional heroic clusters awarded. Courage and valor were among the terms attached to these awards.

Lonn considered himself fortunate. Many who received such recognition never had the opportunity to wear their medals. He walked the young man through them.

The Distinguished Flying Cross, awarded for feats in aviation, hung on a navy-colored cord with two additional bright white stars. This honor was the second highest medal the country offered. A bar of yellow, blue, and red rested above it. The Presidential Unit Citation. Then, presiding over all else, a finely etched metal hanging from a medium-blue ribbon bearing one additional star. Lonn virtually brushed over it.

Brian's mouth opened with no sound. The ribbon supported the Medal of Honor. How rare it was to meet one who received such an acclaim. Most received it posthumously.

Gentle as a butterfly's wing, Lonn's voice continued. "Experience is not what happens to a man; it's what he does from those experiences." He looked squarely at Brian. "I hope you learn that idea, son, before I did."

The medals, representative of numerous days spent in flak-filled skies, still caused feelings to surface in the old pilot. They also provoked feelings in Brian.

"My brother enlisted in the Army Air Force." A long pause ensued. "Served almost fifteen years until he was killed in action. I used to believe him a hero, but I think that notion was only more of our father's bunk. Crap to help serve his business."

Their silence was as deafening as a twenty-one-gun salute.

Lonn's shoulders broadened. "I'm only ashamed of one thing, waiting until my late thirties to become conscious. I still love this country as much as I do my Bessie. It's just…I still know my Bessie well.

"We're at a point whereby Miss Liberty's left and right hands don't know what the other is doing. We've founded all of these religions to support God, same with our country. Dad-blamed political parties. This nation has too many facets of the government, too many divisions of the military and the government, resulting in major communications problems. I simply took orders, figuring someone in charge knew better. Didn't question orders then, not even in my head. The military said that blind obedience was the mark of a good soldier."

Brian looked at the photo again of the late astronaut and then glanced back at his storyteller. "Until?"

"By the time I had served twenty years, I was earning more cash and liberties than higher-ranking officers. Had so much clearance that some of the brass-shoulders thought they had to salute me. I didn't answer to many of them and lacked a bit in my bucket of respect. Schedules were flexible, allowed me to do things like visit J.D. And go with Charlie to get Will's and Wiley's bodies from Alaska.

"I'm not apologizing; I'm talking about the place I occupied at the time. Caring for my family became a priority and I was fulfilling that responsibility really well, financially. The children were attending the finest schools, and the time between special duty assignments allowed Bess and me to grow as husband and wife. If no special assignments, we'd play. But if the service called, I had to be there."

"And they called?" asked Brian, looking for the plot.

"I was soon involved in the preliminaries of Korea and three long years of conflict. He walked over as if to talk to the framed photo. "Gus, although younger, became my teacher. Taught me to be conscious, to be aware. Knowledge was respected back then, more so than age. I never got to be an astronaut but was honored to know a few of those pilots to the stars. Sinker was involved in the growth of the space program, akin to the place I'd been with early aviation. We became friends quickly. We loved to go fishing."

"Sink-er?" repeated Brian slowly.

A broad laugh came over Lonn. "That…this is all before your time, youngster. Gus flew in the Mercury program. Quite a hero and we were already friends. He'd retreat to our place in Martha's Vineyard. Lotsa folks still didn't recognize him yet and Martha's Vineyard wasn't all celebrity hotsy-totsy. TV was pretty different thirty-some years ago, not in everybody's face. No cable. Could count the stations on one hand." He saw his audience remained lost.

"In the early '60s, space capsules landed in the ocean. Gus lost his, *The Freedom Seven*. No fault of his, but it sunk. Got kinda scary. Hell, *he* almost sunk."

"So, they dubbed him, Sinker?"

"Nope, but I did," he said with a mischievous twinkle. "We were talking late one night on the phone awhile after he'd received word he'd been selected to man *Apollo One*." He cast his soulful eyes downward. "*Apollo One* was one of the biggest disasters in the history of the space program. Sinker…White and Chaffee…never had a chance. Gus joined Wiley, an angel pilot on my shoulder."

Although before his birth, Brian knew of the horrific incident with *Apollo One*, atop a Saturn rocket. In a test a month prior to launch, a fire raced through the craft while still on the launch pad, killing the entire crew. Suddenly the catastrophe touched him personally.

The elderly man returned his gaze to the photo of Richard Bach. "I'd become more conscious since meeting Gus. Even changed who became my friends. Vietnam was raging deadly and incendiary, big farce that it was. Not the men and women fighting but the manner in which it was being directed. Something shifted in me with my little buddy's death on the 27th of January 1967. That death and the awareness of Nam shifted my focus. I retired to the States soon after and took to barnstorming with Dick. Maybe it was having Gus and Wiley on my shoulder that really helped me take an interest in life."

Lonn's voice contained dignity as he glanced at the photographs. "Those men and women knew who they were. They weren't the actions they performed. Their value was more important than money. Even with their flaws, I bet each one could stand and say, *'I am safe in knowing my true worth and the value of who I am'*."

AFTER ALLISON HAD PLACED business cards in the soda glasses, she stepped back, admiring the facade of the twelve-foot bar. She was studying the elaborate design, running her hands over the beige wood that had several small frontal doors with heavy hinges and pulls. The raised relief consisted of vines entwined around crosses and goblets. "It's unusual, for a bar."

Bessie laughed. "We'd been in Vermont at a Bed 'n' Breakfast when we happened upon a Catholic Church being remodeled. These wooden doors originally sat at shoulder level," she motioned with her arms, "opening on both sides. Priests served Communion to their parish from these ornate cupboard doors."

"I wouldn't invite the Pope over any time soon," chided Allison.

THE ENTIRE MORNING AND most of the afternoon passed before the two couples, several generations apart, gathered at the long, custom plank-top table in the kitchen to list the treasures. Out of Allison's view, Brian handed a check to Lonn. "Doubt mine will ever be famous," he cracked.

Lonn clasped his hand, his eyes absorbing something deep within Brian's being. "Remember when you shake hands, whenever you touch another person, their body is an altar. It's the same as standing before God."

Although a man of his word, Brian could not speak and merely nodded.

Having returned from a secretive delivery to the Pathfinder, Allison and Bessie finished compiling the list of the reserved items and figured a final tally. Way more finds than she'd expected when she'd begun her mission that morning. The furnishings and fixtures they would be using in their business, without charging unfairly, would multiply several times. She felt both guilt and glee.

Their good-byes were those of long-trusted friends, generations apart.

"The movers will place your stuff in the garage. Then George and Daro can return with your trailer after the long weekend," suggested Lonn.

The younger couple assumed the other one had mentioned the names of their employees as they turned and walked along the neat brick path down the driveway.

Once seat-belted into their vehicle, the weary treasure hunters agreed to call it a day. Brian had not seen Allison so happy in ages and that joy alone tickled his heart. Truly speaking, more treasures than mere antiques had been found. Pulling out of the long driveway, they began their conversation with a simultaneous, "Guess what they told me?"

"Can you imagine being married for sixty-six years?" beamed Allison.

"I can only…imagine," he replied, dreading tomorrow's therapy session.

CHAPTER THIRTY

TRAIN TRACKS

OLD IRON BARS COVERED WITH chipped white paint were in front of the huge dirty windows of the pawn shop. Brian eyed the revolvers and pistols under the glass. Ironic how cheap something so lethal could be. He patted his hip pocket.

When Allison arrived, he was in the counselor's reception area surrounded by magazines.

He rose as she approached.

"We may have hit an iceberg but the ship's still afloat." He attempted to ease the tension and succeeded about as well as if he were chewing aluminum foil.

The blonde receptionist with ultra-teased and frizzed hair looked up, "You're Dr. Feldman's first appointment. He'll be right with you."

They sat on the familiar couch, next to the overly-familiar magazines. He whispered, "Hey, Allison, think she ever found any spiders in there?"

His wife was giggling as the doctor called them into his office. Once seated, the session commenced.

"So, tell me something different this session," prodded Dr. Feldman. The couple looked at each other blankly and then back at the therapist.

"We live in a crazy world and folks do foolish things. One of the craziest is doing the same thing over and over and expecting a change. People get hit by a train, then get back on the track, and then a train hits them again. Surprise, surprise. To obtain a different result, you must take a different action. So, my question is the following.

"After coming here for two months, are you doing anything differently? The marriage isn't working and your past actions have failed. What're you doing differently now? Other than seeing a counselor, are you doing anything differently?"

After a silence, Brian muttered, "Deteriorating."

"Is that deterioration helping?"

"No, 'course not." Less anger sounded in Brian's voice. "I just meant it was different. I'm not exercising, hardly running at all, the time when I used to think and relax."

"Anything different, and good?" asked the counselor.

Allison stepped through the heavy mood. "I've only been doing this for a few days, but I'm giving myself ten minutes alone each day, when I just sit. Usually right after I drive Benny to day-care. Ten minutes when no one can touch me. Ten minutes of quiet time for Allison. And I like it." She looked as if she should question whether or not she should feel guilty. More self-worth issues.

The counselor nodded. "Good. No need to elaborate. Brian? How about you? I know you're reading some again, so that's a positive. What about journaling?"

He shook his head no and then sat up straight. "Well, sort of. Since I was having trouble journaling, George, this guy who began working for us, suggested I use my organizer at the end of the workday before I got too tired or involved with something else. He suggested I write one daily thing I'm thankful for based on one weekly topic."

"One thing?" The counselor asked.

"Right. One thing about the day…I was thankful for about a particular topic that day.

Actually, I picked two topics." The two waited.

"Allison. Allison and our marriage."

"What?" she asked.

"So this week I look for one thing each day for which I'm thankful regarding Allison and our marriage."

"Is it difficult to do?" she immediately asked, only half in self-worth this time.

CHAPTER THIRTY-ONE

HEARD IT THROUGH THE GRAPEVINE

THE WIND RUSTLING A BRANCH against Brian's bedroom window announced daybreak. The scratching compounded virtually into a knocking. For the last couple of years he'd had a regimen of an early morning five-mile run with Oöso and had grown to look forward to it. More than exercise, it was his period of being still and spending time with his buddy. Lately, though, it had fallen by the wayside with occasional poor attempts.

Still waking around four o'clock, he found trouble moving his butt out of bed and out the door. Many nights with good intentions, he'd place his running gear out so it would be readily available. Daybreak arrived and he'd turn over on his side, yet never actually go back to sleep. Depression was beginning to root itself in his psyche.

At 4:05, his eyes were wide open, a lifeless expression on his face. At the same time a few miles away, George's eyes popped open, but he sprouted a slow smile.

Brian was feeling the victim. It all was just not fair. He stirred to the persistent branch outside the window, and saw the parchment pulling loose from the bark. Thoughts ran ramshackle. Of how paper is manufactured from wood pulp. Then he remembered the forgotten newspaper section with the obituary, recalling George's words.

Why do folks get the idea that life is supposed to be fair? He thought again.

The hastily folded newspaper had remained under his bed along with the dust bunnies. He kept Oöso with him several nights each week. Reaching over the bed disturbed her slumber and he heard a low grumble. The newssheet teased his fingers. Finally, feeling a flame shoot through his shoulder blade, he brought the newspaper into his grasp. He didn't recognize the paper with a curious title. The masthead read, *The Vector Point.*

Unfolding it, he noticed the obituary was written in typical format. He began quickly to scan down the left column bearing the names of the newly deceased printed in bold font in alphabetical order. He read unconsciously:

Burns, L.W.

Croce, J.

Deutschendorf, H.J.

Drinkwater, H.R.

Eubank, E.E.

Jackson, B.C.

Kwiatkowski, L.L.

Little, E.W.

Mandino, A.A.

Nelson, E.H.

Northrup, C.R.

O'Rourke, E.S.

Orowitz, E.E.

Peagler, J.K.

A strange feeling overcame him, one of familiarity with an odd ring. He skipped to the opposite page, the section bearing the actual obituaries. No photos, with the masthead only listing the page information and today's date, although it had lain under his bed for almost two weeks. Bewildered, he began to read absently without thought, unconsciously skimming down the mini-biographies.

Loy William Burns, 25, born in Detroit, MI; handsome statuesque young man who loved his parents, family, and horses, died April 4, 1993; the life force crushed from him in a hit-and-run. Would be *enjoying a successful movie career.*

Brian blinked away the cobwebs in his mind, between the fuzzy twilight of the nanosecond after dreaming and immediately before waking to consciousness. This was impossible. It felt like one of those dreams in which he wanted to move his arms but couldn't. Something was bizarre but his eyes read faster than his mind registered.

James Croce, 30, born in South Philadelphia, PA, husband, father, and blue- collar singer/songwriter, died with five others September 20, 1971; on the way to a late-night concert when their aircraft scraped a tree outside the dimly lit runway. Would be freeing all of the songs that were still in his head at the time of his death, raising two more children whose seed never saw the light, bragging about his son AJ's musical career, and praising his wife Ingrid for her successful restaurant in San Diego.

It seemed an invisible fist squeezed in Brian's chest the further he read.

Henry John Deutschendorf, 53, born in Roswell, NM, father of three and friend of the world, died October 12, 1997; left for the heavens as his voice arrived, on a jet plane. Would be healing the world with music and integrity as he healed himself with honesty while continuing the World Hunger Project and the Wind Star Foundation.

Brian flipped back to the masthead. "*The Vector Point?*" he mumbled. Like a college student whose eyes continue onward once the mind has gone numb, he read further.

Herbert Raymond Drinkwater, 62, born in Batavia, NY, father, husband, and former Mayor of Scottsdale, "The politician's politician," died December 28, 1997; continued to live "My time is your time" even when cancer interrupted for 22 months. Would be declining requests to run for Governor, enjoying his wife Jackie setting their schedules, and hassling his son to get married.

Ernest Eldon Eubank, 36, born in Decatur, IL, successful businessman with a wife who loved teaching almost as much as she loved her husband, died February 13, 1959; leaving a family picnic when a driver ran a red light. Would still be teased by folks for his refusal to drive fast. "I'd rather have them say what took you so long? Instead of, my — doesn't Ernie look natural?"

Brian Clark Jackson, *49, born in Biloxi, MI, car enthusiast and collector, died September 28, 1995, losing his race with cancer. Would be expanding their annual Barrett-Jackson Car Auction with his brother Craig, and looking forward to each year's race in Laguna Secamonteray.*

His own stomach felt uneasy but his curiosity dragged him along, looking for a connection, a clue. He felt sluggish, drugged.

Herman Edward King, *66, born in Seattle, Washington. Race car driver, banker and real estate developer who recognized the worth of Arizona's desert. Would be collecting vintage automobiles with his grandson Marc and great-grandson Matthew. Their corporate office in Frontier Town would be the basis for their entertainment, film production, antiquing, and real estate empire – recognized for their generous philanthropic endeavors.*

Ladimir Kwiatkowski, *65, born in Phoenix, AZ; hero to children, died March, 2, 1994; having breathed laughter from the TV for more than 35 years until lung cancer sucked his lungs silent. Would be doing anything he could to make a child smile, to make an ill child feel less pain, enjoying a new-found stardom in film directing, and continuing to shag golf balls with his wife Patsy.*

These death notices. Who dared to put them together? The lives of these folks, they weren't related, nor the years, not even the chronological order matched.

Elroy Wilson Little, *59, born in Turkey Creek, KT; mechanic who never met an engine he didn't like, died May 12, 1995; would be retired to racing in every four-wheel event he could find and learning to express himself to those he loved as well as he did with motors.*

Brian shuttered. Something was hitting too close to home. It seemed like he was attempting to remember a dream as it vaporized with the morning dew.

Augustine Anthony Mandino, *72, born in Boston, MA; husband, father, child-spoiling grandfather, and storyteller, died September 3, 1996; following a fall while trimming a tree at his farmhouse. Would be touring for his 21st bestseller about a lighthouse, living each day as if it were his last, and still bragging upon his wife Bette Lu.*

Eric Hilliard Nelson, 45, born in Teaneck, NJ; singer/songwriter, actor and father of Rockabilly and four children, died December 31, 1985; his tour plane spit from the sky, the heavens taking star of our garden party to join the constellation of celebrities. Would be producing movies and music in a company formed with Tracy and Sam. Having produced and directed "Everyone's Neighbors: Ozzie & Harriet" with his daughter Tracy and son Sam portraying his iconic parents; the three would create a movie and music production company. He would also make guest appearance with sons Matthew and Gunner at his show club The Garden Party.

Carl Raymond Northrup, 20, born in Tryon, NC; a red-headed, freckle-faced, God-loving young man whose love carried him through his four-year bout with cancer; died January 20, 1989; succumbing to a painful death while his friends stood at his bedside. Would be teaching the ministry at Grand Canyon College.

Air went from Brian's lungs faster than it returned. It burned. He gulped hard and the vein in his temple throbbed.

Esther Smith O'Rourke, 73, born in Decatur, IL; mother, grandmother, accountant, died December 4, 1987; her death caused by a needless surgery. Would be advising her granddaughter about sewing and boys, enjoying the success of her author son, and still be refusing to retire.

He stopped abruptly at her name. Fog cleared, names began to register, hitting hard.

Connections became visible. Mother to one of his friends. But she died almost twenty years ago. This newspaper was no longer a curiosity, it was a cruel joke. He wondered how this was done, more so, why such an evil prank as he continued on.

Eugene Eli Orowitz, 55, born in Collingswood, NJ, promising athlete turned actor whose national records in the California State Javelin Throw remain unbroken. Athletic career cut short by insecure teammates when they shaved his head and he tore his shoulder ligaments; died July 1, 1991; insisting all remember his laughter and not the Pancreatic Cancer. Would be starring in his fifth TV series, traveling Africa with his wife, playing with his kids, teaching Sean photography and screening Jennifer's dates.

Julian E. Peagler, Jr., *92, born in Tifton, GA; husband, father and grandfather, owner/operator of multiple automotive dealerships, vehicle lessee to the movie studios during the Golden Age of Hollywood, entrepneur. Lived full live until May 3, 2012; but wuld be helping his wife Beverly and son Marc run Frontier Town when not teaching grandson Matthew to golf and play cards.*

He sat rigid for several moments. "What the…what *is* this?" He gasped for air in fear as he flung the blue comforter aside. Oöso leapt to the floor, scurrying into the easy chair as she watched her bewildered master leap to his feet.

He flattened the newspaper across the bed and ran his finger to the start of the column. Reading and re-reading each line, making absurd associations.

Loy Burns was his young friend who was riding in the back of a truck, the wind reminding him of riding his horse in full gallop. His black Stetson caught air and he reached for it, tumbling over the tailgate, clinging to the bumper for an amazing distance. It was only seconds before the driver noticed, but too late. A low-rider sedan ran over his body, stopped, and then continued forward crushing him. He'd been gone almost fifteen years.

James Croce. Jim Croce. One of Brian's favorite singers perhaps because he was Benjamin's favorite. Tight melodies played on a twelve-string guitar. A nasal tenor voice, drooping moustache, and battered work shirts. Croce's musical poetry inspired him, helped him to remember Benjamin. Croce had died when Brian was younger than Benny. Ironic history.

His album *I've Got a Name* skyrocketed on the charts with nominations for Best Vocalist of the Year. More awards, the medals left behind, dead almost thirty-five years.

Yet another plane crash had claimed the next person way too early, another singer whose work had nurtured Brian's life, another distinguished star that tumbled from the sky, plummeting down in an airplane. Deutsch…he couldn't even pronounce it, but he knew. That was John Denver.

Drinkwater had a familiar ring. Seems Daro had been friends with a guy named Herb who had been Mayor of Scottsdale. But none of this made sense.

Who was Ernest Eubank? Ernest…Eubank. Wait. Impossible. It was his mother's brother, his Uncle Ernie whom he'd never met. He'd heard the story of how Benjamin was younger than Benny when Uncle Ernie had given him a new silver half-dollar at a family reunion and died later that day.

Brian Jackson? How could that be? Barrett-Jackson? Isn't that where the guys got that Mustang?

Brian stopped in an attempt to think, but the mysterious accumulation of obituaries pulled him to read onward. Herman King? More Arizonans. George and Daro were from Arizona. His blue eyes moved down and then stopped, focused on Elroy Little, Elroy Wilson Little.

Roy. Just a really humble man, never affected by the latest style or fad always had his head under the hood with a Pepsi in his hand and an earful of kiss-your-horse country music. He was a fair piece older than Brian, had faith in the young man's company, and had worked on his old truck for no charge. While working on the vehicle, Roy would ask him for advice on how to talk to his girlfriend. One evening Roy came home to discover a simple but elegantly landscaped yard, complete with a steer skull and wagon wheels. Roy. Another damned notch in cancer's belt.

The sight of Carl Northrup's name pulled him forward, grabbed him by the heart, causing Brian to crunch the paper as he leaned forward. His eyes began to well up. Carl was another friend from school, one of his best friends. Together they'd joined Los Hermanos, the Boys' Service Club. The gross foods the initiates were forced to eat created such heartburn in Carl that he had to be taken to the hospital.

Doctors found a non-removable tumor the size of a golf ball. He endured medical treatments silently, as that cancer grew to the size of a soft ball. He gallantly wore a wig when he lost all of his flaming red hair. Courageous to the end as Brian and their teacher, Mr. Ralphie, bid him goodbye in the lonely hospital room. He still remembered the yellow glow of the bedside lamp, the leathering of his young skin. Carl was the first guy he had learned it was okay, even manly, to kiss…goodbye.

Brian threw his head back, mouthing aloud. "Why did I make it, Carl, and you didn't? I've had so much more time than you! What've I done with it?"

He slumped back on the bed, the newspaper across his knee, his mind still confused. His body quaked as he glanced and gaped at the black-and-white newsprint. And then, he remembered George's other words.

Keep an obituary by your bed. When you feel like you've got it bad or feel life's unfair, pull it out. Read about those who'd gladly trade places with you.

His chin hit his chest. He glanced at his track shoes and faithful dog that loved to run with him. "Whatcha think, girl?" as her eyes popped open and ears stood alert in eager anticipation. He sat for a moment and then heaved a heavy sigh. "Maybe tomorrow," and he leaned back against the headboard although wide awake. As he held the newspaper above his lap, gravity unfolded the lower half that'd been hidden by the crease. His eyes snapped to attention as he screamed.

"NO! Nooo!"

Captain Benjamin James Poppy Jr., age 35, born in Olney, IL; military hero with the United States Air Force Special Forces, died December 4, 1993; in the line of duty, multi-decorations due to the courage and loyalty he offered his comrades in various tours of service. Would be retired from the military. Having learned from the mistakes of his parents, he would be building a loving family of his own, working with his little brother, and teaching his nephew to free the puddles.

Tears blurred the print, hot drops burned his cheeks. Unable to read further, he threw his head back and brutally wadded the paper into a tight clump, flinging it over Oöso's head to ricochet off the wall. He fled to the bathroom sink, unsure if he'd retch.

"Gotta wake up," as he splashed water on his face. Anger and fear blended, distorting his face. Staggering against the doorframe, he pulled on his sweatpants. The light from the refrigerator spilled out on the floor. He sipped at some water and pulled some grapes loose, afraid to sleep. Taking in deep breaths to calm himself, he returned to his room, looking for the mystical newspaper. The counselor had warned them about the effects of stress.

His track shoes lay disheveled in the middle of the floor. Oöso was lying by her leash, her chewing catching his attention. "Whatcha got?" as he pried her mouth open. Freeing the newspaper ball he had launched, he found it now a soggy mass returned to its former life, as wet pulp.

He attempted to open the unreadable glob, meeting with complete failure. He glanced to the left, then the right. Oöso nuzzled his hand with her cold nose. Calmed, he patted her head as he lamented. "Never know when we'll be placed on that list."

He moved to the easy chair in the living room and pulled on his running shoes, accepting imagination as a powerful motivator.

Exercise and rising early do not take away from our days. The activity enhances it, energizes us. Brian completed almost six miles non-stop. Not bad at all, especially after he had laid off for so long. The rest of the day was one of his most productive. Rather than tired, his mind actively percolated most of the day. By late afternoon he was now ready to place his brain on simmer.

No such luck.

CHAPTER THIRTY-TWO

WHERE THERE'S A WILL

HEAVEN WAS WITHIN REACH as Brian scaled the squeaky ladder to the tree house. He unlatched the metal fastener unaware that someone was already up there. It was as if he were waiting for him. *As if.* George was seated leaning against the trunk and motioned for Brian to join him.

"This loft is one of the few places where being out on a limb brings me peace," mused Brian, sliding over to sit against the railing. "Allison and I built this little refuge, using the excuse that it was for Benny."

George placed his Pischke's cap on the knob of a branch, signaling there was no rush, that he had his complete attention.

"Man. I had a dream that really got me thinking about life and time. I feel so overwhelmed with it all. I haven't lived in some ways, and feel like I haven't even time to die. It's like I've slept through so much of my life."

"Time remains to climb out of bed while it's still light," offered George. "And I've a feeling you're leading me into something."

"One of my biggest challenges has been learning to release things."

"Such as?"

"Oh, I've had a ton of things. Guilt, love, blame, possessions, women, life and death even. Things have to die in order for other things to live."

Brian leaned to the side to crack his neck. "This dream I had. You mentioned death."

"I strive not to impose my spiritual beliefs but I like the thought of leaving this world with nothing left to clean up. Go without leaving work still left to do. Arrive where we go after death, as clean as possible. Even if you believe you just die and become worm food, maybe at least you'd taste sweeter."

With a slight laugh, Brian leaned forward. "And I just bet you've got some clues on how to do that?"

"You could write a will."

"A will?"

"A Last Will and Testament. Simplify life as well as death. It honors both life and death with a much higher, more deserved value. Some aren't committed to life, shown by their lack of a written will. Without commitment to life, one is still asleep."

"I figure it's those folks who have a lot of stuff who make a will. I mean I don't have what I'd call an estate."

"Remember old Howard Hughes?" returned George.

Brian looked back, recalling recent mention of the whacked-out tycoon's name. "Genius of a man. He accomplished much in so many separate areas. Left an estate worth an estimated $13 billion. Be a great deal more today, an amount closer to $43 billion. But the reclusive industrialist didn't leave a will when he died in 1958. It took almost fifteen years and $20 million in legal fees to settle Hughes' affairs. Then his heirs had to pay millions more in death taxes that could've been averted."

Brian shirked as if an unpleasant taste had invaded his mouth. "I read an article that John Denver left $20 million, but no will. Hopefully, it'll be divided among his three kids, thanks to Colorado laws, but his second wife tried to claim controlling rights. You can bet a big chunk of that inheritance will be lost in court fees. But I don't see how this affects me?"

"No matter your worth or your poor planning, the outcome will be worse if you don't plan at all. Without proper foresight, when you or Allison dies, and certainly if you both die together, chances are those left with your business won't be able to afford to keep it. Or maybe even your home. A simple will can avert that disaster." He spoke with no threat, only fact.

"I just keep thinking there's always gonna be time, but I know that mightn't be the case. But... legal matters tend to bewilder me, so I put it off. That's true any time I don't understand something. I postpone taking care of the matter. I let it scare me off."

"Let's be basic and release the fear. What's a will? A direct interpretation, it directs what *will* happen to things when you die. Not if, but when. It organizes your assets and liabilities."

"Organizes?"

"Many folks don't do it. They make their beds and have to sleep in them. However, one morning someone else suddenly has to deal with the laundry."

"Crap. I never thought of it that way. I don't like thinking someone will have to clean up after me, in anything. So a will is, kind of, an act of completion."

"Death almost always overtakes us unexpectedly. Sudden awareness of a disease. Heart attack, as if your heart can attack you," he chuckled. "Explosion, train derailment, someone runs a light, nailed by a sting-ray while in the ocean, an earthquake. We don't have to depend on terrorists for surprise deaths."

Brian gazed almost thirty feet below. "Like two grown men falling out of a tree house?"

George peered over the edge as he grabbed a dead twig, snapping it off. "Branch cracks. Poof! You're dead. Found dead. How and where don't matter for this question I pose to you." Brian waited.

"Since you probably won't know when or where you'll die, you don't know who'll find you. So, will whoever finds you know whom to contact? If it's strangers, they'll search your wallet first for a name and address, if it's available."

"Okay," nodded Brian.

"Either through the contents or by resorting to fingerprints or dental records, they finally figure out your identity. Brian Michael Poppy. Now, who will they contact to notify folks that Brian Michael Poppy is dead? Is there a *right* person?"

Brian sat silently as he continued.

"Give me three names, just in case two of them join in your surprise death. Or in case you neglect to update this information when any of them dies. Name three folks to be contacted upon your death."

"Allison," was his immediate answer.

"Allison," George repeated. "Your wife or ex-wife, but nevertheless, a friend. She's your business partner and the mother of your child, so a natural choice. Next?"

He winced and returned, "Jason, Jason Johnson."

"Jason's a good choice, close, trusted friend and well aware of your company's operations. You could make an agreement to do the same for each other as you might do with Allison. Next?" He pushed. "Better hurry, dead body's gonna start to stink."

After playing with his chin and rolling his eyes, Brian offered, "Lillian?"

"Lillian?" George repeated. "Can your mother-in-law handle it, even with Hughie's help? Will she find it a burden? Imagine her being the first one to hear, let alone having to call others and tell them you're dead."

Brian's face wrinkled.

"What about Mary-Jean Filusch, our business manager?" asked Brian.

"She should know anyhow and be willing to regulate the business actions to support the person left in charge. She can also help you keep it updated. Good choice."

Brian's face registered a question.

"A will really works best if updated every three years. You're not the same person you were three years ago. Neither is your business."

"Okay. And then what?"

"They receive the call. You're dead. Do they know what to do? Were they aware they were supposed to be contacted? Did you list a pecking order for the person first in line? Did that person give you permission, so they're conscious of their obligation and the responsibility?

Picking up the pieces for someone who's died ain't no cakewalk. Most important, that person must know the actions to take. It's not as if you get another chance to explain it to them."

The young man shifted uneasily.

George prodded, "Put yourself in their shoes. What would you want to know?"

"I guess, sure, I'd want some directions. Some instructions regarding what to do, what's expected of me."

"An ideal plan is to accept responsibility for the same duties in the event of that person's death. In developing the instructions, you can make sure all is clear for both of you, total consciousness and awareness. Chances are that whoever's left behind will be in a bit of shock, some grief, to say the least. Sharing written instructions will enhance the friendship, while ensuring both know clearly what to do."

"Enhancing friendships," smiled Brian. "Takes some of the *ick* out of the job." He reached for the yellow pad. "Do I begin by writing an outline of things I want accounted for?"

"There're no rules. Most people begin with the money, cash on hand or in the bank, plus any income. And you're paid differently, being self-employed. Do you have a file so accounts can be found and contacted? Have any other income?"

"Allison does the bookkeeping with MJ, but I receive a check occasionally from a couple of oil leases I inherited from my mother. Even thirty dollars every couple of months adds up eventually. No sense wasting it." He wrote down *Oil Leases*. "I never thought about other monies, stuff like commissions, royalties. There's that rental property we have."

"If any exist, make a list. Remember the vehicle you just sold, allowing the guy to make payment arrangements?"

"Good point," Brain nodded as he jotted another note.

"Being boss, do you have a job description of your work responsibilities? Or one for Allison? Basically, are there instructions on ways to keep the company running or the way to dispose of it profitably and fairly?"

Brian made several notations before looking back for him to continue.

"Federal Estate Taxes are devastating if the will doesn't exist or isn't properly prepared. The government could prevent Allison from being able to afford to keep the business, or your house. List the people who inherit the business or your share. It's fairly easy but won't do it on its own. Otherwise, it is government chow."

Brian placed several asterisks around *Protect the Business*. He chewed on the top of the pen. "I guess physical belongings are next. Most of that is in the house but I have some things in my... apartment."

"Play the game. You're dead today. Now."

Brian's eyes opened wider, grasping the seriousness of their topic. The truth was that every second that passed brought his actual death nearer. *Apartment Stuff*, he added. Then he spoke quickly, "And I suppose that should be listed even though Foster, my landlord, has kinda become a friend."

"Anything to ensure ease. Not like asking Jason to watch

Oöso when you're outta town. Where do you have things stored or lent out? Be concise, clear," he parsed.

"I know you have some belongings in a separate storage facility as well as the apartment. People tend to forget to list storage units and things like mail boxes, safes, lockers, safety-deposit boxes, and even general bank accounts. If overlooked, the contents go to the highest bidder, not your family."

Brian added to his notes, *Storage and Lockers*.

"I guarantee you can't take anything with you. What if I asked you to name five people you want to inherit specific things? Quick. Give me five names. Couples can count as one."

Brian sat for a moment and then wrote fairly quickly. Aloud he explained. "Allison, Benny, and Jason, as well as Lillian and Hughie." He shrugged, "Those are the only ones I can think of offhand."

"No rules," George repeated. "But good choices. Now, what would each one be given? But first, if your ego can handle this question, would they appreciate your selection? What if you asked them? I figure you have the next piece of this puzzle."

"Got it," chuckled Brian. "Make a list, have it down pat."

"You might also list anything you don't give a hoot about, stuff such as clothes that the homeless might appreciate. You can direct that too in order to help others as well as helping your executor with their job."

Brian's eyebrows rose as his stomach growled, only slightly surprised when George produced a small bag of fruit. Frankly, he was growing less and less surprised by this unique employee, turned-friend-and-guru.

Handing a peach to Brian, he continued. "Here's an afterthought. Of these folks, how many have you taken the opportunity to tell, while you're alive, the reason they're important to you?" He bit into his fruit. "Why do folks wait until they're dead to share such pleasantries.

"And if what you have to tell them is so all-fired important, why in Heaven's name are you waiting to tell them? Why are you taking the risk of having to tell them as a ghost? How're you going to feel if they decide to die before you? I like what you're doing with the library of books and videos for Benny. But think about things left unsaid. It's your business, your life."

Brian eyed him between scribbling on the notepad and slurping the sticky juice of his peach as it dripped on the bottom of his pad.

They munched for some time until George picked up the reins again. "Now then, items which are important to you but others may not know about. Things you'd want your immediate family to have but they may not know the importance or significance." He tossed the pit to the ground for some pigeons. "Along with that, there might be things of actual monetary value."

"Like the Indian jewelry and turquoise from my mother," Brian said.

"Yep. Other things might be stamp or coin collections, collectible sports cards or magazines, even antique toys. Remember the old G.I. Joe dolls? Original ones in good shape, now net $800 to $1,200 each."

Brian looked puzzled.

George paused a moment. "Probably before your time," he added under his breath as he reached into his pocket. He pulled out his buck knife, able to open it with either hand and drew an apple from the cache. "What policies do you have that are paid in advance? Not just life insurance or car insurance. You have home and office policies. Don't expect these companies to go out of their way to offer a refund to your family if nobody contacts them and asks for it."

"I guess I figured refunds would be automatic."

"Nope. Companies will continue the policy until it runs out so they can keep your money unless someone cancels. Allison's premium may decrease with you off the policy if she knows to mention it, but none will honor such requests without an official statement from you. But, oops, you're dead."

Brian wrote for a moment. "Any others?"

"Obviously medical, health, and life insurance policies are the same way, and that blamed Social Security is the same. Social Security, like Military Intelligence, is a misnomer. And speaking of the military, you weren't in but your folks and brother were. The various branches, as do many business associations, have silent pension plans and burial packets or assistance. These plans don't affect you but if your friends don't mention this sort of information, the people left handling the deaths won't know about 'em for sure."

"It all makes sense, when someone stops to think about it." He stretched his arms out. "So, what others will owe refunds?"

George suggested leads. "Any place you paid in advance, even if just the balance for the month is left. Deposits count too, such as telephone, cable, and utility deposits. Some balance may be left on rentals, such as mail boxes and storage units."

"It's hard for me to think of those things immediately. I can't assume others will figure this out on their own." The continual note-taking assured George that the time invested in this conversation wasn't in vain.

In the time it took for said list to be completed, he'd skillfully peeled his apple in one continuous piece. He stood among the green leaves and hung the red and yellow spiral peel as if it were a decorative windsock. Brian always marveled at the way his peculiar employee could move so near the birds without spooking them. The feathered creatures began to nibble the sweet skin before he was reseated.

"Okay," with a mouthful of apple. "In general, now, if we divide all your worldly possessions into three categories of cash, properties, and things, how do you want each divided up? Who gets what? Otherwise the government will take it all and dispose of it quickly." His distaste for certain governmental actions was obvious.

Brian seemed relieved when George reached for the pad and inspected it although he soon learned more needed to be on his agenda.

"Suppose you and Allison bite the big one together?" He crunched his apple. "You both die way before planned. Will Hughie and Lillian raise Benny? How old will they be in twelve years when Benny is sixteen?"

Brian rolled his eyes. "In their late eighties. Ouch. Well, we already have Allison's brother, Corbin, listed as guardian, and Carolyn, her sister." Then he realized, "But it's merely an understanding. Nothing's been put in writing."

"If they die before then, who'd assume Benny's care? For that matter, what happens to your loyal pooch, Oöso? Maybe she only has a few years left but aren't you a bit concerned about her comfort in her final years? I can't see Lillian playing Frisbee with her, and Benny can't if she's at the pound. Oöso, that is. And then there's your faithful feline Polly."

More notes and several minutes before Brian resumed. "What about debts? Not just where money's owed to me, but if I died today, I'd be leaving debts behind, too."

George was visibly impressed by his conscientiousness. "Some folks kick off and figure its tough luck for those they owe money to. Some people don't consider banks or credit card corporations worth honoring as living entities. Those pieces of plastic out there represent the fact that you received and enjoyed goods and services. Those cards are just as valid as anyone you owe money to on a personal level. A major concern often overlooked is the debts left behind. Which ones will be cleared and which will become another person's burden? Methods and policies are available to ensure payments rather than repossession."

Brian wrote more notes.

"Equally important, who owes you money? If you choose to be conscious about your mortality, how do you want the debts others owe you to be handled? The reverse makes you wonder if any of those owing you money would feel guilty if you died before they repaid the debt. And, would they continue to pay?"

Brian entered the conversation. "And make it known if and how they're to continue honoring the payments, or if they're resolved in my mind. Although it's not my responsibility about the guilt they carry, I see if I died and no direction was provided, they might assume they don't have to honor their debts. That action in itself could cause them eventually to carry guilt."

"Very good," nodded his coach.

"What else do folks forget to address, before they die?"

George reflected inwardly about the insight Brian was displaying before offering his reply. "You've learned the value of healing through writing. Many folks have multiple journals or diaries. You said that you keep a journal of things about Benny that you began the day he was born. It'd be a shame for him never to find such writings, never to know they even existed. Imagine if someone discovers them unlabeled, and without knowing the information they hold, throws them away."

Brian snickered. "Remember 'The Brady Bunch' in which the girls were always at odds about their diaries concealing their innermost secrets? Not bad things, just feelings, private thoughts."

It spurred George to respond. "Here's a movie scenario for you. You're on a business trip such as in the New York disaster and your family's notified that you've been killed. Devastating, no body is recovered. Searching through your apartment, they find your journals, poems, and notes which get read."

Brian pulled on his lip.

"Then," George offered, "in the second half of the movie, you return having survived, a victim of temporary amnesia. How do you feel knowing that everyone now knows all of your intimate secrets?"

George opted for reality. "Let's fade, dissolve from the movie scenario back to life. Did you write anything in particular that you want or don't want known? Secrets discovered might be impossible to deal with…from the other side."

CHAPTER THIRTY-THREE

TELL ME NO SECRETS

"A SECRET CAN BE like a pot boiling. Gases build and expand. It can strain the container or erupt. A secret can carry the label of good or bad, but secrets secrete. In one sentence to yourself, what secret may be discovered about you in your journals? But don't tell me."

As Brian's thoughts took flight, he prodded him further.

"Have any secrets in your mind? Your journal may already address them but some folks are so paranoid or ashamed, they won't even write full disclosures to themselves. Now remain silent, but what secret do you have that you protect or hide the most? What do you feel would happen or change if someone knew that secret? Not necessarily the world but no longer secret from those you concealed it from."

"Secrets? Doesn't everyone have secrets?"

"Are we talking about everyone, or you?" he sternly replied. "I repeat that secrets secrete. Allow the answer to form a simple sentence in your head. The first thought that arises will be the truth. Hear the silence and then hear the answer. It belongs to you and you alone. I don't want to know about it."

Brian's eyes darted through the tree's leaves. The secrets of man are more plentiful than the stars.

George stretched his long legs out across the plywood decking. "You shared with me that you have a box of cards and letters from Allison. They could comfort Benny in the years ahead by providing proof of the love shared between his mother and father before their deaths, especially after the divorce."

"Our love before the divorce," followed Brian.

"Before or after. But the love from which he sprang. Enormous comfort in years to come, if they ever reach him. They can help him create pictures of parents in love, become examples for his life. If you both died today, while he's four years old, what are the odds they'd reach him? What'll fuel his memories? What pictures will he develop?"

Brian cringed, wondering if this stranger could read his mind. Impulsively, he pulled his wallet out, gingerly running a finger over a shot of Benny with Oöso.

George spoke solemnly. "I loved looking at the albums in your living room, learning about your family since you and Allison got married. And I shared in your sadness about no pictures of your own childhood and on the brother you lost. However, the photos had no written explanations. Plus Allison mentioned the boxes of photos she'd yet to sort. Who could even identify them other than you two?"

Brian remembered the way he or Allison always narrated the stories when someone looked at the albums. And in showing photos to Benny of his grandparents and great- grandmother, he knew few others would recognize them. "We could pick a couple of evenings and write notes on them together," said Brian.

"Sure, this doesn't have to be work. None of it does. Consider it a labor of love even. For my own curiosity, share with me three moments of time, three Kodak Moments, if you will. Name three favorite photos."

Brian noted *Photos, Describe*. "The first is a photo of Benny and me when he was less than an hour old. We planned for a home birth with a midwife. This was the first photo of him and me together when I was asked to hold him while the midwife checked Allison for possible damage. He was fussing, and I remember wanting to hold him yet so concerned I do it right."

He cradled the memory as he cradled his arms. "My arms melted around him like a second womb, around my baby, my baby boy, my little man. You could've hit me with a semi-truck and I wouldn't have budged."

George understood.

"It began to rain," mused Brian. "Allison looked so beautiful. Precious." A tear escaped as he tightened his lips in a rigid grin. "She looked out the window and then to me, and said, *Don't take Baby Benjamin outside in the rain just yet.*" Until that moment his name was going to be Hugh for her dad."

Both men sat in reverent silence until a breeze stirred Brian. "Our place was pretty raw but we had a couch. My shirt was open a bit and Benny nestled into my chest, his wee hands exploring my chest hair as if he were kneading bread dough. We both fell sound asleep, Oöso at our feet. And eagle-eyed Lillian caught our nap on film. I didn't know it then but that's when Benny and I bonded."

Brian laughed aloud as he changed the mood. "Then the photo I caught of Allison after we built this tree house. She's had a tough time letting that little girl deep inside her come out to play."

George wished more people honored their inner child, without forgoing the role of being an adult.

"She has this rag doll we call, The Little Girl. Any who, Lillian had brought over this tea set from when Allison was little. So later, Allison had a tea party for Rose, Cookie, and The Little Girl.

"I happened to see them from the kitchen and called Jason and he rushed over with his telephoto camera. We caught Allison dressed up in some old costume jewelry of my mom's, serving The Little Girl tea. She had no clue."

Brian grinned. "Then the shot I took the other night. Allison, Lillian, Daro, and Benny were posing on the porch. Oöso was there, even Polly. And you happened out the door and I caught you in it as well. I got you all in a family portrait. That reminds me, I need to get the film developed."

George let the comment pass, turning to dangle his legs over the edge, swinging his feet back and forth. "Books are a type of energy. Many folks surround themselves with books. Care should be exercised not to hoard books any more than one might hoard money. You said you keep a file for the tools you lend out. Do the same with your books. Keep lender and borrower conscious of their responsibility, but don't hoard."

"Good point, but kind of ironic. Allison and I recently met an interesting man with quite a book collection. Next I reckon you want me to name three books from my library that I want placed into specific hands."

"Very good, Grasshopper," said Master George Kwai Chang.

"I have about twenty that are signed by authors I admired and whose writings have helped me. I hope to present them to Benny when he turns fourteen."

"A library for Benny, that's what Daro said. I like that."

"If I were to pull three from my shelves, I'd pull my mom's Bible for Benny. I'd want it in his collection. Her marks and notes, her energy's in it."

He leaned back in thought and then raised his pen as he recalled the book he lent to Jason. "*When Bad Things Happen to Good People* by Harold Kushner. He was a former Rabbi who questioned his own faith when he faced a disaster with his son. Like me, he doesn't believe God does bad things or creates disasters. Losing someone at an early age as I did with Benjamin was eased by the wisdom offered in it. It also helped having it under my belt before Mom died."

"Benny might need the same if you were to clock out early. What we read shapes us. Knowing the books someone held dear might help another person learn about us."

"This one's going to require some thought."

George took a long sip from his water bottle. "So many folks end up in therapy as a result of the pain they inflicted on others, generally by accident. Are there any you feel you owe an apology to? They may not even be expecting it, but you know their names right this minute."

A huge breath issued from Brian's lungs. "Already I think of ones I figured were past and long forgotten. Guess they aren't past after all. Have any clues on ways to go about undoing them?"

"May not be easy. I'd say an apology with no attempt to vindicate one's own butt is most powerful."

Like most folks, Brian had plenty to choose from. "I borrowed money for an emergency vet bill from an older friend, Morgan Woodward. A relatively small amount but it was enormous to me at that time and he was there for me. I finally repaid it but never apologized for the delay, only reiterated excuses. Then there's Lillian. About Allison and me. I never realized I broke a promise to them concerning their daughter. I'm embarrassed, shocked," as he hung his head.

"Some look at things left unsaid as an account running or an energy leak." George's look was one of understanding, prompting him to continue.

"My dad." Brian shrugged, folding his arms over his knees. "Of course he's dead like my mom. But I realized sometime ago that he may have done the best he could do at that time. I figured I was about Benny's age when dad virtually disappeared after Benjamin joined the service. As I grew, I chose to distance myself and disconnect."

It'd been a long time since he remembered referring to his father as *Dad*. "I'd apologize for the child I was, the man I became, the one who held the grudge. I probably wouldn't have let him into my life if he'd tried. Hell, maybe he did try."

Gently George reprised, "You can still apologize or clear the account. You know the way to write letters of forgiveness and release folks from business debts. It works the same way for releasing someone who's died."

After writing some names on his pad, Brian stretched his arms. "You know what? I'd ask Oöso to forgive me, too. That dog has been the most genuine example of unconditional love I've ever seen. Had 'er before Allison and I met. I remember swatting Oöso with a newspaper, grabbing her by the collar, and virtually throwing her across the room for dumping a trash can." He looked away.

"I became a better father through that dog. I finally recognized I'd abused her. I think if humans could see animals cry, they wouldn't hit them. The last five years have been much sweeter for her, but she never loved me any less. Glad to see me, even when I was too tired to give back. And she puts up with my damned depressed state. She gives continually. Back then, loving and playing were great but my punishments were too harsh. I'd apologize for not learning that lesson sooner."

"What about apologizing to Brian? Apologizing to you for a few things? Have any thoughts on that matter?" Their eyes locked.

"To me. Damn." His neck popped. "Not taking my schooling more seriously, procrastinating since my teens about building my body physically, waiting too long for marriage counseling, not going to professionals or classes or college, not asking Mom to teach me to budget and keep books." He looked up. "She was one hell of an accountant, you know. Yeah, there may be a couple of things," he closed satirically.

George nailed it shut. "Now I have a rhetorical question. When are you, if you are, going to get to those apologies and settle these accounts?"

Brian remained blank, knowing actions speak louder than words.

"So, if all these matters were in order, if all had been addressed, all of the potential homework completed, how would you feel? Your will is in order. Keepsakes assigned to special folks. No debts or secrets to harm your family. Apologies all offered. No accounts left running. Remember, you *are* still alive with time to make your bed."

Brian felt an energy surge similar to awaking from his dream about the mystical obituary. His loud sigh, as his head fell back, was sufficient answer.

George wiped his hands as if they were finished. "Okay, everything's taken care of. Everyone knows their jobs and the things to do." His impish grin led into his ploy, palms open. "So, what should we do with this blasted body? You've addressed what to do with your car and trucks, a small fleet of vehicles in your case. What about the vehicle you've been traveling in on this road of life for thirty-one years?"

The young man was taken back by his oversight. "I know some people write their own funeral services and obituaries."

Motioning as if showing the fish that got away, "Here's this body, in your case, in fine shape. Like a used car with a few reusable parts."

Brian knew the direction he was headed in. "Maybe it's lame but…I have a fear of organ donations, as if they might give up on my life in order to retrieve the parts they want. I did give my dad's eyes after he died. Actually, anything else in him had been pretty well pickled by alcohol."

"You can look into the myths about organ donating as you pick up simple literature on trusts, and note your decision about organ donation on your driver's license. However, we still have a decision about the body. Simply put, any reusable parts? What about the remains? Do they cremate or plant them?"

"It averages at least $12,000 for the simplest funeral. Break the expenses down into their specifics. The funeral home operates a business to make money. Limo or Town car here, piece of clothing there, rental of the mortuary, signature book, organist, cement to protect the casket, these are all charges. Plus hidden costs. Folks aren't aware of this until they receive the final bill, but difficult to ask for refunds after the fact."

"I don't take to being buried," responded Brian. "Waste of ground, waste of materials for the casket, and as you said, it's a huge expense. My Mom's coffin alone ran a couple grand and so did my Dad's. They weren't even fancy. Military caskets, since they'd both served Uncle Sam. And then, the limos to transport the bodies cost another $500. My folks wanted a military burial, so I honored that request. But I'll take the torch. Cremate me. Then divvy up the ashes and have everyone take me snow-skiing." He held his arms out like a plane. "And let me fly while they race down black diamonds or tumble down the bunny slope."

George also had thoughts on this matter. "Funny how the body's one of the easiest things to decompose, so easy to return to the environment, yet we do all we can to prevent that process. Invest the same $12,000 in vitamins, massages, and exercise, where you and folks can see the results. Gain a few good years with such an investment rather than all this fluffy foo-foo stuff that will only be seen for part of a day."

He headed to the next subject. "I know you tithe ten percent of your profits to causes you believe in. Some folks arrange so a tithe of all their final worth goes to a cause they find worthy, almost as a last thank you to God."

With this closing point, he saw it was almost time for dinner and grabbed his cap as he raised the trap door. Once his shoulders were level with the decking, he lifted the brim of his cap. "You coming, boss?"

"Yeah," Brian replied pensively. "You go on. I'll catch up. Just making a couple more notes."

CHAPTER THIRTY-FOUR

A GOOD DAY TO DIE

BRIAN WAS FIRST to finish dinner. He gave Benny a good-night kiss and hugged Allison a bit longer than normal, pecking her forehead with his lips. Lillian's eyebrows rose when he gave her a kiss rather than a hug. He turned to us with a "Night, guys."

Allison saw something was up as he grabbed his leather satchel off the counter and threw in two extra legal pads. A few minutes later, she stepped from the kitchen and handed him a linen bag and a smile. He glanced within to see the thermos, corn chips, a wedge of cheese, and a knife. Where would he ever find another who could read him so well? As his fingers clenched the bag, she gently squeezed his shoulder. "Don't let the Boogie Man getcha."

He went out the door as she closed the cupboard, pausing to pull out the popcorn.

Brian took his things to drop in the basket that hung on a long red-and-white nylon rope from the fort before heading to the garage. Glancing upward he saw the little portable light and cord were already in place in the tree, questioning it little as his mind was on the work ahead. He grabbed two red bricks to use as paperweights.

Once situated in the leafy fortress, he browsed his notes and pulled out one of the fresh pads. He saw the last of the sun and flashed on dying at that very moment. "Twilight. Appropriate to deal with the end of life." He was determined whatever he did write would be clear, even if the tree fort collapsed, before completion.

OUTLINE WILL he placed at the top. He pulled the second

pad and gave it the heading, *WILL – TO DO. Brian Michael Poppy,* he added. He smiled at his self-awareness and continued. *In the event of my death, please contact the executor and administrator of my estate. Such is, in this order: Allison Elizabeth Poppy, Jason Kenneth Johnson, or Mary-Jean Filusch.* And then wrote, *NOTE – add contact info.*

He shrugged. A simple start, a step forward. He continued down his list until he had gone through several sheets on both pads before laying them aside. Opening the linen bag, he tore into the chips. After a few minutes he licked the salt from his fingers and folded another sheet over the top.

Dear Dad,

I barely remember any physical contact from you as I grew up so it should not surprise me, the day we last saw each other I remember no hug goodbye, no 'I love you' from either of us. Probably similar to when Benjamin chose to leave home.

Mom <u>always</u> worried she had turned me against you. She tried to get me to send birthday cards, Father's Day cards. I was not overly cooperative. I didn't want to get to know you or you to know me. I tried to tell her that she had not turned me against you. I had decided, on my own. This letter is very hard to write – of course you being dead may make it harder for you to read it. But I feel a strong desire to explain to you how I felt then and feel now.

I told Mom it wasn't her who turned me against you. It was you always working and the way you treated her and my brother. You ignored us. Men in the church took me hunting and Mom supplied so much love and time I really didn't allow myself to think of you. It hurts me to say, but you weren't missed.

Years after she was gone, on the night Allison and I had Benny, your grandson, I walked outside alone in a parking lot and cried so hard. I cried out loud for the fact that I not only missed Mom, but I missed you at that moment. I recall how I shook and was surprised I was crying.

That cry of almost five years ago was very important. I had a lot of hate in me. The tears washed the hate out. I had only our hunting trips in South Dakota for good memories of time spent with you. Even as a kid, I'd worked to bury the bad ones. I didn't know you. I see things so differently, so much more clearly now. I had allowed a lot to be blocked out.

Mom had said that with more support given to you, your life might have been easier. She said so many people loved you, but after you let Benjamin's decision hurt you, it seemed nobody else mattered. No one knew how to tell you they loved you. Didn't know how to be there for you. Strange it was the last year of her life when she shared this with me.

I'm 31 now. Thirty-one years on this planet. And just beginning to stand on my own. Stumbling more than standing alone, failing miserably in my marriage. Still not the son you had in Benjamin or had hoped for in life.

I want you to know, for whatever reasons you handled things in a way which I allowed to hurt me, I forgive you completely.

For all the years I held grudges and offered you no option for healing, no support, I now ask in spirit for your forgiveness because I wanted to hurt you back. I am so sorry.

He bounced the ink pen against his cheek before he scrawled,

I love you, Dad. Your son, Brian

Laying the pad atop the other, he stared up through the leaves, taking a breath, weary and elated in the same moment. Interlacing his fingers and stretching his palms out, he rolled his head. Glancing at his pocket watch given by his mother before her clock ran out, he made a mental observation that his conversation with George took less than an hour, and he had in a couple more now. Another two-to-three hours with writing the other letters all at once, then a day for follow-up on his notes, research, and typing everything, and he'd be finished. He could do it in a couple days if he disciplined himself. The big trick would be not to procrastinate, not to drag it out. Schedule it all in his planner; if the commitment is not scheduled in there, it doesn't exist.

Lunches individually with the three he wanted as

administrators. Type up the agreements and he'd have a complete will, and peace of mind. He'd easily invested many times that potential twenty-to-thirty hours in procrastinating. Glad he could laugh at his own folly.

Following a few slices of cheese, he resumed.

As he began to proofread all he'd done, he felt the vibration of someone climbing the ladder. There was a knock from beneath the trap door. He pulled it open as a bowl of fresh, buttered popcorn slowly emerged. It was followed by a large mug of hot chocolate, tiny marshmallows swimming on top.

The hands were all he needed to see. The door went to close with no face seen or words spoken. As the delicate yet strong hands pulled it closed, a sweet voice was finally heard. His favorite voice said, "Just thought you might need more supplies. I won't bother you unless there's something else you need. Goodnight."

He looked out over the ledge to the ground until he could see her image in the shadows. He watched the sway of her hips, the bounce of her hair. Noticed the brilliant fire she had built for him. He eyed the pen, bouncing the end of it off his cheek and pulled the bowl onto his lap. Some place halfway through the steamy chocolate and three-fourths of the popcorn, his heavenly stare was interrupted by a shooting star. He blinked himself alert and folded to a blank page. As the pen slipped, he wiped the butter from his fingertips. Then he started to scribe, beginning with the title he'd underlined.

CAN ALLISON COME OUT AND PLAY?

Can Allison come out and play?

We can pack up and go in so many ways.

The weather on a picnic with her is always fine, Because in her heart she carries her own sunshine – Brightening a cloudy or even a rainy day

And once her heart touches yours, you'll want to stay.

My energy pulses with thoughts of her hand in mine.

And a new value has been placed on the spending of time. She opened her heart to me and in I dove.

A pirate would die to find this treasure cove.

Her hands like her heart are simply one of a kind.

It took little time for me to recognize she's quite a find.

About her long, smooth neck dangles a fair chain of gold,

On one who once born – the angels broke the mold.

She soars as a lover, as a twin, as a friend –

As her soul ensures you share in win / wins.

And gold links her heart to her spirit running bold.

Her mission as a Keeper is to heal, nurture, support, and hold.

If you like to swim then dive into her eyes,

There is a beauty and warmth you can never buy.

Revel in the mixture of shades laced with darker green – Be wrapped in their gaze just as a sweet dream.

Prepare to get lost without even a try,

Their warmth remains long after goodbye.

Her lovely face framed by blonde hair hanging down on me, Nectar sweeter than her could not be found by a bee.

The flick of a tongue, the brush of her moist lips –

Tickle of an eyelash, delicious drink yet to sip.

The texture, the softness, the aroma of a memory –

I wonder if these wonders – ever will I see.

As a flower unfolding just grasping her power, She can look deep in you to see who you are.

To hope I am allowed to hear and share in her dreams –

More valued and potent it makes my own power it seems.

The faith I hold for her ability is taller than a tower.

One of my dreams is to be her Keeper of those powers.

It once bothered me she was in all that I see – More so as there is no more sharing as "we." Dancing, cabin by a pond, and clouds above,

Through all these, as in her, runs my memory of love.

The ocean, Mount Rushmore, and a ledge in Sedona's trees.

I missed the obvious somehow and just now hold the key.

When she is not around one-half of me is away.

I miss her giggle and funny things she did say.

An unconscious moment can hurt and twist another's feelings –

But action with love can beat fear and support the healings.

Can Allison come out and play?

If the chance comes again, my common sense and strength will stay.

He reread it twice, counting the syllables, thinking the butter stains were rather decorative. He glanced across the vast yard toward what had been their bedroom. The key phrase was *had been.* He searched the stars but found no falling ones to wish upon.

Rereading his poem a third time, his smile dimmed. Action, knowledge, too late again. After dumping the remaining kernels over the side for the birds, he set the mug in the bowl and placed everything in the basket. Next he tore it loose and read the title aloud. "*Can Allison Come Out and Play?*" He faltered. "Syrupy. And too late."

The torrid fire had burned down to glowing coals. He sucked

in his lip, wadded the poem into a tight ball, and flung it at the open fire pit. It hit the border of rocks and then bounced in. "Two points." He lifted the latch and lowered the basket.

Walking through the backyard, a breeze wafted through, a light drizzle began. After he placed the basket on a wicker chair under shelter by the back door, he carried his satchel toward his truck. The tiny droplets sounded like bacon frying as they hit the luminous embers in the fire pit.

CHAPTER THIRTY-FIVE

SAW SOME SKILL

CONSTRUCTION HAS CHANGED over the years. One of the down-sides has been the influx of teens anxious for the higher paycheck. Many misread framing as an easy way to earn a buck, some at the cost of a finger or two in their over-zealous attempts. Tom still had all ten digits. Of course, he was new on the crew.

A person comes to a job with hopes of good wages but tries to skip the education of training. Without education, an apprentice is open to such mistakes as removing the guard from a skill saw to cut faster by being free from setting the guard each time.

The curved saw guard performs two duties. It deflects the direction of sawdust while cutting, especially important to those thinking their un-goggled eyes are invincible, and it protects everything when the trigger's released while the spinning momentum of the blade slows to a stop. The uneducated apprentice believes only the blade's being protected. The truth is that he and all else are being protected from the blade. 'Course, *skill* saw denotes that the operator have common sense and skill to use it properly.

Attitude is easier to read in some folks. The tan new employee was just such a read: easy money and more attitude than education. Clearly Tom put care into his vehicle's exterior appearance, his body, but was lax on the care of the passenger, his spirit and mind.

The saw bucked as the headstrong youth raced through the plywood with the guard removed. A sudden sound of an air gun being used on the roof above caused George to flinch. He missed the incident but witnessed the result. I saw it all.

Comparatively speaking, a coconut's harder than the human skull, and a four-inch wood rod more resilient than a leg bone. Flesh and muscle can be sliced through as easily as a block of cheese with 140 dagger teeth, one-eighth inch in length, traveling at more than 5,300 revolutions per minute, or eighty-eight revolutions per second.

One might expect blood to gush instantly from a slash to the bone. Whether imagination as opposed to accurate memory, Tom's mind clearly saw his flesh peeled back, yellow fat strands hanging loose, the tension causing severed muscles to pull apart. In those micro-milliseconds, his mind questioned that bare bone should look white rather than pink coral.

As the buck and bounce of the saw occurred, just as swift was George's reaction. The electric saw was suddenly unplugged, limping across the ground as his viselike grip clenched the wrist of the foolhardy young man. The focus of George's steely eyes was as strong as his grip. The white-faced teenager a remained silent. Time stood still, resuming as if in slow motion.

The scream of the young man, coupled with the agitated bite of the whirling blade into gravel brought everyone running. The boy stared with horror into the calm face of the human tourniquet. He had his hand clasped over George's, unwilling to have him release his grip, unready for the imminent rush of blood, unprepared to see the way in which one foolish act may have altered his life, as we crowded around to see…the pink mark that stretched from inside his wrist across the top of his forearm.

Rotating his arm, his memory and logic provided no answer. I stared at George. Brian and Justin surveyed the marred plywood, runaway saw, and the redness on the employee's arm.

"You were lucky, kid," Brian barked, remembering less fortunate workers. He jerked at his arm, surprised to find only a scrape, reading the panic in the young man's face that had turned younger. Yet the teenager moved from appreciating his luck to being concerned about ego and his job, physical importance superseded inner substance.

"I'm okay. It's all right. The saw just slipped," trying to excuse the mishap.

"I should fire your ass. You told me you knew how to use a skill saw, that you were experienced, competent." His voice softened, "You lied to me, Tom."

The boy was shamed and offended. "Wood was damp. Give me another chance."

All of us had our eyes riveted on our superiors. Brian and Jason knew the handling of such moments were crucial and so did George and I. Brian quickly ran his palm over his mouth, gripping his chin, rough from the early stubble. He pulled the young man's arm forward for another look with a brief glance to George. The imprinted outline of his grip remained red on the young man's wrist. "Stay off the saw today. Don't touch it." He gestured for me to pick it up. "Nothing electric."

"You're not firing him?" snapped Jason.

The teenager looked fearful, awaiting the answer. He had payments on a new truck, a macho Dodge Ram with lifters.

Brian looked at the young man. "You think you're worth it? I mean, for us to keep you around for another chance?"

The youth regained his composure. With a smirk he responded, "I never met a 2-by-4 smarter than me."

The crew remained silent…as did our boss for a few beats.

"Good," Brian nodded. "Since the saw *is* obviously smarter, you stay away from it. Your job is to find me a 2-by-4 with no end. We'll talk more in the morning."

"But…"

"Tomorrow, I said."

The lower lips and set jaws of the remaining crew were rigid as we turned away to resume our work. I looked at George. *A board with no end*, a Zen riddle with no answer. I was tempted to clap, with one hand. Would the young man hide out for the rest of the shift? Would he even show up for work the next day?

QUITTING TIME COULDN'T have come too soon. The saw incident weighed heavily on Brian's mind. He was anxious to see Benny, finding the lad had made a gallant attempt to be dressed. He'd promised to take him and George to check out the area for the picnic. He also promised that afterward they'd drive to the place where a small footbridge crossed over a narrow stream, a favorite adventure.

The layers of faded and chipping yellow paint were an accounting of the generations that the old bridge had supported. Most of the paint was one with the wood. Occasionally a loose flake could be found. Slight cracks echoed the timber grain, splinters of aged paint more than wood. A good two inches gapped between the heavy, warped planks, some of which wobbled and squeaked. The paint-encrusted nail heads danced under foot, their groans more audible to a tiny child. The adventure ran some twenty feet long, narrow in width, with rails. This place was a favorite for Benny. George allowed father and son to proceed first in their adventure.

Brian walked across the wooden planks. "Hold my hand, so you won't fall in."

The child stopped at the point where the dirt path met the wood of the bridge and looked over the edge. He peered with his shoulders and tiny chest ahead of his toes. Then his little face looked up into his father's face, across the length of the bridge, and up into his father's eyes, "No, Dad-dy, no."

Brian looked back to George, concerned and bewildered.

Benny spoke softly as his toes touched the first plank. "If I hol' you hand, I might le' go an' fall inna waa-er." He edged a bit farther and lifted his arms. "*You* hold *my* hand 'cuz me know you ne'er le' go a' me and le' me fall."

The boards creaked beneath each step as Brian walked back, his eyes glistening like the wet rocks below. When he reached for Benny's hand, he glanced at George, then the heavens, recognizing the magic of the little one's words. He gave thanks for his son, recommitting to his responsibility for the child standing upon this ancient bridge.

JASON WAS WORKING extra hours since Rio's birth and especially since the diagnosis. The insurance company was dodging, claiming a *pre-existing condition*. He figured he'd work through the long weekend without telling Brian. The main thing was that the work kept his mind occupied. Thus, he was alone in the storage yard when the delivery truck arrived with four cartons from *R.M.A., Inc - Richard Ryan Martial Arts* marked for Brian's attention. Dean, the UPS driver, unloaded the boxes as Jason's beeper sounded.

The employees and people associated with Brian's company knew of the life-threatening situation surrounding the crew chief's son, so Dean told him to make his call and he'd stow the shipment and lock the gates, off the record. In hasty thanks, confusion resulted between Dean's left and Jason's. The cartons were added to the shed where boxes of Brian's personal belongings were stacked and stored. Four crucial cartons…lost for all intents and purposes.

Denise waited by the phone for his return call, crying with joy. She had paged to tell him they'd received a package notifying them of a way to afford the next examinations and potential surgery which would allow them to stay closer to Rio during the tests. But she had no explanation for how or why they received the envelope bearing a tiny imprint using a heart as the palm of a child's hand and postmarked from Phoenix, Arizona with detailed information on the Phoenix Children's Hospital.

CHAPTER THIRTY-SIX

UNEASY RIDER

BUGS AND INSECTS LODGED in the crevices of your teeth. Sun beating down on your leather jacket absorbing the hot rays. Sweat for evaporative cooling. Body and vehicle both subject to the elements of rain and sleet. Unable to hear anything above the deep rumble of the machine beneath your legs, feeling more than hearing. Hoping to stay alert under penalty of injury or death. One pebble, one crack in the asphalt, one banana skin away from meshing your flesh with the highway. Some folks just know how to have fun.

Riding a motorcycle can offer the same magic to a voyage as a glider does to flight, the closest thing to being self-propelled. To the alert biker, the land traversed is felt as if on foot, the scoot of gravel and dirt, the single vision of following the glow of headlamp in the night, the hollow reverberation crossing the planks of an old country bridge, the rays of the early morning sun warming the area as he introduces his steed of two wheels to virgin terrain.

Erle Pylett cleaned up his simple campsite and slid his copy of *Zen & the Art of Motorcycle Repair* into the saddlebag, alongside an old leather holster. Boarding his mechanical steed, he looked around to be certain he was alone before using the electric starter. Ego. He revved the engine a few times, loving the rumble, and then he and his Harley galloped down the road.

Brian, Benny, George, and I were headed for what the kid called a Boy's Nite Dinner.

The unmistakable *rap – rap – rap* filled the air as the biker passed our truck in the lot. Rocking his Harley Softtail up onto its stand, Erle climbed off outside "THE Bears' Bar & Grill."

Stomping his feet twice to free some dust, he pulled a map from a worn leather saddlebag and patted his wallet pocket. His stocky hand pulled open the stained glass door and politely held it wide for us.

Walking in, I figured I'd have to buy a souvenir for Emily, my assistant. Autographed pics of *the* Bears covered the walls. Mike Ditka, Dick Butkus, Walter Payton, and even Gale Sayers.

Following us in, the biker looked and surmised it a combination of a "Cheers and Jimmy Buffett"-style restaurant. He placed his NFL jacket emblazoned with *Dallas Cowboys* over the back of the bar stool. He didn't buy it, he'd earned it. He was proud of the team, back in the days when a gentleman coached them, class and respect gone when Tom Landry left. That, and a torn-up knee, told Erle it was time to hang up his pads. He chuckled, realizing where he'd chosen to eat.

Ordering an iced tea, he spread his map out at the bar as he reached into his rear pocket to double-check his thin wallet. He struck up a conversation with Sid the bartender, a guy who looked like he walked off the cover of *GQ Magazine*. After a few refills, Erle hesitantly asked if the place might need a temporary grill cook but learned otherwise.

He'd played semi-pro football, maintaining a good physique and a gypsy lifestyle alluding to the fact he didn't like to be tied down. A popular phrase to avoid responsibility and commitment. He was not a participator, his excuse was that he was learning to master spirit.

Some folks believe they can master spirit and ignore life. He wasn't aware that the challenge was to observe when not participating at all. Be conscious. Necessary when hurling down a highway on a vehicle of steel and chrome, as well as through life in a vehicle of flesh and blood.

I could read something was up as George excused himself to walk over to the bar. He introduced himself and then apologized for having overheard his predicament, suggesting that Hazel's Bed and Breakfast might need a cook.

The biker was standoffish for a few moments then popped, "Just wanted a few hours work is all. All I need is a tank of gas for the road."

Intuitively George sensed the wanderer's concern that the job might smack of some permanence and responsibility.

"Don't want to cramp my chance to see the world," Erle insisted.

"Good point. I remember the scenes from *Braveheart* and *The Gladiator*. The warrior in the thick of battle doesn't know who is winning. He's only concerned with his immediate area. He's participating."

Erle looked, impressed with his words but blank to the meaning.

"The Commander on the other hand, withdraws from the battle-field to the top of the knoll to observe the overall battle in order to direct his soldiers. See the weaknesses, see the strengths. In seeing the world we can master life by learning to observe life. The acts of participation and observation apply to all manners of leadership, all walks of life. Generals, presidents, bosses, coaches, teachers, quarterbacks, parents. Citizens of Earth."

I think old Erle was wondering who let this customer run loose. "I'm not the leader type," he said briskly, hoping to drop the conversation.

"Leaders come in different forms," replied George. "There are three types of leaders. The best, the most powerful, and most effective is the leader who is unknown as the leader and personally does not feel like one. The second best is the leader who people follow because he is loved. Third is the leader who uses fear and intimidation. People follow and obey because they fear him."

The biker stared blankly. All he wanted was a burger and an iced tea.

"It's always wise to take time to examine ourselves. Everyone is a leader as everyone is a salesman," George offered.

"Nope, not me. I'm the fourth," ended the biker looking to the menu. "I don't lead and I ain't nobody's role model either."

George returned to our table, obviously frustrated. Sliding into our booth, he began nervously spinning the scuffed silverware. Then, he stared at Benny and chugged a glass of water. Almost instantly, the kid squirmed in his seat alerting his dad to a restroom run. Once gone and before I could question, he began, "I don't know how to explain it," he said in a low voice.

"What's new?" I quipped.

"I can't explain it but that guy with the cycle is on his path," nodding toward the stranger, "and at a fork in the road."

"Path?" as I quizzically watched the lone fellow at the bar.

"His *path*. He's where he has the best chance to gain the next step in his greatest growth."

Putting the puzzle pieces together I began to grasp the message. "You mean, here? In Hinsdale?"

George shook his head up and down empathetically. "More than that. There are some strands of the tapestry, *his* tapestry, around him now. In this place. And as I got near him and mentioned the inn I could tell the Hazel's Bed and Breakfast is part of it. He's supposed to go there."

"Supposed to?" I asked, thinking of pre-destiny.

George understood my confusion. "Supposed to, in the sense that the B 'n' B is the next best piece of the puzzle he could choose. Some opportunities await him there. But it doesn't look like he's going to take that route. So now *we* have the opportunity to direct him there."

"Or had."

We watched as the stranger stared at his map.

"And somehow, somehow we're involved, and so are the Poppys." George paused in confusion.

CHAPTER THIRTY-SEVEN

BURNING BRIDGES

THE PARABLE OF BURNING THE BRIDGE behind oneself to force a forward motion can be exemplified in many ways. Benny's sleeves were wet, trailing water, as he walked out of the bathroom stall, following a flush.

"Lookit, Daddy. Foun' a nick-ill." He proudly displayed his wet treasure.

The father saw the soggy sleeves and asked apprehensively, "Where'd you find the nickel, Benny?"

"In da toi-toi," he said, holding his hand and prize up to the sink.

Brian knelt down, looking at his proud little fellow. He wondered about the lessons he'd been teaching his child to have him dip into the toilet for five cents. "You reached in the toilet…for a nickel?"

"No," the child answered with defiance. "I no weach in toi-toi for nick-ill." He held out his other dripping hand and opened it. "So, I dwop in my qaw-ter."

A nickel wasn't worth reaching in the toilet, but a nickel and a quarter, now that was a different matter. He lifted his son to wash his hands and the money. After ample towels were used to dry him, the father held the door open for his smiling son.

GEORGE HAD BEEN STARING at the stocky man at the counter. "There's a connection there."

"Think Brian is supposed to give him a job?" I asked as I saw him and his son.

"No, I need time to think." George smacked his lips as he stared across the restaurant at Benny again, who as if on cue, bolted for the candy machine. *As if.*

"Okay."

"Their involvement is indirect. Not direct in-your-face. Ours is indirect too."

I felt foiled as we watched Erle fidget, glance at his watch, and then get up. Both of us were relieved to see he left some of his belongings on the bar top. In addition, his plate wasn't quite empty and from the look of him, food seldom went to waste.

In the parking lot behind the building, Erle fiddled with his bike, tugging on a wiring harness that went up the fork to the headlamps, flipping the switch several times. He glanced to the sky turning dusk, striking the headlamp again. "Double damn!" He spat on the ground and then stomped through the door again.

Benny wasn't cooperating with his father, as he scurried around the candy machine and grabbed the biker's leg. The stranger knelt down, an easy smile appearing. Handing off the curly-headed young lad, he asked where he might find a cycle headlamp, learning from Sid that anything open couldn't be reached before dusk.

Folks consciously and subconsciously run from the things they need the most. "I can make it to the next town if I'm careful. What's life without a little risk?"

George abruptly hung his head in his hands as his keen ears overheard the stranger talking the talk rather than walking it. His look of panic made no sense to me and even less did his comment. "He can't leave now. It's unnecessary, it's not his time." His chest heaved. "He'll have to start all over again."

The riddle worried me. "So what're you…er…what're we gonna do?" Brian and Benny were almost back to the table.

"What can we do? Tie him up? A couple more bites and he's outta here. I'm open. I'd trade a place in heaven for a solution right now."

I seldom saw my pal desperate but I knew for him to behave this way, it was miracle time. As I stood to let Benny and Brian into the booth, I winked and excused myself. "I have to get something from the truck." Guess it was my wink that unnerved more than unsettled him. *Desperate times call for desperate actions*, I figured.

Erle studied his map for several long minutes before refolding it and leaving three bucks as a tip. Rethinking, he looked to see if Sid was in view and sheepishly palmed a dollar, commenting to an elderly man at the bar. "Gas money."

I'd been outside for a bit before he opted for a pit stop, ducking into the restroom. He emerged shaking his hands dry, mentioning the lack of towels as a policeman entered. The layout of the place caused him to cross the officer's path halfway to the door.

The officer asked Sid, "Who belongs to the cycle?"

Erle looked at the only other customers as possibilities and let out a subtle laugh. He misread Officer Jim Kirshner as a redneck and offered up a mouthy reply. "Unless there's one out there with training wheels or a sidecar, that'd be me. What's your problem with it, Officer, Sir?"

On the tail of this scenario, I reentered through the door carrying a small notebook, stepping around the two and rejoining the booth. "What'd I miss?"

George's eyebrows rose in concern about what he himself might have missed.

Meantime, the lawman maintained his civil attitude to Erle's sarcastic reply but wasn't above wit and sarcasm himself, referring to his bike as a *Harley-Frisbee*. The comment lingered for a moment before the biker bolted for the door. The subsequent primal guttural scream from the parking lot brought the few patrons and personnel outside.

Blue, high-gloss finish, custom red-and-white flames still visible though the Harley- Davidson lay flattened. The meager fuel that remained slowly dripped out of the cracked tank…custom flames, custom wrinkled. Although not quite a Frisbee, it looked more like a huge paperweight than a motorcycle.

The officer looked at the unfortunate cyclist and completed the report before bidding him, "Good day, Sir. I hope you enjoy your stay in Hinsdale."

The deflated biker pried the leather side bags free as he sheepishly looked at our king-cab truck, approaching to ask if he might hitch a ride. When Brian asked his destination, he glanced towards George and grudgingly replied, "Hazel's Inn. It's some bed 'n' breakfast place."

Our flatbed trailer had room behind the bobcat tractor, so we offered to load the crushed cycle onboard. It took some effort for us to load the remains.

George had his eyes on me. I could feel their weight. We still hadn't spoken privately and I was determined to remain occupied with little Benny, climbing into the backseat, buckling him in place.

A busy stoplight was two blocks from "THE Bears", leading to the next town. Two cop cars were blocking the road as a result of an accident. The same officer stood next to his patrol car with radio in hand. We slowed to ask if they needed any help. A driver had run the light, having trouble seeing the signal at dusk. We all exchanged silent looks, knowing Erle would have been passing through this intersection on his cycle, with no headlamp.

Brian offered to store the mashed bike at the construction yard. Assured him we'd be able to unload it with the help of other crewmembers. The biker was reluctant to accept help, a believer in paddling his own canoe. Once he was convinced, we dropped our hitchhiker off at the inn.

As the stocky man climbed from the truck, he was coming to grips with his situation. "Thanks." He glared at the trailer load. "Don't scratch it," as he attempted humor. Then with a deep sigh, he headed up the stairs to the lobby.

I remained a chatterbox with Benny until the truck was pulling into the storage yard. Then I made a lunge over the seat for the door handle. "Let me out here and I'll grab a couple of the guys before they leave."

As we were joined with additional muscle, I held Benny clear of the equipment, protecting him and myself a bit. Once the squished cycle was unloaded, Brian asked George to back the small tractor off the trailer.

"Wait a minute," hollered Brian, stepping to the front of the tractor. He pried something off, hooked to the front blade. He held the twisted chrome script letters with the tip of his fingers, tilting his head from side-to-side. "*Idson. Idson. Idson?*" he read aloud before flipping it into the recyclable trash bin as he motioned for George to continue.

I felt my nose wrinkle and my lips pull back as I clenched my jaw tightly. Dismounting the tractor once he had it parked, George's mind was working like "*The Wheel of Fortune.*" He walked deliberately toward the metal bin. Pulling the distorted chrome from the trash, he visualized a *D* and then an *A* and a *V* in front of the chrome letters. Then he glanced toward me, innocently holding the young child.

CHAPTER THIRTY-EIGHT

PUDDLE-BUSTING BENNY

THE IMAGINATION OF A CHILD is the magic from which dreams are made. Do you remember any of your childhood magic? A dark passage to escape the monsters' lair. A place for a time tunnel back to the days of cowboys and Indians. A tubular space ship that carries you to Mars. A cavern. A secret fort.

No matter what's envisioned, the last thing it would be to a child was a dangerous drainage pipe running from a field to a hilly road, the hilly road outside the fence laden with the lure and reward of puddles begging to be set free.

It was just a drainage pipe to the older kids too big to crawl through, their imaginations now perfecting the fine art of flirting. And the adults depending too much on the young teens to watch the youngsters carefully, wouldn't notice the pipe. Both older generations misled by the expansive fence running the perimeter of the park, accepted the false security. All were forgetting the power of a mere moment.

BRIAN NEVER CEASED TO BE AMAZED at the way Oöso could soar for the Frisbee. Maybe she was a bird in an earlier life. Once as white as the Samoyed Wolf's fur, the molded plastic disc now had a dull finish and ample perforations from the eager snap and clench of the dog's powerful jaws.

"Magic Johnson has nothing on her," I marveled, watching Oöso pause in midair amid a variation of twists and turns, latching onto the spinning saucer. Bending her spine into a furry U-shape, her tail curved upward to the back of her head. Craning across her

283

arching body, consistently snagging the sailing Frisbee. Even as it appeared close to escaping her, rolling across her right shoulder in a scoop to snag the toss mere inches from the grass in a move the best Diamondback would envy.

She was completely stretched out horizontally, some five feet above the earth in a lunge, flipping onto her left when the saucer was snared. Hovering more than six feet from the ground curled with paws above the toy, her head forward as a fetus, claiming a pose akin to Dr. J dunking a basketball.

"One thing never changes. She never misses."

"As long as I throw it half decent," laughed Brian when a short toss forced Oöso to paw the Frisbee on the ground to flip it over, to grip the edge with her teeth, carrying it to him with the same exuberance as if she'd caught it a full head above her master.

She maintained the speed and agility of a young dog, certainly the heart of one, too. She ran so fast that she appeared to move in slow motion. *The Six-Million-Dollar Dog* was another of Brian's nicknames for his beloved friend. The stride of her forelegs out in front with the rear ones outstretched, then her front paws seemed to pull her forward as her mighty rear ones pushed off, and she became a bolt of white lightning.

ONCE A THOUGHT SAILS into the air, it becomes available for anyone to grasp. Albert Einstein, Willie Nelson, and Eleanor Roosevelt were just a few who had subscribed to this belief. Rose was the most attentive of the teens. At thirteen, she enjoyed acting as mother-hen to all the younger kids without resorting to bossiness.

Here, she was grasping a thought. Amid all the noise and diversions, she noted the absence of Benny, Justin, and three other children. Her father, Lou Jekel, was the chief of the fire department and one of the captains in the boisterous volleyball match. As a babysitter, she appreciated the life-support training he'd taught her, leaving her well versed in the safety motto *it only takes a second*.

"Bring yer butt over here," yelled Justin through the fence, but Benny and the other three ignored the older boy, teasing him as he called. He studied the wire and posts, wondering how they had slipped through the tall fence. "Benny, Get outta the road. C'mere, *now*."

But the asphalt roadway was laden with curves and hills leading to the deep dip in which they stood, appearing not as a road to the little ones, but merely a place to play. The large puddle held their attention and splashing feet captive. Paper cups serving as boats in an ocean among mountains. The only threats present were the waves to the ship from the splatter of their feet as they freed each puddle.

Not much of the long road could be seen from the valley of the children, the configurations exaggerated by the youngsters' small statures. Even if the road were flat, they wouldn't have seen the other puddles being freed some five miles away, a distance of only five minutes when traveling at sixty miles per hour.

The knobby truck tires kissed the pavement in a rhythmic hypnotic hum. When the Dodge Ram hit the dips, it distorted its shifting weight. The truck sailed across the county road as a snow skier tickles moguls. And as a skier sets his sight on the next hill, so did this driver on the puddles. Water leapt from the road in wet, expansive sheets across his windshield. Thomas laughed with his girlfriend's mock screams although no danger was foreseen on this lonely open road.

Benny looked up as Justin pleaded. "Pleeze, Benny. Grab those guys and c'mere." His knuckles were white, his fingers wrapping the strands of the sturdy fence standing five feet tall. A crisscrossed wire that defied a good climb, bearing three strands of barbed wire across the top for good measure. No holes, not even a gate in sight.

We often focus on the problem, that is, the fence. The culvert pipe extended eight feet to this side of the fence and then ran under the road to the other side. Although the spiral, corrugated metal pipe was three feet in diameter, it lay unnoticed beneath the fifty feet of road and additional embankment.

The pipe lay in plain view to a wee child, and it only took a moment. And in the minute taken to read these last pages, the Dodge Ram traveled a full mile, freeing puddles with every dip on the lonely road. The Ram...four miles...four minutes...from four children.

Rose was concerned for the missing kids, yet not so worried as to alert the parents. She spotted Justin making some sort of commotion at the fence and went to investigate the ruckus. She walked past George who sat in a crouched position, his face buried in his hands as though napping. Farther into the woods, no one could see the lanky man in the top hat seated the same way, the purple tails of his coat rumpled on the grass.

I WAS WELL INTO PLAY with Oöso and Brian as we took turns flinging the disc for the playful dog. Occasionally, we'd include a bit of keep-away that lasted no longer than three tosses with the high-flying pooch. Each time, she dropped the Frisbee at Brian's feet and headed out for another pass.

"Fetch it, girl," he yelled. She sized the toss and made an elegant leap into the air in perfect synchronization with the speeding Frisbee. Jaws opened and inches from a perfect reception, she abruptly turned her head in the totally opposite direction, and the disc careened off the back of her head. She swung her torso around, landing on three legs, her back to us, the Frisbee lying in the green grass at her side.

"What gives?" Brian puzzled when the dog refused to respond. As he moved toward her, she bolted across the field in the direction of the distant volleyball match. We hollered her name and then exchanged surprised looks and broke into a trot after her.

THE LIFTING SENSATION OF the heavy Ram truck created momentary lapses of weight each time it climbed the hill and defied gravity before puddle-purging again. Thomas and Katie could feel their stomachs lift with each rise along the road bordered by the park fencing. She giggled for him to slow down, unaware of the two large puddles that awaited them two miles...two minutes away.

"Yer mom's gonna be mad," Justin screamed.

Rose could now hear his warnings and from atop the knoll, she could finally see the danger, the emergency, and began to run.

WE BEGAN TO SLOW our run increased from the yardage we'd crossed. The dog's path lay straight ahead. Off to our right was the tense volleyball game. Rose seemed out of place racing alone, heading in the same direction as Oöso appeared to be running.

We both slowed to a stop in an attempt to decipher the riddle. Our eyes ping-ponged from the energetic kids to the volleyball match and back to the direction Oöso and Rose were headed. A vector pinpointed by an animated Justin at the fence.

The racing dog froze in her tracks, barking energetically. Her head was fixed on the spot where Justin stood half a football field ahead. Her head shifted twice to the left. From atop a tree stump, I followed her gaze and then beyond Justin to the low spot in the hilly road.

George threw his head back against the bark of the tree where he sat. His defiant *NO* to the heavens was heard above the yells of the game. In scant moments his feet traversed the sand of the volleyball court. The team members scattered while some tuned into the screams of Justin and Rose.

"Lookit me, lookit me," laughed Benny. His leaps sent water careening over their makeshift ships. The kids remained oblivious to all else.

"Watch this," laughed Thomas as a deep puddle sent a sheet of water over their windshield into the truck bed, momentarily blinding them from the world.

Mere seconds passed from the moment Oöso had halted. Her eyes darted between the charging Ram and children and road. She instantly jerked in an altered course.

With her third glance, I grasped the missing piece of the

puzzle. The distance to the children was greater than the distance to the road. The forty-five-degree shift of the dog's path was obvious. She was no longer headed for the boys or the racing vehicle. The unfolding geometry created a vivid scene in our minds. The dog was headed for a point halfway between the children and the truck, both now visible to Brian and me.

Rose's tears were clear, as clear as her occasional glimpses at the truck. Justin was crying too, frustration overcoming his ability to scale the resilient fence.

The valiant. The heroes are those who buck the odds. Parents shouted, parents screamed. The fear in their voices knew no gender. Little Pete's keen eyes now saw the danger, alerting the others. George leapt over tables. Mark joined the charge. Robin moved incredibly fast, *especially for a girl*. Big Pete's long legs gained yardage, only to be passed by the four legs of Zorro, thinking it was all a game.

The valiant. The heroes. Twelve feet from saving them, but for the fence. Justin made an upward leap, higher than his basketball shoes had ever carried him. He grabbed and held tight to the barbed wire as the sharp metal shanks mercilessly chewed through the flesh of his young fists.

We raced to close our gap of thirty yards in the direction Ooso was now headed.

In a full run, George saw the blood running down Justin's narrow wrists as the child continued to search for and fail to find a toehold with his scrambling legs. Rose pushed him from behind as his glasses fell to the ground.

George hit the fence hard, only to be catapulted to the ground. Ever in motion on a roll, he turned toward the two Pete's. "Here," as he grabbed the end of a large picnic table. They charged the fence with the heavy frame.

The valiant. Involved in a perfect triangle. First force, second force, third force...children, truck, and Ooso. Many say a dog can't think, surely not able to figure geometry. Most certainly unable to determine that the distance to the road was shorter than the distance to the children.

"See her, see her," was my breathy prayer as I ran. *Surely on one hill the driver will see the white dog against the green grass.*

I recognized Tom's truck and ripped my shirt off, using it as a signal. No way across the fence, the driver must see the kids at play, their only chance. "Pay attention, Tom. If you ever pay attention, do it now," I screamed.

The valiant. The heroes who buck the odds. Oöso suddenly broke her direction again, akin to the best quarterback dodging a tackle. As in *The Great Escape* when the motorcycle- riding Steve McQueen as the Cooler-King used a hill in a vain attempt to launch himself over the barbed fence, so attempted Oöso the Frisbee-King.

All life turned to slow motion. Oöso didn't scale the fence. She totally cleared it without so much as a tuft of fur being claimed by the vicious barbed wire…as it became evident to our horror and respect, the dog sought not to warn the truck or the little children. She committed herself to altering the point of impact.

With less agility and grace than normal, she hit the opposite ground halfway between the fence and road, unceremoniously upon her chest first, her jaw flattened to the grass. No one saw her quick glance towards the truck but everyone witnessed her next move. Rather than running across the road, she leapt upward some four feet just above the truck's grill directly at the right headlamp.

Katie screamed through her hands.

He jerked the steering wheel to the left and pumped the brakes.

Rather than five hills away, Oöso altered the point of impact into fifteen yards. We couldn't tell if it was the thud of the collision or the escape of air from the powerful chest of the Samoyed Wolf that filled our ears.

Katie's and Rose's screams blended with the screech of the huge tires.

Justin's cry trapped in his throat, he was hanging limp upon the fence, barbs imbedded in his hands. A lady pulled him free, as another boy picked up his glasses.

The crash of the table forced the wire and nails free from the posts as the men clamored over the crumbled barrier, followed in close pursuit by Justin.

Brian's agonized cry issued from both the collision of the vehicle and the flesh that tore from his back as he leapt from another table and dove between the strands of barbed wire.

The chrome of the headlamp broke loose as the furry body inflicted a dent in the unforgiving metallic hood. Hitting her horizontally, the impact propelled her over the hood, tumbling up the windshield, over the cab, slamming with a solid thud in the truck bed.

Momentum flung her past the tailgate down onto the road atop the fresh tire marks.

The truck skidded into the far ditch one dip before the ashen-faced children, three of whom stood statuesque in the puddles. Oöso's body landed on the peak of the second hill in full view of all. Gravity caused her to roll slightly toward Benny, him skinning hands and knees as he ran for his fallen friend. The sound of his terrified voice caused everyone to stop, amazement registered that life remained in the dog who painfully shifted her body as if to check the results of her actions. *As if.* Her brown eyes grew content when she saw her boy-child approach.

Benny, Justin, and Brian's blood spilt more than Oöso's. Her damage was internal, a mere crimson stream running from her pink nose. The mighty heart still beat, but only failing in her mission would've caused it to break. Whimpering as we scooped her up using my shirt as a makeshift stretcher, we moved her to the grass. Little Pete stared, his dog at his side. Zorro barked to keep the onlookers away. It was no game.

Allison reached her family, her face slick from the flow of tears. Brian had arranged Oöso so she lay upon her belly, paws, and legs as if she were merely napping. He kneeled, straddling her back with no weight upon her to create a shield for his dog. He wept to the skies and then bowed his face to her furry crown.

She lifted her head, sensing the silent approach of Allison who stopped behind Brian with her face buried against his bloodied back, one arm around her weeping husband, the other around her crying child who'd now live past age four.

Benny pulled away and moved in front of Oöso to see her face. He sat by her front paw, holding it in his left hand, patting it with his right. Brian whispered her name continuously.

Sometimes in the past, Brian and Allison had sworn the dog could smile. This was such a time.

Allison knelt close to her husband, her left hand touching his shoulder, stretching her arm gently to stroke Oöso's back. Her tearful comments crossed between "I'm so sorry" to Brian and "Thank you, sweet dog" to Oöso. She realized she'd never encountered death. Even with the rabbit and fish, she refused to accept their deaths. Death was a topic avoided...avoided by Lillian and Hughie...and with her son. No wonder he walked into danger, he knew nothing of death.

A bloodied hand reached out for Oöso. Justin's face was stained with dirt, his wire rims marred by tears and blood. His mouth hung open with spit stretching between his lips, still too much pain in his hands and heart to utter a sound.

I took Tom's cell phone to place a fruitless emergency call and then sat cross-legged by Oöso's other paw and began to stroke it. I looked into Benny's confused eyes, Brian's eyes that continued to dart about the area, and Allison's eyes that pondered silently, a way to explain this tragedy to Benny.

She felt guilt. Her family had sheltered her from death, kept it a mystery, making this experience more painful. She'd have trouble being there for her child as this was all new to her. She wished she could somehow go back in time, if not to save Oöso, then at least to allow Benny to experience death through the loss of his goldfish or the loss of the rabbit.

I felt completely helpless. My eyes traversed the area where the four children had been playing. I shuttered, visualizing the other disaster averted. The massive truck surely would have mashed the children before anyone knew what had happened. *How did these kids slip past the fence?* The one unspoken thought shared by Brian, Allison, and George. *The place was safe; we'd checked it.*

The majority of the crowd remained within the fenced area, giving Brian's family space. They kept their children back from touching death as many parents mistakenly do. One person stayed farthest. It wasn't the top hat he carried in his hands but the violet jacket that caught my eye. Our eyes met briefly as the colorfully clad stranger seemed to point with his eyes. I followed twice until I saw it. The mouth of the culvert pipe. *The passage. That's how they did it*, I realized. But upon looking up, the tipster was gone.

I looked at George, standing behind Brian and Allison, one hand on each of them. His sturdy stance, one foot to each side of Oöso. Relief for Benny and the children's safety, yet total frustration for the spiritual dog dying. I knew by George's look that he knew. But I had no clue yet concerning his earlier experience while crouched by the tree.

Benny began to double forward with his little jaw aquiver. "Oöso, I sowwy we cwaad twu da cave."

Through his own tears, Brian looked toward the drainage pipe. Another piece of the puzzle became apparent as he made a silent, personal note to safeguard it later…to protect others. He turned towards George. "Maybe Oöso saved more than these four kids."

Brian felt Oöso shudder slightly and then he heard a low rumble, the death rattle. "Oöso?" said Benny as he lay down with his face at the end of her paws.

Careful to keep his weight off her prone body, Brian felt the space fill beneath his hip as the dog filled her frame with air. If he chose to say anything to his friend, the time was short. "Oh Oöso. You've helped me so much. Why can't I help you? God, I love you."

She turned her head as her master hung his own above Benny's. She licked the wound on his hand. On death's door, she was still caring for him. Then with a final rumble, the air with her spirit escaped, coinciding with several doves on wing overhead.

Brian felt Allison's body quake upon his back as his own cry turned into a roar. His fingers, still wet from Oöso's healing lick, closed the dog's loving brown eyes.

Benny's sob became a scream, causing his father to pull upward so quickly he almost slammed Allison. He looked at Oöso who'd comforted him for so many years.

Instead, it was the crumpled bed comforter. His face was soaked with tears as he looked at the back of his hand that Oöso had licked. It bore a cut, somewhat healed.

"Oöso?" Then he remembered leaving her with Allison last night because the picnic was going to be held today. "The picnic. The pipe. The PIPE! He ignored the ringing phone as he threw on some clothes and flew out the door.

The sledgehammer plus enough rebar and wire to attach a safeguard would be in their garage and so would the double-sided ladder. Allison's Pathfinder was blocking the entrance to the open garage. His mind puzzled as he saw the lovely owner lugging the sledgehammer, a toolbox already in the back of her vehicle.

Before he could ask what she was doing, she interrupted without a greeting. "Where are some long stakes? I had the scariest dream."

"Where's Oöso?" they said in unison.

"Probably with Benny," said Brian in answer to his own question.

"No!" stammered Allison. "Benny had a nightmare, his scream woke me. He was crying for Oöso. She's missing. I tried to call you but you didn't answer. Mom's here to watch him. I've never seen him so scared. And Oöso's gone."

They pulled the tools from her vehicle and tossed them into the bed of his truck with the other materials, the metal bed echoing. Snapping their seat belts, they sped off. Neither noticed George watching all from the tree fort.

Déjà vu laced their discussion as they crossed onto the hilly road laden with puddles. Nothing could be more amazing as they became aware that not only had they experienced the same dream, but evidently little Benny had too.

"Watch your speed," she cautioned, remembering the kids of the dream hidden at play. Together they had experienced amazing coincidences but nothing like this. Both of their dream renditions held the same memories although certain points loomed larger.

She mentioned being sheltered from death and her concern that she'd done the same for Benny. Then she noticed Brian's damaged hand and the long rip in his tee shirt. Neither one could explain the scrape on his back or cut to his hand. Both agreed, as they slowed over the last two rises, nothing could be stranger.

Brian pulled to a halt at the right of the road, seeing the open drainage pipe ahead. Atop the fence toward one end of the pipe, a blue crane was sitting on a post.

"Look," said Allison. "Something is blocking the other end of the pipe." They saw a bundle of newspapers until the blockage of white sprouted a wagging tail and two pointed ears. And a smile.

Their lips mouthed, "*Oöso*," although no sounds escaped their mouths.

Allison unsnapped her seatbelt and jumped from the truck cab, moving to open the tailgate. Brian scooped up the rebar pipes and coil of wire as she reached for the toolbox and sledgehammer.

I missed it all, awakening in a cold sweat, my bed sheets drenched. Normally my dreams were lucid, but not this one. I grabbed my journal to record my horrid nightmare.

CHAPTER THIRTY-NINE

A PICNIC FULL OF MIRACLES

HANDLING THE TERROR of nightmares and potential picnic disasters created quite an appetite. We devoured French toast, eggs, hash browns, and fresh-squeezed orange juice with our conversation of coincidences and construction.

Benny loved to ride in his dad's truck almost as much as Oöso. After chores and eagerness to spend time with his son and dog, he took them along to deliver a special invitation. Another trait that Allison appreciated, and Lillian questioned, were the invites he made to virtual strangers to join group and family activities. An only child knew what it was like to be alone.

Erle smiled when he saw the truck pull up the long drive to Hazel's Inn where the biker had landed a job in order to bankroll some money. The inn-owners' demeanor placed him at ease. He found Hazel to be fussy but a durn good cookie-maker when she stopped talking and actually made them. They'd offered him a horse stall to store his bike and make repairs, which assured he'd be working at the inn for quite a while.

He welcomed Brian's request to join the picnic, particularly with Benny backing up the invite. The boy placed his arm around a stocky leg to lead him to the truck and Oöso greeted him with a wet nuzzle. Pulling up to the picnic grounds, Erle joined the competitive volleyball game in progress as Benny headed off to find Justin.

The small seasonal creek that ran beneath the bridge traversed the picnic site, revealing an abundance of river rocks but barely any water where Jason walked with Justin and Benny. By the river's edge near a cypress tree, they saw George delicately stacking rocks into a tower. The rounded rocks were six inches in diameter and he'd made four columns, one more than three feet high. Jason watched before curiosity overtook him.

"Making these little towers is a means of prayer, a meditation. I learned it in Sedona, Arizona." His column noisily toppled. "Impossible to make much of a column without paying close attention, focusing."

"Looks more like a caveman's version of Jenga. What kind of prayers?" asked Justin, crouching to help him rebuild.

"Just prayers. Can be like this one here for children and animals. Or they can be built for a family, or even a project. No rules." He looked up at Jason, "Or for a change. Prayer doesn't have to be boring. It can be fun. These rocks are like life or friendship or marriage. They can topple and fall unexpectedly."

The two boys continued along the bank, as Jason uttered not a word. He just wandered off in private and began to build his own rock column. He was open to any miracle for his tiny son.

Youngsters can play hard only for so long. Benny had returned to the picnic, his hands clasped together as he lay on the ground, staring at the clouds. Oöso lay beside him as if surveying the changing pallet of the sky with him. *As if.*

I watched for a moment. "Whatcha doing, Benny?"

"Me jus' thinkin 'bout dim clouds," as he pointed up in the sky.

"Thinking what about them clouds?"

"Ooooh," he sighed. "Like da way dey look fwum 'bove dem." He sat up, staring. "Dey look soffer. Bounzier up dere. Like daddy's shavin' cweem. 'Cept dey gots big, big hills an' long sha-ows. And dere's light fwom inside and dey don' move. Dey jus' go f'ever and ya can't see da gwoun. And I wanna weach down and mix 'em like my finn-ger paints." And with the stir of his tiny hands, the sleepy boy dozed off with his dog.

"That ride left quite an impression. How old was he when he flew on a plane?"

Allison looked back blankly. "He…hasn't."

George returned with sodas, catching Allison in camera stance. He opened the soda tab and held it as she focused.

"Look at them lying there." She closed an eye to frame the shot. Both lay on their left sides across the patchwork quilt. Benny's head was propped against a rolled-up blanket, Oöso's head rested against the child's rump. His right arm crossed over the left, her right leg crossed over the left. Right hand the same as Oöso's right paw, a Kodak Moment.

I returned with Lillian as Allison spoke. "Sometimes I think that dog's an angel. She's always been a blessing. I know Brian sharing her is really helping Benny."

"Angel," smiled George. "Animals are spiritual. Unlike children, they retain that innocence, genuine spirituality, because they remain free from ego and the opinions of others." He stepped closer. "So, here's one for you. If one *forgets*, that's mechanical. If one *forgives*, that requires a choice. Which do dogs do? Forget or forgive?"

She closed the camera flap and returned it to the pocket of her tan shorts. She took her soda and sipped as he continued.

"Being free from ego, they can be abused yet still be loyal and loving. By the same token, that's why some folks believe an animal can't reason. Often animal abuse is unconscious behavior. But it can reach a point whereby fear enters the picture. Then animals have trouble forgetting *or* forgiving. The term *break their spirit* occurs when fear is instilled. *Breaking* a horse is completely unnecessary. *Bond* with the horse and one automatically *bonds* with the spirit. The same idea holds true for raising a dog or a child, or our world."

Allison spoke. "Brian's often told me of his surprise he bonded with Oöso after his earlier ways of punishment. He realized some were actually a type of abuse until he learned to discipline without striking her. If folks became aware, maybe they'd learn to bond instead of break. He said it helped him with kids."

"Do you think dogs go to Heaven?" she asked as Lillian

stepped closer.

"I'm asked a great many questions," he began. "And, I strive to offer only the truths I know. Anything else is merely possibilities, even if they're my beliefs. A belief isn't always a truth. But truth is always a belief."

"Can you give me an example?" she asked.

"Many people profess that dolphins and whales are loving, intelligent, and spiritual. From the information I'd read and seen this became my belief. But it wasn't my truth until I met a man in Hawaii. In Lahaina, they call him The Whaleman, and he started a foundation to preserve ocean life. He gave me the opportunity to swim with several of these popular creatures. Now I can verify the genuine love these animals have to offer. My belief progressed from being my belief, to becoming one of my truths. However, in telling you, it can only be *my* truth and *your* belief until you experience it."

"What about angels?" Allison asked as Lillian's ears tuned in, awaiting the reply. "Many believe in angels. I do as well. But it still isn't something I'd teach without having experienced it to be a truth."

"Soooo," Lillian raised an eyebrow, "is it a truth? Do angels exist?"

Before he was faced with answering the question, a freshly awakened Benny tackled his leg. "Wessaw wif me Unca Jaa-urge-val-more. Wessaw me."

Allison beamed at her mother. "I never saw anyone as good with kids as Brian, until I met George. Both forge a connection the way they interact with them. They have a Montessori- way about them, like kneeling when talking rather than merely bending over, functioning on the child's level. More than physically coming down to their level, they become as one with them. Brian said he learned that from his mother. Says she always got right down there with him, down on her knees to play with his toy cars, at his level. George just seems to come by that trait naturally."

Justin saw the wrestling match and leapt across George's back. Once I spotted them, I came to rescue my pal and tossed the boys around until we lay in a heap. As the laughs subsided, Justin stared at

294

some of the older, blue-haired women putting out the settings on the picnic tables.

"What you looking at, Justin?" I asked as the boy eyed them.

"I was jes' wondrin' 'bout panty hose and all. I saw my grandma's hangin' on the line," was the point-blank reply. "When they fart in those things, do their ankles swell?"

Once again, the child had sucked me in. Then, he and Benny, energy renewed by the joke, ran off laughing to check on the bonfire.

The fire pit's flames pulsed while Benny stood completely still with Justin at his side, standing in direct line of the smoke with their eyes closed. When the breeze shifted and they were no longer engulfed in smoke, they opened their eyes, looked around, and then moved into the direct path of the smoke again.

"What're you boys doin'?" queried Lillian.

Justin replied quickly. "Benny's teachin' me to move the smoke with my mind."

Brian and I grinned when she shot a disapproving look in George's direction. Then he did something else she didn't find *normal*. He walked over and began to climb a tree. Another thing I liked about him.

Later, we saw Benny and Justin playing by Rio's crib. To their left were numerous toys. A plastic Spiderman, Buzz Light-Year, a red Ferrari, a few rubber dinosaurs, and some blocks. All piled in several short vertical columns, balancing carefully.

"What's that?" George asked pointing to the first one that had a gray dinosaur precariously perched on top.

"That one's our prayer tower for Rio," said Justin. He placed a locomotive atop a metal truck in a new column.

"And this one?" as he drew closer to the one made of little cars.

"Dat's fow my daddy to com' back home." Benny's reply was calm and confident as he placed a block gently atop the pile. George placed his palms atop the boy's head, delivering his own silent prayer before he moved along. There were more trees to visit.

Stacked prayers completed and once again alone, Justin and Benny peered over the edge of the crib at baby Rio. The boisterous volleyball match loomed nearby. Justin was happy his tiny sibling was having a good day. While Little Pete was Justin's big brother, Justin in turn had become Benny's surrogate big brother. Both had welcomed little Rio with as much love as his parents had. His demeanor was so pleasant today that few at the picnic remembered his illness.

The two boys leaned over the rail, gently tickling the baby into giggling. They looked around but missed George and me perched in the split trunk of the tree above. Yep, we both love tree-climbing.

"Quick," whispered Justin, pushing his glasses up on his nose as he looked down in the playpen. "Tell us everything you know before they make you forget."

The baby cooed sweetly.

George wiped away a knowing tear as I climbed soundlessly down the tree to intercept the ladies as they approached, my arms in a gesture of silence that enabled them to hear Justin coaxing Rio.

"Now 'member. Soon as you can talk, tell us all you know 'bout everything b'fore our parents make you forget." Justin turned to Benny. "They 'member 'til they're born 'n' start to grow. Then they start to forget."

"Me fow-gettin' wot God looks like aw-weady," agreed Benny.

Lillian registered disbelief at this ridiculous idea. Allison revealed surprise at stumbling onto a special secret. George was a wise man who'd spent time, remembering.

CHAPTER FORTY

AS THE CROW FLIES

IT'S INTERESTING WHO we remember from our youth. Who do you recall from when you were fourteen? I can't remember who won the academy awards or World Series. I can't even tell you the vice president's name when I was fourteen. However, I do remember a teacher and a man from church who helped me through that age. Ralph Bradshaw and Walter Cory.

Fourteen was a tough age for me. Boys have two years as a teenager and yet two years until they can drive. Hormones rage inside while macho egos wage war with other guys. Nobody leads, everybody follows. We thought we were rebels yet imitated our peers. Trouble arises when boys do things as a group, things they'd never do alone. Times are just as rough on girls, too.

Mark had been the natural leader of the group since fourth grade. Robin had been his dear friend throughout, unusual because she was a girl. However, many a boy had received a blackened eye when they began the chant, *"Mark and Robin sittin' in a tree."* She could deliver a punch without jarring her wire-rimmed glasses. Then, there were Little Pete and Big Pete.

Little Pete was a keen shot with a slingshot, B-B gun, or water balloon. Nicknamed Little Pete in grade school because a long-legged galoot moved to Illinois from the east coast, also named Pete, who towered above his elementary school teachers. Even Justin called his big brother, Little Pete.

Big Pete won the LaGrange Spelling Bee three years running

and was a voracious reader. He could spout answers to "*Jeopardy*" as if he'd written the questions. Little Pete and Big Pete, they were a team, shadowed by Zorro.

Powder was actually born Kenneth. An all-American boy always picked first when teams were chosen on the playground. His dad dreamed he'd play for the major leagues.

However, he loved to cook. This all-American boy became known as Powder after the day he rushed from the kitchen to the pitcher's mound with a fine coating of flour all over his face and arms. One moment defines a lifetime.

One teen was known as Wiley as in the Roadrunner cartoons due to his mischievous stunts always backfiring. Luckily, he had musical talents also. Loud but still music. Then there was Gabriel who idolized Davy Crockett. On weekends he'd sleep in his backyard tent reading by flashlight. Then there was Gardner who always had cash. Newspaper routes and lawn mowing, already the prosperous entrepreneur.

They were all hanging together when the lead pellet sailed through the air, assisted by luck and skill. Bad luck for the bird knocked off its perch. Black feathers hovered in the air as its body plummeted to earth. The eight young warriors and huge black dog stood horrified rather than excited, the silence broken by George's voice.

"Great shot, boys. 'Course we'll need several more to make it worthwhile to throw on the barbecue." Startled, the youngsters wanted to run but knew George and stood squeamishly still.

"I know you guys would never kill just to kill. To make it a sport, you always kill to eat, to feed your families."

The warriors exchanged glances.

He gingerly scooped up the fallen fowl. "Any of you know how to pluck a bird? Or we could skin it. Which of you has a knife? This was Little Pete's kill, so he gets the honor of cleaning it while y'all gather more game."

Mark unconsciously brought out his buck knife, trembling. George opened it with one hand and offered it to Little Pete whose ashen face began to show subtle tears.

He placed an arm around the boy more to draw him close and prevent him from running than to offer affection. "Here, take your prize." He tried to hand the limp bird to the reluctant marksman. "Feel it, still warm. Life just left it. Nothing's better than freshly killed game. A few more and we'll be able to barbecue these critters and you'll be sinking your teeth into these babies within a couple hours of killing them."

The kids shuddered at the demonic smile on his normally peaceful face. He could sense the young minds at work, wondering about getting out of this jam, wishing they could turn back the clock. One action, one moment was all it took to alter their lives, and the lives of others. One thought shared silently was their search for a possible escape.

Mark felt guilty for offering his knife that had previously been used only on wood. The closest it ever came to blood was removing a splinter from Gardner's hand. In a broken voice, he asked, "What if'n the rest of us ain't as good a shot as Little Pete, Mr. Mazen?" Zorro sat on his haunches as if absorbing the conversation.

"Well then, I suppose Little Pete could be the chief hunter," he held the felled bird out to them, "and each of you could take turns cleaning the game he bags. Maybe Powder could cook them up after they're cleaned."

Gabriel hoped nobody saw his sleeve, absorbing the snot and tears from his face. "Well...well that's not really fair for Little Pete to have to do all the work, Mr. Mazen. And we're 'spected back for volleyball soon. Ain't much time for huntin' more birds." All the young faces tracked a glimmer of hope.

"Maybe Robin would clean and cook it," suggested Powder. "She's a girl." The resulting slug to his pitching arm jarred the Dodgers cap from his head.

She placed her hands on her hips. "There's plenty of food for the picnic. It's kinda dumb to kill somethin' when we don't need it."

George countered all of their reasons to disband the troop of hunters, making ample use of the bird as a prop to drive home his true beliefs, the bird still warm.

"Wasteful. Real wasteful," chimed in Little Pete to support Robin's remark, anxious to have George remove his arm from his shoulder so he could place some distance between him and the dead bird. Zorro's big black head bobbed back and forth with the verbal volley.

I'd remained within earshot and out of view until I couldn't resist any longer. "Wow, fresh crow. Better than hotdogs and hamburgers. Who made the kill?"

Little Pete barely raised his fingers.

Taking the lead, I continued. "Too bad it's too late to bag more. And it's a waste of time to go to all the trouble of skinning just one bird when there's not enough to share." I reached out to grasp the knife and placed the flat back of the blade to my thigh, closing it.

All of the youngsters welcomed me as their new ally until I asked, "Hey, Little Pete. You gonna stuff him as a trophy to remind you of your first kill?"

The young warrior's stocky legs went limp as George lifted his arm from the boy's shoulders. "Don't *need* no trophy to 'member what I did," broke his quivering voice as he hung onto his dog for support.

Feeling content about the lesson learned, George turned to me. "Suppose the only thing we can do…is bless the bird and bury it."

Turning back to the youngsters whose cheeks began to regain some color, he directed, "You guys go over to the volleyball game. Daro and I'll bury the little guy." He reached out with the bird. "But you each get to touch him, so you'll remember this proud moment." This exercise took several minutes as each tried to hide his fear and remorse. Such charades displayed their feelings even more.

Little Pete went last, cupping both hands. His head drooped over his shaking shoulders, chin to chest. I could feel my own heart swell when his comrades stepped forward and each laid a gentle hand on his shaking shoulders.

"Thanks, Mr. Mazen, Mr. Brónach, for burying him," he offered through his tears as he returned the small victim to George's sturdy hands.

I reopened Mark's knife. "I'll return this later." I began to trench a small grave as the kids departed, deep in thought. Zorro remained behind. "Shoo. Go on," I ordered as the black dog stubbornly sat nearby.

George gently stroked the dark feathers of the stilled messenger of God. Knowing his love and respect for winged creatures, I completed the grave in a neat rectangle and stood, hoping to ease his sorrow by acknowledging the lesson delivered. "This incident will stay with them all their lives. I wouldn't have missed it for the world." I grinned at the kids rushing off in the distance.

"I know," he replied, his eyes still resting on the bird in his hands. "That's the reason I sent you the thought to come over and join us."

The comment spooked me as I reached over to stroke the bird's silky chest. Before I touched the animal, George raised it to his face. I half expected a kiss to be delivered prior to placing the dead bird in the ground.

"Thanks, little fella," he cooed. "You did a great job. Hope I didn't scare you." At that, the bird's eyes opened as he twisted his head from side to side, causing me to jerk my hand back.

"Go on your way now," he instructed as the bird bounced upright, glanced at us, and then flew above the treetops.

Zorro gave a high-pitched yelp as if stung by a bee, taking off with his tail tucked between his legs. My mouth hung open until George was almost out of sight, too.

CHAPTER FORTY-ONE

IN HOT WATER

A FEELING CAN PERMEATE the air as easily as scents can evoke memories. Smoked pork chops on a campfire, yellow jasmine abloom in the desert, the refreshing swell of a summer rain. The wet drops exploded on the windshield of the Pathfinder.

As Allison drove, her inner feeling was one of peaceful contentment yet she wondered why. At the very least, peace brought tranquility. The meditations were helping, and she was proud she was making the time daily. She was feeling good while caught in a common, human question of guilt. Why should she feel good? So often guilt and fear remain in the ethers, marring and staining hope and faith…even withstanding the cleansing wash of an evening's summer shower.

She tried to ignore the *FOR SALE* sign reflected in the beam of her headlights. Once parked, she bounded up the stairs to their lovely home, not dwelling on the fact it'd be someone else's soon. Fumbling with her keys in the shadows was common. Attached was a tiny flashlight that Brian had given her but unless he replaced the battery for her, her fumbling resumed. At least the rain had subsided.

As she went to place her key in the door, she noticed, couldn't help but notice, a sunflower covering the keyhole, the stem held in place by the pressure of the heavy Dutch door against the frame. Volumes of memories flooded her within the span of a second. Sunflowers held a special place in her heart.

Like a teeter-totter, her mood slumped, then soared. It rose with the memory of the wooden block with a fabric sunflower on top with the inscription *Just give me sunshine and sunflowers* sitting on her window sill. Then there were the sunflowers she'd stenciled on the cupboards that Brian praised to guests. Sitting on the mantle opposite the rain cap was a large angel holding a sunflower. She named it her Peaceful Angel although he had nicknamed it her Piss-full Angel to irritate Lillian.

So many sunflowers and so many memories. Was this the reason Brian's father sought to obliterate all memories of Benjamin? Was it actually too hard to be reminded of the good times once they were over? Like the sad oldies song by Lobo when the former boyfriend laments, "*So don't expect me to be your friend.*"

Gently, lovingly, she removed the sunflower and inserted her bronze key into the dead bolt. Before the tumbler turned, her mind parlayed back in time. Suddenly it was eight years ago. May 12th. Brian had given her three colorfully gift-wrapped boxes.

The gifts were numbered in the given order to open them. She loved gifts and he loved giving them. Within the first box of red was an old silver skeleton key. The note read: *You hold the key to my heart. Here is the key to our future.*

She virtually shredded the second box of yellow to find an antique doorknob with the proper locking mechanism for the key. She savored the moment with the third box that had a broad purple ribbon adorning the wrapping paper. It held her engagement ring.

Blinking her eyes she returned to the moment as she murmured, "How time flies." Approaching their seventh year of marriage, lucky seven, with a divorce on the horizon.

Allison looked at the keys in her hand. As the tumbler turned in the lock, she couldn't help but wonder what the key to her future now held. Teeter, totter. A somber feeling prevailed as she spied a note on the coffee table.

3 PM.

"Almost three hours ago." Reading to herself made her feel less alone. "*Benny took us out to play, so we're taking him out to dinner. We'll put him to bed, so enjoy your night.*

P.S. We cleaned the house, so no working."

It was unsigned. Looking at the flower, she was relieved and disappointed and entered the family room, she was surprised by the unnatural darkness. Even the aquarium lights were turned off. Automatically, she turned to the nearest light switch.

The dual switch also controlled a wall receptacle, which she was reminded of as she heard the click of the stereo. A tape began to play, Whitney Houston's voice singing the theme from *The Bodyguard*. "I Will Always Love You."

Their song. Whenever and wherever it played, even once in a grocery store, Brian had asked her to dance. Their song. Ironic when much later they realized the lyrics painted a bleak end to a love affair. *Too often we listen without hearing. Was it fate that we'd dubbed it our song?* She thought.

She barely noticed that only one verse of the song played. However, she was well aware of another flower on the stereo. A white rose with a long thin violet ribbon. Her hand refrained from turning off the music. She reached instead for the green stem as Neil Diamond serenaded her, his deep voice aided only by a violin and sole guitar.

"We are two and two of us are one I'm back on my feet again,

Out on the street again,

Looking for love…on the way to the sky."

Memories began to re-surface about a major business trip for Brian to meet with Mr. Duke as they built the company. That evening she called him at the Hyatt of Albuquerque. He said he'd had dinner at a place in which a tram took him to the sky. And she'd told him how proud she was of him and his achievements.

The satiny ribbon went across to the table looping around a wine goblet filled to the brim with Bailey's Irish Creme, milk, and three ice cubes. As water beads ran down the crystal stem, she felt a tear trickle down her cheek. She wondered how long the drink could've sat without the ice cubes melting. She gently raised the beverage to her lips while Mac Davis made her laugh with "You're my Bestest Friend."

As she listened, an arrow beneath the glass caught her eye. It pointed towards the stairway and she gingerly proceeded. The flicker of light at the top concerned her while the music from the upstairs speakers subdued her. "Brian? Hello? Brian?"

He respected her fears, so she knew the silence confirmed he wasn't hiding in the shadows. Now, she was unsure whether to be relieved or disappointed.

The ring of the telephone caused her to jump. It was MJ, explaining that Brian knew the guys were taking Benny out so he scheduled an evening meeting about a high-rise. Her questions met with a general lack of information and cancelled the idea of him or anyone sharing her night. As she hung up the phone, Marshall Tucker was promising,

> "Somewhere there's got to be, Somewhere where you and me
>
> Can get away from this noise and fury,
>
> Just you and I alone,
>
> There'd be no telephone.
>
> We'd never be in a hurry."

Expectations were one of her biggest downfalls. They dissolved as she headed towards the flickering illumination coming from the bathroom. One atom moving affects the whole universe. Her mere entrance caused the flames to waver. Oh there were candles, all right, of all shapes and sizes. Someone must've raided Yankee Candle because they were placed everywhere.

Three were located on the far corners above the antique tub, two small ones by the front of it next to a coaster awaiting her drink. A couple more glowed from the sink and atop the tank of the toilet. Two enormous ones were standing by the iron claw-shaped tub legs, tall enough to cast light above the curled lip of the tub.

Pink candles mainly, the color she used in meditations about her and Brian. Then there were light blue, coral, violet, and dark green. The entire room, a warm radiance of dancing shadows. She no longer cared about who her bathroom benefactor was.

She marveled at the ready suds and the inviting warmth of the bath as her clothes fell to the floor, exposing her pert small breasts and freckles to the dancing candle light. *Whoever* had been thoughtful enough to place a green sponge for her to use in bathing. She piled her long blonde hair atop her head with a clip, revealing her strong, smooth shoulders. Brian used to play connect-the-dots, using his tongue and her freckles.

There was no lack of talented souls to entertain her. Jim Croce offered up "Photographs & Memories" and "Time in a Bottle." Mac Davis returned and stole her smile with "Dreams that Last Forever" and then wrung tears with "Regrets." A youthful Frank Sinatra crooned "Serenade in Blue."

Brad Paisley was joined by Carrie Underwood. *"Deep as the life from God's own breath—Endless even after death—Gone like the sunset."*

As she leaned back, letting the hot water heat her skin, The King delivered a regal rendition of "Can't Help Falling in Love." Anne Murray searched for "A Little Good News Today." Willie Nelson's nasally voice crooned "Somewhere over the Rainbow," followed by The Man in Black performing her favorite version of "Amazing Grace." Jimmy Buffett proved more than a Parrot-head with "Dream Jimmy Dream."

The cool Bailey's and the warm bath lasted only long enough for her mood to be altered by Eddie Rabbit jumping in with "Do You Right Tonight." She looked toward the hall, surprised to notice the emerald green nightgown hanging behind the door. White lace daisies circled the neckline, a long forgotten gift from their first Christmas together. Wendy Webb's haunting "My Beating Heart" played next. "Can't Buy You Money" from Toby Keith. Randy Crawford offered up "Your Precious Love." "Don't Leave Me Lonely Tonight" came from Lari White, the lady he said he'd chase if Allison left him for Clint Black.

An antique cuckoo clock chirped the time. Talking to herself eased being alone. "Eight's a little early for bed." As she rose, the suds clung seductively to her breasts, her long legs, and hid her treasure, a white-blonde treat only for the mirror.

The plush print towel seemed extra soft as it drank the moisture from her skin. "It would be nice to have some assistance now." She somberly snuffed out the candles respectfully, thanking them and their flames. As the darkness overtook the room, the last of the bubbles gurgled from the tub and she slipped into the nightgown. Her mood slumped again, until she looked down the hall and saw the flicker of more candlelight from their bedroom with a trail of fresh flower petals leading across the bed.

The music continued. She was relieved to hear Rod Stewart's "Never Give up on Your Dream" although she felt Barbara Mandrell's "Sleeping Single in a Double Bed" would've been more appropriate. The fabric face of The Little Girl smiled a greeting from the king-sized bed with a new patch-work robe draped over her shoulders.

A long-stemmed red rose poked its head out of a pocket. Draping the quilted robe over her nightgown and her shoulders, she felt the other pocket sagging. A small bottle of perfume with a folded sheet of paper attached. Pulling the collar back, she allowed the cologne to dust her long neck, the tiny beads like a mini-massage as her hair hung down her shoulder blades, past the small of her back. Then, she slowly opened the note.

It appeared to be a simple artist's rendering of a house. Looking closer, it looked like a tree house, but not just any tree house, Benny's tree house. She ran past the empty bed and threw open the drapes with such force that she scattered the dried decorative flowers that hung above the curtain rod. Taylor Dayne's sensual voice offered "With Every Beat of My Heart" followed by "Love Will Lead You Back." Then George Strait, the only man with whom Brian might have to compete. The song from his movie was used in their wedding ceremony. "I Cross My Heart."

From the backyard came a tiny glow, akin to the flicker she had seen in the bathroom. Peering out her window, she saw a star appear, then others. No, not stars, tiny Christmas lights were beginning to show and flicker. The stout ash with massive limbs cradling the tree house looked as if fireflies inhabited every branch.

Returning her focus to the room, she saw a small sunflower painted on their window with the notation *Take a Risk*. She stepped over to the dresser for a paper she'd printed earlier, followed her intuition, and placed it in her pocket.

The music countered with Van Morrison's dramatic voice, turning strong and high, shrill at points, joined by a breathy flute in the second stanza before the band took "Moon Dance" into full swing. Halfway through, a sax solo hit heavy, teamed with deliberate strokes from a keyboard. The strained voice carried her through the French doors.

She wanted to run, only she wasn't sure in which direction. Had she foreseen this, would she have even removed that first sunflower and unlocked the door? It was too late to speculate. She'd opened the doors, crossed the wooden landing, and was already walking down the exterior stairs.

The cool grass yielded to the gentle step of her bare feet. Why was she stepping so lightly when expected by someone? She realized she was releasing control although she clutched her robe against the cool air. "Halfway there but still time to turn around," she uttered incoherently.

In the shadows sat their bikes. She laughed aloud and then covered her mouth. Although Brian was the more outrageous, she was the more adventurous, especially in matters of love. Nevertheless, one summer moonlit night he'd caught her off-guard as they talked of bravery and daringness while they pedaled. Him bare-chested and her in a midriff, they turned their bikes down their roadway beneath the street lamps. A few houses from their drive, he lagged a bit behind her pace.

Momentarily, he regained his position alongside her. His conversation turned a bit chatty as she glanced at him, grinning. Then her hair flared as her head spun around, realizing his walking shorts and purple boxers were hanging on his handle bars. Her shy Brian was clad only in tennis shoes, hairy chest, moustache, and a smile, and not at all sleepy. They barely made it up the front stairs into the shadow of their doorway.

Back to reality, she looked at his green mountain bike and ran her hand along the frame. She gave a playful squeeze to the seat as she found herself beneath the tree house. Her breath became syncopated as she reached for the first wooden rung and began what seemed an incredibly long ascent up the ladder.

From her vantage point, the base of the fortress cut a black silhouette out of the leafy heavens sprinkled with electric stars. She remembered the care and extensive plans Brian had put into building the tree house, amazed at his ability for blending quality work and fun. He'd taken great care in building this little fortress, using his level to run 2-by-6 boards for floor supports. She valued his meticulous work. Helping him on this play structure had allowed her to know and value him even more.

Reaching the top rung sooner than expected, she was engulfed by a wave of fear. Even naïveté. She assumed her suitor was Brian, yet MJ had said he had a meeting. She withheld her urge to knock on the trap door. It certainly appeared that she was expected although she had no proof who was waiting for her. She remembered discussing the topic of fear with George once.

Would you be more afraid to talk with the devil or with God?

She wondered.

CHAPTER FORTY-TWO

LOVE AMONG THE LEAVES

SHE LIFTED HER RIGHT HAND off the top rung, and made a small fist to knock. She found herself wondering if she'd rather it be Brian who answered. Or Daro or George or Madmoe? She rapped five times with the last three more boldly.

"Who is it?" a rather subdued and not fully recognizable voice questioned.

"A scared little girl," uttered a tiny voice.

"Scared? Then we have something in common. Come up. Please join me."

Her hand pushed upward to lift the hatch, and literally, open her surprise.

Two points on the circle. The trap door seemed to lift so slowly for Brian but quickly for Allison. The floor to him was a ceiling to her.

She remembered questioning as they built this leafy oasis, *Why the trap door?* It would have been easier just to run the ladder up the side.

"Because this way is more fun," smiled the happy carpenter. "Didn't you have forts as a little kid? Kids love trap doors, things they can open and close, crawl through. And a door in the floor, it's almost secretive."

He found special hinges so kids could sit on the door without tearing their pants or scratching themselves. Finally, she understood. She saw his child inside was still alive, and she hoped his free spirit would help her trapped little girl to emerge. Help her with the ideas she wanted to believe. Prove a truth, that she was valued and loved.

As the hatch lifted, the blinking lights were framed by the cutout in the plywood floor. To her, the twinkling of man-made stars and God-given stars were intertwined.

His vantage was viewing the opening door from the hinge side virtually as a wall. Breathless to see his love emerge, he was battling to slow his heartbeat. Frozen not with cold but with fear. Worse than their first kiss, worse than the time a security guard cast a flashlight upon them entangled in the cab of his old Chevy truck.

His eyes darted to his right. The hot cider and snacks were near at hand by the popcorn popper. A huge leaf licked one of the mugs. In front of the cider was a tray of cheeses, crackers, and sugarless jelly. His nervous stomach emptied the plate of crackers twice in anticipation.

He surveyed the twinkling lights overhead, strung that afternoon while George steadied the ladder on the fort's floor. The uppermost strings moved slightly in the evening breeze. "Overkill," he'd worried aloud.

"No, figure one string for each year you've been together as a couple," George reassured him as the ladder shook. Brian scaled another thirty feet above the platform as he draped the tree with electric glee, the extra strand for hope of the future, his own idea.

Over to his left was an emerald green vase so dark that one could barely see through it, with an array of sunflowers, baby's breath, and three roses. Two large white in full bloom and one baby rose of red.

Propped on a small ledge atop a limb was his old AM/FM cassette player from the days before CDs, having played reliably through years of construction sites. The places that small music box had traveled with them. The earliest was the first of his birthday excursions that they'd shared. Then the camping trips, bed and breakfast lodgings for her birthdays, and assorted weekend escapes. Passionate lovemaking, too.

He hit the start button when he saw her willowy figure begin to emerge out of the moonlight to be consumed by the shadow of this trusted old tree. The tape softly launched the words of Survivor among the leaves.

"I was living for a dream, loving for a moment.

Taking on the world, that was just my style.

Then I looked into your eyes, the search was over.

You were with me…all the while."

He ran his hand over his chin, not often he shaved at night. His face still tingled. Although cozy in his maroon sweats, he drew the comforter up to his neck only to release it in an attempt to appear relaxed. He reclined on his right elbow against a large branch, having attempted more posed positions in practice than imaginable. All this reran through his mind, and the door was just now opened. He placed a small flower in his teeth, biting through the stem as the crown of his favorite blonde appeared.

Allison had lost track of the well-placed songs, unaware of the time he'd invested in producing the lengthy taped serenade, one to greet her and another for the tree house. The exquisite and multiple surprises since removing the sunflower flooded her senses.

The other side of the circle for Brian was the tension that had resided in him all day. No release, no period of relaxation. He'd rather make the attempt and blow it than lose her from no attempt at all. Losing her and being incomplete, incomplete and broken from not giving his all.

Grasping the top of the trapdoor, he laid it horizontally against the floor. She appeared so radiant that he felt he could've seen her without the glimmer of the sparkling lights. Her green eyes outsparkled anything mortal man could create.

She crossed her arms as she rested upon the edge of the floor opening, playfully placing her chin on top of her forearm. Her bare freckled shoulders were peaking out, slightly forward. Allison's mood was high, her robe low. He could now see the slight freckles across her nose as her smile appeared. Her eyes glanced to the drinks as her right hand reached out. "Is there room up here for two?"

"Have you a reservation, Mademoiselle?" he asked in his worse French accent.

"I've more than that," she played along. No accent could be more seductive than her voice. God, he loved her voice. "I have a private invitation from the gifted young architect of this lofty hide-away." With that, she pulled her robe back over her shoulders to finish her climb.

He was mesmerized by her moves and she coyly accepted his stare. Brian was loyal, but the first one to admit he enjoyed the looks of a fine woman. She was glad to still be appreciated. He held his right palm out as she placed her hand in his to climb up. Her accent turned Southern with, "Well, thank you, sir." Once her hips were level with the floor, she pivoted and delicately sat to his right on the floor's edge.

Lifting her legs up, her robe fell open. He used to tell folks that she had legs that went all the way to her elbows. He was remembering their first night of becoming one. She caught his glance as she turned, leaving the trapdoor opening clear. She was surprised to feel the blush rise in her own face. *Freckle blending*, he called it.

Releasing her hand, he lifted the door to close it. The romantic flickering lights illuminated all the colors in her hair. She flipped it over her left shoulder, exaggerating it out of mischief rather than sensuality. She knew ladies who flipped their hair weren't high on his list. As she turned toward her suitor, she leaned her head so her hair hung down naturally curling on the floor. This, she knew, drove Brian wild, as evidenced by his sweat pants.

He loved her hair. He loved her body. She treated her body like a temple rather than a pup tent. Her hair was like the grains of sand on the beach, each strand a shade different. Thank goodness there was no orange for he could never rhyme that.

In days gone by, he often woke next to her and with the gentlest care rearranged her hair upon her pillow. When he was over-stressed, she dusted his face with her long, thick locks until he drifted off to sleep. She began with the bridge of his nose, his eyebrows, his eyelids, his lips. And when he wasn't stressed, lying naked across his entire body.

Allison studied the fort as if for the first time, marveling at the way he wasted nothing. First on their block to begin formal recycling, finding uses for the things others saw as scrap wood and trash lumber. Behind his right shoulder the narrow shelf made from the last piece of plywood, left over from the narrow three-foot-wide catwalk he'd built in a rectangle to loop around the girth of the tree. Even the small shelf was decorated tonight and hosted a popcorn popper, plugged into an orange extension cord.

She looked toward the rustic railing made from the branches he taught her to strip of bark. Notched with leather ties. He'd insisted on using fallen branches and hated using new lumber even in their business. He felt wood, or a tree, had a life and deserved an honorable legacy. "Life resides in everything, even in plants and rocks," he'd said.

The base of the tree house consisted of two full 4-by-8 sheets of one-inch plywood, arranged into an L-shape with a triangular piece joining the corner. She remembered her surprise at the way that the image formed in his head with no drawings. And the funny pieces of hardware, such as hidden hinges, S-hooks, nylon rope, and pulley, all with the purpose of making this leafy fortress more special.

Behind her a natural wall was created by the two large trunks, each almost ten feet around. The blanket was sewn from old blue jeans. He tossed the edge back across the closed trapdoor, now serving as part of the floor. She smoothed the denim, remembering the mountains it had covered on their picnics, the sensual moments it had embraced, the new baby it had caressed. She smiled as she recalled his insistence on flat hinges.

"There's room over here," motioned Brian as he unfolded the second comforter. His voice was now natural. He was conscious of the importance of the moment and wanted to be real. Fun but real, not hiding behind his humor was a new path for him.

"I hope I can say the words," she began nervously, "so it comes out right."

"Just speak from your heart," he coaxed. "You can. I've heard you."

Her eyes darted a bit. If she listened to her inner self, her words would come honestly from her heart. "You just seem different, not that I want you to change," she faltered.

"I have to change, fix these character flaws I found, if we're ever going to keep our marriage intact and make it flourish. It isn't a change for you or Benny. It's stuff I don't like in myself. The change is for me, and then us."

His words left her less vulnerable as she spoke. "You seem different. As if you aren't acting like you're on stage or selling yourself. Am I making any sense?"

His behavior was changing because his way of thinking was changing. Far from perfect but at least he knew he wasn't imagining his progress.

"I think George has been good for you. I like him and Daro, too. I see you and George talk, maybe because he's a stranger and easier to talk to sometimes."

"Yeah, but he doesn't feel like a stranger. Maybe he was just the teacher who surfaced once the student was ready." He bit into another cracker. "Since George and Daro didn't know me, maybe it was easier for me to be different around them."

"Maybe that different person is the Higher Self coming through. The real you." He wavered as his eyes moistened.

"Maybe the God in you is being allowed to shine, and maybe that's the way He lights the path. I think those two have been a blessing in our lives."

He stared deeper into her eyes. Never had he felt so vulnerable and so safe. "Is that what's happening with you and your mom? You two seem to be talking, really talking, more."

Her hands came to her lips as she gazed out at the fire pit, the wheels of Benny's bike, her wedding ring. The way the wooden fort circled the tree. All were circles. Then she put her head so far back, her hair touched the decking, exposing her neck. The stars, real and artificial, all separate, yet all offering light. "I'm working more diligently at seeing things from Mother's point of view. I may not agree or even understand but if I can see it, then I can drop some of my defenses and really communicate. As Daro thought, *I can understand yet not have to agree.*"

He hung his head, subtly wiping an eye before looking up. "You've been doing that with me lately. I see that now, and I really appreciate it. I see now the places where I've been doing some of that, too."

She chuckled nervously. "Mother, too. George got under her skin. We're both finding that as difficult as it is, it does become easier."

"I finally see I had a bad habit, making everyone wrong if they questioned me, thinking I, frankly, had to cover my ass. George said if I saved my spirit, my ass would follow." Their chuckle eased the tension.

She slid the snacks between them, creating snacks. First was a sandwich of two crackers with strawberry preserves and some mozzarella cheese. She placed it in Brian's mouth. His nip to her finger was gentle. He returned the favor by lifting her glass to her lips. Their eyes remained drinking in the other, long after her first sip.

Brian could hold the silence only so long. "I've been running again. Not that I expect to see any changes yet," as he did a false flex. Humor can live with spirit.

"Why?"

The question seemed innocent enough, once looked at from her point on the circle. Physical health and appearance would've been his answer a few weeks ago. That was no longer his truth.

"I found it was my prayer time, my questioning time, and my listening time. Rather than fighting with myself to sit and meditate,

I realized I needed to get back to what works. The physical part's just an added benefit. George worked with me and I found I was separating the two, making more work for myself. I finally saw I did that in several areas. As in prayer and meditation, I just don't sit well," he flinched.

"No kidding," she giggled.

His face showed slightly red again under the twinkling lights as he continued. "So the running satisfies my need to move while I use my mind."

"Which doesn't sit still either," she teased.

"Well, using it for spiritual thoughts rather than just problems focuses on linking my head and heart, and I forget about the chore of exercise."

Her face softened. For the past few days she'd succeeded in her daily ten minutes as Daro had challenged. Amazing results. It became her time to listen to herself. It cut her fear of being alone, by taking the whole idea of being alone to a higher level.

"Daro got me thinking," she began. "Are you game?"

His eyebrows rose in anticipation.

"Rather than just assuming we're going to see each other." Her nerves were showing, scared because she was about to ask for something directly rather than manipulate. The weight of her chain. "That is, what if we planned an evening alone, once a week, if that's not too much?" She was caving in but pushed onward. "Just us, so we could talk, as we're doing now. Compare thoughts from our meditations, your runs, even our dreams."

"Like a date?" Brian softly blurted.

All was silent, except in her head. The chink of the chain, the rustle of the ribbon. *Chink, rustle, chink.* "A date? Well, no." Color flushed her face. "Yes," she squealed. "Yes, I want a date. Just you 'n' me, once a week."

He saw her strength that he'd seldom witnessed. She fumbled

but took the risk and asked directly for the thing she wanted, and she went from a trot to a gallop before he could reply.

"A weekly date and maybe Mother could watch Benny. We could put some money aside in case we wanted to stay some place special."

"Whoa," he softly interrupted. "I don't see any way that would work."

Her smiling facade buried the cracks in her heart.

"I'm just concerned that we'd be asking too much of Lillian. She and Hughie, well, they seem to be kind of cozying up a bit. And, I don't want to be staying away when we have a beautiful home. I've missed it."

Allison looked puzzled.

"Besides, I already spoke to Denise and Jason. Since we gave him a raise and they got help with Rio's health care, he'll be spending more time at home. So they've agreed to keep Benny on those overnights," he added with a wink, a step ahead of her.

Time twinkled away beneath the lights. Both were surprised they had so much to talk about without mentioning the divorce. At one point, they merely gazed, talking through touch, blue eyes drinking in her emerald ones.

He found himself studying her as never before, memorizing every aspect before she was gone. Her eyes were deep, dark green lagoons beckoning him to dive into their depths.

Fingernails long enough to tease in a tickle but short enough to work with tools. Her hair grew in a light white-blonde from her temples in a way disguising the beginning of her hairline. Her eyes contained flecks of gold that matched her hair.

Allison gazed at his dark natural curls. His piercing blue eyes he credited to his mother, as well as the early gray strands woven throughout his hair. The scar in his hairline showed a bit more tonight, the memento received in high school during a tee-pee job gone awry when a low branch left him with his own knothole. The hair upon his chest was her personal favorite. She had to draw upon her memory. *Darn that tee shirt*, she thought.

"You know," she began, a phrase she hated. "I mean, I know." His laugh was an interruption as she joined him. "This is still going to take work. Okay if I share something I learned?"

His apprehensive look was apparent.

"It's okay. It's about me. I know I don't ask for things very well and I don't often speak directly. Like it was difficult for me to ask for our weekly date."

"I'm so glad, proud that you did. What was the change?"

She rolled her eyes to collect herself. "I began journaling. Surprised to see that half the time I didn't know the things I wanted, so it was pretty lame to think anyone else would know. And, not blaming her, some were due to habits I learned from Mother."

He nodded, careful not to sound judgmental.

"And in journaling, I found a way to listen to myself, and one of the big things I realized was I had all of this faith…"

"The thing I've sometimes lacked."

"All of this faith, and I was taking no action to fuel it. The praying, the meditating is helping, maybe as your runs help you."

People often have their own expectations, behaving in ways they hope others see or will believe them to be. The first is a shadow and the second is often false. Both actions are based on fear. That night the couple found the fearlessness to discuss their fears. Neither one tried to fix the other, save the other, or convince the other to adopt a new belief by saying how well something they were doing was working. They merely listened to each other, joined hands and minds and hearts as they journeyed to various points on the circle.

"Daro said to ask you about some website he showed you, some angel thing. I had no clue he could even turn on a computer."

She beamed as she reached into her pocket and unfolded the piece of paper. "Want to give this a try? Daro said he has a lady friend he calls his Colorado Dance Partner. Her name is Sydney and she created this exercise.

He was attempting to understand but only blinked.

"Daro said this Sydney does counseling and," she paused realizing she was explaining too much. "Oh, here you go." She flattened the paper. "There are four questions that are only to be used between two people very close and trusting."

He waited for the punch line.

"And willing to listen to the answers with no comments."

He grinned broadly. "Gotcha. Let's go for it. Who goes first?"

"Here they are. I printed them out, on faith," as she scanned the four questions. "*What are you thinking? What are you feeling? What haven't you told me?*" She paused. "This last one can be altered. *What do you love about me? Or about yourself? Or about today even?*" She tilted her head. "So, Monsieur, we do all four, and then switch, but no interruptions, okay? At the end of each answer, all the other can say is *Thank you.* Ready?"

He nodded slowly.

"Would you rather I go first?" She handed him the list.

He gazed down at it and saw the four folds in the paper, and the crunch it had received as a bit of a security blanket when she approached the fort that night. He felt her fear and bravery, but more so her openness. "So I ask each question, wait, and listen to each answer with no comment. Then go onto the next?"

Her nod was nervous.

He looked at the page. "Allison, *what are you thinking?*"

"I'm thinking, why on earth I went first," she laughed. "Wait. I want to answer these in the present, not in thoughts of the past or the future. If I answer that right now, I'm thinking that, that if we're doing this question-and-answer game, we do have a chance."

He wanted to speak, even to agree but successfully remained silent as he pushed onward. "Allison, *what are you feeling?*"

"Scared," followed by, "yet I'm less scared by admitting it."

"Scared," he breathed as he caught himself. "Allison, *what haven't you told me?*" Inside he was scared about the information he might be about to learn.

"Funny," she sighed. "I never thought to practice these questions on my own first. What haven't I told you? Give me a second."

Brian found silence difficult as if the clock moved slower in silence for him than for others. He looked up as her lips parted.

Her voice trembled. "I haven't told you...I looked for an apartment for Benny and me." He felt stabbed.

"I wasn't going to depend on my folks, so I've been looking for a place for Benny and me to live."

He remembered the rules and gulped back his fears and accusations. He scanned the possibilities for number four and opted for the first choice, figuring it must be the most important. Or maybe he wanted assurance. "Allison, *what do you love...about me?*"

Her face warmed. "Brian, I love that you have or at least show no fear even when I know you're scared to death. You may like to be the life of the party, but you don't hang in cliques, don't care if people accept you. You just care that you're true to you, and I love that trait."

He rolled his tongue against his lower lip as he handed her the sheet. He was scared to death and realized this was his call for a chance, to be scared to life.

"Wanna take a break?" she offered in her role as lifesaver. Before he could take advantage, though, she said, "Brian, *what are you thinking?*"

He blinked, thinking about his thoughts, wondering why he couldn't think of words for what he was thinking, and then he understood. "Right now, I'm thinking I don't know what I'm thinking. No, that's what I was thinking. I'm thinking that I want to be here in the now. In the now, answering these questions."

"Good," she slipped. "And…*what are you feeling?*"

"Guess I'm scared, too. Scared of losing you and Benny. No. Hell, I'm scared of losing myself. I'm scared I won't stay in the present, in life, won't stay open to the stuff I've learned."

She was finding this question-and-answer game more difficult than Daro had warned. She expected the worse with thoughts lingering that Brian no longer wanted her. "*What…haven't you told me?*"

He was having trouble seeing her through the tears in his eyes. Of late, he sure hadn't told her he loved her. Instead he blurted out, "What I haven't told you is the thing I won't tell anybody. That I need help, that I'm scared that I can't do it all myself."

Silence as they both blinked absently.

Then she asked…"*what do you love about yourself?*"

His mind skidded to a halt. He wanted her to ask it the way he'd asked her. He wanted to tell her the reason he loved her. He didn't want to talk about himself. Finally he blurted, "It may sound like bragging but I love I'm smart enough to know I love you and could never find someone I'd love more even if I wanted to. I love myself because I'm wise enough to tell you that if we work together, we can be together. I love myself because if you're willing to give me another shot, I won't give up and hide." He exhaled deeply. "Wise enough to suggest that we use this little game each week on our dates."

Nothing is wrong with having needs and asking for help rather than pretending to have all the answers, nothing weak about voicing one's shortcomings or flaws. It takes great courage to expose oneself to another's observations.

Serving fear is living a lie, supporting secrets. Expectations are often kept as secrets. Eventually, all secrets *secrete* as do infections. Exposing our fears means lancing them open. Energy once used to preserve secrets is released to serve in a higher vein, allowing us to hear our intuition, to see more clearly to move to the next level.

The white in her eyes showed as brilliantly as the star upon which he had wished. Just a touch of teal green in her right eye, some moss afloat in one of her pools. Generally her hair was locked behind one ear or the other, her left at the moment, due to the stroke of his hand. The tiny pierced holes in her earlobes had healed closed after she learned the acupuncture points, ending her sinus problems.

She loved his eyes. Even at the worst point in their relationship, she'd loved his eyes. Folks asked if they were really that blue. She'd been insecure when ladies, total strangers, complimented him. Right in front of her. Eventually, she learned he only had eyes for her. Windows to the soul, and his held many facets, his eyes speaking louder than words.

Many learned those blue gemstones retained great power. They could discipline and melt Benny with a single stare. Cut through the taunts of a bully, a verbal switchblade to his throat. Settle and reassure a new employee and lost child alike. And at times, cause her clothes to shed as a tree sheds leaves in autumn.

The cup clinked as he set the glassware down. His hand went for her shoulder. She reached for his hand and he feared he might've gone too far. She eyed his hands, bringing the fingertips to her mouth, suckling the ends. She laughed at the shudder it sent through his body.

The blaze in the fire pit below had been reduced to a small steady glow, not made for heat but for ambiance. Their minds were completely focused on each other or they might've realized that neither of them had built a fire that night.

"If I take this off," as she touched the tie to her robe, "do you think I'll be warm enough?" A subtle, yet polite, safe approach to inviting the arms of the man she trusted but arms that hadn't enfolded her for many months.

He glanced at the comforter and thought of the word. *Comforter. She had come to the fort. Come-fort-her. Comforter. Comfort her.* Then he blinked, wondering if his thoughts had kept him away from the moment too long as he placed a nervous arm out to her. So much was realized in silence, alone with each other's touch. He fought his urge to talk. Words and humor were the places he hid behind when scared. This risk, he wanted to see through to the end.

The thick comforters were more for atmosphere than necessity. Their bodies warmed each other. The heart can fan the flames of faith. And the lessons in awareness from the recent weeks continued to fuel their hearts.

The popcorn popper popped its last kernel. The cassette player played its last song. The fire pit offered up its last spark. No one noticed.

The nightingales bore silent witness to the unique love nest among the leaves. Few of the birds would've been able to see the details of the evening bloom of passion unfolding in the night air. And fewer still would've recognized the green nightgown as anything more than a large leaf as it drifted down, appropriately alighting on Brian's bicycle seat below.

CHAPTER FORTY-THREE

THE BOOKSTORE

FINDING A PARKING SPOT was never tough when George was with me. Some would say coincidence, much like the *coincidence* when we spied a full double rainbow the first day we hit Hinsdale, and a mailbox. He believed such a rainbow sighting was a prelude to good, almost magical happenings. Not sure what he got from the mailbox. Brian and I climbed out in the crowded parking lot. Jason would be dropping George off.

Entering the mall, we examined the brightly lit directory. A bold black *X* marked that we were *HERE*. I traced along the path, looking for a bookstore we could meet at later, and then we parted company. Brian had his own list. He was stuck buying makeup for Allison.

I stopped by a couple of other shops, first to buy some film for Allison. It was getting hard to find actual film anymore. The pungent odor of the film developer assaulted me before the chocolate aroma from an old-style See's Candies store lured me away. The white bag rustled as I pulled a second vanilla crème from it, slowly mashing it against the roof of my mouth, and turned the corner toward the bookstore to meet up with George and Brian.

I still have challenges with panhandlers. I stiffened as I neared the exterior of the storefront where the gaunt bearded man in a rust-colored poncho stood. I noted the cleanliness of the beggar as well as that of the two basset hounds patiently sitting at his feet. Rummaging in my wallet, finding no singles, I pulled out a Lincoln in preparation.

The towering lover of hounds turned toward me with a smile. Before even offering a nod, I held the five-dollar bill out with, "I don't have any change."

"Certainly," countered the homeless man who grasped the fiver and handed the limp leashes to me. He quickly made change with four crisp singles and the appropriate mix of shiny quarters, dimes, and a nickel. "Here you go, sir. Peaceful day," he beckoned as he grasped the leashes again.

Man. My eyelids blinked as if sending Morse code in my attempt to recover from my faux pas. Outside this bookstore, I certainly should not have judged that book by its cover. I thanked the tall fellow, then luckily found a pay phone and pretended to make a call with the change. Finishing my act, I mouthed another *thank you* and walked into the bookstore.

Two aisles over, I glanced at a book about birds and rolled my eyes as I saw the *Firemen's Hot Calendar. Every good fireman can handle a piece of hot ash* had been my motto. Spying copies of *Arizona Highways* and *True West* Magazine, I felt at home, settling into one of the store's easy chairs.

TRYING TO HIDE THE HOT PINK BAG from Victoria's Secret, Brian walked a few aisles over.

George was bent over in an aisle below a sign designating *Motivational.* His eyes scanned the bookshelves, a multitude of colors and titles flashing before his eyes. Aloud, he ran his finger across the authors' names on the bindings. "M. M-A. M-A-N. M-A-N-D. There you are," as he kneeled lower. His shoulders seemed even broader due to the bulk created by his olive flak jacket. With his index finger, he flipped out three different pocket books covering the colors of the American flag. Then he reached for an adjacent hardcover trimmed in gold mustard with white panels.

With the bag folded as small as possible, Brian went to find a clerk, hoping to find a book on writing poetry. He noticed a man intently watching George, two aisles over.

The elderly gentleman looked rather dapper. He had a high forehead. What white hair that remained was parted on the left and cut fairly short with a few dark hairs shadowed near his temples. Clean-cut although a day's growth of whiskers peeked from his chin, clad in a collarless Perry Ellis shirt that was woven in black, tan, and white checks. An alpaca jacket of tan hung loosely over his long arms. The brown Italian loafers moved deliberately without making a sound. Pausing behind George, the man reached down to place a massive hand firmly upon his shoulder. Brian moved an aisle closer.

The touch startled George, glancing at the hand upon his shoulder and then up the long arm to the owner. From his point of view, the man looked even taller than six-feet-one. Silver-rimmed glasses with rectangular lenses framed the piercing blue eyes.

"George Valmore Mazen. How are you?" His smile turned impish as he eyed the books. "I see you still have good taste in your reading materials." As two smiles of recognition exploded, Brian wandered away, giving them their space.

Placing his left hand atop the gentleman's hand that still rested upon his shoulder, George turned clockwise as he rose, never breaking physical or eye contact, obviously thrilled at this chance meeting. "And what brings you here, my friend?"

"Some unfinished business around Chicago, and I never could pass a library or a bookstore. How has it been for you?" The question was one of a concerned nature.

"I still take it one day at a time. Certainly enjoying the caseload, but this one seems different. This is unlike any of my other assignments."

"Are you placing judgments or expectations on this one?" queried his elderly friend with a tilt of his head.

"No, no." George paused, uncertain about himself. "Just anxious for the outcome, I reckon. I'm anxious to see where the story takes me and where it ends." He looked into the gentle eyes. "Why? Do you know something?"

A sly dimpled grin accompanied the smile lines on the gentleman's face. "If I did, would I be at liberty to tell you? And far be it for me to divulge the way a book concludes, without telling the story. Where would that leave me?"

"Where, indeed. And where *have* you been? I always wondered how it was when you awoke."

"Actually it was quite peaceful. And, a shorter lag time than most. What is time anyhow?"

George grimaced ever so slightly.

"I left there as I arrived here, embraced in love. Left in the arms of my gal at departure. Then Simon was waiting to greet me and he even had Slippers with him. Seems he and Lazarus were watching over my old buddy until I arrived. Those two pooches make quite a pair." His long fingers squeezed through the padded jacket to the younger mate's shoulder. "I understand your trip hasn't been as smooth."

George forced a smile loosely as he shook his head slowly to the side. "Much seemed like a dream. Some, more like a fog. Guess even now I'm learning patience as I look for answers to questions. Repeating some of your exercises helps, and I work to instill *right thoughts, right action,* striving *to remember to remember.*"

"How goes it with your sidekick, your student?"

"I'm often his student. It's interesting that as he learns, I gain clarity. I enjoy the ongoing contact. It used to be that I'd have a project and then move on. Having Daro assisting me creates an ongoing project within the projects. I can see when he actually learns by putting things into practice or just resorts to a band-aid."

The gentleman retracted his hand and smiled knowingly. "To break a habit, one must replace it with a good one, can't leave a hole or a vacuum."

George agreed with a tap of the pocket books against his friend's sturdy chest.

The man continued, "I just wish more of the AA folks would opt for habits of juice and exercise over coffee and cigarettes."

"What's this?" George animated his eyes. "Is that judgment and expectation I hear from The Great…"

"The great who?"

Curiosity had the better of Brian and his voice startled them with the interruption. He thrust his hand forward to greet the stranger.

George stuttered an introduction. "The Great... The Great. That's it. Just, The Great."

He looked warily at George, his hand still hanging in the air. "Hello, The Great. I'm Brian, Brian Poppy, The Mediocre," he smiled.

The man was almost offended. "You aren't mediocre; you're one of God's greatest miracles, and He doesn't make mediocre ones." His sincerity sent a chill through Brian. The touch of his hands, cupping the left one over the top, encased his hand completely. The warmth and gentleness were akin to a hug. Enormous strength resided in this man some years his senior, yet all he could identify was simple love.

"And, does The Great have a formal name?" Brian's hand was still encased and keenly aware of George's eyes doing a volley between the two of them.

George tried to shake off his uneasiness, mystified by the calmness with which his tall friend was handling this unexpected meeting and the resulting inquiry. He shuffled in his combat boots. "Name? Oh, his name. This is, well, you're Brian Poppy. Of course, you already said that. This is..."

The gentleman calmly intervened. "Augustine. Mr. Augustine."

"Riiiiight," sighed George as he placed himself behind them, blocking the section of books in which he had been searching. "This is Mr. Augustine."

"And how do you and George know each other, Mr. Augustine?"

The gentleman calmly replied in a mild New England accent. "He and I worked together once. Actually, I recruited him for a type of team I was assembling. Turned out later, we had a mutual friend."

George nervously toyed with the safety pin beneath his lapel. "What type of business did you have?"

"Environmental reclamation."

Evidently, Mr. Augustine knew Brian wouldn't be satisfied with less, so he continued confidently. "We dealt with the masses, that is to say, mass material. Items that others discarded, we retrieved and salvaged." The man employed his large hands in gesture. "We... searched out their value. We...assisted in finding proper use for them again." His eyebrows rose momentarily above his silver rims.

"Have we met? Should I know you? You look like someone I might've seen."

"That's quite possible as we're all connected, a part of the chain and deeper, a part of the ribbon within. A research study found that we are all within three people of knowing everyone. For example, do you know any of the Presidents or anyone who does?"

With a roll of his eyes and feeble attempt at humor, Brian replied, "No, they had the wrong address when they mailed my invitation to their Inaugurations."

The statuesque fellow was conditioned to people using humor when entering the unknown. "You are within three people of knowing *any* of the past living presidents. Many such associations are already shared between you and me, of which we are unaware. In this case, I know a couple, so you are only one person away. And others in your life further verify this theory. You may not realize it, but you know several other people within three, two, or even one person of knowing each of the living Presidents intimately."

"Does this thing work with others? Like with Sandra Bullock...or Taylor Dayne...or Leann Rimes or the Playmate of the Month?"

"You have five questions," was the immediate response. "The answer to the first one is 'Yes,' most assuredly."

"And to the others?"

"Regarding do I know the ladies you mentioned? The answer is..." His reply was cut short by the saleslady.

"Here is the book you requested, Sir."

A warm welcoming smile radiated from his face. Brian saw the author's name on the binding. *Thoreau.*

The saleslady turned to Brian and continued. "And the books about which you inquired are over here!"

Before he turned away, he extended his hand again. "Nice to meet you, real nice, Mr. Augustine." Then he followed as the lady led him to another aisle.

"How long will you be staying in Chicago?" asked George.

"Actually, I'm leaving now," responded the kindly man.

"I thought you had a project to complete."

The benevolent eyes softened even more as his gaze spilled over him. "I did. It was just conducted, and concluded, in this bookstore."

George nodded, suddenly understanding. "We're never alone."

"Let's just say, we were all concerned about you, my friend. Time is meaningless. Sometimes merely one gentle word turns the tide, which fortifies the faith. Faith is important to the teacher as well as the student," he winked.

George felt as if everyone knew the unfolding script but him. Knowing that the elder's project was concluded, he realized their time to visit in their new world was limited. He asked about the next project for the older gentleman.

"Well, thanks to you, I finished here early. And after more than a quarter of a century of airports, I rather enjoy this astral travel we are sometimes allowed."

"Is Bette still raking in those Blue Ribbons?"

The older man beamed at the mere mention of her name. "My gal is still the best at quilting, and still watching out for everyone. Now she's becoming a film producer and public speaker, all about her time with some old fly boy out of World War II. And, I had a hand in directing a fine gent into her life."

He ran his fingers over the cover of the book the saleslady had handed him, clutching it tightly to his breast. "Damn, I'm proud of that lady." Emotions were thick in the air as he shook his head and continued. "Now, for my quick sojourn to Arizona. It's pleasant to be in a place where time is everything…and nothing."

"The boys?" queried George.

"Well, they still have a little trouble yet, even still, with the thought of their mum having a new beau.   Poor Matt, he wouldn't give Jesus a chance to date his mother."

Both laughed heartily. "Other than that, the boys are doing great," as he beamed a perfect row of pearly teeth again. "Up North, Dana is always coaching or playing soccer when he isn't re-computerizing the company for which he works. Wish he'd go hit some balls for me," as he imitated a golf swing. "Carole's nailed her doctorate for her college degree, bless her heart. Danielle is writing poetry and growing up too quickly. She and Grandmom could double-date. Ryan is shooting up like a weed with a great sense of humor and playing in a band."

George visualized the ripples of love carrying this man's seed.

"And Matt and Lori are dealing with their family growth in Colorado. Now our marketing mastermind son is assisting a huge homebuilder, oversees three states. He still races around as he did when he was a tyke on his trike, pretending he's Parnelli Jones on the flat track when he has a chance. Not too popular a pastime with Lori.

"Lori's mother and I take turns visiting with William and Ben since they're almost past the age of still choosing to hear us. Their grandmother Carolyn has acclimated really well, doing lots of good for folks. We've done two projects together but this upcoming assignment I have in Scottsdale is a solo one. It's something to do with another writer, but that's all the information I know."

Brian returned with a couple books as he saw the two embrace with unguarded love, unconcerned if patrons witnessed their display. They released each other, and tears glistened in George's eyes. Both raised the books they held and bumped them together as if it were a toast using a fine aged wine. Books are the best of spirits.

The elderly gentleman turned and whispered, "Take care, Babe."

Softly George returned, "You too, Sir, and give Margaret my love."

"Who's Margaret?" Brian asked.

"His mother."

"His mother. Wow. That's great. She still alive?"

George didn't answer.

"You must have learned a bunch from that gentleman." Brian began to fish. "Quick, top of your head, what lessons did you learn from him?"

A mischievous grin followed as he turned slowly. Without a moment's hesitation and absolutely no stumbling with his words, "Begin a new life, greet everyone I meet with love, persist until I succeed, remember I'm a miracle, live as if this day is my last, master my emotions, laugh at myself, constantly increase my own worth, take action rather than procrastination, and pray." Then he turned and headed for the register.

Conversations with George often left a person speechless.

Standing at the cash register, neither noticed as Mr. Augustine took one of the dog leashes from the old man outside the bookstore and walked off with their two basset hounds in loyal pursuit.

CHAPTER FORTY-FOUR

HOT DAMN AND HALLELUJAH

MONDAY MORNING WAS a Norman Rockwell spring day. The air was crisp and clean, everything vivid and clear. Even the birds were enjoying the weather. We were in the shadow of the garage, having attached the trailer so that after work we could pick up the antiques from the Smith house. First, however, we had to load some left-over bricks for a job site. Working in assembly-line fashion, we were almost finished when George pointed to the blue heron making a low swoop over the house.

I looked up and then found myself staring at a red brick in my hand. "So why do we place a higher value on these old used bricks than we do on old people?" I was having one of my astute moments.

He was visibly impressed and surely would've entered into an exploratory chat had Lillian not come running out of the house in full trot. Her heels echoed on the wooden porch and then clattered once on the cobblestone walk. What was most impressive was that her feet never touched the stairs. She vaulted from the porch to the pavement. If not for the radiant smile on her face, we'd have been worried. I caught her moments before she'd have tumbled to the ground, the force jarring my cap off.

A giddy, "Stop," was all we could translate as she made no effort to conceal her glee. Her arms flapped with sporadic phrases. "Forget the truck, forget bricks, unload the bricks, take the truck."

Grasped the words, yes; comprehended them, no.

As I zeroed in on her, she caught her breath, burst into giggles again and planted a playful slap on my chest. "Oh, and make sure you take the big trailer. Brian says you have to retrieve something extra from the Smith's place."

We finally slowed her down enough to learn we were to swing by Brian's apartment for his belongings and retrieve some boxes from the office storage before driving to the Smith's farmhouse.

Taking a second for her words to register, I turned to George with a huge grin. "His apartment. His stuff! Brian's coming home!" I bear-hugged the lady spinning her in a circle before setting her down and bursting into laughter.

"Here're the instructions. Oh my, where did I put…"

"It'll be okay, Lillian," George said, laughing. "I know where the Smith place is. Brian already told me."

She smacked me in the chest again. "Allison says they decided that if they can build a successful company together, they can certainly grow a successful family." She began to race away but remembered more and spun around in a tight circle, "And besides, they build beautiful babies!"

As I turned to George, she leapt forward grabbing my ears to pull my head down and planted a solid kiss on me. The last we heard above the clattering shoes was that everyone was in store for a celebration dinner that night.

We unloaded the bricks in quick fashion, the old clay breaking on a couple of them. I brushed the stubborn red dust off my jeans, beaming with success at the image of Allison and Brian reuniting. "Piece of cake," got me a third chest slap from George. It was difficult not to smile.

Arriving at Pendley Place Apartments, we found Brian's, designated by a metal number three on the door. The two-bedroom was clean and spacious. It was going to be easier to load his belongings than we'd figured as much had remained in cartons. His heart hadn't been in moving into his own place. He knew keeping his spirits up was important, so he went for an apartment with a fireplace, lots of windows, and a room for his study and meditation. However, after three months, that room still served mainly as storage.

Only able to bring himself to deal with so much at one time. Most of his belongings still remained with Benny and Allison. Neither of them had found divvying up personal items easy, certainly not enjoyable. Few evenings went by in his apartment without some beeswax candles offering warmth via their simple glow. He'd switched to beeswax, knowing no petroleum was used in their production, more healthful for the environment. Hypocritical to think maybe he could sustain the world when he couldn't help himself.

He'd brought only a handful of books from his collection, arriving one book at a time when he remembered one that might provide an answer for his tumultuous life. Most recently he'd pulled Bach's *Nothing by Chance*, after noting some of the unusual coincidences surrounding the arrival of his two new employees, their new friends. Us.

His lack of unpacking was evidence that his heart wasn't into the split. Personal items were on the slim side as so many brought reminders of Allison and Benny, reminders of his failure and loss. Once they offered comfort, but now they inflicted pain.

On the mantle was a small 5-by-7 close-up of Benny shot at a cabin after Allison had scrubbed the child in a metal washtub. The tip of Oöso's pink nose was peeking into view. There was a shot of Allison in a green-yoked shirt, holding Benny. Brian had used scissors to remove himself surgically from the image. Subconsciously for him, it was easier not seeing himself in a family scene, one to be nevermore.

The narrow vertical frame holding four black-and-white images were pictures of Brian's mother. Matted in charcoal gray, the photographs were ones of her at age eight, posed for school; age seventeen, graduating from Decatur High School; age twenty-something, in her dress uniform of the United States Marines; and finally, one made three weeks before the fateful surgery. He felt he'd come so far since her death, but now felt more alone and a bigger flop than ever before.

Another photo revealed a tiny hand with sausage fingers clenching the smallest finger of a feminine hand. The wedding ring on the lady's hand identified them as Benny and Allison. In their first mother-and-son portrait, he proved less than cooperative. Finally in frustration, Brian had them take a shot merely of their hands. To the dismay of the salesman, it was the only photo they purchased.

As I started out the door with an armload of Brian's clothes, I was confronted by the manager. Reddish beard, wire-rimmed glasses, and striped suspenders. At first, I figured he was concerned about the reason we were in Brian's apartment, a situation I'd let George explain since we'd neglected to bring a key. Although the rent was paid a month in advance, the landlord only saw the matter from his point on the circle; a move out months before the end of the lease.

My attempted reasoning didn't work with him and my assurance of a win-win situation fell on deaf ears. Tilting my cap back on my head, my anger rose to the surface. "What's the matter? Someone take the red off your apple?"

George approached. With a gentle touch of his hand to the irate manager's shoulder, the leathery face softened, introducing himself as Foster Pendley.

"I get a little short-fused when folks skip out after trashing the place. I know that Brian fellow isn't like that. I just have lotsa repairs to do. Frankly, I hoped I could enlist his help." A complete shift of energies had occurred as he offered to help load the truck.

Passing with my arms full, I breathed low to George, "Love it when you do that."

It was evident Brian had hit Target or K-Mart. Matching green for the kitchen, dish- drainer, sink stopper, towel holder, trash can. Blue for the toiletries, bathmat, towels, tissue holder, and various articles. They were a far cry from the personal touches he and Allison had in their home.

Soon after moving out, he'd invited her for dinner. She left him two mementos as a surprise. Large half seashells they'd gathered in Benny's bucket from a sandy beach. They'd used one as a soap holder and the other as an incense tray. He thought of her each time he reached for the soap or lit some sandalwood. And the memory pained him.

He couldn't separate the memory, yet couldn't bring himself to put the items out of view, so he opted to take no more chances on her leaving surprises by not inviting her anymore. Had she only known, and had he only told her, that her loving gesture pained him. So both figured the other one was faring better at this separation. George could read all of this heartache with the mere touch of his fingers to the shell. The pain was unnecessary, brought on by Brian's choice to remain silent, pain that could have been avoided merely by speaking to the other person. Just by living the truth.

I dropped a carton in the hall and announced, "Here's one for the towels." Brian said to deliver all the linens and kitchen and bath stuff to The Luna Homeless Shelter."

Mr. Pendley noted the care with which George lovingly folded the towels, neatly packing them in the box. The landlord unaware, I knew George was bestowing a prayer on each item, a blessing to the souls of each downtrodden recipient. As he ran a finger along a fluffy blue towel, I passed with the last of the clothing.

I returned and stepped into the bathroom with a small box. "S'cuse me," I pulled open the medicine cabinet. Lifting the glass shelf out and tipping it over the box, I allowed the items to slide freely. "Hair mousse, shaving cream, deodorant. Check." Grabbing the next shelf, "Nail clippers, floss, more deodorant, eye-contact solution. Check." Then the last shelf, "Toothpaste, razor, hairbrush. Check."

"Nice job, Daro" as he rolled his eyes and handed me the shampoo from the shower. "Want to begin on the kitchen?"

Folding the last of the linens, came the clatter of cans and plastic jars. "Okay, George, the kitchen pantry's finished. Counter only had a blender, some Arbonne shake stuff, and his Murad vitamins. At least he's smart there but in the fridge is only leftovers and... Yowzer! These are pretty ripe. I'll trash 'em."

With most of Brian's belongings still in boxes and Mr. Pendley supplying assistance, the truck was quickly loaded. The bed and entertainment center would require another trip as we had to save room for the stuff from the farmhouse.

The landlord walked us out, expressing some concern about

re-renting the place, apologizing as he admitted he was just plain sorry Brian was leaving.

George was reassuring him that he'd have little trouble finding a tenant and that the Poppy's would honor the contract until rented. Then I subtly nudged my buddy after sliding behind the steering wheel as I saw a stocky man in an NFL jacket walking up the drive.

He nodded at us. Then the biker nervously thrust his hand forward to Mr. Pendley. "A pretty blonde lady driving a Pathfinder told me you might have a place to rent, possibly even a furnished place. I have no references. I been staying at a bed and breakfast."

George leapt into introductions, joining their hands together. "Foster Pendley, this is Erle Pylett. He's new to town but the Poppy family will vouch for him. He'll be working at Fussy Hazel's, the bed 'n' breakfast that Brian's company will be remodeling."

A broad smile sprang to Mr. Pendley's face. "That's good enough for me." Unexpected kindness can unnerve the biggest man. I found the scenario most amusing as I watched in the side-view mirror.

Sheepishly, Erle began to question the owner about necessary deposits but George countered. "Erle here's quite a handyman and might be useful with those repairs."

George turned to the bewildered man. "There's also a full-sized bed we couldn't fit in the trailer. It only has a couple months' mileage on it. I know the Poppy family wouldn't mind if you used it. Merely needs some sheets. TV and stereo are still in there, too."

I decided this scene was too much fun watching the heart of the landlord open, coupled with the confusion of the Harley-less biker receiving so much good so I selected a couple of boxes.

"Pardon *moi*. This saves us a trip. Here's a box with some towels and a set of sheets for the bed. Some other stuff, too. They're all yours," as I loaded one into the overwhelmed arms of the newest resident of Hinsdale.

Erle went to speak but nothing came from his mouth.

George left a gracious goodbye with Mr. Pendley and his new tenant, then winked at me as we bounced back into the truck. "Nice touch with the towels, Daro."

"Nice touch with the doubletalk, George Valmore." By the time we made a slow loop around the parking lot, Mr. Pendley was leading Erle to number three, guiding him in a fatherly manner, his hand resting on the biker's broad shoulders.

Erle looked over his shoulder, his mind in overdrive. "Who *are* those guys?"

Our second stop had us heading for the construction yard where we attached one of the small flatbed trailers to a second truck. This way, we could load the boxes from storage in the first with Brian's apartment things, then head to the Smith's farmhouse with the second. I opened the huge garage-style door to the musty storage unit, surveying the area. The dust irritated my eyes. "There's too much stuff in here. How on earth we gonna know what goes and stays?"

His glance made me wish I could retract the statement. It made sense then for him to pull the cartons and me do the grunt work loading them. Typical. After a couple trips, I asked, "You sure this is all Brian's?"

"I'm only pulling the things he'll want," he said, running his palms about an inch over the sealed tops of various boxes. Those that he selected had been sealed, using entire rolls of tape.

The truck loaded, I hopped in the other rig and followed to the farmhouse. I puzzled over the instructions that Lillian had finally given me as we pulled over by a large weathered barn. I continued to study the map, though maps are not my specialty, and looked all around the area. Nothing made sense. One building was apparent, a peaked barn with a tumbled-down silo. Slats had fallen away in many places, and the once red-stained wood was now a gray brown.

He pulled up next to me as I parked across the brick drive. "Hey, George, I'm surprised Brian didn't buy these old bricks. We should tell him. Maybe come back and haul them away."

Steering around an old mailbox with yellow paint chips and *343 Sunrise Avenue* barely visible, he pulled along the barn. The large sliding doors had rusty hardware with webs glistening in the sun.

"Here's the key, Daro."

"Sure this is it?" I glanced at the colored keys, surprised that the padlock opened easily. "I thought there was a huge farmhouse. From the looks of that foundation, hasn't been a house here in fifty to a hundred years."

Dusk was nearing when we arrived at the Poppy home with both trucks. It provided an ideal veil so we were able to park one next to the garage unnoticed. Making sure the Pathfinder was gone I backed the other truck in and we pushed the trailer into the garage and closed it. Lights gleamed brightly, lawn manicured. The home seemed to leap off the cover of *Phoenix Home & Garden* Magazine.

Brian had successfully concocted a story with MJ that necessitated Allison's return to the office. He ran onto the porch rushing us. "Hurry, she just left. Unload it so Hughie and I can set it up. We already have the other one out of there."

His father-in-law had joined us for dinner and Justin was staying over while his folks flew to Phoenix Childrens Hospital with Rio. There were plenty of helping hands available, including Benny's, whose lack of carrying capabilities went unnoticed due to the glow of the son seeing his daddy returning home. The excitement was even evident to Oöso who managed to squeeze in and out of the flow of people, sustaining only one stepped-on paw and a few near misses of her tail in the door.

Brian assigned Benny the job of being in charge of Oöso. George walked up to the dog, eye level as she leaned out from the porch, and uttered a few words as he caressed her white head. From her resulting actions, had people not known better, they'd have suspected George had instructed Oöso to take charge of the boy-child.

I knew the truth. Not as much slipped by me anymore.

CHAPTER FORTY-FIVE

THE LONG GOODBYE

THE MOOD IN THE POPPY HOME was one of unbridled joy. Bouquets of flowers brought the colors of the garden inside. We used the entrance through the dining room to join the rush before Allison returned home.

While Hughie and Brian broke a sweat carrying things upstairs, George and I attacked all nine gritty cartons along with those from his apartment. The heavily taped cardboard was cool to the touch. We placed them next to the window seat of the French-paned alcove in the living room, the regular spot for the Christmas tree. It was an ideal setting to release memories and contents to a world of renewed love. Taking care to wipe them clean with a cloth on the porch, he brought the dustiest boxes in last.

Brian was now the complete opposite in his behavior, almost overboard as he shared his fears openly about surprising Allison. The tension was breaking more sweat on him than the labor. Actually it was a toss-up about who was more nervous, Brian or Lillian. The general consensus favored Lillian because she kept secrets so poorly.

When Allison returned, her own excitement of her family reunited kept her from catching the obvious suggestions to go upstairs. Suggestions to freshen up, change her slacks, help put away Brian's clothes, all went by the wayside.

"I've an idea," I grinned at George.

"I'm afraid to guess," he winced.

So much for forgive and forget, I thought as I turned my attention to the boys and whispered. "Come on, you two. Let's have you guys play in Benny's room until dinner's ready." The little boy bounded ahead as Justin and I joined from behind, the stairs echoing like hollow drums.

A few minutes later, I returned and cast a wink at the men. On cue, the happy voice of Benny began. "Momma, Momma, c'mere. C'mere. Mom-m-m-a."

"What's that about? Brian, would you check on him?"

"Gosh, Hon, sounds like he really wants you," he flustered in reply.

"I'll go," was Lillian's response, surprising us all.

Hughie caught his wife and rolled his eyes to tip her of her faux pas. "Oh, you'll have to go, Allison," as she abruptly ducked into the bathroom.

Allison shrugged her shoulders, as the child's happy voice grew louder and more impatient. When she reached the first landing, her mother peeked out from the bathroom.

We controlled our chuckles and once she was upstairs, trotted to the stairway. Then we crowded upstairs to be outside their bedroom door. Jason kept Oöso from jumping into bed with Benny.

The wait was momentary, mere seconds before Allison's squeal was joined by Oöso's bark. Lonn and Bessie's former bed was stretching its posts toward the ceiling. Benny was on the bed wearing his mom's patch-work robe, bouncing as he clapped his little hands together in glee, the draping of the gauze canopy swaying.

She ran her hand gingerly up the mahogany posts almost eight feet tall, her mouth opened but only silence came forth. The floral comforter from their former bed fit perfectly. The crowd parted for Brian to receive a loving embrace.

"No time for a road test," cracked Hughie to his wife's dismay. "It's dinner time." Benny and Justin ran for the stairs with Oöso's paws clicking across the floor.

Dinner proved to be a celebration despite the phone calls. The first was their neighbors' call from the Phoenix Childrens Hospital in Arizona…in tears. Both Jason and Denise were on the line with news about the diagnosis of the tumor behind Rio's eye.

Surgery for the baby was still scheduled, but none of the medical specialists could explain the findings. The latest opinion supported by complicated tests, rechecked three times, diagnosed Rio as having a non-carcinoma blood clot. Translation? While the young baby would still lose his eye, the degree of surgery and concern for additional complications associated with cancer were alleviated. Virtually vanished.

The word *miracle* escaped the lips of the medical community and mother alike, echoed by all receiving the news at the homestead. Justin leapt into my arms as I staggered backward, regaining my footing. I saw George shared in the joy but was avoiding eye contact. It appeared as if this diagnosis was news to all, except him.

Another phone call came toward the end of dinner, slightly dampening the festivities. It was for George. He took the receiver, leaving me a bit bewildered although used to surprises around my compadre. The conversation left little to the imagination. When Lillian heard the mention of a UPS package, she dashed with embarrassment to the animals' shelf and laid the cardboard envelope addressed to *George Valmore Mazen* by his plate. He nodded but didn't elaborate until he returned to the table. The disappointment of the family was obvious and for me, too, kind of.

Apparently, or allegedly, once we went to work for them, George had given their number in connection with us delivering the car. And in order to honor that agreement, we had to leave that evening. All talk to reconsider was thwarted when he explained it away as a prior commitment and that delivery of the classic car was slated for a surprise to a young man, necessitating a specific date of delivery. Following dessert and hasty packing, we'd load our simple belongings into the Mustang and hit the highway.

"This way will be better," as he looked towards the cartons. "Opening those boxes is just for the family." With a smile, he looked into Brian's moist eyes. "Enjoy the now, creating the memory of your first night home."

Allison saw Justin fidget about spending the night. "It's all right. You're family."

The celebration meal appropriately included mashed taters. After the kids and I inhaled several helpings, Lillian picked up the empty bowl as if it were a trophy, proclaiming proudly that the mashed potatoes were made by Allison.

While I enjoyed the announcement of dessert turning out to be Devil's Food cake, George had the last laugh when Lillian placed the large chocolate cake in front of me, decorated with a small mailbox that Allison had scoured the toy stores to find. Even Benny and Justin squealed at the joke. Pure coincidence it was our last meal together. *God Wink*, I thought.

George excused himself early from the table with a subtle look to me to ensure I keep everyone entertained. I deserve a B.S. degree in BS-ing. Upstairs in the guestroom, he easily unzipped his satchel, removing the bag of books he'd purchased, stacking three pocket books on top of two hard covers.

Pulling his pen from his pocket, he inscribed four of the five books on behalf of us both. Deliveries in a fashion so they remained surprises were next on his agenda, determined none be found until we were long gone. From the landing on the stairs, he saw I was still entertaining while Brian and Allison were finding chores more fun with love, so he began his clandestine mission.

He placed the white paperback, *The Greatest Salesman in the World*, on Allison's computer. She detested salespeople and insisted she could never be one. He'd suggested, "We're all salespeople in life, just as we're all students and all teachers."

Slinking into the laundry room he spotted Lillian's laundry basket atop the washer. Inside it he placed the blue pocketbook, *The Greatest Miracle in the World*. He reached inside his denim shirt and then paper-clipped a tiny white cloth with a little golden safety pin inside the rear cover.

The two hardcover books were next. With the same care as when he'd stolen popcorn from Allison, he sneaked into the living room. Under a couch pillow he placed *HoHo!HaHa!HeeHee!HaHa*. The cover had a man in a pipe hat with two other jovial characters.

He stealthily passed the bookshelves and eyed the section with Benny's books and made a spot for a mustard-colored one, *The Greatest Mystery in the World*. This book was the only one George did not sign for it already had a personalized message. He wondered when the parents would spot it. More so, he wondered if they'd note the odds of the author personally inscribing it. In green ink the notation read:

To Benny,

I have always liked that name, too. Love, Og Mandino

March 15, 2017

He kissed two fingers and touched them to the author's photo on the back cover before easing it into the space next to *Charlie the Caterpillar*. Slipping out the rear door, he headed for Brian's truck and placed *The Choice* on the dash.

After this secret stash, he headed for the locked garage. As usual he didn't use a key. From inside, he threw a clear plastic tarp over his shoulder and then removed two pieces of furniture as if they were weightless. Grasping the dark cherry arms of both, he sneaked along the far end of the house. Once in the rear yard, he effortlessly hoisted them above his shoulders, clearing the railing as he ascended the stairs.

On the balcony outside the master bedroom, he fished in his pocket to remove a small envelope. He taped the note securely to the French doors and arranged it so the message was obvious from inside the bedroom, next to the one still painted on the window. It'd be harder to overlook the matching, hand-rubbed rockers placed outside the doors. However, just in case, the tarp would protect them.

Dear Allison & Brian —

We know these went to a home where love would surround them. Be well, be love —

Bessie & Lonn

Back in the kitchen, Brian had begun to shelve dishes while the gals created a huge care package for us. I'd requested they include deviled eggs, insisting they were George's favorite. Private humor shared on the road, even if I'd be the only one laughing.

Brian and I watched the closeness of the ladies working together. It was unparalleled to previous times when we had seen them in contact. As George re-entered with our bags and laid them by the couch, he, too, noticed the love.

He relished the progress made by Lillian, demonstrated as she announced she and Hughie would leave, *when the big boys do*, no longer needing to manipulate love. George winked, appreciating that she wouldn't intrude on the couple's first night back together.

"Oh," exclaimed Lillian. "I almost forgot." She ran for her huge purse and pulled out an envelope of photos. "I got two-for-the-price-of-one."

"Great." Brian took the package and shuffled through them. "Here it is. Huh?"

The group shot clearly depicted Allison, Benny, Justin, Oöso, Polly, and me. Brian scratched his head. "Where's George? I could've sworn I caught him in the shot."

The attention shifted when Benny spoke. He'd been frowning since he saw our traveling bags. Oöso put her head atop one of them when Benny walked over and defiantly sat on the other. His voice began to quake as he turned his cherub face upward. "I 'il mizz you Unca Daaaw-oh. I 'il mizz you, Unca Jaa-urge-val-more."

The kid nailed us both. All emotions were bared.

Justin insisted he and Benny could carry our bags to the car. Turned out, they had plans of their own. Once out on the dark porch, Justin easily opened George's bag. Innocence.

He placed two items in each bag. A toy fish in there for George, and with a giggle, the red flag from a mailbox for me. Benny added a picture he'd drawn of me sitting in the tree writing and one of George flying a plane over water.

As everyone headed out the door, we saw Benny back on the porch step holding his head up while he blinked rapidly with alternating eyes. The shift of a child's mind.

"Careful, Benny," yelled his mother. "What are you doing?"

He pointed to the twinkling fireflies. "I winkin' back at dem."

She walked down the stairs between George and me, holding our hands until the end of the walk. At the car, she hugged us both and then made me blush. "You had your chance." She reached for her husband's hand, "We're together...for good."

"*Believe* it." George squeezed her shoulder.

Lillian wrung her hands intermittently, still carrying a dishtowel. "You two are angels. I've so much to thank you for, so much I've learned."

Hughie shook our hands. He felt he'd missed out on something, but the ripples caused within the family would lap up to the shoreline of his soul in time.

As I approached the car, Brian handed me the UPS envelope and a company envelope with two business cards, having additional information jotted on each. He explained he'd written three letters of endorsement, two concerning us individually and one commenting on us as a team. "There'll always be room on my crew as well as in our home for you guys."

Then he turned directly to me. I extended my hand but he declined, delivering a heartfelt hug mimicking his son. "Sorry, Daaaw-oh, a handshake just won't do."

Benny noticed the way his Dad pronounced my name. I was *his* Daaaw-oh. His reaction was as if someone were making fun of me. His buddy. His sandcastle friend. Most adamantly he grabbed the leg of my blue jeans. Distinctly the child voiced a clear, "I luff you, Dare-oh."

Lifting him, I held him close and buried my face in his tiny shoulder. The little hands tangled in my hair as the youngster snuggled closer. George was then drawn into the frail moment as Benny doubled over backwards to him, into the arms of his Unca Jaa-urge-val-more.

Justin pushed his glasses in place and braced himself, squared his shoulders, standing tall. With a gentleman's dignity, he shook hands with both of us. Struggling to look strong, he tried to make light of the goodbye with a joke. "Hey there, Daro, here's one for the road. Know what Noah's wife's name was? Joan of Arc."

I knelt down, face-to-face. He melted against me and we shared a long hug.

George initiated the next move to hug the young child within whom he saw the heart of a man. "Enjoy your little brother, Rio. Take great care of him, just like you do Benny." Justin clung to him as tightly as he had to the fence. And then Justin took a deep breath and turned away.

The chatter of the birds and time grew still as Brian finally walked over to George. Everyone knew this'd be the tough one, although interrupted by Oöso's bark. Curiously, she was sitting in the backseat of the Mustang. Not wanting to leave her home, she was merely intent on getting in her good-byes. Getting her licks, so to speak.

Scampering out, she cleaned a speck of icing from my face. She and I had also come a long way. How I missed my dog at home being watched by Emily. I gave their dog a hearty hug in return. She stilled as George knelt down and cupped her white face in his hands, her pink nose inches from his. Only the pooch heard the blessing he offered, her tail wagging. "You did a good job, girl. Thank you. I'm proud to know you, Fur Face."

Then George rose to face Brian again. Both looked forward to the moment, yet dreaded it. It began with a handshake in which both men clasped their hands over the other. They offered token but valid statements about the memories shared, how long they'd remember each other, thanks on both fronts.

Brian began. "I decided not to let *normal* be a buzz word. I'd rather be a creation, than an imitation."

"Be the best vision of you, rather than the second best version of someone else," nodded George.

Brian reminded him of all the appropriate numbers in case we ever needed anything. Then, as if both of them were riding on a carousel, all of us spun away and the world was just them.

"Well, George Valmore, if I ever had a brother," he began to quiver, "If Benjamin had lived, I'd like to think he'd be like you."

George bit his lip aware he might break down if he didn't speak. He moved his right hand up to Brian's shoulder. "There's a little of each of us, in us all. If I share some of Benjamin's traits, I'm honored. I know wherever he is, he's proud of you. You're not keeping still anymore; you're going all the way."

His eyes pooled as the evening rain clouds closed in, looking up as if to catch air in his lungs. Then he looked back into his face. "And if I were to have had a little brother, Brian…there could be no finer one than you. Benjamin could be no prouder of you than I am."

A conflict of chill and warmth went through us all as we watched the embrace of unguarded love. Brian softly uttered within inches, "Thanks for everything. I love you."

George was unprepared for his own emotions. "I know, Brian. Me too. Just, remember to remember."

Lillian placed her arm around Hughie's waist, and he in turn moved closer. Allison, Benny, and Justin clung to me. Oöso appeared as the observer while Polly rubbed alongside her white furry body.

I figured I better get us moving, so I climbed into the driver's seat, the beige leather squeaking. I pulled the creaking door shut, stilling a curse when Benny reached through the window and handed me the window crank. Oöso and child then bounded up the porch stairs, followed by the others.

George set the envelopes in the backseat and then buckled his seat belt. He noticed the glint in my eyes when Benny reminded, "Dare-oh, look out fer arr mailbox."

As the family waved from the porch, Lillian walked arm-in-arm with Hughie to their car. I fired up the Mustang, avoiding eye contact with George.

"I got an idea." I adjusted the rearview mirror to sight in on the real estate sign as my target. *FOR SALE LESLIE McDONNELL* was all I had time to read before the rear bumper toppled it, the chassis squarely crossing over the sign. I hit the horn three times to signal it was no accident.

George and the family broke into an uproar of laughter as the clouds broke into a downpour of rain. Then, with another wink to my buddy, I gripped the chrome t-shift, pressing the black button in with my thumb, and pulled it forward until the red line signified *DRIVE*. I pressed the gas pedal a bit harder than necessary.

Through the rear window of the car and from the front of the house, all parties watched until the distance and the rain washed the scenes from view.

CHAPTER FORTY-SIX

MEMORIES Á LA CARTE

TOUCH AND SMELL, lasting memories. Driving home, Lillian asked Hughie if he'd like to find a spot to park and *watch* the rain. He needed no coaxing, taking in a deep breath of the moist air and smiling.

Brian soon had a crackling blaze aglow in the fireplace. By the time Allison had returned with the two boys ready for bed, the glow of candles was also dancing off the walls. White, green, rose, and lavender with flames dancing. The incense of white sandalwood and love permeated the room as they drew near the nine boxes from storage.

"More boxes than I remember," he puzzled, tapping his lower lip, absentmindedly running his finger over the label. *RYAN MARTIAL ARTS.* He envied the love his friend Richard had shared with Katrina.

As Allison strolled by, she gave him a kiss, whispering her eagerness to test their new bed. Thoughts harmonious fueled moving through the first four boxes quickly. Benny and Justin gladly helped, dragging a stool to return things to their original places. The kids sniffed at the clothes removed from the carton. Cedar laced with mothballs was an unfamiliar smell. All smells are new to us at one point.

Allison and Brian shared the childlike love of surprises as much as giving or receiving. Not all the boxes were Brian's things, simply being returned to their home. He paused, silent and perplexed, given another chance to honor a commitment made to his wife, one he felt he'd botched badly.

When Brian's mother died, he'd boxed and placed her possessions in a storage unit belonging to his friend, Richard Ryan. These belongings included boxes of toys from his childhood. As with all things, months became years and then many years. After he and Allison began to date, she heard of the long-stored childhood memories. With her love of children and antiques, she wanted to examine these boxes with him. And he kept promising they would.

In his procrastination, he lost contact with Richard. He made a couple attempts to reach him when Benny turned two. Then at three, he pursued for a couple more months. Alas, another promise broken as a result of the foolish belief that there'd always be time.

She always cited that his procrastination had cost him something valuable and had prevented her from enjoying that time of touching his past. More than mere curiosity, she'd seen this as a way to become acquainted with his childhood and his mother. Had he only known, but she had not shared this except through guilt trips.

He hadn't recognized the importance. He misjudged the value of time, of personal responsibilities. She hadn't clearly communicated her desire. The failing husband-father was saddened by the personal loss but most disheartened at believing he'd once again disappointed her. It had echoed throughout their marriage.

She found her husband standing by the remaining cartons in silent awe. With no concern for explanation regarding the *how* of it, he spoke. "Honey, remember the boxes of my mom's with my toys? Those boxes I always promised we'd go through?"

She began to cry her amazement, her bewilderment. Generally, she'd have buttered popcorn ready. Now, she sat in eager anticipation, knowing she was witnessing a miracle even if she wasn't attaching that label to it.

Opening the first of the unexpected boxes, he pulled out wadded sheets of newspaper stuffing. She smoothed one to see the year was 1980. More than twenty-seven years ago, this box had been packed by his mother at a time when he was taking that treacherous step from a toddler's toys to teenage boy. She now had a virtual time capsule of her husband from 1980.

They could see several clear plastic containers, shoebox sized storage units. Heavily scratched, the varied sizes served little Brian as a way to sort and protect his playthings. His mother instilled a powerful sense of caring, a trait of respect. Allison began to understand her husband and his mannerisms more. She was well aware of the way he handled the property of others, assuming that was an inborn respect.

He returned things in better shape than when borrowed. Honored elderly people and older buildings alike, abhorred litter and destruction. Felt there should be no needless destruction. Everything should pass into the next state of being in a peaceful manner, one that supported the environment, the world, and the universe. His beliefs weren't inborn but inbred by his mother.

Obviously these toys had seen many miles of merriment, but Allison learned that a great many had first belonged to his brother. They'd been thoroughly enjoyed, yet treated with respect by Benjamin before being inherited by Brian at five years of age.

Where were her toys now? All were worn out. The toys of her nephews and nieces never lasted a year. What'd happened to Benny's? They lay somewhere in between. Allison couldn't even master keeping track of the covers for her music.

Brian demanded his son respect property, yet it was a soft demand, one given in love. His own actions served as examples. She was never aware of it until this moment. It made her love her husband, her partner, her friend, even more. Now she felt a love and respect for his mother, Benny's unknown grandmother, for she had instilled this ribbon of respect within Brian and certainly within Benny's unknown uncle.

While acknowledging that Brian's mother and brother were Benny's grandmother and uncle, she never considered they were also *her* mother-in-law and *her* brother-in-law. She'd always thought of them more as Brian's and Benny's losses. Now she felt the loss for two of her family members she'd never met. Their bodies had died, but their lives continued, and their lives were touching her right now. Suddenly she was actually meeting Brian's mother and Benjamin.

Such awareness sprang from the mere appearance of some boxes filled with toys. She bit her lip in nervous anticipation. Brian had no idea of the awareness and growth she'd experienced in mere seconds. Could she ever explain? Now, might break the moment. Not words but actions would let him know. She knew she'd just changed. A major shift had occurred, and she'd let him see it through her actions.

She joined him as he lifted out a carton packed full of small metal cars of the Matchbox series, before Hot Wheels and well before Transformers. He balanced a replica of an old open- seat Model T in the palm of his hand, green with bright red seats. She reached for it and rolled it across the box flap.

He told the way his mother had helped him paint a huge sheet of plywood with roads and parking spaces. Allison remembered constructing a similar setting for Benny and how much joy that had brought Brian. He often compared her to his mother, a compliment she appreciated more at this moment.

"What are these? Trees for a train?" she asked, pulling out a container.

"Ah, man, my kingdom, my knights." Brian went back in time. Popping the lid, he grabbed several medieval characters, three inches tall.

"You have to make a shadow box for these," as she tenderly inspected a knight. Much more colorful than the molded olive-green soldiers that most kids had.

"And those," as he reached for a ten-inch tree, "were for the landscape. Mom cut the branches off an old fake Christmas tree. She glued rocks to the bases of the branches. Man. She was mighty creative."

"I see where you get it," hugged Allison, relishing this time together.

He looked at Benny and wondered what traits of his mother coursed through his veins, dearly hoping some flowed through Benny.

"Mom, Benjamin, and I used to go to Marshall Fields at Christmas. Visiting the huge department store had become our tradition. We'd ride the train there and window-shop, then have lunch beneath the giant Christmas tree that towered up several stories through the center of the store. The ornaments were as big as Benny. At least in my memory.

"All the store windows had elaborate, festive displays. Scenes to tantalize all of the children. Animated elves were in Santa's workshop, trains running through tunnels. She started these trips with Benjamin and then both of us, but we kept going even after he was gone. I can still feel the cold window pane, all us kids with our noses pressed against the windows, our breath steaming up the glass."

"Tell me more."

"Obviously, Benjamin was long gone by the time I was eight, but it still remained *our* tradition. Montgomery Ward's was still flourishing. The store had gigantic windows with a corner display. One year they had a huge castle complete with a drawbridge and towers. The price was huge, too." He made grand gestures with his arms as he handed a couple of the plastic knights to the boys.

"Bitchin'!" exclaimed Justin.

Allison giggled with a wink as the boys watched the animated man.

"Every boy wanted that castle as his own. I don't remember the price but it wasn't in our range, so unknown to me, Mom began to build me a castle for Christmas."

His excitement flourished. "She secretly made two train trips back to figure the dimensions, making sketches from the icy sidewalk, the overhang barely protecting her from the blowing snow. Then she figured out the shapes, cut all the wood, and built two towers from cardboard cylinders. So clever. Decorated the edges of all the walls and lookout towers in little mosaic tiles someone had discarded."

His look was distant, his mind's eye vivid. "The castle itself was about four-feet around and the base rose up about a foot with a tunnel running underneath it. Had another building within the walls that stood a couple a feet high. She glued tiny gravel from our driveway on all the walls and towers. And then, a separate ramp about three-feet long led to the drawbridge that used a wooden thread spool to raise and lower it. We'd put the whole thing up in the basement on our billiard table when my dad was away."

"Surprised it's not in here," she joked as she pretended to look.

His eyebrows rose as he sucked on his lip and then shrugged. "One year the basement flooded when my castle was on the floor. I was as devastated as the castle. One of my early lessons in nothing lasts forever."

No longer amused with the little knight Brian had handed him, Benny had wandered over to the window box. He climbed upon a cushion and patted at the window while the rain increased. "Jaa-urge-val-more. Jaa-urge-val-more," he repeated softly in sing-song fashion as he flipped the pages in some books.

Allison looked up to see their son's tiny frame in the window box. "I know, Honey. He and Daro are gone. We'll miss them."

"Hey, Benny, look at this." A tiny paper wad a quarter-of-an-inch bounced off the window. Brian held a miniature catapult. "Mom spent money on the important stuff, like weapons. We had two of these, so we could do battle."

The boys rushed over as he shot another little paper wad overhead. He patiently showed his son the way to launch a couple more until the young knights had mastered the contraption, taking them over to the windowsill while Justin made more paper wads. Even these were fair game for Oöso to chase.

Allison wore a bemused look as she lifted out some brown fabric. Raising it to her knees, she unfolded it, adorned with bright green leaf cutouts. Her face puzzled for a clue.

"I wanted to be a tree for Halloween. Man, I could never stump her," grinning at his pun. "I had seen talking trees on The Wizard of Oz and "Captain Kangaroo." That Halloween I wanted to be a tree. So, Mom had me gather several large leaves for templates and she began the painstaking endeavor of cutting out fabric leaves and creating a costume for my trick-or- treating." He puffed out his chest. "I won yet another First Place at Gower Elementary School's Halloween Party."

An outrageous laugh surfaced with the next outfit and he detailed the incident of the Peter Pan costume, complete with green tights. "After finishing the sewing, she dyed everything forest green, and it stained her hands. She had to wear gloves for two weeks."

Well into the third box, Allison's voice turned shrill. Here was a toy she'd heard about so many times it seemed legendary, emphasized as his favorite Disney character from all the ornaments they'd collected. "Here's your Donald!!!"

His visual mind took him back. "*I wanna Dona' Duck com' liv' wif me*," a three-year- old Brian had requested for Christmas.

"*You know, it won't be the real Donald, don't you?*" countered his mother.

"*I know, dat's 'kay. I sti' wan' him*," was the toddler's reply.

Allison's soft hand caused him to blink as he returned to the present. "Benjamin was the hero, even then. He finally found a Donald Duck. It cost more than twenty dollars, quite a bit for a stuffed animal back then.

"That was the year my dad's business began to soar. Gifts galore, yet I only cared about the foot-tall, duck-billed creature imprinted with his trademark blue naval jacket. And on Christmas morn, Donald sat, patiently awaiting me, in the rear of the wagon of my new red tricycle."

He grinned as he looked at the duck in Allison's arms.

"*Oh, Donald, you did com' liv' wif me.*"

Turning aside, he added, "I understand my dad was a bit miffed. I kind of ignored everything else, all the other gifts." His look turned distant. "Benjamin was only around for one more Christmas."

She placed Donald in his lap as if to console him and laid her head on Brian's shoulder, running her nail about a small circular

Band-Aid on the duck's left temple.

He blinked to clear his eyes. "That's from the time I gave him a haircut. Mom sewed the Band-Aid in place." He tapped the four brass buttons on the jacket bearing chipped red paint. "And those were white 'til I painted 'em with her red nail polish. I really liked to paint things."

They turned towards their child. There was the time he'd painted Brian's hammer. There was the tree house basket he'd painted. Then of course he'd painted Allison's hubcaps when they painted the house.

Attention shifted. "Okay, make an amendment to the will you said you just wrote. I want this." She laughed. She'd heard of Grandpa's woodworking.

About three-feet long, a foot-and-a-half high, and a foot deep, the log cabin had a peaked roof of dark Masonite. Two windows of gold screening sat next to the brass-hinged door. A wooden peg fit through carved guides to latch it. The logs measured about an inch in diameter, cut and arranged to create a crisscross-stacked effect. It was another one of Grandpa's creations, all hatched from scrap wood, no doubt.

Brian had shared tales of visiting and Grandpa used to take him as he had with Benjamin, out to his workshop to select a piece of scrap wood at random. The old carpenter would then hand it back to the child.

"*What's this?*" the kindly old man would ask holding out a piece of pine or hickory. "*Whadda you see?*"

And whatever he envisioned, as had his brother, such would be the next life, possibly the third or fourth life, the former tree, ex-scrap piece would reclaim. A bat, a horse, a gun, a wolf, or a train. The seed of creativity and imagination planted and nurtured. Fertile seed placed in the rich soil of a child's mind.

What had felt like a myth assumed the image of reality with her ability to touch the stories kinetically. There, wrapped in newsprint, she found the visualization of a child's mind turned tangible. A piece of redwood transformed into the silhouette of a pistol. The barrel and handle showed residue of a glue repair. "What happened?"

"Major lesson in taking care of my toys. Left it outside once. We looked all over for it. Mom found it in the grass a few days later…with the lawn mower. I was so upset because it'd been made for Benjamin. He didn't play with it anymore, but Grandpa was gone. He'd died the previous year. Brush One with death." The term hurt her ears.

"Later that year Skipper, our dog, was hit by the school bus. I found her as I came home. Brush Two with death. Although Benjamin was still living, he was gone from our lives the year following that. Brush Three with death."

She looked back to the wooden toy. "You respected other people's belongings," she said almost to herself. The valuable trait was sinking into her being, as well as death adding respect to life. Belief becoming a truth, perhaps.

He pulled out two more plastic cases, larger than shoeboxes. Nervousness began in his throat. "These were the toys handed down to me by Benjamin. At least some of his belongings remained in my life for a while."

Little Brian knew he had, what adults would call, *pulled the wool over his old man's eyes.* He had a piece of his brother that his father knew nothing about. He still had Benjamin's toys, still had a memory his father couldn't touch. Still remembering his thoughts as a child was the reason Brian did so well with youngsters.

Allison was unable to speak, knowing many of these toys came from a generation older than Brian's. Antique, certainly, but treasures of more than monetary value. Brian's favorite toys were those that Benjamin had shared with him. Antiques, all containing love.

Justin and Benny began to peek impatiently into the next box. It looked like a care package from Battle Creek, Michigan, the mysterious Mecca of a time long ago when children mailed their allowances and newspaper money in anticipation of a *three-to-five-week* wait for delivery. Mattel and Wham-O were the kingdoms of the toy world. Many of Benjamin's toys were popular worldwide before Brian's time. She imagined elaborate plans for her husband to make more shadow boxes.

"Look, guys, I have super balls," laughed Brian as he used his thumb and two fingers to create a backspin and flip one forward. The black ball hit the floor, bounced straight up, went forward in a curve, and then shot straight up again. Polly wasn't amused but the patterned bounce was an instant hit with the boys, and Oöso. He expected his wife to remind them, *no bouncing balls in the house.* Instead, she just impishly looked at him and asked, "You have what?"

Realizing his choice of words, he was glad to hear Justin's voice interrupt.

CHAPTER FORTY-SEVEN

SILLY PUTTY

"ARE THESE PANTYHOSE? He held a small yellow plastic egg. Both parents laughed at his association of Leggs Pantyhose with the package as they opened the plastic shell and released Silly Putty to the world of Benny and Justin.

"I remember this stuff," squealed Allison before the boys could claim it. She stretched the putty-colored substance until it snapped, and then kneaded it together. She leaped up and the children followed her into the kitchen. Pulling the comic section from their stack of recyclables, she rolled the putty into a ball and selected a cartoon from *The Family Circus*. Flattening the clay upon the cartoon, she then peeled it back up. The colorful images of Jeffery and his mother were clearly captured.

Next, she stretched the rubbery substance to distort the faces. At the boys' cries for a turn, she split the Silly Putty in half and returned to join her husband. She faked a disappointed look. "I forgot to show them the way it bounces, but I did tell them they have to put it back in the shell or it runs away."

Suddenly, vivid scenes from their personal childhoods of the damage that Silly Putty had done to their parents' carpets. "And stay in the kitchen with it."

Many of the objects simply caused the couple to laugh, such as the creations from an entrepreneur known as Big Daddy Roth who played up the vocabulary from the era of the Beatniks. Proof of reincarnation with the introduction of Hippies. Toys from the marketing hipster included the Weird-O Model series, colorful tee shirts, and most popular was the long-snouted rodent whose name is still heard today. Rat Fink.

Christmas cookie cutters of crimson plastic brought tales of two boys helping punch out gingerbread men, Santa Clauses, Christmas trees, and snowmen. His wife assured him they'd be put to good use that winter. Next were tiny plastic Disney characters, their paint chipped and faded. They were on display in a box made by Brian's Mother from an old typeset box she'd acquired from a print shop.

"Benny's room," Allison smiled.

Brian pulled out a red wooden racecar, *Pinewood Derby* emblazoned on the side. "Did you do scouts?" she asked.

"No, but Dad did Cub Scouts with Benjamin. They made this car together." He spun the black plastic wheels that used nails as axles. "The cars were fashioned from a uniform block of wood already in the basic configuration. Benjamin carved it to the shape he wanted, and then Grandpa drilled holes in the wood, filling it with copper B-B pellets until it was the proper weight. Won Second Place."

She smiled, handing him three plastic car models of 1/32 scale. His mind's eye transported him back and saw them on his brother's desk. He gingerly reached for them as if the paint might still be wet, recalling his brother building the finely detailed cars. The memory of the smell of paint and glue as Benjamin sat at his desk by an old brass table lamp. Always building models, but never too busy to play with his baby brother. She turned a turquoise and white Corvette Stingray over in her hand.

He nodded, his head looking about and then above. He stared back at the model now cradled in his hands. "There must be something after death. I can't believe these plastic models have a shelf life longer than my brother."

It sounded like a champagne bottle when the ping-pong ball bounced off his head. "Oops," she giggled, drawing her head down and shoulders up as the two boys charged her. She held two pliable red rubber guns. By wedging a ping-pong ball into the barrel and then squeezing the handle, she could shoot the ping-pong bullet. In self-defense, she handed them off to the boys before Brian could grab one. "Go into the family room, boys." Soon multiple *pops* were followed by the sounds of a fleeing kitty.

Next were stacks of bubble gum cards, certainly collectibles.

The bundles were held with rubber bands turned brittle. Black-and-white, vaguely familiar to the couple. They showed Napoleon Solo and Illya Kuryakin of "*The Man from U.N.C.L.E.*," the TV series that enthralled fans from '64 to '68, Benjamin's era. Allison recognized the pathologist on the TV series "*NCIS*." He hardly looked any older.

A popular feature of the spy shows was the gimmickry. "*The Man from U.N.C.L.E.*" featured a pistol, converted into a rifle with the addition of a clip, shoulder stock, barrel extension, and telescope. "Mom told me Benjamin took this to church once, wearing it under his jacket in a make-shift holster, becoming a secret agent. Secret, until Mom found out when his gun slipped out in church."

Allison always wondered if it was wise for Benny to hear of his father's escapades as a child. It appeared she now had his uncle's shenanigans to deal with, too. However, she welcomed them with an open heart.

The boys returned and began looking through another bundle of cards. Benny held them to his nose, the sweet bubble gum smell alive after decades. "Hey," motioned Justin. "This guy looks familiar."

Allison shuffled through the characters of Odd Job, Goldfinger, Dr. No, Pussy Galore, and 007. James Bond. However, when she attempted to explain who the debonair gent was, Justin wasn't buying it.

"That's the dude from the submarine movie and *The Rock*? No way!" he argued.

They tried to explain that Sean Connery was the original James Bond. He'd out-lasted all of the others in hits like *Goldfinger*, *Dr. No*, and *From Russia with Love*, the time of the early '60s to the early '70s, a span of almost ten years.

When the rubber band crumbled on the first stack, the cards fell to the carpet. Justin scooped them together as he asked, "Who are these dudes?"

"Oh man. Your generation missed out. That's '*The Man from U.N.C.L.E.*'."

"Uncle who?" asked Justin.

The United Network Command for Law and Enforcement. James Bond saved us on the silver screen while Napoleon Solo and Illya Kuryakin saved us on TV."

"Illya Cure–ee-who?" asked Justin.

Brian spread several of the cards until he found one of the suave young gentleman with shaggy blond hair. "Here," as he held the card up. "Illya Kuryakin. David McCallum."

The silence was deafening until Allison attempted to explain. "You know. David McCallum. That's Ducky on 'NCIS'."

Justin suggested, studying the card quite suspiciously, "Maybe this guy is Ducky's son."

Allison resumed her exploring until her guttural "*Blech*" brought everyone to rapt attention. Having opened a new carton, she stood over a box within a box, slightly recoiled with her right hand pulled back to her shoulder. Her blonde head tilted as she looked at the dark hairy object held captive under a plastic bag.

The two boys joined Brian peering over the sides, with some caution. He grinned, pulling the bag off and setting it on the table. The dark hairy creature was more than a foot tall with arms menacingly outstretched over its head.

Apprehensively, Benny stepped behind his friend. "Wot's dat?" "The Wolf Man." Brian's laughter put his son at ease.

"Too cool!" hollered Justin.

"There used to be a series of models that kids could build, like cars. Frankenstein, Dracula, The Mummy, The Creature from the Black Lagoon, and The Wolf Man. Monsters made famous from drive-in movies and black-and-white TV."

They stared in silence.

"Mom told me about this. Benjamin was probably eight or

nine. I wasn't around yet, maybe an afterthought in the mind of God. Anyhow, he entered this contest where kids customized the monsters. He used real hair he got the barber to save for him." Brian's laughter filled his eyes with tears. "But Mom said he ran out of hair, so he caught this old black tomcat and tried to shave it. Dad heard all of this noise in the bathroom and when he opened the door, it scurried up Dad's bare leg."

His audience squealed with laughter.

"So later on, Benjamin opted to make do with the materials at hand, and used his own hair. Mom came home and the model was done but Benjamin was visibly short a few locks. Took First Place in the whole state of Illinois," he added proudly.

Allison was beside herself wondering what their boy would be like at eight. "Wot dees?" asked Benny as he struggled with several flat pieces of cardboard. It seemed strange that these were alien to the boy.

"Record albums," Brian offered as he looked at his son holding *Herman's Hermits* and *Gary Puckett & The Union Gap.*

"And these?" echoed Justin holding an orange rectangle of plastic and a similar gray one. The labels showed *Johnny Cash, Chicago,* and *Three Dog Night.*

"Those are 8-Tracks," Brian offered, suddenly feeling ancient.

Allison pulled out a flexible coiled spring. Most of the red paint had worn off. She rotated the Slinky between her outstretched arms as she moved over to the boxes by the window. She arranged boxes and books in a stair-step fashion. Two demonstrations were all the boys needed. Loving a simple spring four-to-five times their age, they soon graduated to using it on the staircase. The old slogan came back to her: "*It's Slinky. It's Slinky. It's fun, it's a wonderful toy. It's Slinky. It's Slinky. It's fun for a girl or a boy.*"

Rejoining her husband, she grasped the leather collar of a lovely suede jacket, burnt rust in color. A lady's jacket with thick leather buttons squared off at the hem and lined in gold satin. Brian sat with his head cocked to his left, his lower lip out slightly.

"What's the story?"

"As you know, my dad was really into having someone continue the family business, especially after two miscarriages before Benjamin. They still had no kids and felt they might be getting too old. All the relatives were older, had their tubes tied or had given birth to girls."

She didn't interrupt.

"My folks had struck a deal. If mom birthed a girl, she had to buy dad a bowling ball. And a carrying case," he gestured as if to increase the value of the deal. "But in the event of the long-awaited boy to carry on the prized family name, Mom would be awarded a leather jacket." He rose and held up the suede prize. "See the dark spot? Benjamin did that."

He reached for his wife's hand and she stood. Words were unnecessary. Stepping behind her, he held the jacket open. Her arms slipped inside the smooth lining. He pulled it up over her shoulders, closing the lapels, placing a gentle kiss upon the trail of a tear. She wrapped her arms around herself, feeling the embrace of her newly found mother-in-law, and brother-in-law.

Next were a couple of containers with soldiers about a foot tall. GI Joes, one Navy, one Air Force, and two Marines clad in the appropriate cloth uniforms. The plastic molded face of each bore the telltale scar on its left cheek.

"You had dolls?" she teased although she recognized their value.

"*Action* toys," he rebuffed in a most masculine voice. "These were Benjamin's, the original GI Joes, before they sissified them with fuzzy hair and cropped beards."

Thrusting her shoulders back, she posed the soldiers, causing them to attack each other as she rotated her wrists. "*Fighting* dolls," she assured him.

"Yeah," he laughed pulling out an accompanying comic book. Inside the cover was a monochrome advertisement. He sang aloud. "*GI Joe, GI Joe, fighting man from head to toe. On the land, in the sea, in the air.*" He shook his head. "Boy, they suckered a couple of generations of boys with that one."

"What are these?" She held a beanbag of brown rough burlap, scratchy in her palm. Brian smiled as his shoulders slumped forward, his head tilted in reflection.

"Sandbags. The GI Joe paraphernalia was expensive. There was as much junk available for him as for Barbie. Mom bought the burlap, made bags, and lined them so they wouldn't leak. She filled them with gravel from our driveway, again. Made Benjamin fifty of them. He had the only sandbags in the neighborhood." A deep voice resonated. "Sandbags, ma'am, a necessity of war."

He tossed a bag back and forth in his hands. "She was always sewing. I remember hearing about the time Benjamin was in seventh grade. My folks didn't have much money. She bought non-brand name clothes and embroidered *OP* on his clothes for Ocean Pacific. That was the big name in clothes then, none of that Hilfiger whatever. Nobody ever knew the difference."

A smile graced her face. She'd have liked this woman. Would've loved her, in fact.

Bored with the latest toy, Benny crawled back onto the window box with a couple of books. Occasionally he pressed his face against the cool window glass.

Justin tapped Allison's shoulder. She sighed while Benny repeated the surrogate uncle's name again and again, "Their departure might be more difficult than I expected."

THE RAIN MADE A HOLLOW plunking, careening off the roof of the Mustang. "You done good, George. Pulled off some great miracles," I offered in hopes of breaking the silence.

"We're a team, Daro. Whatever I pulled off, as you put it, we did together. Nothing, none of the so-called miracles, was anything someone else couldn't have done."

I sucked at my cheek. The gauge lights glowed off his face.

"It's up to them…to remember to remember. They got some of their beliefs shook up."

"How do you think they'll do?"

"Beliefs won't last. Truths will, especially those shared." Experiencing the let-down one sometimes feels after a vacation, he sighed, "Depends on their actions."

"Do I dare ask where we're headed next?"

"Due Northeast," was his curt reply. "Catch a motel for the night."

"Can you be more vague?"

"Get some sleep, drop this baby off tomorrow, and fly home."

CHAPTER FORTY-EIGHT

SPLISH, SPLASH

SOME FOLKS STEER A CAR, but I tend to aim. Aimed for puddles in the long stretches, freeing them in an attempt to lighten the mood. The rain poured heavy sheets over the hood with such force it was difficult to tell the puddle freed from the rain.

I turned to George as he scooted down in his seat and finally laid his head back. I glanced at him a couple of times before I tried to initiate a conversation, speaking to be heard above the rain echoing off the roof.

"Hey, George, how about another shot at how you describe meditating? I mean, what's it like for you?"

"For me, it's akin to a meeting with God, a type of prayer. It's a way of remaining in touch with my inner self."

"Like that super-conscious stuff you're always talking about?"

"When you dream…between snoring," he winked, "you have dreams. Some you remember." His eyes closed again, bringing darkness. "Some folks say they don't remember their dreams. Some think they don't dream at all. Others remember going to bed with a problem only to awaken the next day with the perfect solution."

"Okay, I get that. Continue."

"Such solutions arose in your sleep because you allowed yourself to listen to your super- conscious, your link to God when He spoke to you." He leaned forward to turn the radio low. It crackled as the green light glowed on his arm. The familiar nasal notes of Willie Nelson were half into "Angel Flying Too Close to the Ground."

"Good example," I motioned with my head. "When he writes songs, Willie says he hears the music all the time and simply pulls it from the air."

"Another such creative force was Henry Ford. Said all the ideas he forged were already in the atmosphere; he was merely the first to make them public," I shared.

"How 'bout the way Thomas Edison did things? I heard he had a backless leather couch that sat in the middle of his lab in Menlo Park. When stumped for a solution, he'd lie down. After a while, he'd have new answers. Did you know old Thomas?"

He laughed before regaining his thoughts. "No, I don't think so. What else do you know about Edison?"

"In 1862, Edison published the *Grand Trunk Herald*. He printed this weekly in a freight car, which doubled as his lab. We talk of rhythm and ripples; here's one for you. He saved the life of a station official's child and was taught telegraphy as a reward. Then, as a telegraph operator he created his first recognized invention. He made a telegraphic-repeating instrument enabling messages to be transmitted automatically over a second line without an operator. Just think, if not for that child…where would we be?"

"Ripples," said George. "Whereas Alexander Graham Bell invented the telephone, Edison's carbon transmitter propelled it along. One helped the other."

"Most folks only remember his electric light."

"By far his greatest creation occurred when he publicly exhibited his incandescent electric light bulb in 1882. He developed and installed the world's first central electric-power station. Imagine the flickering gas lights of New York City dimmed to darkness. To witness the streets aglow even brighter, bathed in a constant flood of light." Reaching over, he shoved the knob into the dash, turning off our light before I jerked them back on.

"Turkey."

"Edison knew the alpha state of the mind was the bridge to

creativeness and being an invent-a-holic, he didn't want to waste time sleeping more than necessary. That couch was part of his method of slowing the vibration of his mind.

"In Menlo Park, Edison's lab was surrounded by glass panes and filled with wooden work tables. Right out in the open stood that custard-brown leather couch. The early type used by psychiatrists, no back but elevated on one end. To the right, on the floor, Edison kept a bucket filled with water. When he got stumped, right in the middle of all the hustle and bustle, he'd lie down on the couch while still wearing his heavy lab coat." George repositioned himself and continued the story.

"He'd place a steel ball the size of a grapefruit in the palm of his right hand. He sought the balance between blocking out all the noisy interference in his physical lab, yet not nodding off to sleep, to enter that alpha state. If he dropped off, the steel ball fell into the water and woke him up. This way, he trained himself to enter, under any conditions, his own inner lab. There, devoid of time and costly mistakes, he continued his work, returning to his lab in Menlo Park and West Orange with new insights."

"Wonder if Edison saw his inventions as miraculous?"

"Like Einstein, Edison constantly credited those who lived before him. He recognized the unity, the continuation of all knowledge. Over a twenty-year period, he breathed life into the shaping of modern society with the light bulb, the generating system, sound-recording devices, the phonograph, the alkaline battery, the diamond record needle, the electric pen used in lie detectors, the mimeograph, the talking motion-picture projector, more than one thousand patents," as George snapped his fingers.

I shook my head. "Wonder how many inventors and scientists work that way by going inside themselves like that?"

"Hard to say, but the humble man often stated '*I'm not a scientist. I'm a technologist. I've added little to original scientific knowledge. I've pieced together the knowledge others have learned*'."

"More than a thousand patents." My fingers danced on the steering wheel working the math. "That averages almost fifty per year, about four per month. He perfected a new invention, a patent...once a week for twenty years."

"Ever think he lost precious time thinking about where he'd spend his vacation? Giving your life doesn't necessarily mean dying. With Edison it meant living."

"Imagine, if more people had his passion," I mused.

BRIAN REGRESSED in time as he scooted another box across the floor. "Here's some more stuff made by Grandpa."

Allison assembled the yellow, black, and red wooden pieces into a four-car train. White pine pegs slipped through holes to connect the pieces. "Benny, look. Toot, toot."

The child ran over and dragged the wooden train toward the window. Her love and words traveled generations and touched Brian's heart. "He has a piece of your grandfather, his great-grandfather, a memory of him."

TO THIS DAY, CHICAGO REMAINS a land of tracks and trains. The Mustang slowed to a stop at a railroad crossing, the headlights dancing on the flatbeds and cattle cars flashing past. Faded maroons, an occasional blue one, dull yellows corroded with rust. Lettering of white-to- black predominated. Most of the cars were accented by the soft spray of graffiti added in train yards across the country.

I watched a few more clack by. "Wonder if any of these cars ever passed us before in our travels? You ever think about being a hobo? I always liked trains."

The kaleidoscope effect of our headlights and the stroke of the windshield wipers had a hypnotic effect. "Me, too," finally came George's distant reply.

When the flashing red lights lifted, the rapid succession of solid thuds from the trestle beneath the wheels jarred the vintage Mustang. As the tires cleared, he was looking down the track to the caboose disappearing and pondered aloud about my comment, tying it to his own thought. "Funny the way folks' lives touch each other, sometimes more than once." He sighed deeply, "Sometimes, never again."

Man, his mood was coming down and starting to bum me. "I once had an old Ford Falcon. It was a station wagon, weird style with only two doors, white with red leather interior. I added red shag carpet and an 8-track stereo. Anyhow, I remember making out at the drive-in to Gary Puckett & The Union Gap." I dropped a couple verses of "Lady Willpower" before I continued.

"Never would've guessed my path would cross with his and I'd meet Puckett." I looked at George. "And we never know when such paths may cross again. But sometimes, it's like this," and I swerved to hit a puddle, sending a torrent of water over the car. "Sometimes, George, that one touch, makes quite a splash."

He knew what I was hinting at. We'd certainly remember this trip. The Poppy family would occupy our minds for a long time, an eternity for him. I thought aloud. "Wonder if Benny will remember us? When he gets older and has children of his own?"

George's thoughts were almost a mumble. "Difficult to say for sure, Daro, but I'd like to think so, but you never know. The brain is fallible."

Wanting to believe we'd made a difference and that the little guy would remember us, I countered. "What about that subconscious and super-conscious stuff?"

"Your subconscious remembers but it has its ups and downs. It works more on memorization and training. Now your *super-*consciousness remembers everything."

"Super-consciousness," I repeated, "as in our God link, our Higher Self, that messenger- of-God stuff?"

"Yep, the trick's in learning to listen to it."

We drove in silence for a spell. I was reflecting on my middle-of-the-night visit with Allison, about whether the info I shared had been the truth rather than merely my belief. "How do you really know when you're plugged into it? Plugged into your Higher Self, that all-knowing power?" I wanted assurance that my belief was a truth as lightning began to flash.

He groped for words, his thoughts punctuated by a roll of thunder. The syncopation and softness of his voice seemed as though he were talking to himself. "It's a feeling, a realization. When we listen, we learn. We begin to reach…perfection…as we realize more about ourselves. We begin to reach, the level." He drifted off as the thunder increased. "The level God lets us know when we still ourselves to listen."

As a child, I'd watch the flash of lightning and count the seconds until the thunder rumbled to figure out the distance of the bolt of lightning. If this exercise works, the flash crack of the next lightning bolt and blast of thunder were virtually inside the Mustang. The reverberation of nature peeled George's eyelids wide open. He jolted upright, like the time in bed at the Poppy's house.

"Stop right now. Turn around. Turn around," he cried.

"What?" I looked around. "What? I just hit a puddle. That was only thunder."

Seat belt fastened, he managed to turn almost completely around in his bucket seat. "Go back," he ordered.

CHAPTER FORTY-NINE

RIPPLES

THE WOODEN FRAME IN Allison's hand held a two-dollar bill and a silver fifty-cent piece mounted alongside two photos. The bill, new in 1959, had a red seal stamped to the left of Jefferson's face. A white-haired man held a small boy, both gleaming. "Look. Your grandfather and Benjamin won a contest." She read the note below the picture.

"August 15, 1959, The Poppy Reunion. Effingham, Illinois.

Grandpa Edward Poppy was the oldest descendant present. Benjamin Poppy Jr. was the youngest.

Each received a new two-dollar bill."

Beneath the photo was a silver coin sealed in its own clear envelope, next to the second photo. She read the typed inscription.

"This half-dollar was given to Benjamin, February 13, 1962, by Uncle Ernie Eubank who told him, a boy big enough to have a pocket is big enough to carry a half-dollar."

Brian sat in silence, remembering the mysterious obituary he'd been given by George, the one that Oöso had chewed up. Rather, he remembered the dream connected to it. He figured he could never explain it to his wife.

"Do you remember much about your Uncle Ernie?"

"No. As a little boy, I got short-changed. He was gone long before I was born."

"STOP. STOP." George demanded. "Turn around. *Please*, Daro. Find the next exit.

" Having just hit the freeway from the turnpike, I pulled onto the shoulder, stopped the car, and looked at my animated friend. "What's goin' on, George?"

"Turn around. I want to go back." He grew calmer though forceful, "Now."

Confusion crossed with trepidation and fear. I understood the rules. I'd challenged a few, but I knew once a mission was completed, you were never to have contact with those involved. Never were folks to learn of George's secret. Though not sure of the consequences, I didn't feel crossing The Boss was a wise move for either of us.

He rolled the window down and the rain pelted his face. He blinked and then sucked air into his lungs deeply. "Daro, it's okay. Turn around."

Should I believe him or was I being conned? How much power did I have over him?

The gas gauge registered *Full*, yet he'd made it clear that an angel wasn't that much wiser. No better or more capable of miracles than you or me, merely operating from a new perspective. I stalled, "Can't make a U-turn. I'll catch the next exit."

SHE HAD NO CONCERN when she saw Benny and Justin looking at the scrapbooks she'd pulled from the box and stacked for them to use for the Slinky. "Two boxes left. The big one or the little one next?" she asked.

"I dunno. What're these? They aren't mine."

The cartons were actual shipping boxes, taped securely, almost severely. A sheet of old stationery was taped to each, covered with clear tape for protection.

"*Personal?*" she knelt closer. The letterhead read *Benjamin J. Poppy Construction*. "Wasn't that your father's company?" She was surprised at his reaction. No anger or hatred anymore. She was unaware of the miracle a release-letter could reap.

"I thought I'd discarded all this. It's probably just his office stuff." He stepped away from the box to show no interest or curiosity in opening the cartons.

Although curiosity was a commodity that was fairly non-combustible in Brian, it was definitely aflame in Allison. It was only her creative suggestion that there might be some office paraphernalia now possibly antiques, which persuaded him to open the box.

I WASN'T DOING TOO WELL at soothing George. Frankly, his adamant insistence to return scared me. We weren't to be seen again by those in an assignment because the people might reconsider things that happened. To return to the Poppy household meant the chance of being seen as some kind of miracle worker. They might forget their own worth, crediting him with miracles rather than themselves, devaluing their own work, their own personal power.

Plus, I was really concerned about the way Benny might react. Such a return and repeat departure might not be understood by the little guy, let alone by the adults. And George wouldn't explain why he felt the need to return.

Against my better judgment, we left the interstate, soon approaching the intersection where a few days prior, Erle had been spared a deadly encounter. The memory made me quiver as the stoplight changed and I slowed.

An evac-copter flew over. As the long blades sliced through the air and rain, George cowered at the sound but continued to search the skies. I began to search too. But I had no clue what I was looking for.

THE CARTON OPENED much too slowly for Allison. Once opened, Brian motioned for her to proceed, allowing it to be her quest. In truth, he was apprehensive about touching his father's past, afraid to release the monster from the dark. She threw one of the wads of paper to Oöso who scooped it up.

"There. See? This is nice." She unwrapped a foot-long, cedar-and-cherry-wood box. It had an ornate Japanese appearance with a detailed robust tree in bas-relief. Finding it locked, she turned it over where a small silver key was held in place by tape yellowed with age. "Well. What treasures will we find in here?" she playfully acted.

Three pieces of jewelry fell out with some other trinkets, probably broaches from his mother. Once out, they revealed an old yellow envelope wedged into the box. It was torn open at one end. She pulled out a thin paper, folded three times. Small succinct typing was spread across the center of the telegram. Then, almost in horror, her tears began as the telegram read itself into her mind. "Oh," she broke, "Brian."

Her husband was distant, studying the jewelry. A slight heart shape of gold with the silhouette of a face. Fine fabric, ribbonry attached. Violet, the highest color on the spectrum, accented the Purple Heart. Two additional clusters were attached.

Next a long navy-blue cord fell free, with the Distinguished Flying Cross. And among the campaign ribbons and embroidered badges, the Congressional Medal of Honor, awarded posthumously.

Now he knew what the piece of paper said. He remembered the two men who arrived with a large manila envelope. The telegram was dated *December 21, 1993*. His mind had buried the image that was now resurfacing. Two servicemen dressed immaculately, creases so sharp they could slice cheese, Class-A uniforms he later learned, delivered the package. Twenty-four hours later, as they had promised, a telegram arrived. It was addressed to his parents from the United States Armed Forces.

Allison read the telegram aloud although he already knew the contents.

"Dear Mr. and Mrs. Poppy:

We regret to inform you that on 04 December 1993, your son Captain Benjamin James Poppy Jr. was killed in action while serving the United States of America in a classified capacity. Stop. Due to the nature of his duty and his death, Captain Poppy was awarded full honors and memorialized at sea. Stop. The Flag of the United States of America is presented to you by a grateful Nation. Stop."

Rather than signed personally, it ended in the same informal type,

"General Daniel K. Stringer,

United States of America, Air Force"

The words left her mouth and lay there as still as the medals, as still as Brian's heart. These two cartons were filled with items his father had packed, things all others believed had been thrown out. Obviously, the telegram had been added years later. He looked empty, staring at the yellow telegram.

"When he enlisted, I lost him. Smiles, wrestling, model cars, mud puddles. He was just…gone. Thirteen years later, when that arrived, I lost him all over again."

Under the carved box was a large finely crafted shadow box. Brian remembered his father building the strange triangular case, yelling when the seventeen-year-old questioned him. It disappeared before he saw it completed. The dark-blue fabric bearing brilliant white embroidered stars showed through the glass. He opened the case and removed the triangular-folded flag, pressing it against his trembling jaw.

Allison opened another envelope. The contents brought back his smile. It revealed report cards, class awards, news articles, and sports ribbons, all charting Benjamin's young life. She read one of the report cards aloud.

Leadership qualities. Works well with others. Could do better if he applied himself. Sometimes a rebel. She eyed Brian. "Hmmm."

He pulled a note on stationery from Gower Elementary School and read:

"Dear Mrs. Poppy,

Please do not help Benjamin with his mathematics homework. He's having enough trouble.

Thank you.

Mrs. Switzer, 5th grade."

Brian was always amazed at the way his mother had been a phenomenal accountant but never mastered the New Math.

A long plain-white envelope held a folded birth certificate detailing that a seven-pound, seven-ounce baby boy was born at Richland Memorial Hospital in Olney, Illinois at 6:50 in the morning on November 17, 1958. Benjamin James Poppy, Junior. The certificate was signed by Dr. Frank Webber.

THE LIGHTS OF the Victorian home in the distance seemed to calm George but unnerved me. "Look, I don't mean to pry but I've a right to know what the…what are we doing here? Just what do you have planned?"

Rather than feeling attacked, he turned to stare at me. Silently, he agreed with my concern. And, he appreciated me having the nerve to confront the issue, to confront him. I think he spoke only because he felt he owed me that much. "I…don't…know."

It took all of my control not to slam my fist against the steering wheel. I slowed a bit, torn between the designated rules and genuine compassion for my friend. "I don't know either, George, but I know we can't, whatever *can't* is. We can't go back."

THE PORCH LIGHT FLICKERED before burning out, causing Allison to glance at the front window. Her arms around Brian, both were weeping openly as the flag lay between them. A release was being completed by his saying goodbye to Benjamin. For her, it was a love and a grieving process for her brother-in-law she'd never expected.

Benny was visibly concerned and offered a hug to his mother. Justin watched, feeling helpless, again. It was Oöso who brought all back to the moment with her nuzzle of the paper wad into Allison's lap. As she assured both the boys that everything was all right, she picked up the clump. She threw it twice for Oöso before it began to unfold. Rather than newsprint, it revealed the hand-written poem that Brian had thrown in the fire pit.

"'*Can Allison Come Out to Play?*' What's this?"

Brian chewed on his lip, dark eyebrows raised, as she read the long poem aloud before she placed a kiss on his cheek. He stared at his dog, who stared back.

The cartons revealed treasures greater than any garage or estate sale. They contained Benjamin. And they contained the unknown love of a father who packed everything away thinking that there'd always be time. What folly. Packed away the memories of time wasted and time lost.

Next, a bundle of envelopes, some six-inches thick, tied with two pieces of rough twine. Allison saw they'd all been opened. Years of letters postmarked from a period of 1980-1993. Originally sent from Private Benjamin Poppy on up through the ranks until they were sent from Captain Benjamin Poppy. No notation of *junior* on any of them.

Written to Brian and his mother, but never received. Captured, raped, trespassed, read, and secretly preserved by a misguided, insecure father. Prisoners of a private war, collected through the years, eventually buried. Guilt hidden in sealed cartons by an enraged and pained man. The first act was one of haste and to continue as he did was a sin.

"Maybe now we can get to know Benjamin," hoped Allison.

He was not ready to open the package of letters and handed them to Justin, asking him to put them by the other boxes.

When Brian's father died some ten months after his mother, he became sole beneficiary. Not that he cared. In his mind, he had no connection with his father and in his mind he'd ceased to exist. By the time a key to his dad's safety-deposit box was forwarded to him, he had already sent most of his father's possessions to charities. The contents of the bank box led him to a storage facility which he had Jason deal with.

Jason found furniture and boxes. With no sense of urgency

or attachment, Brian had him get rid of the furniture and place the boxes with his mother's possessions in storage. He examined nothing, never chose to view any of it. He wanted no part of his father's business or his life.

The first thing Brian pulled out of the carton was a book atop several others. A hardback copy of *The Greatest Miracle in the World*. The book fell open with an envelope tucked inside. A place marker they thought, until they saw a note was scrawled in neat penmanship across the front.

"Mom —

Please save these books for Brian's 14th birthday. Each one is inscribed in order for him to get to know me. Always remind him that I am, as he will be, who he is as a result of the people he meets and the books he reads. Those factors will determine who he becomes. Maybe these books will help him remember who his big brother is until I see you all again.

Teach him right thoughts, right actions. Love, Benjamin"

"My God, he compiled a library for you. Benjamin made a library for you years ago Brian, just as you're doing for Benny."

He smiled, feeling his mother's and his brother's lives course through his body. Emotions blocked them from noticing the envelope being carried away by Benny, addressed to Brian's mother, still unopened. Anything in his mother's name transferred to her sole surviving son upon her death. The retroactive military insurance for a captain lost in a tour of duty, collecting interest for more than fourteen years, a welcome addition to Benny's college fund that would more than cover it in fact.

The envelope just felt important to Justin, so he took it from Benny without incident and tucked it in a safe spot with the bundle of letters. Call it child's intuition.

THE RAIN BOUNCED OFF the metal real estate sign, still lying on its back where I'd toppled it. I pulled well past it, parking out of view.

George stepped out of the car, leaving his door wide open. Eyeing the sky as if attempting to look past the clouds, he began a slow walk and then a trot. I leapt out to follow when he burst into a run. His eyes began to mist up with the weather. We were getting soaked from the rain as puddles continued to form.

TO A CHILD A SEALED BOX of any type is an invitation and a temptation to find surprises, or at least stuff off limits. Interesting stuff. While Justin was playing on the stairs with the Slinky, Benny had managed to open the last remaining carton and put some of the items in the window box. He patted the window glass, lyrically repeating George Valmore's name as if it were his own self-composed ballad or mantra. His wee voice had a happy lilt. He giggled as he scattered photos from his father's childhood, black-and-white images he couldn't associate with his bloodline for years to come.

Brian found a little pill bottle in the bottom of the box they were still emptying. It contained what appeared to be tiny bone fragments. He rattled it and then looked closer. "Allison, here's Benjamin's baby teeth. C'mere, guys and look at these."

She looked toward her son at play. He called Benny again to show him, but the child's rapt attention was focused on what the little boy held in his hands already. Both stood and walked over to investigate.

Brian reached out. "Easy, guy. Whatcha got?"

Allison saw the trophies from Benjamin's high school days. She reached for what Benny clutched, a gold metal frame etched with a rough pattern. "Careful, Honey, the glass is broken."

"Me," Benny patted his chest. "Me an' Donal'."

She blinked several times at the enlarged black-and-white glossy that had a Christmas tree in the background. Atop a three-wheeler with a wagon compartment behind, was a child in sleeper pajamas with little feet. Clutched in his right arm atop the white handlebars was a plush Donald Duck. Nobody knew how much

Benny looked like little Brian, until now. She handed it to her husband who began explaining to Benny and Justin who was actually holding Donald Duck.

Allison took the frame and shook loose the broken glass into an empty carton. The gap caused the enlargement to slip out revealing another picture, back side out. She held the frame in her hand, recognizing the handwriting she'd seen earlier. It was the penmanship of Brian's Mother.

Taking one album and the frame, she and the boys walked back a few steps, sitting down next to Brian. She reread it aloud: "Freeing one last puddle before going off to serve his Country-April 1980."

Benny crawled upon his father's lap as she placed the frame in her own, careful of glass still clinging to the edges. She had to fiddle a bit to separate it from the thick brown matting. Her fingernails pinched for the snug photo, carefully beginning to slide it out. Black-and-white again. The ground appeared shiny before they identified it as a large puddle stretched across the bottom of the vertical shot. Muddy feet and knees appeared next.

Pulling it out an inch at a time revealed a little body in a rain slicker, clinging to the left leg of an adult who stood alongside wearing muddy combat boots. Allison glanced at her husband as his breath stopped. Both fear and happiness were registering. At his nod, she continued.

"Daddy?" patted Benny on the photo with his head tilted. The child's face in the picture could be seen, clad in a familiar vinyl rain cap. "Dat Daddy too?"

"Yeah, that's me, Benny, when I was your age."

Their eyes studied the photo. They continued up the long arm of the combat jacket, resting atop the child's shoulder. An adult, bent over slightly.

Brian understood the treasure unfolding. The image was now half-exposed, half- concealed. There, in his mind's eye, was the vision, the dream, a remembrance of a small child's feet at work, freeing a mud puddle. His feet. The vision of one or a vision shared. He was dumbfounded by the memento.

"That year, 1980," he repeated as he began to remember days gone by. "That's when he left for good. That's when I lost him."

GEORGE AND I WERE STANDING on the dark porch out of the direct storm. Torrents of water were falling, the wind gust rushing along the deck carrying much of the moisture.

Although out of the elements, the planks and even some of the windows were slick from the alternating rain patterns created by the winds. We remained out of view of the Poppy family but well within view of the photos Benny had scattered on the window seat. We struggled to see without being seen, taking care to remain in the shadows.

"**DO YOU,**" began Allison, still struggling to free the second photo, "look like him?"

"I don't know." He tried to regain his composure. "I can't remember."

The focus was on the stubborn photo. The broad shoulders were to the child's left, and total joy washed over his small face with a fair share of mud. Reality raced anticipation, sadness extinguished by joy as realization slammed him.

"Allison. It must be me and…" he battled with the frame for the photo held snuggly as a prisoner by a single glass shard. "Let go, Allison."

As the photo fell free from the matt and frame, Justin's eyes bulged, in a silence broken only by Benny's squeal of delight.

"Jaa-urge-val-more." Benny clapped.

"George Valmore," Brian repeated in a whisper.

"BENJAMIN," I SPOKE BREATHLESSLY, looking through the glass pane to the photos on the window box and then to George standing silent in the black veil of the porch. The images, although younger, were obvious to both of us.

In the brightly lit living room, Brian's hand rested open on the photo, favoring the recognizable face. In the dark of the porch, George's open palm was resting on the windowpane, framing the happy family. A tear fell from Brian's eye to the photo as his lips trembled.

George's tears flowed as freely as the rain, trickling down the glass pane.

BRIAN'S EYES LOOKED at the small vinyl cap in the photo, the cap that now rested on their mantle. Only Oöso knew who else was also gazing at it as she stared out the dark window to the shadow figures. George saw her intense gaze and placed an extended finger against his lips. Was her canine smile imaginary?

Suddenly Brian's heart was heavy, as if weighted on the right. A twinge, then a vibration ran across his chest, up into his right shoulder. His breath quaked as he attempted to use it to ground himself. His stomach tightened as the moisture pooled in his eyes. Jaw clenched, lips pulled thin. The lower one quivered, stretched tight as a board, the upper rolling over slightly. Nostrils flared involuntarily as breath heated his nasal passages, passing warm into his eyelids. His vision out of focus as if under water looking up.

The tear escaped from the corner of his left eye, and the logjam was broken. Allison pulled Brian to hold him close, allowing him to weep into her arms.

GEORGE'S TEARS FLOWED FREELY and with no shame as his lip quivered below a slight smile. "I didn't mean to scare you, but I didn't know. I didn't know, until…in the car." He forced a chuckle. "Kinda blows the theory of angels knowing everything."

"Yeah, I got that, now. C'mon partner," I prodded. "We better go." I pulled up the collar of my jacket before I stepped off the porch, remaining out of view.

He followed me into the rain that was now turning gentle. A female rain. He looked at me before stepping away from the porch. "Thanks."

The rain shifted as we headed for the car. The delicate drops camouflaged my tears of sheer joy as they did George's.

Suddenly he turned his head up in the night air with his eyes wide open in the rain. He pulled his soaked cap free, shaking his wet curly locks. As the rain massaged his forehead and cheeks, he repeated softly to the heavens. "Thanks." And with that, he took another glance at me and took a mighty leap into the air.

I recoiled too late to avoid the tidal wave…of the puddle he set free.

CHAPTER FIFTY

YOUR WORD IS YOUR WAND

"THERE ARE MORE THINGS in heaven and on earth," Hamlet said to Horatio, "than are dreamt of in your philosophy." And neither George, nor Horatio, nor Hamlet was talking. We checked into the motel in silence. I fell asleep fully dressed and awoke completely alone. The room clock showed midnight, and the cardboard UPS envelope was propped against the bolted-down lamp on the round table by the window.

The TV remote sat atop our permission slip for transporting the car with a one-way ticket from Chicago's O'Hare Airport to Sky Harbor in Phoenix. First class booked for the next day, just past noon at 12:06 PM departure. Five-hundred dollars was tucked inside. I recognized the handwriting scrawled across the still unopened envelope:

Daro,

Use your intuition to finish the Mission. The gas tank is full.

Take a hug – George Valmore

I had nothing unpacked, so I pulled out my toothbrush and wandered to the bathroom, carrying the packet. As I tore open the flap of the envelope, I wanted to cry. I wanted to laugh. I wanted to ask more questions. But what would I ask?

George made it clear from the get-go that he didn't have all the answers. This trip pretty well debunked my belief that angels knew everything. I'd only believed angels existed until meeting George. With my belief now my truth, I still couldn't prove it anymore than proving if there was love. Come to think of it, I couldn't even say how many angels I might've already met.

I walked around the motel room, going no place, yet my mind doing laps. George had said that life wasn't all scripted out, that we were gifted with the freedom of choice. Maybe God only had a synopsis because of that. The Grand Producer-Director worked six days and then rested on the seventh, with only a synopsis and a hopeful plan for life. No script, just notes to allow us to ad-lib with that freedom of choice.

I watched the pellets of rain turn to droplets on the window glass. What was it that George, or Brian, or Allison called them? Silver ships of souls.

An astrologer makes predictions from the stars. Same goes for weathermen or meteorologists. Those colorful weather trails moving over a blue screen are just guesstimations for the weather. Yet men and women have proven they could change the weather at times in grotesque fashion as Al Gore and others have warned. There are some healthful ways, such as cloud-seeding. Maybe that's what an angel is, God cloud-seeding with silver ships of souls for us to ad-lib with our freedom of choice.

For the first time I had an inkling of the weight God had placed on His own shoulders the day He or She gave us...freedom of choice. Probably the last time God was able to take a day off. Heck, most of us just pretty well ignore the Sabbath as a day not to work and keep holy. If we can't keep one day holy, it's hard to imagine us respecting all seven days. If only we did the obvious in our ad-libs, just merely listened to ourselves to hear the right thing, and then did it. I should have learned by now only to speak for myself. At least I knew I could do that more than I had. And if enough of us succeeded, I'm sure God would appreciate another day of rest.

There was no map for delivering the car, just a simple address, and the original title which for me clarified how the car managed to have such low mileage with only two previous owners. A young buck purchased it new from a dealership in Valdosta, Georgia. The parent kept it in storage, signing it over to its third owner to whom I was now committed to delivering it in order to honor our mission.

Intuition told me it was best to be seen and not heard, so I parked the Mustang at Lillian and Hughie's house, leaving the keys in their mailbox where it all began. Two keys hanging from a silver chain with a small, rectangular metal dog tag. Five stamped lines of information, beginning with Captain Benjamin James Poppy Jr. That should explain as well as anything.

Wet, overcast morning and not much traffic on the road, I began to wonder if I'd make the airport in time for my flight. Having never hitchhiked before, I thought I might be able to write a column about it as water began to darken my tan cowboy boots. I was due for another pair from Saba's once back in Scottsdale. I prayed for an angel when I felt the highway rumble from thunder, or so I thought.

Once encircled, I recognized the famous, or infamous, indistinguishable winged death heads. I prayed for an angel, and received nine of them.

Be careful what you pray for.

THE END

Acknowledgements

Mom agreed with the Native Americans' belief that it took a village to raise a child. Well, I've come to recognize that it takes one to write a book. She was my greatest teacher and friend, gone before my author days. Mom also said it was better to thank people and risk missing some than to overlook everyone, so thanks out to my hamlet – some of which led up to this moment.

Bette Mandino took the reins of riding shotgun over me after we lost her beloved Og Mandino, my favorite author and first mentor, and the one who convinced me to write books. She remains my greatest support of long-standing faith. Big heart and a big boot, both shared with love. We've laughed, we've cried, we've shopped.

Michael Landon knew the premise for this novel. My favorite actor and the man I would have chosen as a big brother from his days as Lil' Joe. On that somber day at his memorial, as I went to leave the memorial to fly home – Cindy Landon placed her hand on my shoulder and asked, "Are you going to finally write those books?" I still get God-bumps when I think of that and will always thank her.

Judy Worman translated my scribbles and lasted through laborious edits. Her second career was pup-sitter for Nubble. She also helped me recover after some major injuries from a drunk driver. If not for her and therapeutic counseling from Duffy McMahon, I am not sure I would have made it back to Light. Sherry Hays was remarkable for edits and research skills, and long-distance friend at all hours. Mary-Jean Filusch Davis and Robin Cleveland who typed in my early days. Brian Jasper has done a few re-types while generally keeping me organized, and Mindy Bond for keeping Brian organized. And Edward Ellsworth gets a bucket of thanks for serving as my web master, computer guru, and taco maker extraordinaire, keeping me in line, on track, and blogging. Thanks to his wife Valerie Moore for sharing him, her proof-reading, her crafts skills, and their doggies.

Love still lives on for Oöso, Polly, & Nubble - my past four-legged old souls who sat beneath my desk and no doubt directed Gibbs my way. And there is my warrior of heart, my girl-cub Erin Rose Bunzel Kraus, my daughter who kept getting back up when life knocked her down. She is my shining star.

Life presents hurdles and downright hells, the trick becomes finding the rewards. Joel Erik Thompson is a great attorney and fellow author. Hell was worth it to meet him and his lovely wife Shandaé. A gateway from hell was also provided by Marc Peagler as I was endeared to Beverly and Matthew Peagler, Juan Oglin, and Frontier Town.

Walter Jeffry 'Iron Butterfly' Curl was my cohort in high school and church. He shared his family, we T-P'd much of Scottsdale, room-mated through college, and he helped me outrun bullies – and still does. Another life gift includes Rich DuPuis who invested countless hours with me, solving the world's problems over a pool table. I hope they have a bookstore with a billiards hall in Peru. Mom loved you both as her own sons.

My publisher TechPress and ELM Tree Books with Angela Totman and Michael Lechter at the helm made all this happen. One hears of horror stories with publishers so it is quite the blessing to be finally surrounded with creativeness, quality and integrity.

Harry Flynn, master of publicity, saw something in me before many others, certainly before me. He opened the stage doors to the world of entertainment, introducing me as his peer, forever changing my life for the better. Publicists Sean Mahoney, Henry Rogers, and Lori Ames also welcomed and guided me into a whole new level of book, publicity, and stars.

Although Stanley O'Rourke did the best he could, I grew up fatherless and brotherless. Walter (& Bobbie) Cory, Jack Elwood (& Bessie) Curl, Bill Cory, Mayor Herb Drinkwater, Gene Ramsdell, Ed 'Carbonation' Leavitt, Gary Simon, Ernie (& Dana) McEntire, Rich O'Brien, and Reverend Dan Stringer all picked up the slack.

Arriving in Arizona from Illinois to a man's world and glass ceilings, Mom had to work two jobs to provide for our home, so cooking was a rarity. But I never went hungry thanks to the families of Donna Cory-Garner, David & Carrie Page, Mark Turcotte, Dan Zapata, Steve and Kevin Goodenberger, Jim Vance, and Roger

Scurlock - meals always served with love.

Coronado High School provided a solid part of my foundation. I've had such an unexpected resurgence of friends all these years later with the alumni. Virginia Eades, Ralph Bradshaw, and Larry Halbert receive credit, or blame, for my interest in the written word and my passion to rearrange letters. Other teachers willing to work with me rather than banish me include Marshall Trimble, Clyde Kidd, Larry Bell, Muriel Vandenoever, Thema Wortman, Joseph Gatti, Evelyn Caskey, Gary Stephens, and Mary Stoltenberg. I often use the words blessed and honored, as I'm keenly aware that I have an abundance of both in my life.

My work as a Media Host to Authors created my own writers' workshop on wheels in repeated drives and ongoing chats with some of the greats in literary entertainment. Some such as Tasha Alexander, Deborah Coonts, Lisa Gardner, Andrew Grant, Kathi Kamen-Goldmark, Sharon Lechter, Robert B. (& Joan) Parker, remained in close touch and were a phone call away.

Others that gave as I drove them to signings included T.A. Barron, Dr. Marty Becker, Barbara Taylor (& Robert) Bradford, Rita Mae Brown, Ken Bruen, Meg Cabot, Bruce Campbell, Lee Child, Deepak Chopra, Jackie Collins, Rita Davenport, Wayne Dyer, Joy Fielding, John Lescroart, Michael McGarrity, Christopher Moore, David (& Donna) Morrell, Lauren Myracle, Jodi Picoult, Karin Slaughter, Gerry Spence, Michael Stackpole, Laura Van Wormer, Victor Villaseñor, Susan Vreeland, and Randy Wayne White. All shared wisdom and I am a better writer thanks to each.

Not many get to meet their heroes, let alone befriend them: Og Mandino, José Silva, John Randolph Price, Michael Landon, Richard Bach, George Addair, Johnny Cash, SQuire Rushnell, and Stephen J. Cannell. I question why God smiles on me so. What a life!

Bear with me as I rattle on through more names and they'll know why. Bob 'Boze' Bell, Jana Bommersbach, Erle Braugher, David & Don Bellisario, Julie & Michael Biodrowski, Linda 'Tiger' Bird, Pat Boone, Chris Bowen, The Boys of Cypress, Jimmy Buffett, Keith Buchanan, Leslie 'Bunny' Bunzel Pfleger, and Rosemary Bunzel.

Ed Cooley, Janice Bruce Corak, Alex Cord, Changing Hands Bookstore, Cherry Creek Lodge, Rolf Dale, Foster Davis, Dead

Mule Ranch, Ellen DeGeneres, Betsy Dornbusch, Mark Drinkwater, Louise Ann DuArt, Ford Dudley, Georgia Durant, Dr. Alan Eads, Buddy & Dorothy Ebsen, Mark Erwin, Morgan Fairchild, Darci Lynne Farmer, Mike Farrell, Fiend 2 Clean, Beverly Ford, Deb Foster, Jerry Foster, Esther Fuller Deacon, Sue & Dr. Emil Faithe, Wayne Futch, Ann-Marie & Marc Geyer, 'Professor' Mike Gilbert, Gabe Gomez, Gower Elementary, Joseph Grizone, Joann Hamilton-Selway, Dan Harkins & Harkins Theaters, Camille Hartz, Fussy & Hughie Hays, Big Pete Hermann, David Hess, Dan Horn, Rich 'Hank Plow' Howard.

Brian & Craig Jackson & Barrett-Jackson Auction, Susie Alcott Jardine, Cindy 'Flame' Jordan, Bill King, Kohl's Ranch, Donna Kortman, Noah & Kerby Krause, Bill Kuraz, Patsy Kwiatkowski, Emily Laisy, Linda Ambrose & Jerome Allan Landau, Jennifer & Sean Landon, Michael Lanning, Melody Laubach, Chelsie Laws & Murad Vitamins, Dr. Joseph Lillo, Alan Lundgren, Dr. Sandy Mazen, Matthew McConaughey, Jami McFerren-Beams, Pat McMahon, Dorothy & Robert Mitchum, Sandy Neddermeyer, Harriet & Rick Nelson, Tracy Nelson, Willie Nelson, Virginia & Hugh O'Brian, Omega Vector, Larry O'Rourke III, Brad Paisley, Steve Parker, Joey Robert Parks, Luna Patterson, Chris Pease & Chelsea's Kitchen, Teri Peluso, Poisoned Pen Bookstore, Boe Pfleger, Phoenix Children's Hospital, Gary Puckett, Sidney Pirkl, Chris Pischke & Pischke's Paradise, Dave Pratt, Jim Pruitt, and Gary Puckett.

Anna Ransom, Prissy & Jerry Reed, Larry Reese, Rehab Burger Therapy, José Rivera, Coach Don Robinson, Chuck Rogers, Will Rogers, Giovanni Rosati, Rural Fire Department, Oregano's Pizza Bistro, Richard Ryan, Chuck & Tora Schrader, Barbara & Bob Sickles, Karen & Howard Smolin, Kat Steele, Dr. Dick Stolper & Scottsdale Ranch Animal Hospital, Stephen Floyd Stradling, Joan & Bobby Surrette, Melinda Vail, Elden Von Lehe, "Wallace & Ladmo," Lyman Ward, Betty Webb, Mary Jo West, Greta Wood, Morgan Woodward, Rob Word, Jim Worman, Michael Yarman, and Tim & Laurie Zunk.

If I missed you herein, buy a book already and I'll write your name in it by hand. I hope I do you proud.

Hugs, Pierre